The Collected Short Stories of

Mary Johnston

by Floride Green

MISS MARY JOHNSTON

The Collected Short Stories of

Mary Johnston

edited by

Annie Woodbridge

and

Hensley C. Woodbridge

The Whitston Publishing Company
Troy, New York
1982

Table of Contents

Preface

Mary Johnston is a writer whose personal life and history show contrasts as great as those of her stories. Her health was frail, yet as a teenager, after her mother's death, she undertook the care of her five siblings and shared the management of the household with her father. She was a highly educated woman, especially in the fields of literature, history and philosophy; yet her health prevented her school attendance for more than a few months. She was deeply religious, but she felt religious dogma one of the worst ills of our culture. She didn't attend any church in her mature years. She was a suffragist and a feminist, but after strenuous efforts in support of votes for women, once the nineteenth amendment passed, she refused to join the League of Women Voters. She avoided anything that might create division instead of unity for all humanity. She was a pacifist who wrote the two most epic novels of the Civil War, a pacifist proud of the military heroes of her family and her state. She wanted to conserve the history of the South and her behavior was that of the Southern aristocratic conservative while her ideas were the most advanced of her day. She was a most popular author and a most neglected author.

Mary Johnston's personal history began in Botetourt County, Virginia, November 21, 1870, and ended sixty-six years later May 9, 1936, in Warm Springs, Virginia. The history of Virginia, her life and her family history are as intertwined as the history of Virginia and her writings. Fifteen of her twenty-three novels have Virginia settings and deal in part with Virginia history. She also wrote a history dealing with the days of the colony, *Pioneers of the Old South*, Vol. 5 of the *Yale Chronicles of America Series*.

Mary Johnston's father, Major John William Johnston, served the Confederate States Army under his cousin General Joseph Eggleston Johnston, highest ranking officer of the US

Army to resign and fight for the South. Her two Civil War novels are dedicated to these two members of her family.

During Mary's youth her family moved several times, both to New York and Alabama and in Virginia. Mary's early education came from her grandmother, tutors, and the reading she did on her own. Her family sent her to a private boarding school in Atlanta, but her health was so bad she returned home after a few months. These few months were the only formal schooling this scholarly woman received. After her mother's death, in spite of her own poor health, Mary, age sixteen, took care of her five brothers and sisters and helped her father manage the household.

She began writing in an effort to help the family finances, and her novels did just that. Five of MJ's seven novels published between 1898 and 1912 made the list of best sellers. This was during the first twenty years that such lists were kept. Her most popular book, *To Have and To Hold,* topped the list for 1900. These figures as well as recent studies in popular culture substantiate George Longest's[1] statement that Mary Johnston is one of the most popular writers Virginia has ever produced.

In 1911-13 MJ built a beautiful home, *Three Hills,* near Warm Springs in the mountains of western Virginia. She and her unmarried siblings lived here the rest of her life. Though frail in health MJ was never a recluse. She traveled in Europe, Egypt, and the United States. She became interested in many social issues: woman suffrage, labor, pacifism and socialism. Her philosophical and religious study led to an interest in Theosophy, reincarnation and transcendentalism. She experienced mystical awareness.

In the first book containing a chapter devoted to MJ in 1901 a friend is quoted,

> The author is not very tall, and her figure is slender and fragile. She carries herself well and has that high-bred air that gives her a distinctive charm in any assembly. Her eyes are large and brown, with flecks of gold. Her light brown hair is soft and wavy and she wears it simply. She dresses quietly and fashionably. Her tastes are those of a charming woman, who, although unconventional, respects every propriety. Briefly, her life is that of any

high-bred, aristocratic girl of the South.[2]

This description seemed to hold true in all later discussions of Miss Johnston. It also shows how early her unconventionality was recognized. The dichotomy between her advanced ideas and her "high-bred aristocratic girl of the South" conduct first attracted wide attention in her prodigious work for woman suffrage. In 1909 she helped organize the Equal Suffrage League of Virginia. She wrote letters to the Richmond *Times Dispatch*, articles for the *Atlantic Monthly* and the Virginia *Suffrage News*[3] to which she was a contributing editor. She spoke before the General Assembly of Virginia, the legislatures of Tennessee and West Virginia, a conference of governors of all the states of the Union[4] and to audiences in Boston and Birmingham, Alabama. She joined feminists from other states in Washington, D.C., and marched until her friend Ellen Glasgow considered her a martyr.[5]

At the suggestion of Fola Lafollette of Wisconsin, Mary Johnston wrote *Hagar,* a feminist, suffragist novel to present the cause of women to her readers. The readers were fewer. Many critics condemned the book as propaganda, but Lawrence G. Nelson pointed out many good things in it[6] and "Despite all its shortcomings, it has been recommended in Tillie Olsen's reading list as a 'classic of its own kind'."[7] MJ continued to tell the story of women in *The Witch, The Wanderers,* and to a certain extent in *The Fortunes of Garin, Sweet Rocket, Silver Cross, The Great Valley* and *Miss Delicia Allen.*

In support of causes other than feminism Mary Johnston served as co-editor of the pacifist women's journal *Four Lights* for the fourth issue (March 10, 1917). She contributed a poem, "The Artist," to this issue. She later decided that these pacifists were too militant and broke her connection with them. Her interest in Theosophy and humanism appears in her fiction as do her mystic or transcendental ideas. For example, Edward Wagenknecht, one of the two critics to publish critical studies of her works since her death, says she died "a Socialist, a pacifist and a mystic."[8] However, the other, Lawrence G. Nelson, whom both George Longest and Ronald Cella consider her best critic, describes her as ". . .patrician, conservative and traditional to the core of her being."[9]

Wagenknecht prefers her later novels containing surreal or mystic elements. Nelson prefers the historical fiction, especially the Civil War novels. The reading public overwhelmingly agreed with Nelson. These early books, first called historical novels, later termed historical romances and recently classified as gothic or gothic romances,[10] appealed to many readers.

In spite of this popularity and considerable critical attention during her early career, her public began to wane even during her lifetime, and in 1961 Nelson said only two of her books remained in print: *Pioneers of the Old South* and *To Have and To Hold.*[11] In sharp contrast to this the 1980-1 *Books in Print* lists twenty-nine entries for Mary Johnston; five of these are editions of *To Have and To Hold.* In 1978 G. K. Hall of Boston brought out the first bibliographic study of criticism of her work: George C. Longest, *Three Virginia Writers.* The Twayne United States Author Series is to publish a book length critical study by Ronald Cella in 1981 and Louisiana State University Press has contracted for the publication of a biography by Jeanne Nostrandt. Recent shorter publications include a biographical sketch and bibliography of first editions by William W. Kelly in *Southern Writers,*[12] a biographical and critical article by Dorothy Scura in 1980 in *American Women Authors* (N.Y., Ungar), another article by Scura for a Richmond journal and two critical comments I wrote for the *Jack London Newsletter* in 1978.

Although most of MJ's writing was fiction her first short story did not appear in print until 1920, twenty-two years after the publication of her first novel. From 1920 until 1935, one year before her death, she published twenty-one short stories in nine magazines and one newspaper. These stories have never before been collected. However, *The Wanderers*, fictional sketches of the relations between women and men from prehistory to the French Revolution, is considered a collection of short stories by the *Short Story Index* and some critics. Gayle Melton Hartley, in her dissertation on *The Novels of Mary Johnston,*[13] includes *The Wanderers* and feels that the lovers in each story are "reincarnations of lovers in preceeding eras" and that this gives a continuing narration and "a sense of unity to the work."[14] *Sweet Rocket*, a frame novel, also contains separate stories told by the guests at a Virginia farm, a Utopia.

All but three of the separately published stories are listed in O'Brien's *O. Henry Memorial Award Prize Stories* for the year in which they appeared. The three unlisted were in publications not considered for these selections.

The twenty-one stories have great variety. Some, like "Black Lace" and "Elephants Through the Country," build suspense through sequence of events or psychological tension. Others, i.e., "The Church Festival" and "The Return of Magic," lack plot entirely. For women faced with financial exigency in "The Angel" and "The Tree," a sentimental solution rescues one while a bitter realization that the poor must always give in to the rich brings change to the life of the other. Most of her stories show a positive, hopeful view of life and humanity, but "There Were No More People" shows Mary Johnston's fears for the future if competition, conflict, and wars win out over cooperation, mutual understanding, and peace. In direct contrast to this gloomy view of the future, the delightful Christmas story "Doctor Barbary's Vision" shows men from three races, the humanitarian country doctor, the Indian of his vision and, of lesser role, the black man on the farm who hangs a lantern to guide the doctor, all working united to bring about the birth of a new life, a new future.

Unlike MJ's novels, almost all set in the past, these stories, except the one fantasy and the one science fiction story, occur during MJ's lifetime. One, "Buried Silver," begins earlier but continues into the prevalent period. However, they record the history and social customs of the period: the lynching, the revival meeting, the church festival, the women's culture study group, foretelling the end of the world, the excitement stirred up by the coming of a circus to a remote community, the services performed by the blacks for the white population of the South, the masked ball on a cruise ship. The characters of the period appear too: the overworked country doctor, the unmarried female relative in the homes of the Southern families, the loyal black servants, the poor with their superstitions, the witch. In addition to recording history and sociology the stories represent the popular culture of their day.

One of the most unusual features of these stories, twelve of which appeared in popular women's magazines ordinarily credited with publication of formula stories, is either the almost total absence of competition or else competition changing to cooperation. Mary Johnston believed substitution of cooperation for competition to be one of the three greatest needs of our contemporary world. This idea figures as a major theme of her novel *Foes* published in 1918 just two years before the appearance of her first short story. In this story, "One Night," the two Johns, one a labor leader, one a capitalist, in their mutual understanding after death give an example of the desired cooperation. It is interesting that the feminists of our day have the same hatred of competition felt by the feminists in the early years of our century.

Unusual for women's journals also, there are few stories, three or four of the twenty-one, with love between the sexes as a main theme. The principal characters of these stories are black. Miss Johnston depicted very few black characters in her novels. Only in *The Long Roll, Cease Firing,* and *Miss Delicia Allen* do their minor roles attain importance. In the short stories love affairs furnish the main theme for "That Cold," "After the Storm," "Lion Loose" and "Mockingbird." In "Mockingbird," however, the most important conflict occurs between the Bogey Vinnie bought from the witch Maum Ann and Cynthia whom Vinnie wishes to scare to death. After her family, her friends, her preacher and even the magic grains she walked ten miles to get from Daddy Joe all fail to break the Devil's hold on her, Cynthia, like a feminist of our day, works out her own salvation. This is an unusual story for MJ to write in 1928 because in her later fiction she almost never has a villain, one person trying to harm another. Also of the many witches in her novels all are white witches, warning of evil, healing, telling the future. This is the only one who uses her powers for evil. In her interest in witches MJ with her historical knowledge of the persecution of innocent women shares the indignation of our present day feminists once again.

The other three love stories are given one star each by O'Brien, but I think "After the Storm," a skillful adaptation of the Cinderella tale, presents more interesting characters. In all these stories the black characters show a simple, unsophisticated enjoyment of life, and love of the opposite sex contributes to this enjoyment. Four other stories have love as a minor theme. Of these only the white couple in "Buccaneer" have doubts, fears, a general lack of trust in love and marriage. Of the eight stories with love as a theme only this one leaves the reader doubting if a marriage will result and if so if Philip Blackwell and Rosamond Hart will live happily ever after.

Black characters play major roles in nine of the stories and the lynching of a black man with the subsequent psychological hell on earth for the four leaders of the mob form the plot for another, "Nemesis." The servants in "Black Lace," "Buried Silver" and "If a Weasel Crosses Your Path Turn Back" are loyal, honest, devoted to their employers. Just as Roxy in *Miss Delicia Allen* risked her life to save Delicia, Melissa in "Black Lace" returned to the flood-threatened home and lost her life but saved her Old Miss's grandson. Dauphin lived in poverty, almost starved in "Buried Silver" rather than dig up the treasure only he knew about. He saved it for Young Miss's baby. William in "If a Weasel. . ." risked his life in spite of his fears to deliver a message for his employer.

All the short stories were published after MJ began to write of transcendental experiences, reincarnation and the super-natural. Ghosts appear in ten of them, women called witches in two, and fairies in three. In all but one story the ghosts seem so real and their materialization so natural that the other charac-ters talk to them with no fear and the reader too accepts them as true. These ghosts want to settle misunderstandings in "The Two Business Men," "One Night," and "Nemesis," give aid and comfort to the living in "Doctor Barbary's Vision," "The Tree," "Attic Room," and "Black Lace," seem to be checking on a descendent who may be a reincarnation in "The Buccaneer," but in "If a Weasel Crosses Your Path Turn Back" the ghost tries to haunt William Carlisle. The other dead who return are trying to instruct, aid and comfort those they have left behind.

The only real fairy is Magic who is also Truth, Science or some other earthly benefactor personified. Her story, so beauti-fully told, shows how well MJ could handle pure fantasy. It re-sembles the fantasy of Lord Dunsany. The old deaf woman shut off from communication with others by her deafness and time spent in "The Attic Room" is really a fairy princess in her tower to no one except the young author with whom she shares the attic. He discovers her poetry as well as her fairylike qualities. The third fairy, the fairy godmother in "After the Storm," also has no supernatural powers. She enchants children with her stories and she produces clothes and a carriage for Pallas reminiscent of Cinderella's fairy godmother, but this fairy is called a witch by Octavia, the mother of the family with whom she lives. These fairies are all old, all wanting to give help to others. The most original of the surrealistic characters is the strange creature who evolved after "There Were no More People upon the Earth." This story reminds the reader of early science fiction by Lovecraft.

The style of the stories like the stories themselves is varied. In the introduction to the *O. Henry Memorial Prize Stories of 1929,* the editor says of "Elephants Through the Country" "That it is consummately written is clear" and quotes Professor Burrell: "That it is a study of phantom fear interested me very much. But the 'study of fear' did not for a moment usurp the stage to the detriment of the people who were involved in this human situation."[15]   Sylvia Chatfield Bates, who included this story in her collection, *Twentieth Century Short Stories,* "finds the piling up of emotional effect in the hero's dread like the ponderous footsteps of Shiva the great elephant himself, coming over the mountains."[16]

In "One Night" the style and sentence structure suggest the jerks, stops, whistles and movement of the train described as a monster breathing rhythmically. Repetition in these two stories effectively builds up this feeling of movement. These two stories use another MJ characteristic: careful selection of names to add broader suggestion to the narrative. Shiva, like his namesake in Hindu mythology, turns out to be a destroyer. The name John for both the capitalist and the labor leader suggests that both represent many men and eventually that both are one.

The editors of *College Readings in the Modern Short Story* comment on the use of the teacher of mathematics as a narrator in "The Two Business Men" as an especially effective "means of bringing the dead Mr. Beckwith into contact with the living Mr. Arnold."[17]   The narrator skillfully lends reality to the unreal. Only one other short story, "Nemesis," has a narrator and this rather long story uses the narrator in only a few sections.

The device is effective here as it gives the reader an eyewitness account of the lynching. More than one man's account, it suggests the version of the event accepted by the community. MJ used a narrator in several of her novels: *To Have and To Hold, Michael Forth, 1492,* and *The Slave Ship.* Her language, which tends to be a bit stilted when it imitates the language of the 17th or 18th centuries, seems more natural and believable in these narrators.

The use of archaic language adds a poetic quality to MJ's writing even if it makes her "a living anachronism" in her own day as Louis Untermeyer said of Edna St. Vincent Millay.[18] To quote further, "The archaic idioms, the quaint inversions and rhetorical images, are those of three centuries ago; but the voice is that of a woman aware of the modern world and radiantly responsive to it."[19] This description of Millay seems to apply equally to MJ.

In addition to inversions and archaic words, which at times may irritate the reader, MJ's punctuation, the excessive use of exclamation marks, dashes and even the unpardonable sin in a freshman English theme in her day, the comma splice, must have been anathema to composition teachers and some critics of her time. However, these distractions never impede MJ's sure sense of a good story.

Most critics of the novels commend the beautiful descriptions of nature. These descriptions enhance the stories too. One outstanding example is the warm autumn foliage and autumn weather brought miraculously by the Indian to aid the doctor across the icy, wintry mountain also accurately described in the story "Doctor Barbary's Vision."

MJ's "unerring sense of finish" causing her to "stop short, rolling down the curtain with. . .swiftness. . ."[20] characterizes both her novels and her short stories. She closes her two volume epic of the Civil War as the Army of Northern Virginia tramps toward Appomattox on the last page of *Cease Firing.* In the stories of this collection again and again the reader is left with a feeling of a complete story yet with the idea that there is more to come, life is going on. Or as MJ says in "The End of the World," "The world kept on coming to an end and beginning afresh."

This type of ending is one of her great narrative assets.

In spite of the contrast between the surrealistic stories such as "Return of Magic," "No More People" and the stories of social and psychological justice like "Nemesis" both contain unreal elements. The unreal appears in most of the stories. Any reader unwilling to look beyond empirical knowledge, or at least suspend belief for a time, might miss the charm of some of them.

May these stories induce you, the reader, to transcend the humdrum concepts of real and accept the possibility that, "There are more things in heaven and earth. . .than are dreamt of in your philosophy."

Annie Woodbridge

NOTES

[1] *Three Virginia Writers,* Boston, G. K. Hall, 1978, p. vii.

[2] E. F. Harkins, *Famous Authors (Women),* Boston, L. C. Page & Co., 1906, p. 312.

[3] *Woman's Journal,* National American Woman Suffrage Association, October 17, 1914, n.p.

[4] E. D. Coleman, "Penwoman of Virginia's Feminists," *Virginia Cavalcade,* 6 (Winter 1956), 8-11.

[5] Ellen Glasgow, *The Woman Within,* New York, Harcourt, Brace and Company, 1954, p. 187.

[6] "Mary Johnston and the Historic Imagination," in Richard K. Meeker, *The Dilemma of the Southern Writer,* Farmville, Virginia, Longwood College, 1961, pp. 61-62.

[7] Iris Biblowitz, et al., *Women and Literature: an Annotated Bibliography of Women Writers,* 3rd edition, Cambridge, Massachusetts, Women and Literature Collective, 1976, p. 35.

[8] *Cavalcade of the American Novel,* New York, Holt, Rinehart and Winston, 1952, p. 197.

[9] *Southern Writers, Appraisals in our Time,* Charlottesville, University of Virginia Press, 1961, p. 78.

[10] Kay J. Mussell, "Gothic novels," in M. Thomas Inge, *Handbook of American Culture,* vol. 1, Westport, Connecticut, Greenwood Press, 1978, p. 156.

[11] *Southern Writers, Appraisals in our Time, op. cit.,* p. 87.

[12]Robert Bain, et al., *Southern Writers: a Biographical Dictionary,* Baton Rouge, Louisiana, Louisiana State University Press, 1979, pp. 251-252.

[13]University of South Carolina, Ph.D. dissertation, 1972.

[14]*Ibid.,* p. 120.

[15]Garden City, Doubleday, Page & Co., 1930, pp. xiv-xv.

[16]*Ibid.*

[17]Edited by George R. MacMinn and Harvey Eagleson, Boston, Ginn, 1931, p. 18.

[18]Edna St. Vincent Millay, *Lyrics and Sonnets,* New York, Editions for the Armed Services, Inc., 1941, p. 3.

[19]*Ibid.,* p. 4.

[20]*O. Henry Award Prize Stories of 1929,* p. xv.

Acknowledgments

We are greatly indebted to Capt. J. W. Johnston and the Rev. Robert Q. Johnston, Mary Johnston's great-nephews and literary executors, for their permission to allow the publication of these short stories.

Prof. Ronald Cella of Murray State University, author of the forthcoming Twayne series volume on Mary Johnston, first provided us with the addresses of Mary Johnston's great-nephews. He also provided us with a xerox copy of one of the short stories.

We also wish to thank Edmund Berkeley, Jr., curator of manuscripts of the University of Virginia Library, and his staff for their assistance to us when, during the summer of 1978, we used the Mary Johnston collection of this library's manuscript division.

I (Annie Woodbridge) thank Dean Kenneth Peterson and the Morris Library for aid with the travel expenses to Virginia.

Elline Long carefully prepared the final typescript.

Most of the stories were available in the Morris Library of Southern Illinois University. We also used both the Cincinnati Public Library and the University of Illinois Library.

We are pleased to thank the authorities of the Virginia State Library, Richmond, Virginia for permission to produce the photograph used as a frontispiece.

Annie Woodbridge
Hensley C. Woodbridge

Textual Note and Short Story Bibliography

As no manuscripts, typescripts or proofs exist, the text of the short stories is that of the published magazine version. Typographical errors have been silently corrected and marked with a footnote number with the incorrect form noted at the end of the short story.

The short stories are published in this collection in chronological order. The following is a listing of the short stories with pertinent bibliographical data concerning their first published appearance and any known reprints.

"One night," Chicago *Tribune Sunday Magazine,* July 25, 1920, pp. 1-2, 6.

"The return of magic," *Reviewer,* 3,1:359-363 (April, 1922).

"The tree," *Good Housekeeping,* 76,5:54-57, 232-234 (May, 1923).

"Nemesis," *Century Illustrated Monthly Magazine,* 106,1:2-22 (May, 1923).

"There were no more people upon the earth," *Reviewer,* 4,1:3-8 (October, 1923).; *The World Tomorrow,* 7:58-59 (February, 1924).

"The buccaneer," *Ladies' Home Journal,* 45,6:6-7, 68, 70 (June, 1928).

"Black lace," *Ladies' Home Journal,* 45,8:16-17, 66, 68, 70 (August, 1928).

"The two business men," *Harper's Monthly Magazine,* 157:

445-455 (September, 1928).

Reprinted in G. R. MacMinn and H. Eagleson, *College Readings in the Modern Short Story*, Boston, Ginn, 1931, pp. 318-337.

"The mockingbird," *Ladies' Home Journal*, 45,11:10-11, 83-84, 86 (November, 1928).

"The angel," *Ladies' Home Journal*, 46,1:10-11, 102, 104 (January, 1929).

"The baptizing," *Ladies' Home Journal*, 46,4:16-17, 91-92, 94 (April, 1929).

"Elephants through the country," *Virginia Quarterly Review*, 5:59-83 (1929).

Reprinted in *O. Henry Memorial Award Prize Stories of 1929*, selected and edited by Blanche Colton Williams, Garden City, New York, Doubleday, Doran & Co., 1930, pp. 165-186; Sylvia Chatfield Bates, ed., *Twentieth Century Short Stories*, Boston, Houghton Mifflin, 1933, pp. 235-259.

"Buried silver," *Ladies' Home Journal*, 46,9:6-7, 158-162 (September, 1929).

"Church festival," *Bookman*, 70:66-72 (September, 1929).

"That cold," *Ladies' Home Journal*, 46,11:28-29, 222, 224, 227 (November, 1929).

"The end of the world," *Ladies' Home Journal*, 47,3:10-11, 172, 178 (March, 1930).

"After the storm," *American Magazine*, 110:36-37, 139-144 (August, 1930).

"Lion loose!" *Ladies' Home Journal*, 47,10:14-15, 130, 133, 135, 138 (October, 1930).

"Doctor Barbary's vision," *Pictorial Review*, 32,12:10-11, 76-78 (December, 1930).

"If a weasel crosses your path, turn back," *Virginia Quarterly Review,* 9:87-107 (1933); *Scholastic,* 23,11:5-6, 11, 30-31 (December 9, 1933).

"The attic room," *Ladies' Home Journal,* 52,12:5-7, 80-81, 83, 85, 87 (December, 1935).

One Night

The one was a trades unionist and the other a capitalist. One drove the locomotive through the night, and the other slept in the stateroom of the Pullman Arcady. The name of the one was John Gordon, and the name of the other John Douglas. The one belonged to a brotherhood, and the other to an association. At the moment association and brotherhood were in conflict. Quite bitter conflict. The man of the association traveled east to a war council—industrial war. The locomotive and the man of the brotherhood were bearing him there, through the night.

The fireman, Jim Smith, and the brakeman, Guy Howard, carried union cards. The train stood at a small station somewhere east of the Mississippi, waiting for No. 4 to pass. It was between 9 and 10 at night. There had been rain and would be rain again. Just now occurred pause, with lanes of clear sky among the clouds. Stars shone in these like lit crafts upon rivers. The station roof and platform glistened with the wet, the rails ahead glistened, hanging lanterns turned rain pools into fire pools, swung lanterns had a shadow light following below. The air felt wet and fresh. The engine, big, black, metallically shining, a good monster with a chitinous body, stood breathing restfully. John Gordon leaned out from his window. Jim and Guy came and stood below. Jim spread a newspaper that he had just bought from the station newsboy. A neighboring light permitted all to read. What they were reading was strike news.

No. 4 lingered its coming. The passengers in the Pullman displayed some restlessness. It had been all right, this standing still, a little earlier when they were in the diner. It was pleasanter to dine without the swaying, rushing of the train. But now they ought to go on! The delay continuing, quite a number of men and women left the train and began to walk up and down the platform, in the moist air, between the lighted cars and the badly lighted station. The station loungers and the patient folk of the waiting room, waiting for a later local, watched them dully.

John Douglas' secretary, who was also his nephew, had brought him an evening paper, printed in a neighboring town, available now at this station. Others within the Pullman obtained the same paper. The sheets turned. Faces were hidden behind them, but the hands, holding closely the two sides, showed interest, in some cases tenseness of interest. Three men in the Pullman Arcady were members of the association. Others were bondholders in the industry affected. There were also a banker and a stock broker. All read the strike news. It was when the paper was exhausted that they left the train and walked on the platform. They took overcoats and hats, for there was a chill in the air. The three or four women walking were wrapped up, but they wore high heeled, thin shoes. For several turns they kept beside husband or father, then, having enough of it, they turned back to the sleeper. The white jacketed porter helped them aboard. The men continued to walk up and down, up and down.

John Douglas walked alone. He had with him neither wife nor daughter. His wife was dead and his daughter married. Young Browne, his nephew, after sending a couple of telegrams for the uncle, had foregathered with a newspaper man from the forward Pullman Sparta. John Douglas walked with a bent head, chewing the end of a cigar.

Bonham, the owner of the Chickasaw mine, came alongside. "What d'ye think, Douglas, of this flareup in Egypt?"[1]

"In Egypt?   I don't know! Ask me something nearer home."

"It's as near as anything else! I've got papyri and a queen's necklace at a dealer's in Cairo. Unless he's already sent them on, as I devoutly hope he has----"

"I don't collect," said the other.   "So I'm not anxious about my birds' eggs and stamps."

Bonham dealt in blandness and had taken the thirty-third degree in turning corners. "It is an anxious time! Armageddon's lasting longer than it ought to----"

John Douglas grunted.   "I hate sentimental catch-words! Armageddon and Waterloo and Appomattox and such! So long as men are men they fight! Who fights the hardest and longest gets what he fights for! I'm not at Armageddon, nor at Waterloo, and I'm not anxious."

Bonham seemed to give ear to someone on the sleeper

steps. "Well, I don't think they'll win this time!" Going, he said to himself, with reference to the figure moving up the platform. "Don't be too sure you aren't collecting!"

John Douglas, cigar in mouth, head bent between shoulders, walked on.

The engine breathed rhythmically. The night air moving shook the open newspaper, blurring the print. Howard steadied it with a grimed hand. Jim Smith seemed lost in the columns, he read so intently. He was the enthusiast, the idealist. Every concrete thing seemed transparent and pervious to him. It might be said that through these items of strikers and constabulary he touched Wat Tyler and the Spartan helots. Howard, the brakeman, lacked this intension. He was on the surface, but he could be quite violently excited there. Now he sucked in his breath and expelled it. A small cloud of vapor joined the night. "Railroad men next, don't you think, captain? Gee! If it had been left to me I'd have gone out last week!" He probably expected no answer, for John Gordon was a silent man, or had a spell of silence on him. He read, leaning down from his window.

Far up the line a whistle blew. A start seemed to go through the train and the passengers in the cars or upon the platform. "There she comes!" said Howard, and moved to look at the light like a star. Jim Smith lifted wide, brown eyes, nodded, and folded the newspaper, putting it in the pocket of his overall, blue when it was clean, but now so grimed with coal and stained with oil that one was left guessing. John Gordon stirred. He said, "It's a fight to a finish. Well, let us finish it!"

Those who had walked the platform were returning to the cars. But John Douglas, who tonight felt so unsociable, had walked farthest, off the platform indeed and upon the gravel bordering for some distance the siding. Going by the engine he had noticed the three reading. He felt a throb of hostility. "Enemies!" It was as distinct as if he had been a savage in the bush. Probably, in the moment, that was what he was. He had gone on, but they stayed there reading—reading news of a colossal, preposterous strike—reading it with sympathies not on his side. They were rebels and heretics, they were adversaries. Now he came back by the engine. They had folded the paper, they were about to get to their work of driving the train. Passing, he came in for what John Gordon said.

John Douglas halted. There was in the voice coming across to him through the night just the hostility that he himself felt.

Measure and degree, it was there. Each to other had the precision of an echo.

He stood in the ring of the station light. John Gordon, feeling him, looked over from his engine. The conductor had told Howard, who had told him, of two or three of those who were upon the train. Moreover, John Douglas' picture was in the morning paper.

"That's John Douglas. Well, Mr. Douglas, suppose you go back to your sleeper? This isn't your end of the train!"

He did not say this aloud, but he said it to himself.

No. 4 was coming like a dragon through the night. John Douglas looked hard at John Gordon. Perhaps it was the night, so misty and shifting of lights, with the sense—and he had noted how heavy this was—of something waited for, something coming. Perhaps it was simply his mood that was growing more and more harsh and strained. He was aware of this. "And yet I have been—I am—a kindly man!" He had told himself that the fewest of minutes before. However this might be, John Gordon's grimed face summed all that he was fighting and that was fighting him. It made a person of the word "antagonist." The word was a lit window. How many foes were behind it were useless to inquire. They crowded the rungs of the ladder of the ages. Space, time deep, John Gordon looking out of his window----

No. 4 shrieked. John Douglas moved abruptly, walked away, cigar between teeth, down the platform to the Arcady.

As he mounted the step Bonham spoke from the doorway. He was talking to young Browne. "The born collector at first collects all kinds of things. Then, life being short, comes in selection---"

John Douglas pushed by him without any especial suaveness. "Good night, Bonham! Tom, I want you presently to take a letter----"

No. 4 was in. Jim Smith shoveled coal. John Gordon, taking his post, put hand on throttle. No. 7 moved—moved faster. Passengers breathed a pleased acquiescence. Night, night, beyond the station lights—wide dark, a country not thronged with inhabitants—going east, going east—rain in the air, rain lines upon the windows, slanting, tying together right hand and left hand corners. There was a college professor aboard, and he was talking diagonals. "Something like your compromise----"

John Douglas entered his stateroom. At first he would shut the door on all these fools. Then he opened it to hear the fools in their folly, and feed his sense of all their mistaken ways. That he could see that they were mistaken meant that he was in the right way. It was comfortable to have every grain going of that assurance.

Tom Browne entered. He had him close the door while he dictated his letter. But "Leave the door open!" he said when the young man rose to go.

"Is there anything more I can do for you, sir?"

"No. I am going to bed. Good night—Tom!"

"Yes, sir?"

"Go ask the conductor what the engineer is named." The nephew went and returned. "John Gordon, sir."

"John Gordon. Scotch enough. Good night!"

"Good night." Browne went to the smoking car. They were talking the strike in there.

No. 7 crossed a river, turbid from the rains, with the water high and adding its voice to the resonance of the bridge. John Gordon kept his eyes on the track ahead. Jim Smith shoveled in coal. "River's high. It thumps, thumps the bridge. Thumps and sucks. Tom Wilson was driving the night the first bridge gave."

He took the fireman's seat. No. 7 was running with a dull sound after the drum like sound. A wood rose on either hand. The fine rain whipped in. He watched his side of the track. Behind the sentry part, and behind the almost automatic feeding of the engine, his mind went afar.

The night settled to its happenings and its rhythm.

Half past 10-11. The express roared by the villages where almost all the lights were out. It was raining. The lights winked and blurred in the night. Wet track, a speeding of telegraph poles, trunks of trees, shocks of corn in fields, glare on them all from the great head light, black night where it did not pierce. A cut, and the roar flung back from banks of wet clay intensely lit—and the short tunnel, and the road imprisoned with engine and train, the roar and the heavy smoke—an embankment, and the light and noise thrown off into the night—fields again and the shocked corn close to the track, and the blown rain. Jim shoveled in coal. When, finally No. 4 had passed No. 7 was an hour late. Now it was fifty minutes late.

Ahead, to the right, lights clustered. No. 7's whistle shrieked for a town so big that the express must stop. This station was brightly lighted. Passengers were in bed, there was no walking the platform, save the hurrying feet of the few who now became passengers. No. 7 moved, quickened, rushed on and away. Still country now, deep night and rain. Jim Smith dug coal from the tender and fed the engine. Flame flashed out of the furnace door at him. There was a roaring white heat in there. The telegraph poles ran close together. No. 7 was making up time.

John Gordon kept his hand on the throttle, his eyes upon the rolling track. He was as good an engineer as the road possessed—as any road possessed. So far as his powers went he would carry No. 7 safely through the night. He had a name for watchfulness, for knowing when to go fast and when to go slow.

He ran his engine with the usual engineer within him in charge. But tonight, in other respects, there was hardly the usual John Gordon. He recognized this himself. "What is it in the old Bible about wormwood?" As the moments fled it grew bitterer and bitterer. "Wormwood." That was it! Wormwood and gall.

The strike. He had visions all along the line of it. It was now the thirteenth day. Yes, he thought the brotherhoods would inevitably come in. Must come in.

With his bodily eyes upon the track ahead, and his bodily hand upon his engine, and the mind that must serve here serving like an industrious gnome, there was left bulk and volume to be absorbed in the strike and in what lay back and ahead of it. It was in this bulk and volume that there grew wormwood, and the wormwood all grew and leaned toward, and overran and developed the other side from the strikers' side.

His inner state grew hotter and bitterer. There was much to encourage and excuse the growth of wormwood, and he knew it.

The abyss of things rushed up, and every ill there was he laid to the exploiters.

No. 7 made the long curve. Track and train took the shape of a bent bow. Now, leaning forth, he saw behind him all the farther length of the train, the three sleepers and the last one the Arcady.

Behind the engine the mail coach, behind that two day coaches, then the three Pullmans. The small coach, with Bob and Overton, were out of the wormwood, and out of it the two day coaches, and out of it conductors and porters and whatever there was of train crew. In it, in varying degree, were the sleepers, Sparta and Thessaly, men and women from which had walked up and down the platform while No. 4 was waited for.

In the heart of it was the sleeper Arcady. He saw it with his bodily eyes, at the end of the train, on the long curve, just opposite the engine. The inner vision entered it and sought John Douglas. Of course he would be in the stateroom.

There was the center of the heart of wormwood! It was all gathered up for John Gordon right there. There was his exact nadir and opposite. There it was so truly, at the bottom of the curve. There for him stood unlikeness, opposition, antagonism, foe! John Douglas became the emblem of the Idea, and the emblem became hated. He was employer, he was capital, he was the other side. He was the controversy, the long, historic controversy. He was the figure on the platform that stood for all the rest. He was Exploitation, he was Injustice, he was Injury. John Gordon became all the strikers everywhere, John Douglas the struck against, and the battle was holy. It was right to hate with a perfect hatred the opposer, the withstander and withholder walking the platform with a cigar that glowed in the dark, with his bull head sunk between his bull shoulders.

No. 7, the curve behind it, straightened through the night. Jim Smith fed the engine coal.

The train, the mail and day coaches, the sleepers, vibrated. "They're making up time," thought young Browne as he stretched himself in the lower berth of No. 11. John Douglas had the stateroom alone. He disliked close neighborhood of sleeping bodies—said it was not healthful. The porter made the bed at half past 10. The Negro gone, the door shut and blinds drawn, John Douglas finished his undressing and got into bed. He was tired, and the feel of it was cool and comfortable, restful. The car, for a wonder, was not over heated nor under heated, nor was there the annoyance of coal dust. He liked traveling in rain. Why not, then, rest?

For certainly five minutes he did rest, in a subjective relief and ease, with his mind quiet, just aware of the fringe where rose and sank vague, impalpable, not unpleasing forms. Then by degrees the frictionless state vanished.

The train vibrated. After an hour John Douglas gave it up. He turned on the light at his head and drew his watch from under his pillow. Nearly midnight. For a few minutes he debated with himself, then rising with a jerk, he turned on the full light, put on his overcoat, took a book from the suitcase open on the sofa, lit a cigar and climbed back into bed, prepared to read and smoke until he was sleepy.

The strike—and other strikes flying up, all around. "Pshaw! I can't read. I can smoke still." He threw the book upon the sofa where it lay face down. Then he sat, propped up, his overcoat about him and his cigar in his mouth.

He knew so well how Pullman sleeping cars looked that, sitting there, staring before him, he saw as it were through the door and down the darkened aisle. He saw the bordering swaying, bulging, green curtains, and the beds behind them. He supposed they were all sleeping, Bonham and the others, including the college professor. He saw Bonham's long, lank shape, like a grasshopper or a devil's walking stick. "I hope a mummy's haunting him!" He saw in passing Tom in No. 11. He was fond of that boy. The check he sent the other day must have reached Lucy (his sister) by now. Jean (a niece) was growing a fine girl. "I think I'll buy her a watch." He made a mental note about china for the other girl who was soon to marry. And he was going to Brentano's for books for his daughter. She liked the new, foreign things that he never read. The book that the strike wouldn't let him read was one of Rosa Nouchette Cary's.

He looked through the Arcady into the next car, Sparta. The like darkened aisle, and bulging curtains, and suitcases annoyingly projecting from under berths. The like sleeping forms. He knew two or three in this car. Here was the newspaper man of whom Tom had spoken. Of course he wanted an interview. Well, he couldn't get it! There was too much talking about this strike. John Douglas knocked the ashes from his cigar. "Bonham might give him one about mummies, or that damned college fellow with his fourth dimension—" He grinned and puffed out smoke. He was feeling better. He had a sense of relaxation, and could see sleep with the tail of his eye. He looked into the third car, Thessaly. Swaying curtains, darkened aisle, men and women asleep, porter nodding in a corner, conductor just gone through----

Consistently and usually his vision would have stopped there. The sleeping cars were the train to him. Tonight, before he knew it, he found another train. Two day coaches, the mail coach, the engine—the fireman and the engineer.

With a flash sleep was gone. Relaxment was over. He stiffened himself in bed. Presently he sat upright. John Gordon. That was the name of the strike, or the strike was the name of John Gordon—all strikes—the whole, culminating fight, the question and the duel. Slowly, with a smooth, automatic action, he put up his hand and removed the cigar from his mouth to the window ledge. A thousand ages of strife rose out of the dark well. He became delegate for an association that was very old. It summed itself up in him, and he moved a right hand that knew stone hammer and sword and machine gun, that knew orator's gesture, that knew pen and check book. The volume of all that side seemed in him, and the volume of all the other side in the engineer of No. 7, with his hand upon the throttle, and they were at odds and would stay at odds until the engineer gave in.

"It's 1 o'clock," said Jim Smith, and shoveled coal.

The rain came down steadily. Where there was running or standing water anywhere near the track, the headlight showed it full and muddy. The telegraph poles glittered, the tree trunks, the chance buildings past which rushed the express, the sides of cuts, the mouths of tunnels.

John Gordon was bent upon, John Gordon inclosed the strike, the whole of it in its vast light and shadow. "Mr. John Douglas, Mr. John Douglas, your end of the train isn't the whole train.—No! By no means!"

The stateroom of the Arcady thought. "At the meeting I'll advise---"

Said Jim Smith. "If it comes to the general, captain, how're you going to vote?"

"I'll vote the strike."

He looked out and ahead along the track. "Here's the big embankment. It's raining like the beginning of the forty days!"

A moment, compounded of dropping down, of turning over, shocking, impregnated, if one had time to taste it, with terror. "O, God!" cried Jim Smith.

The stateroom of the Arcady went black.

. . . .

Evidently a stream from which the fog was lifting. It was not so wide after all, and still it seemed somehow wide. Evidently trees where had seemed but a streaky nothingness. Little willows and hazels with an occasional taller tree. A shore line with pebbles such as boys make skip upon the water. That was what was underneath instead of an emptiness harder than granite. Evidently dawn—not a sick and vacant gray lacking any application as had at first appeared. Evidently cheeping of birds, evidently spring.

A man moved—sat up. His hand resting upon a round pebble, it seemed to him that the thing thrilled into his palm and was understood. He remembered having once had a long sickness, a fever, and when he was getting well and just lying on the porch looking at things, this was how he felt. That is, somewhat like this. He remembered how all the mornings seemed then so lovely. Well, this was a lovely morning—a very lovely morning.

He looked, and a little way off was lying another man. He thought dimly. "Some one hurt," and crawled over to help. But at that moment the other man, too, sat up. "Hello!"

"You aren't dead then! Hello!"

The second looked at the stream. "I dreamed that blessed line was an ocean and I had to swim it."

"That was just about my dream, too. It's a lovely morning. It's good to feel the sun coming!"

They sat side by side. Said the first. "I suppose I remember a billion dawns."

"Let's call it a trillion. We were going soon to begin to think in trillions."

"All over, all around, everywhere. And thick through. Remembering so much must give the powerful, delicate, and delicious feeling. And yet—it's curious—but I don't seem to be able to remember particular facts."

The second sat looking at the trees emerging from the mist. "I love this air, and the sweet bird singing. Well, sir, we seem to be intimates, but the mournful fact is I cannot remember your name!"

"For the life of me I can't call yours!"

They laughed. Humor played like a warm light over things. "Then we'll just say comrade or brother."

They sat still, their eyes upon the stream and the trees. The mist held strongly upon the further bank. They could see nothing over there. Upon this bank, too, it made a lacework, but the trees were indubitably greening. And there held the same great lightness and exquisiteness. "There's some ingredient in this air---"

"It must be that! I feel as though I could move mountains— if they wanted to be moved."

As though the word had evoked them they saw mountains— a range of them against the sky.

"I ask you, brother," said the one, "have you any idea what is this country, and how we got here?"

"I haven't. It's strange. What do you think we had better do?"

"We might hunt around. There must be inhabitants."

They rose to their feet. Doing this, they turned from the stream to the mountains. Distinctly these drew them, so purple and wonderful they were, with a pale light atop.

They walked and walked, but they met no man. Moreover, what vaguely gave them concern, the dawn held. It was no more day than when they sat by the water. But the mountains grew nearer. They were now seen to be stupendous.

For a time it was yet very easy to move and the strange lift of things continued. But the first ease—sense as it were of the vastest relief and inconsequence—was departing. Instead they knew that something portentous was ahead, and yet they did not know what it was.

They were among mountains, wall within wall. Mountains were around them, before and above them. And they were climbing with a strange insensible swiftness. They were up high, high. And still it held dawn, but brighter than it was. There was no mist and there was a redness in the sky. But their anxiety was growing, and a sense of myriad touches. "What's going on here, brother?"

"I don't know. I was going so lightly. Now I've got a burden on my back."

"The same here. I wish I could call your name!"

"I was just thinking the same thing. John!"

"John! We've got that far."

They climbed. The air was still, but through them, around and across them, seemed to go moving currents, holding many forms if only they could remember or divine them. They now began to have a terror of where they were.

All kinds of reverberations seemed to come toward them bringing crises. The reverberations were not understood, nor the crises which seemed to impend, then broke and passed. They talked for company. Then, suddenly, like a wave of dark heat, one looked at the other and found something of ugliness. So quick it was! They both halted. "Something comes up----"

"We are all alone. Yet I wish that I were lonelier----"

They could not keep from saying what they thought. Word and thought and mood and act had grown one. Certainly the land was strange, for as though they had said "Open Sesame!" there were four where had been two. The newcomers were dark shapes, and at first they made as though they would love the men, but as soon as their arms were about them they tried to crush them. The two fought with them, man and shape, and now they fought weakly and now they fought strongly, but always interminably. Another frightful thing was that the dawn seemed to have gone back. They could hardly see the mountains. There was nothing but the sound of fighting and struggling, and it lasted so long that they were like to forget when the shapes had appeared. The shapes were fearful, and twisted and cowed them. Not the least horror was that they looked like themselves, each shape like the man it would bind, only grown thick armed and monstrous.

They seemed to struggle for a thousand years. Then first one man and then the other got breath and took hold of a kind of a gleam. The shapes grew thinner, weaker. One man cried across to the other. "How are you faring?"

"There's more light. How are you faring? Look out! You'll slip there! It's where I slipped."

"Thank you! You, too, look out. There are loose stones there."

"I've got your name now. It's John Douglas."

"I've got yours. It's John Gordon. After all, you mean to be a decent fellow."

"So do you."

It seemed that the dawn was coming back. Moreover, certainly, those dark shapes were weaker. Presently they dropped their arms which were withered and fell behind John Douglas and John Gordon. There was again the dawn and the red in the sky and the mountains, wall on wall. The shapes were sunken, no man knew how far. The lift was in the air again, the taste of peace. There came taste again of the misty stream and the pebbly shore and the trees. But here were the mountains, and they must climb; they knew not why, but they must climb. They climbed, and their hearts beat, John Douglas, John Gordon; John Douglas, John Gordon.

They came to a niche in the mountain side. The terror had gone, but an enormous loneliness was upon them. They sat down, each upon a stone. "They are like grave stones, but who cares? Can you tell in the least how we got here?"

"No. I ought to be driving No. 7, on the East and West

road."

"I ought to be in bed in the stateroom of the sleeper Arcady."

"We seem to have come a long way and lived a long time in practically no time at all. That stream down there with the mist. It was dawn then, and it is dawn now."

"Well, there's one thing. I used to feel a hatred toward you."

"The same here. I to you."

"I don't feel that any longer, Mr. Gordon."

"I don't either, Mr. Douglas. I didn't at first down there by the stream. Then I did when those terrible old dark prize fighters happened along. But now I don't. I suppose we're all in the brotherhood."

"Or the association. All in."

"It's too lonely here for us to fight. It would be one hand striking the other—one foot kicking the other."

"I believe it is really lonely everywhere."

"Well, it is lonely here all right, or it would be if you weren't along."

"The same to you. Well, we'd better be walking."

They bestirred themselves. As they walked the mountains took a more kindly aspect. The two seemed to go moreover with something of the lightness of the first starting out. Suddenly, by the wayside, under a mountain wall, they came to a cottage. It hung there of brown wood, with trees about it, and the dawn for its prospect. They went in. There was fire upon the hearth, and beside it a cradle with a baby lying in it. John Gordon and John Douglas stood and looked down upon it, and it opened its eyes and looked up at them. It moved its hands and smiled.

"It is I! I know it for myself."

"It is as certainly I! I know it for myself."

"We must have both descended from him. That college fellow might say---"

As they looked the figure of a woman formed itself behind the cradle. It was seated, bending over the cradle. It became luminous, the face became luminous. "Mother! Mother!"

It faded, but the babe in the cradle stayed distinct. Whatever the college fellow might have said, John Douglas and John Gordon felt now a body bond, a warmth and sympathy. It was quite as though between them, passing through the babe as it were, sprang tissue, vein, and artery and net of nerves. "If we were one there, could it ever depart?" They felt a warmth and care each for each.

The cradled babe vanished—the brown cottage fell away. Here was the great ascent of the mountains, and the dawn that was a little redder. But John Douglas felt love for John Gordon and John Gordon for John Douglas.

"Strike and lockout are hard words, and poverty and riches, and labor and capital. They sound like stones thrown against glass."

"Against flesh. They sound like the stoning of Stephen. Or like the Roman hammers at the cross."

They climbed. All manner of reconciliations and unions seemed to take place within them. The light was strengthening and fear had gone from the mountains.

It rushed back. They were on a plateau, then all the mist lifted. The plateau dwindled. They were standing on a peak, and it was a dizzy one. All around them it dropped sheer into abyss. They saw no bottom, but a purple and terrible twilight down there. They had climbed what seemed a mountain, climbing by a mountain path. Now they saw that the way they had come was vanished. Behind as on either side hung the gulf. Moreover, as the plateau had narrowed and shortened, so now the peak was narrowing. There was growing scant room for two to stand.

The light increased, but it increased only upon a further shore from this peak. Across the abyss shot up sheer a vast rock. Over here the sun was under the horizon, but over there there seemed sun. It was golden, the rock. Moreover, it was no mere wave crest with scarce footing room. It was of the foundation of a land. They dimly saw the land, they faintly heard sounds, fragrance was blown to them. What they saw was rich and dear, what they heard was sweet, the fragrance thrilled them. Something cried, "Home, that I had forgotten! Home, home, home!"

To reach home—it became the one desire.

They stood now on a shaft, as it were, a pillar uprisen through night. Around, below, was dusk and emptiness, bottomless, despairing. Only in front was that land, but between them and it hung abyss.

"If there were a bridge----It is too far to leap."

"The ground beneath us does not cease to crumble. If we

stay here we shall sink into the pit."

One plank led across. They saw it now, gray and thin, laid from edge to edge. A voice spoke from that land, and it spoke with an authority they might not dispute. "Just one may cross."

They were not able to dispute it. They consented, and felt no quarrel with the speaker, whoever he might be. But it was to cross—for just one to cross—and the place where they stood was growing unstable, like a quicksand.

John Douglas said: "If only one can go, you'd better go. You've had the hardest time here."

John Gordon said: "I'm used to roughing it. You'd suffer more. So you go---"

"No, you. I want you to be happy."

"And I want you, John."

"I can see plainly enough to see that there wouldn't be any joy yonder---"

"If you won't go, I won't go."

"The ground is vanishing. You go, John. It's heaven."

"Yes, I see. Won't you go, John?"

"No."

The ground trembled beneath them. They took hands, they put each an arm around the other's shoulders. "Meet the gulf then together. It's all over! We are one."

There was speech in their ears. "One crosses."

There was one on the gray plank, gray and thin like a nerve. One went into heaven.

. . . .

Lanterns swung in the night about No. 7. Loud and excited voices beat the air. Hands, arms, feet, the whole body pushed and hauled at the wreckage. Over and over rose a statement, "The marvel is we weren't all killed!"

It seemed a miracle in the dark and wet night. There were bruises enough, flesh wounds, a few broken bones, but nothing like the entire and desperate hurt that might have been. Only—the engine lay on its side, down the bank. The fireman, Jim Smith, had escaped, having jumped. But the engineer lay dead beneath his engine. "Instantly killed,"[2] said the examining doctor.

The sleeper Thessaly, the sleeper Sparta, the sleeper Arcady escaped with little injury. It was the day coaches and the mail coach that had been dragged from the track and overturned. The Arcady, being the end sleeper, appeared indeed to have gone scot free. Its occupants had received a violent jolting and some had been shaken from their berths. Some had thought it an earthquake, others waked at once to the knowledge of accident. All were excited, all were talking, all had dressed or were dressing as fast as they could, with some in attention to fullness of apparel. The readiest were gone forward through the Sparta and the Thessaly to the rain and blackness, wreckage and voices ahead.

Young Browne had thought it an earthquake. The window pane had struck his head he told Bonham and the college professor when he encountered them in the aisle. He seemed dazed. A trickle of blood went down his forehead. Bonham looked. "It's nothing much. Come into the air with us."

Young Browne started, then he rubbed his brows. "I'd better see if my uncle wants anything."

"Hasn't he gone forward with the others?"

Young Browne didn't think so. "I'd better see." He went into the stateroom, whence his frightened voice came immediately, "Mr. Bonham! Mr. Bonham!"

They found John Douglas dead, thrown from his berth and his neck broken. "Instant death," said the examining physician.

Notes

[1] Egypt! in Chicago *Tribune*.

[2] " " around instantly killed omitted in Chicago *Tribune*.

The Return of Magic

Magic stepped softly over the forest floor. "Is the cave clean and the fire lighted? If I go to sleep do not wake me for at least a day and a night!"

"The cave is clean and the fire is lighted," replied the gnome. "Are you so tired? You had best eat and drink before you sleep."

"Give me then," said Magic, "manna and dates from Fez and a bubble glass of Hippocrene."

Magic ate and sipped slowly. Green light and violent light entered from the forest to visit the red and gold light of the fire. "What have you been doing?" asked the gnome. "You work too hard nowadays!"

"I feel rested," answered Magic. "It is good to come home to the old forest and the old cave, and to you, my little old man! It is true that I'm kept going around the clock! There's but one other I know who's as hard worked, and that's Romance!"

"I began to notice everything quickening," said the gnome, "about two thousand years ago. And now there is another thrill and leap! As you say, you're busy all around the clock."

"It is nothing to what it will be in the twenty-first century!" said Magic dreamily. "Yes, yes, it is quickening! I'm not let alone nowadays even in sleep. But I enjoy it! Every one enjoys real work. It's[1] only toil and drudgery when it is unreal."

An azure and ebony butterfly fluttered into the cave and perched a moment upon Magic's knee, then sailed across the firelight and out again into the green forest. "I was thinking just then," said Magic, "of Daedalus and Icarus. I was there—naturally—the day they flew from the walls of Knossus. But I was weaker then in the air of this planet than I am now. Their wings—they were blue and ebony, I remember, like that butterfly's—crumpled up and they fell. But I am stronger today. Beyond this cave and this forest where I come to rest, Daedalus and Icarus by the thousand are flying in the blue air! Look through my eyes. Now! Can you see them?"

"I am looking," said the gnome, "from between a pair of huge wings. Below me is the ocean and it is tumbling in green hills. So it looks to the albatross!"

"Again!" said Magic.

"Wings so far from tip to tip! Here are mountains. They are so high that they are snowy. Yet I am above them. So they look to the eagle!"

"Again!"

The gnome said, "I am over golden, endless desert. There are date palms, ruined temples, half buried sphinxes. So it looks to the stork flying from winter!"

Magic stretched her arms. "Daedalus and Icarus their tribe, learning victory! Some fall, it is true, and I am sorry! But as soon as I am stronger—and, little man, I grow stronger forever—they will not fall! Flashing everywhere, men, women and children—oh, far beyond and above the sea mew and the eagle!"

"I do not put it beyond you!" said the gnome. "Here are grapes of Eschol. I do not believe you want to sleep! Stretch yourself in the firelight and talk."

" 'Talk!' " said Magic. "A little while ago I left two groups of men talking together about markets and meetings and so forth. One group was dressed in woollen and sat in a heated building because it was winter in that city. The other group wore white duck, and palm trees cast their shadows across the court. The two spoke without shouting, but the table between was an ocean and three hundred leagues of land!"

"That," said the gnome, "would have surprised Roger Bacon!"

"Oh, I am not sure," answered Magic. "He expected great things of me! He was so interested in telescopes, which he called 'optical instruments'. If he could see the ones that I am now turning out, and the tales that they bring! Let me tell you, I have great surprises there up my sleeve!"

"Whisper one to me!" Magic whispered.

"By Einstein!" said the gnome.

Magic stretched her limbs in the firelight. "I remember so many darlings! There was Michael Scott,

'A wizard of such dreaded fame
  That when in Salamanca's cave
He listed his magic wand to wave
  The bells would ring in Notre Dame.'

A wizard of another department said that of him. I remember when we cut the Elidon Hill in three. And we were good at bridges, Michael and I! But all that was 'prentice work. Now I am engineer full grown—or almost full grown."

"There stray little winds through the forest telling things," said the gnome. "Mesopotamia waving with wheat and barley, and Sahara a garden, tulips blowing on the Zuyder Zee, and a road to Timbuctoo—"

Magic laughed. "Straws! Straws to show that the wind is blowing. Important, but there is a Within and an Atop to all that!—Mark now!"

She sat up, in the firelight, on the smooth cave floor. She was very fair, Magic, and growing fairer every day. Suddenly to the gnome the cave walls were gone. The great-trunked, green forest, tall and waving, also disappeared. Just Magic and he, and Magic showing him. Out of her hands, as though they were spun from her fingers, ran moonlight coloured ribbons, swift as light and finer than ether and stronger than steel. The gnome saw a marvellous thing. They began to tie together the earth which during his whole memory had been crumbled and loosened, a muddy space around each frayed bit. Now he watched piece brought to fit with piece. The pattern began to show. He heard an enormous singing and laughing and clapping of hands. Then the pattern which was growing clear, and which seemed to him the only fair and only significant thing that he had ever laid eyes upon, faded a little, faded a little more. The gleaming lines were invisibly thin, broke. "I can't hold it!" said Magic disappointedly. "But patience, patience! I will hold it one of these days!"

"Show me something more!"

"I have blue prints for all kinds of things. One by one they will arrive! Have you noticed that in the last hundred or two years men have taken to calling me Discovery?"

"The old name is dear to me," said the gnome.

Magic laughed. "You always were a little backward!" She raised her arms above her head. She was so fair, Magic! "Since the beginning of time the fullest Finding has ever been to come near and nearer to one another! Now I'll show you a farther lap of the way. Shut your eyes! Also do not bother with outward ears."

The gnome obeyed. Silence in the cave, then he said, "There is a rush of voices and of sights! . . .They grow clear. I begin to understand desires, feelings, thoughts. Currents and masses of desires, feelings, thoughts! I share and I understand.—Telepathy? Intuition?"

"Myself, I prefer the word Communion," said Magic. "But the name does not so much matter.—Look and see what I am beginning to do with Absence!"

"I see," said the gnome, "a man sitting in a desert. He has been digging for old buried cities. His camp is over yonder. The men there are asleep. He sits upon an old, old column, honey-yellow, that they have partly dug from honey-yellow sand. It is a starry night with a young moon. He speaks across a great way to one he loves.—I see a woman. She sits beside a window in a farm house, in a land of orchards. It is snowing. She listens and answers within and turns and goes where it does not snow. The man in the desert stretches out his hand. He says 'Emily!' She is there in the desert. She gleams. I see him, too, gleaming. They walk together, under the stars and the young moon, out in the desert.—Absence! You, and they with you, are climbing past Absence!"

"Faint old powers growing stronger as the sun shines," said Magic. She waved her hand and again sprang the cave and the fire and the vast, emerald, waving forest. "How I love the winds heard from this cave! Do you remember the wind in the oak of Dodona?"

"Aye," answered the gnome. "Every leaf had a mouth to tell of Wonder-to-come!"

"Now every forest tells," said Magic. "Every tree in forest, and the tree by the house door."

"Let me see something more!"

"What do you wish to see?"

Said the gnome, "It was ever Death that your great servants and lovers pondered about. They said that it was a wall far greater than the wall of China, and they worked all their days to see over or through it."

"They could only do that," answered Magic, "by being greater than Death. Nothing can be done but by being greater than the thing to be done. That's the secret of Magic! I", said Magic, "have another name—a Sunday name."

"What is that?"

"It is Truth," said Magic. "I am seeing through Sleep and presently I shall see through Death.—Now look again!"

The gnome looked. The cave grew very still, the fire burned

to a point, blue and gold and electric white. The forest without hung depth on depth, and there rose in it an effect of new blossoms and of bright birds from afar. "I have no words for what I see," said the gnome. "But I see! Are they going to meet, the dead and the living?"

" 'Dead,' " said Magic, "is by no means as final as it sounds."

"If you conquer death—"

At that Death stood outside the cave. He was thin, and the stars showed through him, for suddenly all without had grown a clear and splendid night. "O Magic," he said, "there is no better place to die in than this cave of yours, by your fire! Bear me witness that I never said I was immortal! They have said it for me, but I have never said it of myself. When my end approaches, and I do not think it far off as the gods count, may I lie down in this cave, draw my last breath, and leave my great bones here? I ask it of thee, O Magic, whose other names are Love and Understanding and Might!"

NOTE

[1] *The Reviewer*, 3,1:359, last line, gives Its.

The Tree

Anny Smith, in a blue gingham dress and a brown apron, turned the toast for Mr. Nixon's seven o'clock breakfast and with the other hand moved the coffee pot. A red light from the range, striking upward, illumined her high-nosed, long, firm face. Anny Smith had been cook for ten years in Mrs. Lamb's superior boarding-house. Elvira, the cook maid, dipped an egg out of boiling water. Henry, the waiter, came from the pantry with Mr. Nixon's tray.

"It's a fine day, Mrs. Smith!"

Anny glanced out of the kitchen window. " 'Tis!"

"I noticed yesterday the buds were swelling on your tree."

"Yes. Down in Maryland things will be getting green."

Henry poised the tray on his hand and vanished, only to reappear with a tray for Mr. Page, who was taking an early train. Baked apple, cream of wheat, poached egg, toast and tea.

"Jennie and me are going to the beach this afternoon."

"That will be fine!" said Anny Smith. "Put out the 'lectric light, Elvira."

A tall, raw-boned figure, she stood before the sink, washing her hands. As she spoke, her eyes sought the window. Out there, at the further end of a walled-in back-yard, stood a really giant tree, uppermost branches and twigs and rosy buttons at ends of twigs drawn against a saffron morning sky.

"I hope you'll have a good time, Henry!"

Henry grinned. "We will! You won't be going any further than your tree, Mrs. Smith?"

"It's not my afternoon."

"You don't go when it *is* your afternoon."

"I'm not," said Anny, "as young as I once was. I can't gad like the rest of you. My legs and back get tired. I'm on my feet all day, for this ain't an easy place! When I can get a bit of rest time, I just want to *sit*!" She spoke in a harsh, rather deep voice, with a note in it of, "I don't want to be teased about *that* again!"

Henry, going, said peaceably: "Well, it's a great old tree!

It wouldn't seem like Number 27 without it, or without you, Mrs. Smith, sitting on that bench with your head against the trunk and your eyes on the sky!"

"They ain't always on the sky," said Anny. "But we've all got to have mountains and seashore somewhere!"

Operations in the kitchen pursued their usual morning path. The sky was growing blue; a million sparrows made a fuss in the tree. Elvira placed oatmeal, bacon, corn-bread, and coffee upon a table at the end of the long kitchen, and Mrs. Lamb's household staff gathered for their breakfast. Anny Smith; William, the butler; Henry, the waiter; Wilson, the general utility man; Jennie and Martha, the maids; Elvira; and Rupert, the boy, made the staff. Number 27 meant two old houses put together and twenty boarders besides several for meals only. Anny Smith took the head of the table and William the foot.

"It's going to be a fine day, Mrs. Smith! Your tree's putting out buds."

"Yes, 'tis."

Jennie buttered her corn-bread. She laughed. "Mrs. Smith wouldn't take a thousand dollars for that tree!"

Wilson had a gloomy mind. "What if some day they cut it down?"

Anny's harsh, deep voice came in at that. "Who'd do it? Nobody! It's an asset. All the rooms on the back like to look at it. Mr. Page says some moonlight nights it's the past and the whole forest and God to him. It's worth more than if 'twas firewood."

She poured the coffee with a long, bony, elderly hand. Over the back and up the arm to the elbow stretched a great, dead-white scar where once she had been badly scalded.

The kitchen ate rapidly. There was much to do and little idling at Number 27. Still they talked. And what they principally talked about was the prospects of the house, by no means as full as it should be this time of year, and that after a dull winter. Last evening Mr. Warner (Warner was Mrs. Lamb's son) had come downstairs and made them a little speech about hard times, and the need for general spryness and economy and eagerness to please.

Martha now fell upon the last item. "If he means the boarders, I don't see that they do awful much toward pleasing us! I'd like to put them in our place for a bit and us in theirs!"

William, who was a model butler, spoke placidly. "That's

anarchistic, Miss Martha!"

"No. You stick to the Golden Rule," said Anny Smith.

Henry stood up for Mrs. Lamb and Mr. Warner and for the majority of the boarders. "I've been here five years, and I wouldn't ha' stayed if on the whole they hadn't been practicing Christians!"

But something had soured Martha. "Oh, they practice a good part of the time! But if Mrs. Lamb and Mr. Warner got a notion they were losing money by you, they'd turn as hard and send you packing! That ain't the Golden Rule either."

"They've got to look after making money," argued William. "They aren't taking boarders for pure pleasure."

Anny Smith said, "I don't see much to complain of."

The staff of Number 27 pushed back their chairs and rose from the table. The big clock said twenty-five to eight. At eight the breakfast gong would vibrate through the two houses turned into one. The glow from the range struck upon Anny Smith's face and gave it an illusory look of color and youth.

Breakfast, and after breakfast, deliverymen and such. At her regular time appeared Mrs. Lamb, large and dressed in black, broad of face and firm of mouth, with an agreeable, drawling voice.

"Good morning, Anny! Good morning, Elvira!"

Inspection, consultation, and decisions. When everything was done, said Mrs. Lamb:

"The second floor suite is taken at last, Anny! I had a letter this morning."

"I'm glad of that!" said Anny. "It pays you more than anything when it's full, and seems more aching empty when nobody's there."

"I was beginning to feel rather despairing," said Mrs. Lamb. "Times are hard, and one never knows what makes a neighborhood pick up or the reverse. It's Mrs. Lascelles, two children, and a French maid. She takes all four rooms, and if she likes them and the house and the service and everything, Anny, she'll renew at the end of three months for a year. It's important. I shall be awfully glad."

"When she's coming?"

"Next week. She's a widow. The children are four and six, Bobby and Janet. The maid, Marie, has been with her a long time." Mrs. Lamb rose to go. "It's a perfectly lovely day! I wish we could *all* go into the country! Well, sit under your tree for a bit anyhow, Anny!"

She departed. A likable person, Mrs. Lamb, though with lines of Old Care about her eyes and mouth.

The rear yard of Number 27, brick paved save for two rather forlorn flowerbeds, and divided by high, brick walls from the neighboring houses, was a quiet, tidy place, at once sequestered and under observation. It was used only by the domestics of Number 27, but all the rear windows regarded it and its one great, ancient tree. The tree stood in a corner. Trunk and a great branch and the angle of the wall made one small, withdrawn place, away from eyes, an almost woodland shelter. Here, against the trunk, was fastened a bench, and it and the corner were Anny Smith's, hers by prescription, ancient and old and continuing usage. Every one at Number 27 recognized it.

Anny sat down, the mighty trunk between her and the house. At eight feet rose the brick wall hung with ivy. The tree and it together made a fastness, a hermitage. Bare branches, little, rose leaves, small, green leaves, great leaves darkly green, crimson leaves, russet leaves, leaves loosened from the twigs and falling and falling, leaves in the yard, in a great drift in the corner —ten times had she been around the year with it all. Unless the weather was very bad, she might be here as often as three or four times a day. Even if one had only ten minutes! Light rains the tree kept from her; sometimes she sat there with her old umbrella raised. Light snows she rather liked. It was a grand place for the brooding weather before a thunder storm. Once a rainbow got caught in the branches. Today the sky was without a cloud.

Anny sat down, drew a long breath, and relaxed. After a bit her memories or her visions began to play. Dead and living folk came about her, and each wrapped with a bit of Maryland. Sometimes it was just Maryland herself. Sometimes just country without putting any name to it. Lilacs and blackbirds and meadows and a stream. Sometimes it was wider and deeper and fuller than that. Anny Smith, her head against the trunk of the old tree, went afar. She, the old cook at Number 27, based all her days upon her minutes beneath this tree. Here she drank the wine and ate the bread of busy rest.

Anny's body sat still. Anny herself was moving with her mother along a path between grapevines. . .

Upon the appointed day Mrs. Lascelles moved into the

second-floor suite. Whoever occupied this thereby and in the act became the star boarder.

Marie, the maid, ate with the children in the alcove of the big dining-room. The children and Mrs. Lascelles thoroughly kept Marie from eating the bread of idleness. But she found time each day and sometimes in the evening to slip down the back stairs to the basement. That portion of Number 27 liked Marie well enough.

The Lascelles children also were not bad—for children.

Jennie reported: "They're cute youngsters—but, my! 'They're *my* children and must have what money can give them!' That's Mrs. Lascelles."

"She's like a lot of others then," said Wilson. "She ain't a bad-looking woman, but I never did like a long upper lip!"

Jennie laughed.

Wilson turned red. "I didn't mean just that, Mrs. Smith!"

"Oh, I don't mind!" said Anny. "My father used to say that anyhow a long upper lip knew what it wanted."

"Mrs. Lamb's got one, too."

Upon the tree the buds were now opening into tiny, rose-velvet affairs which later on would turn into green leaves elegantly cut. Young ivy leaves on young sprays rejoiced over the red brick wall. Up among the tall branches, light clouds were caught like lace. Sun and shadow fingered the surrounding houses. Somewhere a street organ played.

Anny, her head against the tree, shut her eyes. A journey she had taken with the man who died, a journey clear to New Orleans. Ships, ships! She had been on a ship down Chesapeake Bay. Ships over all the big ocean. The carrying of things over all the world in ships from shore to shore. Things and folk. She was going without a ship.—Music.—Christ Jesus in a boat on Gallilee. —Blackbirds in March and the smell of the woods.—Music.—Her mother's Paisley shawl that she had lost in Philadelphia at the Centennial. Her mother. The tree was growing green. Old friend! A woman had seen and felt a lot under this tree. It was better to own this tree than a Paisley shawl, better to own it than all the diamonds at the jeweler's. A woman named Anny Smith for ten years sitting here every little time she could slip away.—Music.—Ships and trains and travel. They could have them who had the money, but Anny Smith could travel without money when she sat down in this corner.—Dogwood and Judas tree in Maryland.

The kitchen clock struck five. Anny opened her eyes and stood up. As she crossed the yard, a third-floor window opened, and Mr. Page looked out.

"Anny, you and the tree are our oldest inhabitants. I do believe that corner's a house and establishment and three vacations a year to you!"

Anny's long upper lip twitched. She looked up at the pleasant, rosy, middle-aged gentleman.

"'Tis something like that, sir! 'Tis my remembering and thinking and seeing and praying place."

"Well," said Mr. Page, "I hope you'll always have it! I like to see you there."

Mrs. Lascelles, it proved, possessed nerves. They were shattered, she explained to Mrs. Lamb, by her husband's death and the resultant sole care of money and two children. The estate was being settled; there was not so much money now, but later there would be more, oh, a good deal more! Among the consequences of her shattered condition were nervous headaches when she was alarmed or crossed, headaches and restless misery, and "Let us go to some other place!"

Mrs. Lamb spoke of it to Anny in connection with the precise degree of softness for Mrs. Lascelles's breakfast egg and crispness for the accompanying toast.

"Mr. Warner and I are anxious, Anny, that she should be pleased. It's very difficult, life, just now!"

Anny nodded. "I'll try my best, ma'am. But it's a pity some folks don't have to do it themselves! Money's the hardest bed to lie on."

"Lord, I'd change mattresses with her!" said Elvira, who was listening.

The children were dears. They went to a kindergarten, Marie taking them thither at nine and going for them at noon. Sometimes in the afternoon they drove in a hired car with their mother. But usually they trotted off with Marie to a small park not far from Number 27.

They had lived in the second floor suite a month when, one afternoon, they came home with great eyes. They had seen a child run over. Bobby and Janet wanted to tell all about it.

That night Mrs. Lascelles had a terrible headache merely from thinking, "It might have been my children!"

The next morning Bobby and Janet went to kindergarten, but in the afternoon with their mother in a taxi. She told Mrs.

Lamb:

"I can never trust them in that park again!"

It was Anny's afternoon, Elvira in the kitchen with Rupert to help. It was May; there were young, green leaves on the tree. Anny brought her mending with her, and now she mended, and now she rested garment and needle and knobby, elderly hands.

Jerusalem the Golden, with milk and honey blest.—A little church in Maryland.—Little churches over all the earth and the sound of bells.—Forest. This tree was once in a forest, or its parents were. That was much the same thing, very much indeed the same thing. Forest and forest and forest!—And Indians.— Away back upon her father's side a Hartwell had married an Indian woman. A red woman with straight, black hair, and black eyes and a high nose and a long, straight upper lip, sitting under a tree, by a cabin, in a clearing—

As she returned to the kitchen, she happened to raise her eyes. Mrs. Lascelles, an elegant figure in a black and white kimono, was standing before the open window of the children's room. She seemed to be regarding the yard and the tree with a new eye.

Two days after this was Sunday. Marie, who had been to early mass, stopped by the kitchen. "Oh, Meestress Cook, there goin' be sand-pile under the tree!"

"Sand-pile?"

"*Ah, oui!* Bobby and Janet shall play there. No more in the park!"

The Maryland woman turned the waffle irons. "You're crazy! Or it's a joke. French jokes are mighty curious."

"It isn't my joke," said Marie. "I didn't think of it. I'd rather go to the park."

"You can still go all right," said Anny Smith. "That's my tree."

At ten appeared Rupert. "Mrs. Smith, Mrs. Lamb say, will you come to her room for a minute."

Anny went. Mrs. Lamb had her bonnet on for church.

"Sit down, Anny. I want to have a little talk."

Anny sat down in her clean Sunday apron.

"It's Mrs. Lascelles, Anny. You know the children were almost run over in the park the other day."

"No'm. They only saw some one else run over."

"By this time she's got it the other way. Of course, no one can say they mightn't be run over. She's a nervous, fanciful woman, but of course a mother's a mother."

"Thousands of children go to that park and aren't run over. —But of course she's got money."

"Did Marie say anything to you this morning?"

"She said there'd be a sand-pile under the tree out there. And I said that was something that wasn't possible."

"Would you so much mind, Anny?"

"Yes, I'd mind."

"The children are away in the mornings except Saturday and Sunday. She wants them to play under the tree afternoons and those two mornings. Marie will be with them, so that they won't disturb the house. A sand-pile's the obvious thing, and she pitched right away upon that corner. I suggested that she take the space between the flower-beds. But no! It's the corner between the tree and the wall. She's set upon it."

"Hasn't she noticed? She's been at the window enough."

"Yes, she's noticed. But she says she'll make it all right with you."

"She can't—poor, poverty-stricken creature!"

Mrs. Lamb looked at the clock. "I don't think you should take it this way, Anny! Mr. Warner and I are obliged to keep those rooms filled. It's a hard season. There are notes and things. You might understand and be helpful, Anny, being with me so long. She's that kind that if I say no, she'll take all manner of offense and leave at the end of the month. She's obstinate."

"It ain't just!" said Anny. "It ain't just! It ain't just! And you're taking share with the oppressor—"

"That isn't the right tone, Anny."

"—With your church bonnet on!"

Mrs. Lamb reddened. Her long upper lip drew down. "Hard words butter no parsnips, Anny!"

"Then, you've said that she can have it?"

"I haven't any choice."

"Then I'll give you notice, Mrs. Lamb. I'll not leave till you've got a cook, but the day after I'll leave!"

"That's nonsense, Anny!"

Mrs. Lamb, already too late for church, settled down to argument and representations of the rights of things. All in vain!

"Yes, Mrs. Lamb, maybe 'tis your tree. Maybe 'tis. And maybe money and self-support has got to be considered. Maybe it has. But still there's justice. The way I look as it that's something that belongs to God! And I'll stand up for it."

Mrs. Lamb's color stayed; her long upper lip rested very stiff. At last: "Very good, Anny! You're making a mistake. There's a lot of unemployment, and you aren't so young as you were. But that's your look-out! I'll set about getting some one tomorrow."

"If you pleas'm. When," asked Anny, "is the sand-pile coming in?"

"As soon as she can get it. Day after tomorrow, I suppose."

Sunday afternoon and a kind of peace over the earth. Mrs. Lascelles, the children, and Marie drove in the park. Anny Smith, leaving a clean kitchen, crossed the yard to the tree. Green leaves and the sparrows and the ivy. Old brick wall—old trunk of tree. Sunshine fair on a vista of the backs of houses— a broken sky-line—above a hotel at the street corner a flag flying, intensely picked out by the sun.

Anny gazed at the flag, her heart hot and tempestuous. "It's double-faced!" she said.

Presently she broke down and cried, her head in her apron. She had not cried for years.

But the tree—but the tree—the tree and the corner that for so long had been to the old cook at Number 27 a magic carpet and a prayer rug and a home of contemplation.—When you go into a cathedral, presently you take the cathedral tone. When you pass into far, clean, desert space, the crowded heart and mind widen. When you lie in ancient, wondrous forest, you rest. —Anny wiped her eyes and lifted her head.

The great tent of the tree rustled and shone. The warm, red wall and the ivy sprays—the high, distant flag.

"I will do justice—I will do justice—I will do justice among the peoples, saith the Lord."—Lilacs in Maryland, and a little girl playing at keeping house, and a boy coming by and breaking her doll. Mary Miriam, the old doll. Lilacs, white ones, roses, bees.—It's a queer world!—The big willow tree by the barn, the weeping willow.—Trees and trees and trees everywhere. God everywhere.—Her mother rocking on the porch, and the whip-poorwill in the thicket, and little Anny Hartwell so tired after the day's work and play, in her mother's arms. . . .

AT SUNSET, when they returned from the park, Marie slipped down to the basement and the kitchen. "Mestress Smith,

jus' a moment! I wan' tell you I didn't have *nothing* to do with
the children taking your tree."

The basement supper table had found out. Anny Smith
going away from Number 27! It seemed incredible. They tried
to dissuade her, Elvira and all.

"It's got its faults, but 'tis a good place. You won't get a
better!"

"If it's just that tree, you'll miss it for a bit! But it isn't as
though they were going to cut it down."

"You'll just have to go about more," said Henry, "and that
won't be a bad thing."

"They don't any of them understand," thought Anny.
Aloud she said: "That corner meant a lot to me. It's my play-
place—just as much as those children! It's been my play-place
for ten years. It isn't just to say, 'No, now you can't, for here's
somebody's got money to pay for her likings!' It isn't just!
So I'm going."

But they understood just as little as ever.

However, she was easy to live with, and they regretted her
going. Where was she going until she could get another place?

"To the Browns," she said.

"The Browns" was always her statement when asked if she
had friends in the city. But Number 27 had never seen the
Browns, and were inclined to believe them a myth.

Anny slept very little that night. At four she left her bed
and went to the window. The moon in its last quarter hung over
the tree, and below the moon the morning star. It was warm.
Anny dressed and, opening the basement door, went out into
the early dawn and across to the tree.—Just here would be the
sand-pile, practically filling the corner. Bobby and Janet's shrill
little voices, and Marie with her sewing, and up at the second-
floor window Mrs. Lascelles.

She sat down and shut her eyes. "I can't go! There isn't
anywhere else. I can't stand up for justice."

Quiet—quiet—quiet! Treasure, old treasure, a treasure
chest. "Where thieves break not in nor steal."

The great tent of the tree rustled in the rose and the pearl.
The wall was growing clear, and the ivy sprays. Color increased
in the high, distant flag.

Maryland and Maryland.—The old fairy-story book, with
the Frog Prince and Cinderella.—The ocean, and ships sailing and
crossing, sailing and crossing.—Forest and calm, ocean and calm,

mountains and calm.—O Lord God, I've got Thee!—*Suffer the little children*—.Maryland and the old poplar tree with the swing.—The earth's round. The round earth swinging among the stars.—If the idea of joy's within you—you get over tying to any one place. Seeing that now you've got all places. . .

The dawn drenched the great tree. The sparrows talked it all over.

When breakfast was done, Mrs. Lamb sent Rupert to ask Anny Smith to come to her room.

"Sit down, Anny. Well, are you still going?"

"No'm. I've been thinking about it, and I don't reckon I will."

Mrs. Lamb drew a sigh of relief. "It isn't that I don't think it's hard on you, Anny! I do. It has got to be a word in the house, 'Anny and her tree.'—Oh, Anny, money-need's a strong man!"

"Yes'm. Strong as Goliath. Well, I'll go now," said Anny.

The sand-pile came in the next day. Mrs. Lascelles with the children and Marie came down into the basement and out into the yard to direct its disposition. "Yes, right here, if you please! This corner, between the tree and the wall. So they'll be out of the way and won't worry any one! Marie, we'll get a park bench for you—this old one won't do. Isn't it a lovely place, Bobby? Janet, right here by the ivy you can have your doll-house. You'll be just as happy and safe, and your poor mummy won't worry her soul out and get a nervous headache."

Re-entering the house, she came upon Anny Smith in the passage.

"Oh, one moment, Anny! They say you've sat there a good deal, but I'm sure you don't mind changing a little. We all do things for children, don't we?—This is from Bobby and Janet and me."

"This" was a twenty-dollar note.

Anny gave it back. "No, I haven't any room for that, ma'am. And I'd do a good deal for children, but children have all along gone to that park and loved it better than backyards. And the best people think there ain't any especial danger. That tree and that corner meant a lot to me."

Anny passed into her room, Dignity with her. Both shut the door.

Mrs. Lascelles shrugged. "Oh, well, if money can't pay for

it—and I'm sure I've been pleasant enough! Pshaw! what a little thing—just to sit somewhere else in that old yard!"

That afternoon, after luncheon and nap, the children came quietly enough into the yard and to the tree. Marie kept them in order. Mrs. Lamb had made it plain that the other boarders mustn't be disturbed by loud playing.

It chanced to be Anny's afternoon. Elvira had the kitchen, with Rupert to help. She looked large-eyed at Anny in her black silk and her bonnet and gloves.

"Yes, I'm going to the park," said Anny.

Nemesis

They said that the man, a black man, had done the crime. Perhaps he had, perhaps he had not. The probabilities seem to indicate that he had, but it is not certain, was not certain then, and is not certain now. Those who conducted the lynching proceeded, of course, upon the assumption that he was guilty.

His guilt might make a difference, and then again it might make no difference at all. In the way you take it, I mean.

Cottonville, top crust, middle, and bottom, is a place of something like two thousand souls, counting in dogs. There are the big mill and the operatives' houses, long rows of them all alike and jammed together. There are the stores and two churches and the school and the doctor's office and the Y, including moving-pictures, and the nurse and the welfare-worker—everything that the company puts in. If there weren't any company, there wouldn't be any Cottonville.

Cottonville runs into Pleasantly, which was an old, out-of-the way village when the Civil War armies manoeuvered in these parts. It is the county seat, with an ancient brick court-house and jail and three churches and an old tavern—Bell's. The company's officers, with the doctor and the preachers and the lawyer and so forth, live in Pleasantly, in the old brick and frame-houses under big trees, sycamores and live-oaks and magnolias. There's a lot of crape-myrtle, all rosy pink in midsummer. The owners live neither in Pleasantly nor in Cottonville, but somewhere up North. But the upper crust, salary folk, live in Pleasantly.

The country is flat, though on a clear day you may see hills in the distance. It is rich earth still. Cotton gets a big growth. The Choccawalla' goes winding by and gives pretty good fishing. There are bayous, Big Bayou and Jessamine and Laurie's. The railroad is the X. & Y. It's a good enough country, hot in midsummer, frosty in winter, with often a skim of ice. It has its good points and its drawbacks, just like the rest.

Once this region held big plantations, but they've been cut

up and sold. Every three or four miles you may come upon some old, rambling, big house, and in the distance ancient, tumble-down quarters. But no one lives in the quarters, and in the big house few and poor beside what used to be. Harrison Laurie still owned five hundred acres, if you can call it owning when there are mortgages up to the hat-brim.

The Cottonville people come from all over. The greater number are Southern, but there's north of Mason and Dixon's, Middle West, and so forth. Some foreigners; not many. Negroes, naturally, but not in the mill. We don't mix labor there; can't. But they drive the company's teams, and they're in Pleasantly and on the railroad and the boats of the Choccawalla. They have a settlement called Washington down on End-of-Creek, a mile away. Out in the country they're everywhere in the corn and cotton. There are cabins enough. The South, you know—make the image yourself.

Owen Adams was a Northern fellow, nephew of the mana-ger of the Cottonville mill. When he wasn't fishing or dawdling with some woman in Pleasantly or out at Harrison Laurie's, he sat in his uncle's office at the mill. If he hadn't been a nephew, it is doubtful if the company would have found his services for-ever and eternally valuable. There had been some row at college, but college was well behind him. He might have been thirty when the lynching happened.

He ran with Harrison Laurie, far North and far South, New England and Dixie. Laurie was the older man. Jim Nicholls hailed from the Middle West. Jim was long and red, and as dry as tinder in August. Occasionally he gambled, and liquor could turn him into a fighting devil; but three hundred and forty days out of the year he was a still man and a good druggist. Tom Wherry had come east from Nevada when he was sixteen. Vari-ous places east and south, and at last Cottonville, where he was ticket man at the X. & Y. station.

Those were the four, Harrison Laurie, Owen Adams, Jim Nicholls, and Tom Wherry. If they weren't all the leaders, they were certainly among the leaders. It's known, for all that the court couldn't discover it!

The old Laurie place hid itself away until you were almost upon it. The trees around had been growing for Lord knows how long, and they were all hung with Spanish moss. One heard the dogs before one saw the house. When seen, it proved to be dilapidated enough. It belonged to Harrison Laurie, and he belonged to it. It had gone down, and he had gone down. There was an air as though they had been going down for ages and were carrying it off together. He was a long, thin man, Harrison Laurie, with a long, thin face, wearing tolerably white clothes in summer, and a wide white hat and carrying a cane. Or one saw him on horseback, and there he looked best. He had his good points; a reading man, and powerfully fond of that great dog of his, Canute.

Laurie's Bayou is as crooked as a zed. The road to Lane skirts it, then passes Dargan's house. It's a big double cabin and sets right in the cotton, with some heaven-trees around it, and sunflowers and the like. Dargan's wife planted them.

Dargan's wife was still young, a quiet woman who did her work well. She had been pretty; there was a kind of gentleness about her. She liked out of doors, they said, and, when she could, would wander through the cotton or sit for an hour under the pine-trees or down by the bayou, where it's all great cypresses. Often she was alone in the house. John Dargan had his thirty acres to look after, or he went to Lane or to Cottonville in his mortal old car. His sister lived with them, but she had a way of visiting for two or three days at a time Matthew Dargan's people over in Jessamine. So there might be hours when no one was around. John Dargan had two dogs, but they always followed that car.

§ 2

It happened in July. Dargan, returning from Jessamine with his sister, hunted for his wife for two hours, then roused the neighborhood. At last they found her in the thick wood by the bayou, where she had been left for dead. They carried her to the house. A little life came crawling back, just enough to tell and to say good-by and after a day and a night sigh itself away. They got the doctor from Pleasantly. He held her here for so long, and that was all.

They were hunting for the negro. Two hundred persons had suddenly started up and were hunting him—the sheriff and his posse and all these others.

A big negro who worked on the railroad—Jim Lizard they called him. He was found in the cane beside Big Bayou. It was the sheriff who put down his arms and yanked him out. Sheriff wanted to get him to Pleasantly and into jail right away, before the crowd knew that he had been found. So they hurried him to Dargan's to see if she was still alive and could identify. Of course he swore that 't wasn't him. He had been up river and was coming home when he heard all the fuss, and got frightened because he had picked up and spent a ten-dollar bill that fell out of a car window and said nothing about it. He thought it might be that, and got rattled, and just turned off the road and laid low beside Big Bayou. "Fo' Gawd, that's so, Mr. Smith."

She was about gone when they brought him. They had to hold John Dargan. Her eyes were glazing. It's likely enough that she hardly knew what was wanted. But the sheriff got her to answer something. "It was a black man?" "Yes." "A big man?" "Yes. Yes, he had on a blue shirt. No, I can't see. It's all a dark cloud. Voice? Yes, I reckon that's his voice. I reckon it is. It's terrible—O God!" And she died, sinking down between our hands.

It's hard to tell; perhaps it was identification.

The sheriff considered that it would hang Jim Lizard; he wanted to get him away before the crowd could collect. So they put him on a horse and galloped him into Pleasantly and to the jail. It's a strong enough jail to look at, and Smith's a strong sheriff.

That was Wednesday. Farrar, the physician who had tended her, went back to Pleasantly. Something was in the air; he thought he knew the taste of it. About sunset he walked down High Street, wanting something from Nicholls's drug-store. Owen Adams caught up with him.

"Hot weather, doctor!"

"Yes."

"This place blazes! Harrison Laurie's the only cool spot, behind his great trees. I'm going out there in the morning." They walked a little way, then Owen said in a kind of remote and dreamy voice, "The law's too slow!"

"I don't know about that."

"I do. We've got to—"

"No, we haven't got to," said the doctor. "Don't let the climate get into your brain! Here's Nicholls. Come in and have something cool to drink."

But, no; there was something he must get from the office. He went on, and Farrar turned into the drug-store. There were men inside, and they and Jim Nicholls had been talking. They stopped when he entered, and one said, "Hot weather, doctor!"

Jim Nicholls had been drinking. Farrar thought, "I'll watch you fill that prescription," and did so.

Forth from the place,—it was past sunset now,—he made out a crowd before Thompson's livery. As he neared it he heard Tom Wherry haranguing. Owen Adams had not gone to the office; he was here, leaning in his big-shouldered, handsome way against the oak before Thompson's. Farrar thought he would go hear the harangue; then a distaste seized him, and he turned in the other direction.

Night came down hot and close, with a sense of storm. As the physician turned in at his own door a voice floated to him from the street:

"Three to one they'll lynch that negro!"

Town and country—the thing brewed that night and the next day. A number, known and unknown, were concerned in that lynching, but Harrison Laurie, Owen Adams, who ran with him, Jim Nicholls, and Tom Wherry were certainly concerned. Of course the day afterward nobody remembered or recognized anybody. That's in the convention; but all the same—

Hot and still. Owen Adams had ridden his black horse Firefly out to Harrison Laurie's. Farrar, the doctor, going by the office, was told so. Old Miller crossed the street with him.

"There's been a lot of talking and gesturing today! Jim Nicholls at the drug-store—he's drinking—is doing his share, and Tom Wherry is doing his. Cottonville and Pleasantly have got their roughness and thick, hot blood just the same as elsewhere." Sunset came with a great dark, long finger of cloud pointing out over the red sun. Dusk fell, and the fireflies were thick that evening.

§3

It might have been eleven o'clock when Harrison Laurie rode into town, with him maybe thirty mounted men. A number were masked. As the county said afterward, it would be guess-work! The sheriff on the witness stand named half a dozen, but the court couldn't find corroborative evidence. It's known, all the same.

Owen Adams rode beside Laurie. Jim Nicholls and Tom Wherry brought the town crowd to join the horsemen. It was all arranged.

Farrar heard the noise about midnight. He got up and dressed and went out. A neighbor out under the stars accosted him.

"Lynching, that's what it is! No, I don't approve; but what can you do?" The street had a sound of running feet. Youths, boys, went by. "Come on! It's at the jail!"

Farrar thought to himself, "Well, I'll go see; but one man can't tame the lions!"

The vindicators and regulators were massed before the jail and the sheriff's house, built alongside. The crowd may have numbered three or four hundred, but not a few weren't the real actors. Men and youths waked out of their beds, running to the light and noise, just *there* to see who won, sheriff or the mob. But perhaps they and all may be held concerned—Pleasantly and Cottonville and the county and the State and the United States. More than that, maybe.

One person who was there was old Mr. Dempsey, minister of the old Brick Church in Pleasantly. He was trying to make them disperse and go home. Somehow he had managed to reach the steps before the sheriff's door, and there he stood on the top step, calling out sayings from the Scriptures or the substance of them. He had a high, carrying voice: " 'An eye for an eye and a tooth for a tooth. Nay, but *I* say unto you—' "

Certain ones there were fond of Mr. Dempsey.

"Parson, Parson, you get down or you'll be hurt! You're out of this."

"I'm not. I'm in it so long as one of you is here."

He pleaded with them to go home, but they were growing impatient. A voice, perhaps Jim Nicholls's, shouted:

"Get out of it, Parson, or it will be the worse for you. Shove him down there, some of you!" All the place was now in red light. Some one had set a heap of pine afire. It showed Mr. Dempsey pleading hard.

"Let the law act—"

"We'll save it trouble. Get down, Parson!"

"It will come back on your own heads! If you want to get a thing, give it!"

"Get down!"

"What you are doing will be done somehow to you."

"Get down!" They grew impatient.

It was Harrison Laurie who dragged him down. He was

wearing a mask, but it was Laurie. The minister was pushed from one to the other until he was pushed out, expelled. Farrar, the doctor, had also tried remonstrance, though in a far lower tone. It was no use. He was drowned out, crowded out.

The sheriff wasn't in his house; he was in the jail. When the mob found it so, it turned with a roar to the jail.

Smith had a thundering big voice, and he argued with them; but they wouldn't listen. It was Jim Nicholls who shouted: "Hushaby, baby! We are doing *right*!" With that came a rush.

They swept around and over the sheriff and his half dozen. They got their guns away. Smith had threatened to shoot, but there wasn't any shooting. Perhaps he didn't have time. Down came the jail doors. It isn't a strong city jail. They got the negro.

To John Dargan's—they took him out there.

Half a mile from the house, near the bayou, are big trees that have been girdled, and stumps where the trees have fallen and been cut up and carted away. They had a dog-chain, and they fastened the negro to a five-foot stump. They brought armfuls of dry cane and broken wood. They got kerosene from Dargan's house.

The negro kept it up.

"O Lawd, have mercy! O Lawd, gent'men, 't wa'n't me! 'T wa'n't Jim Lizard! I didn't do it! O Gawd, I didn't! Mr. Dargan, you know yo' wife say she didn't fully recognize me; jus' thought so. I was over in Granite, twenty miles from here! O Gawd an' Jesus, right here listenin' to me, I was! Don't you drop that fire in those leaves! O Gawd!"

One of the four men lighted the pile. They say it was Harrison Laurie. The cane blazed up, and the night turned red and horribly loud—like hell.

When it was over, here was the dawn stealing in. There were ashes and the gray, dead trees, and the cold light creeping toward them, and they all looked shrunken and frayed and ashen themselves—the fields and Dargan's house and the girdled trees and the bayou and the stake and the crowd.

The crowd was to dissolve into twos or threes or ones and go off in this and that and the other direction, stealing through country or in a roundabout way back to town. And everybody forgot that he saw anybody else, and everybody produced an alibi—made an "elsewhere" all by himself and stood to it. Those who weren't concerned produced an outcry, but it died down.

The thing was all through the community. Nobody liked to say, "No, I haven't got the sickness, but there's my nephew or my second cousin or my neighbor or the man I owe money to who ought to be quarantined!" So it went. By sun-up there were just the cotton-fields and John Dargan's house and, near the bayou, a heap of ashes. There wasn't anywhere a mob. It had vanished off the face of the earth.

It came on to be a hot, still day, and Tom Wherry was quietly selling tickets for the noon train, and Jim Nicholls was sobering up in the drug-store and talking to a drummer who had a line of fancy goods, and Owen Adams was reading a New York paper in Robert Adams's office. Probably Harrison Laurie was sleeping, he being about the only one who didn't have to account for himself, there in his old castle behind the trees and the Spanish moss. That was all, in the sense that no one went to Magnolia County jail.

§4

Owen Adams sat in Robert Adams's office, reading the Northern paper. It was the second morning after the field out by Dargan's. He read with some particularity of a flower show, a wedding, and a boat-race, and then he dropped the paper into the wastebasket, stretched himself, and rose. His uncle was not in the office. Over by the north window young Wilson typed letters.

"Tell my uncle, will you," said Owen, "that I promised to help Mrs. Linley fix things for her children's party?"

Young Wilson nodded. Owen, turning to go, felt suddenly a diffused malaise. He might have said, had he ever used such words, that subconsciously it had been present for some time. Just how long it was impossible to say; perhaps for a night and a day. But now it stepped into consciousness. There was no localizing it; it simply was there, all through.

"Go play and forget it." He had listened to that advice through much of his life, so now he left the office, caught the street car that went up and down between Cottonville and Pleasantly, and presently was advising Mrs. Linley how the tables should be placed, so that they would get the magnolia shade and view the crape-myrtles.

For the rest of the day he thought he had forgotten it or

crowded it out, but at night he found that it had bided its time. It was growing stronger. By dawn it was pain, positive and prolonged.

He went, in the first light, to see Farrar, the doctor, who told him that he was sound in wind and limb, quite physically all right. Owen seemed relieved, but in a moment again talked of pain. But he was not able to tell where it was, and Farrar could not lay hand on the source.

From the doctor's he went to the office. It was natural to go to bed when you were in pain, constant pain, but he developed a repugnance to that. He wished to be upon his feet and moving, and also to be in company. He had no fever, he couldn't say that he felt weak, he could walk all right, he could even work. There was simply pain. "It'll wear away; something obscure." He accepted the doctor's perhaps over cheerful word and determined to forget it.

You are not to think that all this time there was not discussion enough, suppressed and open, about what had happened out by Dargan's. There was. The law made a considerable show of action; the law could act when it wished to. There is no doubt at all that it would have hanged Jim Lizard, but every one knew that in this other quarter nothing startling would happen. So many were implicated, or would be if it came to accusations and prosecutions, that such a thing could not be looked for. The company ruled Cottonville and Pleasantly and even Lane. As for the farmer and country folk generally, Dargan as one of them, and some Laurie or other had always led.

Owen Adams went to the office, but could not rest there. For a moment he might forget, or it might seem that he had fought it forth, clapped door, and drawn bolt. But through some crack or crevice it came back—pain. In the middle of this night, after an instant in which he thought it had gone for good, it suddenly came battering in with a reinforcement. He was now in something like agony. In the morning he went again to the doctor.

This time he wanted morphia. Farrar couldn't conscientiously give it to him. It looked like a fixed idea. The physician told him so; and that probably the remedy was mental or moral or, so to speak, spiritual, and must be applied by an act of will. But Adams insisted that he was in constant and intense bodily pain. Farrar put him through a thorough examination and found nothing. He tried suggestion, hypnotization in fact, but it wouldn't work. Something immediate and strong was already in possession. At last the doctor did give him a little morphia. He seemed relieved and went away smiling,—he was a big, handsome fellow,—but in the afternoon he came again and wanted more. He said that the first had not lasted any time. Farrar refused, telling him that he was sure the whole thing was a notion; to be a man and overcome it. Adams said that he was in the greatest pain, and begged, and when the physician still refused, he flamed into an ugly kind of anger, and said that he would find a doctor who knew extremity when he saw it.

Later, Farrar understood that he went from him to the drug-store and got some kind of dope. Whatever it was, it did him no good; but after that first day or two he ceased to try anything of the kind. He seemed to know that it was useless.

Here in the drug-store, for the first time after the night by Dargan's he spoke to Jim Nicholls.

"I'm in pain, Jim!"

"Are you? Well, I'm not." Jim sold him the stuff, and he went away. Pain, and the stuff like water. No, not like water. Water was all right, like—like *oil*.

The strange thing, if he thought of it at all, was that he could keep his head. He had never been regular at office, but he went in and out much as he had always done, and listened to his uncle's dry expositions, or dictated a letter to young Wilson. His uncle looked at him askance and was dry and peremptory, but that was because he was virtually certain that the nephew had run with Harrison Laurie the other night, and he abhorred what had happened. But he did not mean ever to bring it out into language. Owen had a pleasant boarding-place in Pleasantly, and he came to table and talked when it was necessary. One of his fellow-boarders, a woman, said to him, "How well you're looking!" But that very night it strengthened again and became hideous—hideous pain.

In the morning he determined to ride out to Laurie's. Maybe exercise, maybe getting away from town, maybe Laurie, with his drawling voice—So he went.

On Firefly he passed the X. & Y. station, and Tom Wherry, in the ticket-office, saw him through a window. Tom Wherry had the greatest stab of envy.

"He's free! He rides away! He can go as far as he pleases—as far as Europe if he wants to! I wish you were me, tied here, chained here! If I had your horse!"

§ 5

A young man, twenty-eight perhaps, rather short than tall, rather stout than lean, having a golden voice and a gift of the gab —that was Tom Wherry. People liked him well enough, and in various societies he was often pushed forward to make a little speech. And he liked in his turn Cottonville and Pleasantly and Magnolia County and his job. If ever he said, "Some day I'll go further and wider," still "someday," like heaven, remained distant and airy. He found, where he was, a theater and a good part, if a minor one, and an appreciative audience, if not one at the top of the cultural tree. If he had been used, with all his saying, to say such things, he might have remarked that the tree was bushier, bigger, fuller of sound and movement where he was. He was pretty content.

For recreation in snatches he kept within his desk a detective story, and he knew everybody who paused at his window, and his imagination never anticipated or followed the trains that roared in and roared out.

Something in him too fluent, too much of the theater, good, bad, or indifferent, made him for the crowd wherever it did congregate, and his trick of language, together with that really precious organ his voice, did the rest. As he would have said, he was talking before he knew it. And usually he advocated that in which the crowd was interested. To reprehend would have been too violent a start from home. Again, he might have answered: "But I *don't* reprehend. Isn't it all right?" So the crowd got under him and pushed him up, but he was never anything at those times but the crowd.

The morning after the happening among the girdled trees by Dargan's house Tom Wherry sold tickets, made entries, and answered questions behind his grating in his very narrow quarters. It was natural enough, with lost sleep, and the excitement subsiding, to feel a kind of distaste. "My life! I'd like to go fishing or to a circus or something out of this hole!" He sold tickets, made entries, answered questions. Station tongue, station ear had to do with the jail-breaking and lynching. When the ten o'clock train came in, people jumped down and talked about it. Of the buyers of tickets and askers of questions some looked at him curiously and others winked. "You look as though you hadn't slept. But of course you went down to jail just to see what the mob looked like." "Mum, isn't it?" "I hope you had pleasant dreams last night, Tom Wherry."

"Sure I did," said Tom. "Old rising bell rang too soon for me! Lane? Train's fifty minutes late, but making up."

When after a time waiting-room and platform and tracks settled into the doldrums, he reached for his book. It opened easily; it was what he called an interesting one, keeping a man guessing. Now, with a clapping suddenness, arose between him and the page a desire to quit. Ticket office, waiting-room, platform, station, Pleasantly and Cottonville and Magnolia County became hateful places. Get away from them quick!

He pushed back from desk with a gasp as of one who has been down in deep water and up for the first time. Reaching for his linen coat, he slipped it on and went out upon the platform. Somebody immediately engaged him in talk. He found himself expounding abstractly—oh, without any personal application!—retribution. Not having been there, he could not tell the composition of the crowd; but to his mind what they had done wasn't so God Almighty far from good! No, sir! Got to stamp it out, sir, got to give the whole kit-and-biling of them warning and example! What do they think of it in Washington? Which Washington? I don't care which. Of course he was guilty! Thought it, if he didn't do it, and I'm morally certain he did it. No, I don't know who was in the crowd; don't even care to know. I take it impersonally, so to speak. That's the way Pleasantly and Cottonville and Magnolia County should take it—impersonally."

He liked the word. Open air and the discussion in which he had come off well had restored him to himself. He walked down the platform. It was a gorgeous, hot summer day, but here hung shadow. Right nice place, after all!

As though the sun had barbed and sent an arrow against it, his environment shriveled and withered and became horrible. He gasped. "This town's a jail! Get away! I've got to make a get-away! It's a vacation Tom Wherry's needing!"

The hot sun crossed the meridian, slowly went down the west, dipped beneath, and vanished. "Make a get-away! make a get-away!" Tom Wherry sat in his room, which was not a palatial one, and his table was spread with railway folders. They showed pictures—mountains and lakes, cities, scenery, rivers, even ocean and ships waiting for trains smoothly running to the dock. North, east, south, west, and the quarters between. Everywhere save straight up and down.

His holiday was not due, but perhaps if he went and told those over him how imperative it was, he might get away. If they said no, and the going cost him his job—. He drank ice-water, and looked out of his screened window at the moon. It was late.

He slept upon it, and in the morning laughed at the folders scattered all over his small room. When his holiday came in September he was going with Rangeley, the telegraph operator, to Rangeley's father's farm, up in the hills. There was a town near by, and a lot of pretty girls in that county. He had been hectic last night. That was it, hectic.

He hummed as he dressed. Every-dayness lasted through going downstairs and across the street to Tony's Restaurant.

But with the coffee-cup half-way to his lips it returned. He set the cup down. Get away! get away quick! This place was dangerous, hateful, and horrible. The ten o'clock express.

He went to the Cottonville bank and drew out his money, two hundred and fifty dollars. Then at the ticket office he sold himself a ticket, and began to write a letter of explanation to be left upon his desk. But in a moment this seemed unnecessary, and he tore it up. He looked at the clock. Half an hour. He sold tickets, answered questions, looked at the clock. Quarter of an hour, ten minutes. Closing the ticket window, he made a step toward his hat and a bag, which he had brought with him from the boarding-house. There came a feeling, quite definite and horrible, of fixture. "I can't! I can't! Everything will get in the way; see if it doesn't! I'm fastened!"

He let the express go by without him. All day both feelings increased, the inward, consuming, terrible hurry and desire, and a miserable conviction of helplessness. In the afternoon he set foot upon the step of the day coach of Number 5. Behind him one called "Wherry!" It was Rangeley. He drew back to the platform. "I thought I saw a man in there that I knew." He had no movement toward confiding in Rangeley or in any. "They'd tell." Escape by himself! Escape from what? He did not know. Men spent their lives, didn't they, trying to escape from death? It was like that; only it was all quickened and run together in him right here and now. Make a get-away! Break the chain! The horror was that he *knew* that all kinds of things would set foot in path to trip him, running.

The next day he tried again, tried thrice. Each time something happened. The express was gone before he was out of the

door upon the platform. Some one came into the ticket office
and deliberately buttonholed him, and the east bound went by.
A crowd got between him and Number 5, and he could not face
it. That evening after hours he started to walk to Burbridge and
thence to Lane, where he might take the night train. He went
a mile or two upon the dusty road, and again encountered
frustration. A man driving an ox team pulled up beside him and
spoke. "It's a hot evening, and you must be ready to turn.
Want to go back to Pleasantly with me?"

He did not want to, but he went, sitting beside the driver.
The man left him at the dusky edge of Pleasantly, going on with
the oxen toward Jessamine.

Make a get-away! Plunge toward it and always be brought
up short! He had tried, and it was of no use. He knew it now
inside. He would try and try, try because he couldn't help trying, and yet he wouldn't be able to do it. The ox man was gone.
Folk in Pleasantly were able to go. They escaped! Mr. Linley
had gone that day on the private car of the X. & Y., going North
somewhere. He saw him at ease, in one of the car's big leather
chairs, Magnolia County growing less and less, fading out. Envy
devoured him. "O God! I wish I were him and he was me!"

Under the big live-oak at church corner he met the secretary
of the Y.M.C.A.

"Evening."

"Evening."

"I'm going tomorrow with three or four of the fellows to
Sea View for a week. A dip in the big water will feel good these
dog days. Wish you could go along, Tom."

"You don't wish it any more than me."

When the other had passed on, it was devouring envy that
he felt. "If I could take his trip, I'd steal it all right! I'd knock
him down for it. But it isn't in a week that I'd be coming back
here! O God, why should he be out of it and not me? Everybody but me!"

"Ocean. Sail across the ocean. Swim across—"

What was keeping him? Nothing and everything.

There grew within him a forlornness, changing now and
again into a vivid and frightful envy. By the fourth day he
might not know if it was Cottonville and Pleasantly from which
he ached to go, or if it was Tom Wherry, or what it was. A
throbbing aversion, and an envy like poison oak, and it did no
good to take trains or to plan to take them. He began to cease

from the attempt. Misery had come to live with him—a misery like homesickness a million times deepened, and all aforetime likable folk now were taunters and flaunters of a property theirs, not his.

From the station window he saw Owen Adams on Firefly riding out from Pleasantly. He seemed to Tom a happy king. "He can get away. He's free. Nothing holds him." The condition of any one not Tom Wherry appeared a condition of bliss. Envy ate him. He was shaken and blasted by those inner great starts to get free. Inner now, not outer. Pictures continually rose of Tom Wherry elsewhere and at ease and happy again. Now he sat upon the deck of a boat, something cool with ice in the glass beside him. The shore receded; it was all right. Now he quite happily hoed corn on a hillside, with the deep woods in view, and the crows cawing, and no other neighbors. Now—but the pictures were endless.

It all increased; only the pictures ceased to appear. There was nothing but a dreadful feeling occupying him and devouring him. At night he shed scalding tears.

Farrar's sister was going to Lane to do some shopping. Farrar went with her to the station, took her ticket, and put her on the train. Tom Wherry said to him as he was paying for the ticket, "You all seem to me quite enviable." Farrar repeated it to his sister, who didn't want to go to Lane this hot weather. "Tom Wherry says he envies travelers. If you had to sit in that blazing place in there, even moving off to Lane would look good. Everything's relative."

Tom Wherry and Jim Nicholls were friends. Jim was a still man when he wasn't drinking, and Tom was naturally drawn to any listener. He might now, one would think, have gone to the drug-store and Jim Nicholls. But he did not go. *"No help there; no help from him."*

§6

Jim Nicholls was not drinking. He had been, but he stopped the day of the lynching. When he stopped he always stopped clean short. He might not touch liquor again for three months. He had been known to go for six months. Short or long in abstinence, he was a tall, red, silent man and a good druggist.

That morning after Dargan's field, going home alone in the

faint dawn, he felt very quiet, everything clearing up after a spree, sense coming back to a Malay after running amuck.

The air was quite still; it was going to be a hot day. In the east hung sheets of green and yellow, and above the low horizon a long piece of faint red. Suddenly Jim Nicholls, his outward eyes regarding this dawn sky, saw in some inner way bloodshot eyes, his own. "I suppose they *are* bloodshot," he thought. He seemed to be regarding Jim Nicholls's eyes through another's eyes. The sense disappeared. He had stopped short, but now he went on with long strides. "Funny thing, that!"

The flat earth slowly colored. Pleasantly and Cottonville stood against the hot, still dawn. He was not upon the road; he was going back to the drug-store by way of the old, cast-out fields. He passed a number of little pine trees. Around spread coarse grass with sedge. There was no dew.

Without further warning, so soon as this, Jim Nicholls began to hate. Certainly, when he was drunken he acted as though he hated, though probably that was only a part of what he felt; and, sober he had a considerable power of disliking. But this was not that, though it may have given the hand-hold. But now suddenly, as though he had leaped into a sea of it, he hated generally and vindictively. If there was anything that was not hating him, fiercely and unpardonably and striving to injure, he could not see it! He hated back, fiercely, unpardonably, and injuriously.

The dawn sky became a face hating and to be hated. The old fields and the little pines and the sedge belted themselves into another face and were hated. Pleasantly and Cottonville, half a mile away, house and trees, church-spires and mill-stacks, ran into a hating third, and were hated.

He came into town. The mill whistle blew, and became another thing to hate. Were his eyes bloodshot? Of course they were bloodshot! What had happened? He did not know. He only knew that another Jim Nicholls had found Jim Nicholls. The two were roosting together, but the first Jim Nicholls was fast being crowded off the perch. By the time he reached his drug-store, with the two rooms behind, the three making all his home, the two Nicholls had coalesced. He conceived that the world was slaying him, and he simply and impartially hated it. He was hate.

Unlocking the door, he entered the drug-store. As he did so he had the thought, "Something must remain unhatable." For

one moment the world cleared. "I wouldn't hate an angel
coming down with a sword to help." The thought closed. There
wasn't any angel; the sun went out. Hate and hate. Even, even,
to get even!

Ancient affection for his drug-store[1] went out like a blown
lamp. Great bottles and jars; labeled canisters; glass case filled
with a medley of brushes and soaps, creams, and salves, and
perfumes; dangling, high-colored cardboards picturing damsels
and flowers and children and the virtues of this or of that; the
cool, compounded smell; the dim sense of ages behind those jars
and great vials, ages of gathering and learning, the hidden romance; all that, though he had never named it, had hung in his
mind with a sense of rightness and fond habit—all grew venomous, hateful. Pleasantly, Cottonville, all the world.

He made his own breakfast. He owned a dog, a terrier
named Barney. This came up to him. He kicked him away, with
a "Damn you!"

Throughout the day folk dropped in to buy, and some with
a wish to talk or merely to look knowing. He hated them all
alike, those to whom he sold and those to whom he stated that
he had a headache and that there was nothing to talk about
anyhow, and those whose stare he gave back like a blank wall.
He still had the sense of his eyes being terribly bloodshot. A
looking-glass hanging in the back room showed him that they
were not actually so, or very slightly so; but the illusion persisted. Well, was it not enough to make eyes bloodshot, the hateful-
ness, the enmity, that met them whichever way they turned!
He wished to fill all other eyes with blood. Pay! pay! pay back!
He sat or stood or moved in an anguish of wishing ill. All things
had come to one throbbing point of hating.

In the afternoon he closed the shop and threw himself
upon the bed in the farthest room. He would sleep. So he did,
heavily. But when he waked, it was first to dull and then to horrible, intense anger and hate. He did not know against whom it
was directed. Why play favorites? It had become an impartial,
horrible emotion.

Hate! hate! hate! Tear them to pieces inside, if he could
not do it outside! *Because they were hurting him.*

By the next morning he had come to self-hatred. There
was one Jim Nicholls. Destroy him, too! Hate and destroy
everybody! Hate and destroy God, Who made him to suffer!

He kept the shop open till noon, then he closed it. In the

evening, a hot sunset light filtering in, he went and stood before a glass vial in a certain division of the shelves. Take from it and mix and drink! But even while he looked he wished wildly to live. It would please them if he died. He remembered a maddened bull. He felt that rage.

Night went, and the next day went. Cottonville and Pleasantly looked at him with bloodshot eyes, and he at them with bloodshot eyes.

Pleasantly and Cottonville were used to a close-mouthed Jim Nicholls, selling drugs and various articles in a drug-store rather shadowy, ailantus-trees before it casting dimness. Not so many observant persons came his way. Drug-store and the pavement without had never been loafing-places, as were other stores and bits of pavement. He had never had Tom Wherry's light popularity.

It was the third day when Owen Adams stepped inside and asked for something to dull pain.

"I'm in pain, Jim!"

"Are you? I'm not!"

He sold him what the law let him sell. He looked at Owen with bloodshot eyes. He knew that his were bloodshot, and he thought that Owen's were the same. When the latter departed, he followed him to the door and stared after him going up the street, out of the ailantus shadow into sun, then again into shadow. He hated him and hated all men. The odor of the ailantus struck his nostrils. "There is a tree called Hate. I got under it somehow."

The weather was hot, the weather was dry. Each night a thickening moon rained down an antique influence; oh, an antique! In Washington, which was the colored settlement out at End-of-Creek, they began a camp meeting, a revival. Thick of the moon meant singing and shouting, and perhaps old Africa coming up in the bones. If you will notice, it brings to us all a certain restlessness of body and mind. Something very old comes up in all our bones. Night by night the moon thickened, and in the day the sun was hot. The drought held.

§7

Owen Adams, riding to see Harrison Laurie, passed by the station and out upon the bayou road, a mile, two miles, three.

Laurie's cotton-fields, Laurie's negroes moving in them, Laurie's cabins in the distance, with umbrella-and heaven-trees and pine and live-oak. Opening the gate, he passed from the high road into one through Laurie's, a narrow and weedy road. Sky so blue it burned, sun with a quiver as wide as the air, and arrows no man might number. Ragged cotton, ragged cotton. At the end of the road stood Laurie's house in an island of trees, trees enormously tall and herding close. In the outpost trees began the swinging moss that was a feature of the place.

Owen Adams, riding under, disliked the moss, as he had always disliked it. But now it seemed to weave in with pain. The road became soft, and sunk into deep shadow. Harrison Laurie's house. Once it had been gray stucco, with white pillars, but now all was of an indistinguishable yellowed and darkened hue, like a November leaf under heel, or a toad's back. The trees hugged close to the pillared porch and to windows. When the wind blew, the streamers of moss flapped like banners of a host in panic; when the air was still, they hung with an aspect of dark finality. "Why don't you clear them out?" "They would grow again." "Then clear it out again, keep clearing out." "You are too energetic."

Ordinarily, in summer Laurie's door stood wide, showing old bare hall and wide stair. In such weather Laurie himself was oftenest found in the porch, in a chair long and low and deep, with a book and a cigar and something in a glass. He might be reading or he might be drowsing, or simply lying, looking at the Spanish moss with narrow slits of blue between. The dog Canute kept beside him. When he put down his book and roused himself he was good company, or so thought Owen Adams.

He was not upon the porch, and the door was shut. Owen, dismounting, fastened his horse to a hook driven deep into a live-oak. As he mounted the steps he caught the fact that a closed window-blind of the room to the right, Laurie's room, was pushed slightly and noiselessly, as though some one would see and not be seen. It was unusual, the blinds being closed.

There hung a knocker upon the door, an old one with a dusky face. Owen knocked twice, then pushed against the door, to find it locked or barred. Again that was surprising. He knocked the third time, and now through the broken side-lights heard Laurie coming and slowly opening to him. The door swung back.

"What's the matter? I've never known Laurie House closed

and barred like this!"

"It never felt the need. Let's shut the door."

He shut and bolted it. The action brought him into the light. It was not sallowness alone; it was pallor, and his long, loose frame and his long countenance, with its small mustache and even, fine, straight eyebrows, had a curious aspect alike of shrinkage and tension.

"Are you all by yourself?" asked Owen. "Where are Ailsy and Creed?"

"I sent them away. No, sir; a man can trust himself, but he can't trust others."

"Where is Canute?"

"I don't want him springing at me; so I've tied him up."

By now the door was stoutly closed. They crossed the hall, Laurie with a soft step, drawn together, and tip-toeing as though some one at hand lay dying. What with the natural shade about the house and what with the drawn shutters, the room that they entered was dimly lighted. But it could be seen to be in disorder, and though the bed had been made, it was creased and crumpled as though Laurie had been lying or sitting there. Pillows were piled high; he seemed to have robbed the one or two other still furnished bedrooms.

"Do you sleep sitting up like that?"

"It's safer so. You are half ready to start—one movement from the bed. Lying down, it takes two. I haven't slept much."

His voice sounded strained and reed thin. Owen stared around, but he had given time enough from his own preoccupation.

"Laurie, I don't know what is the matter with me; I'm in constant pain—the worst kind. The doctor says it's imaginary. He's a fool, or he doesn't know what 'imaginary' means. It's real, I tell you, and it's hell!"

"Pain?" said the other. "But you don't *fear*." He went back to the bed, and sat huddled. Somewhere in the back of the house Canute began to howl. "Perhaps I had best shoot him," said Laurie. "If I didn't think that perhaps—"

His voice trailed off. It was evident that, as time goes, he had long been in terror. He was in terror, or terror was in him.

Owen regarded him.

"What is there to be afraid of, Laurie? If you were in pain, that would be different. Pain's real."

"What I feel is real, too. It's hellishly real. Fear! I tell you,

I've got fear of everything!"

"Fear of Canute? Fear of me?"

"Fear of Canute, yes. I may presently have fear of you."

"I came out thinking you'd do me good. I thought maybe you'd ride back to town with me."

"Why should I go there? God, no! I haven't been out of the house for two days. There's food in the storeroom; I get myself a little. But then I have to pass Canute."

"What's the matter?"

"I don't know. The whole world's one danger. I'm danger to myself. It's terrible! O God!"

He quivered, and sat staring into vacancy. Owen said in a whisper:

"Do you suppose, Laurie, something or some one got *into* us the other night?"

But the other only sat shaking slightly and staring. Unselfishness had not been Owen Adams's strong point. If Laurie wasn't going to help, be interested or sympathize; if he could do nothing to remove or to render more endurable—The spasm of hope toward a friend was spent. Owen felt that the friend came short. He felt dislike, almost hatred, for the figure seated on the bed.

"There's nothing I can do here—"

"No. I wish you would go! It's stronger since you came."

"I wish you had my pain!"

"I'd change. Terror is my master. He's got a long, black whip."

The room, with the shuttered four windows, received light by the spaces between the slats. Coming from opposing sides, these rays crossed and were broken like spears. The objects in the room and the room itself appeared to shift ground like a fencer. There came an apprehension of slipping cohesion, disintegration, deliquescence. Bones turning to water seemed hardly a figure of speech.

Owen backed a little.

"Yes, I'll go. I won't get any help here!"

"You don't give any. I wouldn't have let you in except that I thought, 'Maybe he'll help.' But it was a mistake." He rose from the bed. "I'll let you out. You go ahead."

In the hall they again heard the dog.

"Loose him, why don't you? He's no company there!"

Laurie shook his head.

"No; he'd tear my throat out—".

"He's not mad!"

"No; but he would come at me. I know."

His voice trailed away. He unbolted the door. Said Owen:
"If you knew what terrible pain I'm in!"

A hot wind poured in at door, breathing from fields and
wood and bayou. It seemed to bring with it a draft of anger.

"Damn your pain!" said Harrison Laurie.

"Damn your senseless fear!"

They stared at each other. Anger stiffened them slightly.
At the back of the house Canute was heard again. Laurie's face
became livid. His eyeballs seemed to start, his hair to rise. He
closed the door in the other's face. Owen heard the bolt drawn,
and through the broken glass foot-steps down the hall. He himself leaned against the wood. "Pain! O God!"

He rode back to Pleasantly. It was very dry and hot, the
katydids making a great fuss, the cotton and corn asking for
rain.

About five in the afternoon Robert Adams sent for Farrar,
the doctor. The nephew was then at the uncle's house. Farrar
talked with the latter, who said that as much as three days ago
he had seen that something was wrong. What, he asked the
physician, *was* wrong? Had it to do with that miserable night
out by Dargan's? He hadn't pressed for knowledge. He didn't
want to know Owen's proceedings, refused to talk about them,
had no information at all; but what did the doctor think?

Farrar answered that he didn't know what to think. He
hadn't been able to find any physical cause. He added that in
his own opinion "physical" was a very deep word, containing
more than we thought. So it might be physical, after all.

"I suppose 'obsession' is as near to it as you can come?"

"Yes. If there was such a thing as 'possession,' I might say
possession. Or vibration kindling vibration. But we haven't
come to that in the medical books."

Robert Adams drummed upon the table.

"Owen came here two hours ago. My wife and I persuaded
him upstairs into the spare room. He's losing all command;
people mustn't see him so. Come up and do what you can. He's
my brother's son. I want him un-possessed."

They went. Owen was not in bed, but dressed, seated upon
a chair in the middle of the floor. He said he was in extreme
agony. By now, whatever was that thing, it was working for

itself outward expression. His frame was contorted, his face convulsed. The doctor did not know. He might die if this went on.

Farrar stayed there through the night and had to believe the other when he said he had been caught by pain as a dog takes a rabbit. He said he wanted to die; and wouldn't the doctor kill him, put him out of it quick!

It was a dark night, powdered with stars. Outside the room ran a gallery. Farrar, stepping now and again out upon this, watched the tremendous field, then returned to Owen Adams. About two in the morning he felt a change. Leaving the room, he found Robert Adams sitting up in his library, coffee at hand.

"It's weakening," said the doctor. "I think he'll pull out."

Back with the nephew, he stood in the gallery door watching the dawn. He heard Owen sigh and move, and was not surprised when he came to him in the doorway and whispered:

"Doctor, I feel better." A little later he said, "If ever I get out of this, I'm going to be a better man!"

Farrar long remembered the light coming up over Pleasantly. He had thought a good deal that night of all the strange things in our life. He thought of how things are one. Anyhow, it was a dawn light that was very cool and pure and kindly.

The physician went home and slept some hours. In the afternoon he found himself upon High Street and saw before him Owen Adams coming down the old brick sidewalk. They met under the big tree before Bell's. It was a hot afternoon, a hazy, remote sky shutting all into desert glare, the leaves drooping, and the pink crape-myrtle at the end of Bell's long porch. Farrar asked:

"Well, how are you now?"

"Better; still better! It's the loveliest, quietest feeling!"

Farrar said that it had been an obsession and that it was dying out. The other answered that, anyway, he felt now like seeing his fellow-man.

Half a dozen came out of Bell's, traveling men and others, with two negroes carrying bags, and turned toward the station— the six o'clock express. Owen looked after them, then said:

"I think I'll go speak to Tom Wherry." In a moment he was walking away after the other. He had to pass the drug-store.

Farrar turned for a moment into Bell's. He had taken from the office table the Lane "Messenger" and was reading the foreign news when he heard the shots. The loungers in Bell's started up and ran out, Farrar with them. A hundred yards down the street, as though it had come up through the pavement, was a crowd under the ailantus-trees before Jim Nicholls's drug-store.

When the doctor got there, Owen Adams was dead, Jim's bullet through his heart. Jim's old six-shooter that Tom Wherry used to take from him when he was drinking, and Jim firing right and left at what he said were bloodshot eyes! When they got him down and the weapon away, he had emptied its chambers. The balls went wild, save that one that found Owen Adams. Jim Nicholls!

Early that same hot afternoon in which the loafers in Bell's heard the shots Tom Wherry wandered out of Pleasantly. He went to the thick pine-wood still standing between Chocca-walla and Big Bayou. Everywhere else was heat, but in here was coolness; the ground was not thick dust, but firm and dark and cool and covered with purplish needles. He threw himself down, with his head in his arms. For a while it was a week of misery still, today as bad as yesterday, yesterday as bad as day before, tomorrow coming up as wretched as today, day after tomorrow as wretched! Misery and wretchedness!

He lay like a log in the pine-wood. Time passed; he did not know how much. Within him some one began haltingly to speak: "I am not worth a mite! I am not worth a mite! Sorry for all I have ever done! Sorry for all I have ever done!"

It was night when he came out of the grove, and the moon was shining. It shone over Pleasantly and Cottonville and the fields and the road. Faintly, like moonlight too, entered into Tom Wherry's heart a *liking* for it all. Instantly the brain made words for the feeling. "The old place isn't more than half bad; it isn't so bad."

He went along the dusty road in the moonlight. It shone upon little pines and heaven-trees and where once had been a cabin, a great clump of crape-myrtle. Before him plodded a negro—Daniel, who drove one of the company teams. He caught up with him.

"Where have you been, Daniel?"

Daniel had been to see old Daddy Joe Ferris, who was dying.

"He gwine make er good end—Daddy Joe. He remembers cl'ar back to creation, and he's tellin' erbout it all to-night!"

The two men walked together.

"I've been feeling very badly, Daniel, but I'm feeling better now. It's a lovely night."

"'T is that," agreed Daniel. "The Lord's looking down. Some he takes now, and some he takes later."

Going together into Pleasantly, they heard about Owen Adams and Jim Nicholls.

The heat held over Cottonville and Pleasantly and all the fields and roads and Jessamine and Laurie's and Big Bayou. It held around Laurie's house, and the huge trees and the long moss seemed ranged there not for shadow, but for suffocation. Moreover, it was silent, silent, silent.

Creed and Ailsy, who had been born upon the place, at last determined to break in. Creed got two or three men from the fields. After calling and calling, and only their echoes returning, they used an ax against the thick front door. "You'd think we'd hear Canute!" In the dim hall they turned a little gray, looking at one another. Ailsy began to whimper, "I's frightened!"

They broke in the door of Laurie's room.

"Lawd hab mercy!"

"Lawd hab mercy! He's shot Canute!"

"Lawd hab mercy! *What's dat hanging dar?*"

§ 8

Harrison Laurie was the last to live in Laurie House. A month from that day it caught fire, no on knows how, burned to the ground.

What became of Jim Nicholls? The night after he shot Owen Adams he slept or did not sleep in Magnolia County jail. In a few days there was a commission. It adjudged him crazy. The asylum at Lane.

Did he stay there? No, he did not. He got better. Some time after this, Farrar, going North, and meeting on the train Clarke, the asylum physician-in-chief, asked about him. Clarke lit his cigar and said, physician to physician, that he had never known just what was sanity, and so naturally, had an insecure position on insanity. Jim Nicholls? Jim was missing his drugstore, and the notion of bloodshot eyes had faded out. Also, he didn't hate as much as he had done.

That was in November. At Christmas-time Cottonville and Pleasantly heard that Jim Nicholls had escaped from Lane.

They never found him. No one knows where he is. Once there came a drummer who said that he knew in Arkansas a long, red, dry man, a druggist, who had told him about this part of the world.

Tom Wherry? For another year he sold X. & Y. tickets; then he married a girl up Rangeley's way and moved into the hills. After that Cottonville and Pleasantly heard that he had become a preacher.

§9

Harrison Laurie, Owen Adams, Jim Nicholls, Tom Wherry, But there was a fifth man, and that was John Dargan.

John Dargan was a slow, country fellow, used to mornings and noons and afternoons in the fields, and twilights on his porch, with his pipe and the scarlet running bean and the gourd vine, and the whipporwills calling, and the stars coming out, and pictures then of his childhood and boyhood, and of a year in New Orleans. Used also to his wife, her work done, coming out of house to sit there too.

All had been grief and rage and action of an unaccustomed sort for John Dargan. All was yet, he thought, grief and rage. It was twelve days from the lynching. His sister was over at Jessamine; old Matthew Dargan was lying ill and needing her. Dargan sat alone under the scarlet bean, twilight walking up the west over the fields. His pipe lay beside him. Now and then he took it up and smoked, but in a moment put it down again and sat bent, with locked hands. His dog slept beside him on the warm, brown earth.

Over! So much was over, never to come again!

"Anyhow, we burned him," said John Dargan. "He deserved burning."

When he had said that he again fell silent. Sky and earth lay in dim purple, very far spread and quiet. A white star became visible, then another. Afar in the wood began a whippoorwill. "Whippoorwill! Whippoorwill! Whippoorwill!"

Edie! The day they were married in the log church! Edie! "Till death do us part."

"Edie, we killed that devil—killed him slow! Edie! Edie! We did that for you, anyhow. Edie!"

"Whippoorwill! Whippoorwill! Whippoorwill!"

Two or three more stars came out, but still the sky spread dim rose and purple and umber, and still the fields and wood and road could be discerned.

"O God, I don't understand this world of yours! Edie! Edie! can't you speak to me?"

"Whippoorwill! Whippoorwill!"

A meteor shot across the sky, the evening wind began to move, the pines smelled, the fields smelled. Very quietly there opened within John Dargan a picture—opened like one of the homely flowers about the door: the Choccawalla, and he and his brother going fishing with Jim Lizard, long ago, when they were boys.

He tried to kill it with another picture, but it persisted, it was there. It seemed that it had as much right to be there as had the others.

"Whippoorwill! Whippoorwill!"

"Edie! Edie! I know the kind of thing you would have said! But you are dead."

A blur came over the bayou and over the trees, but the flowers, the heaven-trees, and the cotton about the house grew brighter. The zinnias, the lilies, and the sunflowers, the double row of them, grew very long and shining, and somehow they seemed no longer flat to earth. They lifted, they stretched afar, beyond the dooryard and the cotton, afar up a vast, gentle slope, like a road to heaven. He felt his wife among them. That which went out quietly, dying in the twilight, was the word "dead."

Perhaps, sitting there after a long day's work, he nodded and dreamed. Perhaps he simply became more awake. He heard her speak. Yes, it was within. He recognized that, but it was she. He cried out, within:

"Edie, it is all so dark! Edie, we did that thing for you!"

She had her own trick of speech, and she did not depart from it now.

"John, don't ever say that you-all did that for me! If you're asking me—no! no! no! What good could it do you-all or me or him or anybody? It didn't please and it didn't serve—not anything—not anybody! And as for dying, nothing dies, John. We don't do things that-a-way where I live and where I want you to live. John, let me show you—"

That is all that can be put into words; but John Dargan was simple and humble, and he learned.

John Dargan! It is probable that the zinnias and lilies and

sunflowers never quite settled back again, flat to his dooryard in the cotton-fields stretching beyond it.

Note

[1]*The Century Magazine,* 106:15 gives drug-shop.

There Were No More People Upon the Earth

There were no more people upon the earth.

The poisons that had been manufactured were peculiarly dire. Moreover, the opponents used malignant germs of many species. Pestilence swept away populations. Famine, the gleaner, came after. War had begun among three or four nations, but speedily involved all. There were but two parties on the face of the earth, and they killed each other. War had been general before now, but it was in the old days when the Advisers knew only primitive and partial ways of extermination. Now all was different.

Death rained from the air and swam in the seas, lakes and rivers. Methods had been devised of attaining conflagrations that licked up life. Old ways of slaying still abode, but the new ways were fearful—fearful and effective. From the one to the other pole they let loose Fury, and the skill to which by now man had attained armed her. And now there was none—no, not a man nor woman nor child of ten who was not engaged, and none—no, not an infant—that either side would spare. Long ago it had been that invaders chiefly blasted the coasts and borders of countries, leaving hinterlands to which remnants of populations might flee. But now there was no mountain village, no minute isle of fisher folk, where was not invasion. For now men did not need to accompany or follow up their black vials of black wrath. Cities chose cities a thousand miles away, and mutually they were destroyed in a night.

Neither side wished for the other's complete annihilation. Each preferred that masses of the foe should live, but live in something approaching a condition of servitude. Neither, when the war began, foresaw its own fate. There arose prophets, but they were stoned.

There were no more men and women upon the earth. A force of destruction was discovered, a power, a vibration, deadly to human life, though only to human life. The discovering side strove hard to keep the formula of generation for itself, solely for itself, but failed. The secret was stolen. Now two could play at that game. They played.

But when the very great danger was seen, and they strove for cessation, it was too late. The movement of death went on. At last they were few and weak, and still they died. A cluster of Advisers with some men of science and the mechanics who served them, dwelling in a certain fortress and laboratory and experiment station, outlived the rest, lived long enough to slow down and weaken and put upon disappearance that death pulse to all their kind. But when it was done, they too died of shock and exhaustion and mortal grief.

There were no human beings upon the earth.

The domesticated or herded animals, the horses, the cattle, the sheep and others, were already to a vast extent devoured or wantonly destroyed and gone. The vibration used at the last was not fatal to the remainder. But when man was departed those that still lived in pens or stables or enclosed fields quickly died. Others escaping roamed at large for a time, then perished of famine. But those that might reach the forests or the open, grassy plains lived and grew feral. The dog became extinct. He died with man. The cat survived. For long she clung to the ruined houses, finding her food where she might. But at last she withdrew, stealing away to the woods, where presently she forgot houses and men and women and their ways.

Most of the cities had been thrown to the ground, but here and there, in each continent, yet stood in whole or in part the dwellings and buildings of men. A man might have found these cities, towns and single houses fearful things in their vacancy and functionlessness, but there lived no man to think it. The sunlight and the rain did not cease, the wind nor the snow. Through the years the cities stood soundless save for the low noise of disintegration. This went on always. Timbers, the smaller first, then the greater, rotted through. Walls collapsed; the empty streets became blocked, were buried. Wharfs, bridges, rotted and slid at last into water and were broken up and carried to sea and ground into sand and ooze. All ships upon the ocean when their sailors died went derelict. For a time they roamed with the wave and the wind, but one by one they sank in storm or beat themselves to death against the coast. At last the ocean flowed clear of them.

Time passed, though now the globe did not count time. The cities crumbled down and weathered away. At last they became mounds, great or small, in wildernesses. The grass and the bush and the vine and the tree grew atop. Climates altered, running up or down the scale of warmth. Where had been realms of long winter the palm trees waved above buried marts. Where once in courts and gardens had stood palm and pepper and acacia now the first threw down their cones and the northern maple turned scarlet in the autumn. And coastal plains subsided and the sites of ancient cities became sea floor, or they rose, and the stones of old port towns, had any sought for them, would have been found inland, among hills. But none searched. The restless mind that searched, and called its search Policy or Science or Religion or Art, was departed.

The forest returned and covered the earth with its waves. Forest, ocean, desert, the green, treeless plains, and about the poles and on mountain heights rock and snow and ice—such again was the earth. Nowhere showed a work of man. The pyramids were levelled.

But how great and green and triumphant was the forest! In the last years of man it had feared for itself. Now was no longer fear, but expansion, flourishing and joy. How greenly the universal forest waved, how broad and tall it grew! How the sun loved it, and the shadow, and the moon at night!   The mahogany tree and the pine tree, the palm and the oak and the beech, the breadfruit and the larch forgot their names, but name or no name lived and throve and made music. The fruit trees and the nut trees went on as best they might. So did the olive and the vine and the maize and the wheat and barley and the rice and tea plant. All lived now for their own ends. The rose and the lily and all the garden flowers had long, long ago turned sylvan.

The sea was filled with fish. The whale and the seal renewed their generations, with their great foe dead. The littoral swarmed with life, from the limpet to the rose flamingo and the great turtles. In the air moved, upon the earth settled, the bird clouds. The busy, intelligent life of the insects continued. All animal life returned to its ancient freedom.

The wild horse and the bison rose into mighty tribes upon the plains. They moved in armies—the dust clouds rolled—earth thundered under their hooves. The deer in the greenwood moved or couched in their thousands. In the winter was heard the long howl of the wolf, and the fox trotted down the glades, and the bear sought out the honey tree. In that zone where the sun is strongest the elephant, no longer slain for his tusks, revived and grew numerous. His huge bulk moved through sun and shade. Male and female, he fed and pursued his loves, and journeyed with his offspring by his side. The tiger held his jungle depths and no rifle cracked against him. The lion and the lioness lay at the desert edge, but their golden eyes saw no caravan, no wayfarer walking upright. The baboon, the gorilla, the chimpanzee sometimes caught by young trees and stood upright or moved a few steps so, but that was all. As for the average monkey folk, they scampered in trees and threw down nuts and jabbered incessantly, but that was all. The serpent glided and basked in the heat and cast his skin, but every animal and bird was against the serpent, and he never regained his old prestige.

The Earth lived and was vocal and intensely interested in herself. There were no men upon her surface, but the horn of plenty was not exhausted by that fact.

Ages passed, though there was no clock, ages and ages. There was another pole star than when man had looked into the skies; all things had slightly shifted. And all things kept on developing. The bird and the flower and the grass and the tree, the mammals, great and small, and all other living things continued to unroll a pattern that grew always more vital, intense and significant. The inorganic was modified. The plant had stronger and stranger dreams. By insensible degrees the animal approached putting one and one together. Sensation and emotion had not departed with man, no, nor rudimentary thinking.

Ages passed. Rain fell, sun shone, the great bow sprang in the heavens. The moving air, the falling water, the waves upon the shore, the bird in the trees, the frogs in the marshes, the humming and violining insects, the voice of the packs when they hunted made a music of and by and for Great Nature. All things learned though they learned very slowly.

There was a creature who must be classed among *aves*. He was small, two-footed, feathered and winged. . . . There were no more men upon the earth. . . . Slowly, taking aeons to do it, he put out, in addition to his wings, rudimentary arms that grew, taking a vast number of generations to accomplish it, into true arm and hand. At the same time he began, very, very slowly, to heighten and broaden his skull. Man would have thought him— as he would have thought man—a strange looking creature. But he had hand as well as wing, and below his bird crest room for brain and its manifold convultions. He waxed in size. Feathers,

not hair, covered him, and he could fly long distances very swiftly. And he had song, and, male and female, love for each other
and great care for the young.

It took time, but at last there dawned self-consciousness.

The old vehicle for sensation, emotion, memory and
thought that had been called man was gone. But sensation, emotion, memory and thought are externals, and a new vehicle had
been wrought. . . .

It is not a perfect vehicle. In much it betters man, but it is
not perfect. The new Thinker resembles the old in that he knows
selfishness and greed and uses violence. . . . It rests to be seen if
he can outwear and lay aside all that and remain—as man could
not remain.

The Buccaneer

The cruise steamer was running, swift or slow as you take it, along the mountainous coast of one of the major islands of the West Indies. Yonder it banked—the land, long and purple-peaked against the sunset sky, to the eye and the feeling gorgeously lonely, though the mind knew it to be populous. The sunset itself presented a fantastic splendor, piling peak above peak, creating and uncreating castles and cities and seas of its own with havens and fleets. The light it flung painted the smooth Caribbean with jewels, with ingots of gold, with red. A passenger leaning against the side remarked upon it to a second passenger. "It is as if all the old sunken ships were talking from below——"

"Come to the other side if you want to see a full moon like all moons rolled into one!"

The promenade deck was being prepared for the dance that evening, one of the three important dances of the long cruise. Stewards and sailors working busily had it almost wholly to themselves. Passengers were in their staterooms, dressing for dinner, dressing for the dance to follow. It was a fancy dress dance, a masked ball. Of those who intended to take part many had spent days in improvising costumes. Others, wiser in the ways of these cruises, had included in their wardrobe a dress for the probable event.

"That moon is extraordinary!" said the first passenger. "It might raise the dead out of this sea."

The bugle sounding through the boat, the two left the deck. The red from the west died out of the sea and the silver and gold from the east took its place. The moon loomed truly vast; she rose like a sorceress through the still, warm air.

In the dining saloon all was chatter and gayety. Many not caring to dress twice were dressed now for the dance and came to dinner so, and with masks and without masks. There could not be much deceiving anyhow in so genial and well acquainted a crowd. Masks were for the added romance, that was all. The majority of the costumes were improvised, meagre material served by imagination; the correct and elaborate were as one in ten. But the improvisations were daring and ingenious and the dresses brought aboard had flavor. As the one and the other entered and found their tables applause rippled through the great, intensely lighted, vibrant saloon with the music playing above. Pierrots and Columbines, Indian braves and Indian maids such as Columbus found or did not find, witches and warlocks and princesses from fairy tales, gypsies and pirates and buccaneers had been easy to devise and abounded. The appropriateness to these seas of pirate and buccaneer had occurred to a number. Gaudy handkerchief around head, burnt cork mustaches and ferocious scowl, shirt of sorts and sleeveless jacket sewn with tinsel gold pieces, vast sash and pasteboard cutlass, loose white breeches—three or four dressed so wound in and out among the tables to shrieks of mock terror.

But Philip Bracknell came in austerely alone to his table near the entrance. His table mates made him stand for a moment while they admired. "It's the real thing----"

"Yes. Brown and Brown copied it for me from an old print. Once he lived, whoever he was."

He sat down, then turned squarely to watch the entrance of Rosamond Hart, who was a singer known to North America and to Europe and now on her way to South America, her impresario and others with her. Not only did she possess a noble contralto voice, but she had of her very own a strange dramatic ability. She was a ballad singer, and it was an experience to hear her sing; spellbound, to watch her illustrate with gesture, movement and expression these passionate, tragic, wistful songs. She was a slight, rather tall woman with a clear olive skin and black hair and eyes, the eyes large and expressive, the mouth wide and finely cut. There breathed about her when she wished it an air of power as well as a certain dusky brooding and sweetness. Now she wore the dress in which she sang an especial group of ballads. It was seventeenth century, of some dark and heavy silk, with full sweeping skirts and a falling of rich lace from her beautiful throat and shoulders. She entered unmasked and quietly, but it ran through the saloon: "Rosamond Hart—Rosamond Hart."

As she made to pass Bracknell's table he rose. She paused a moment: "Why, you are the King of the Buccaneers."

He said: "Your dress is beautiful and of the right century." He was on this ship because she was here. She knew that, and at times was impatient with the fact, and at times endured it well enough. They had quarreled this afternoon; she told herself afterward that he was quarrelsome and bitter, and that she must break it all off while there was time—this, now, was neither breaking off nor not breaking off; it was mere courtesy. But he found it hard to get over sullenness; he was sullen now. She smiled faintly, bent her head with her enigmatical look and passed on to her table. Bracknell gasped, sat down and drank water, and remained silent and arrogant throughout the meal. Certainly silent, and the others at table thought arrogant. He had charm, they granted, and he gave a sense of power, but he was certainly terribly proud and had black moods.

Dinner proceeded with a steady rush of voices, with lights so bright, with gaudy blossoms from the last port of call, with the music threading in and out. Dinner ended. Those who were not yet dressed for the dance went away to do it. Those already in costume resorted for the most part to the drawing room or smoking room or winter garden, where attires might be compared and admired. Those who did not mean to dance or to put on fancy dress—the elderly, the unco sedate, the feeble, and all with their reasons—first looked for their chairs where they were set out of the way of the dancers and then departed to their cabins until the bugle should sound. The bare decks were left, and the sea and the moon.

Rosamond Hart with four or five of her familiars stepped from the companionway and walked up and down viewing the floor prepared and complimenting the moon, the sea, and the fantastically peaked and indented shore that the moon showed plainly enough. It was a still night and warm, the dark-blue, just-breathing water caught in a miraculous net of silver and gold. It was the singer who proposed that they mount to the boat deck the better to taste the night. They went, and found an enchantment up here where the moon streamed unencumbered.

The sea was like a floor; it was like glass—a sea of strong golden and silver and sapphire glass. They determined to stay here and watch it for a while, and someone found rugs and cushions and they put these upon the deck in an angle forward where the colored sea was straight below them. Their talk proved broken and murmuring; it turned into a kind of crooning to the sea and the night, and then into stillness. Then a woman said, "O Rosamond, sing to us a little! It needn't be loudly and everyone is away. This moon and this sea ought to be sung to— it's a kind of rite!"

She began to sing:

> *"This ae night, this ae night,*
> *Every night and a',*
> *Fire and sleet and candlelight*
> *And Christ receive thy saule----"*

"More, more!" they cried when she stopped.

She sang capriciously, a verse from this ballad and a verse from that, and as she sang it seemed to her suddenly that the sea was listening:

> *"O I forbid you, maidens a'*
> *That wear gowd on your hair,*
> *To come or gae by Carterhaugh,*
> *For young Tam Lin is there.*

> *"It was mirk, mirk night, and there was nae stern light,*
> *And they waded thro' red bluid to the knee;*
> *For a' the bluid that's shed on earth*
> *Rins thro' the springs o' that countrie."*

"Ah, sing on, Rosamond!"

> *"She set her foot upon the ship,*
> *No mariners could she behold.*
> *But the sails were o' the taffatil*
> *And the masts of the beaten gold."*

It was a mistake, it appeared, as to there being no people about. It seemed that they must have been massed upon the stair, or been in hiding among the boats or where not. At any rate shadowy groups now appeared, with a clapping of hands and a cry for more.

But the singer laughed and stood up, drawing her cloak about her, while her companions gathered the rugs and cushions. She leaned against the rail and watched the sea. It lay burning silver, streaked with gold; there were paths in it, squares and circles, welters of darkness in the glistering, of glistering in the darkness. "Ships," she thought. "How many ships have passed this way or been sunken here?

> *"O where have you been, my long, long love,*
> *This long seven years and mair?"*

She sang it beneath her breath, giving the words to the flowing sea and the moon that drew the sea, and the earth that held the moon to her side. As she stood there watching the shifting light that certainly was marvelous tonight and made one think of many things, she met of a sudden a wave of loneliness. How lonely she was, how remote, how laid idle somehow on the brink of time, where yet could be yearning, yearning for what was no more or for what could never be—how desperate, and yet with nothing to do with one's desperation. . . . It was her ballads doubtless; she had to live too fully with them; they had terrible moods—ballads. They could evoke—evoke—evocation—why such words?

> *This ae night, this ae night,*
> *Every night and a',*
> *Fire and sleet and candlelight*
> *And Christ receive thy saule——*

She left the boat deck. On the promenade deck a few very young folk already were dancing, fantastic figures whirling up and down. Onlookers were gathering, the masks increasing, the violins tuning. It seemed to her that things had subtly changed—the ship, these folk and herself. She felt enlargement, remoteness, a fine, thin fear—and what was all that about, she wondered. At any rate she was not such as these eager boys and girls who must begin to foot it now and meant to keep it up till the last fiddler groaned and stopped. Nor was she among the idle and the vacant who must sop up every drop of entertainment. She would go to her stateroom, rest and read there an hour, and get rid of this mood.

In her quite luxurious cabin she curled herself upon the couch beneath the window and took up the book of verse that she was studying. But the music throbbed not far away and she knew that the moon was shining in at her window, the moon and the sea, the sea that followed its beckoning finger. She shut the book, turned off the light and lay in the silver shining with violins in her ears.

Rosamond Hart stayed so a long time, dreaming of many things. But at last there grew in her a stirring of conscience. A woman had to do her part in life. She must go dance, too, in the medley out there. She rose from the couch, shook out her skirts and smoothed the lace at her bosom and the rich hair piled high above a wide forehead, put on her mask, took up her cloak and left the stateroom.

Outside the door, in the passageway, Bracknell was waiting for her. Inwardly she shrugged. He was over his temper, it appeared. Sometimes she thought that she would marry Bracknell, and sometimes she thought that she would not. He was himself a ballad. At any rate, they did not have to make talk, being used to each other's silences—and nowadays the gentleman did not give the lady his arm. They moved down the long corridor together, and yet in some way separated. He also was masked. She noted with approval, in the somewhat dim light, the way the crimson handkerchief was knotted about his head, one end hanging down over elflocks. She must have looked at him hurriedly in the dining saloon, she thought, for she did not remember the elflocks. The dim, frayed, once gorgeous sash about his waist and the knife in it—that was right. He was a little taller than herself, and lean. His arms were bared to the shoulder; she had never seen them so, and she thought, "How sinewy!" Evidently he had made slight changes after dinner, not wanting perhaps to be too realistic there. His shirt was stained and torn; there ran across it a streak of faint red. She thought: "He has imagination." And a moment later: "He has achieved atmosphere." She could feel it, dark and thin and somber about him, and that it spread and wrapped her too. She felt "fey," like the moon, like the sea tonight.

She drew her cloak about her; it seemed to her suddenly that the boat was gone and the night was wide. Fright came about her heart, and yearning and sadness. Of what she was frightened she did not know; certainly never before of Bracknell, unless it was fright at times to thrill a little coldly when she thought, "I may marry him." As she did not like the mingled sensation and emotion she thrust it from her with vigor. She laughed. "It's hard to keep from being fanciful on such a night as this, with that moon and that sea beneath it.

"On such a night did. . .
Something fearful doubtless once occur!

"Brown and Brown dressed you well, after the old print."

He did not speak, and she thought of their last quarrel, occurring only a few hours before, and supposed that he was sullen. He was often so; it was one of the things that kept her weighing and weighing. Yet she liked him sullen, too; he gave forth beautiful brown and green and purple lights; he was not truly venomous in his moods; he was only wild and unfortunate. Now they did not speak and they did not touch. Well, who cared? Let him come to his senses at his leisure!

They stepped upon the deck. The music had begun anew. As for the lights, they seemed to be fiery and golden—great glowworms, phosphorescence of these tropic seas, caught and globed; and among them, in and out, streamed the moonlight. Many were dancing—Pierrots and Pierettes, witches and wizards, fairies, undines, shepherds, wigged lawyers, kings and queens, Spanish gypsies and sea rovers. Rosamond Hart said, "There are at least four pirates, besides you, Philip!"

A highlander met them. "'Twas you, my lady, for all your mask, that promised to dance with me first." She remembered that she had done so in the afternoon, putting off Bracknell, still sullen. Bracknell was remaining so. Without a word he moved into a piece of shadow.

She danced with the Highlander, and then she danced with a troubadour whom she knew well enough for all his mask. She thought, "Philip is sulking still. But why then did he wait for me at my door?"

The troubadour was a man no longer young and not so tremendously fond of dancing. Nor was she herself so tremendously fond of it. Her singing, and the drama that she devised always with her singing, gave her release enough. The two, at the end of this dance, found a bit of space from which they could watch the scene and then, turning, watch the moon, now riding high, and the glistering sea. Now they looked at the one and now at the other. "On the whole, we've done well with our dresses," said the troubadour, who was a writer of note, "and these colored and not too many lights and this moon hide deficiencies and outrageousness of interpretation. I wonder what the sea and the moon think of us!"

"Probably we're just one more fantastic dream."

"Very likely. The galleons and the captains and the pirates under sea turn in their sleep. That young witch is well done. You know, there is a flavor of Saint John's Eve, far as we are from it! Or maybe it is Walpurgis Night."

"Have you seen Philip Bracknell? He has copied an old print."

"No. Here he is."

Indeed, at that moment Bracknell appeared. He was masked as she was, but even without their knowledge of costume there would have been no deceiving each other. He had, she saw, drawn down the sleeves of the shirt, whereas a little while ago the whole arm had been bare. Moreover, he had rid himself somehow of the smear of red; perhaps he thought it too realistic. She had certainly received the impression that beneath the twisted red kerchief dark elflocks had hung about his neck. But now she saw that the kerchief was only twisted around and hiding his own hair. Well, she had been mistaken as to that, that was all, and mistaken as to the extent of the worn and ragged and stained. The whole ship was a place of flickering lights and shadows tonight, and one mistook. Again, she felt no longer that cold and startling air about him. He was Philip Bracknell, as usual. Certainly he could not frighten her—though she liked him. He was not too quick, superficial—like so many others. He had something deep down that smoldered, that was fire for all its ash and slag, something real, something that would last, that you might warm yourself by, that would rise intact at the last day. Yes, she liked him, and was willing enough to dance with him. They danced.

He was over his sulkiness. "I'd rather have you treat me badly than all the world be giving me favors."

"Did I treat you badly? I did not mean to."

"Yes, you did. I thought, 'I'll just keep away from her. Why shouldn't the moth exercise its free will?' So I kept away until I couldn't any longer, and so took you from that damned poet."

"That moth and candle thing is quite outworn. Besides, you didn't keep away. You waited at my door and squired me to the deck, though certainly you were as silent as the grave!"

"Waited at your door? No, I didn't! And this is the first

time I'm 'squiring' you, as you call it."

"Why, Philip, what a fib!"

"What do you mean?"

"Let's stop dancing. Didn't you come to my door and wait there, and didn't you walk beside me down the corridor and out here?"

"No!"

"Then who did? Let's rest here. It wasn't Walter Burke. He's shorter and thicker. I saw Captain Todd at dinner—his dress is very different. There's one and there's one, but it was neither of them!"

"What is the matter, Rosamond?"

"Nothing, nothing, but—a mask that I thought was you, dressed like you, waited for me. He did not speak."

"There are half a dozen buccaneers just as there are gypsies and clowns. He had his impudence with him, as I'll tell him when I see him! You must have been mistaken as to the dress. This dress was taken from the genuine article, not the species but an individual. I bought the print. I'll show it to you when we get back. In short, there's but one Dromio aboard tonight."

They had drawn aside from the dancers. "Regard that moon, will you, and those paths upon the sea? Let us get out of this and go up to the boat deck for a while! Let us, Rosamond."

But Rosamond Hart would not do that. He would begin to make love to her, and if she turned it aside then the deep smoldering, the baulked strength, the revengefulness, would creep up through the fairer parts. She did not know that she wanted his love. Sometimes she thought she did, but tonight, no. . . . And besides she felt a lassitude, a loneliness, a wish to weep, and yet to sit dry-eyed, and watch the dark. So she said no, and when he urged her, no again, whereupon the sullen pride in him began to stretch like a tiger cub. She thought, "If I marry him I shall not be happy, and yet it seems to me that I shall marry him, and that I would rather have it so."

A man dressed as the King of Spades bore down upon them and asked her to dance. "Yes, I will." They danced.

He said, "That was a fine mask you were with. Down to a T!"

She said, "There are two dressed alike. Can you see the other?"

Both watch as they danced in and out. "No, there is only

your mask. He is dancing now with the court lady."

They touched in the dance. Yes, that was Philip, all right! Gloom with fiery lights—what was the word—fuliginous?—because she would not go with him to the boat deck. She felt resistance to him, her own indignation. Pirate was his dress and pirate was his nature. And then compunction, "Well, and what if it were so!... Oh, this night!

" 'It was mirk, mirk night and there was nae stern light.' " Only it was not mirk night, but marvelous moonlight. . . . Richer up there on the boat deck, with the music streaming up to one and the sea talking. Lonelier and richer. Loneliness—how lonely it would be, down on the white sands of this main.

She danced with the King of Spades and then with the King of the Gypsies, and then she escaped from all and, unnoted amid the sudden excitement of some new figure, went to the boat deck alone. Others doubtless were here, but not many; none near her. There were lights, but chiefly the golden moonlight. How great it was, the moon, how potent! Music should always sound at this distance, and laughter come up like that, in far away waves, as though one listened from the edge of the world or from the moon or from the bottom of the sea.

Her dress was stately; heavy silk, full-skirted, sweeping the bright deck. She had a deep collar of rich lace; her dark hair was coiled and heaped above her brow. She stood in the full moonlight looking at the sea, then moved forward until now she had before her the great prow dividing the Caribbean, and the direct path of the moon. It shone so strongly and livingly. She looked up to the flag. She seemed alone. Stay here and think of this sea and all they who had sailed it and were buried in it. She found a place where she might sit, her cloak drawn around her, elbow on knee, chin in hand. The Caribbean, and all manner of ships, and they who had been at home in them. What was time, a scale that you could run up and down. Lonely, it was lonely on the white sand. Some human souls had wings and some had chains.

> *This ae night, this ae night,*
> *Every night and a'----*

The Caribbean—violins playing—Philip Bracknell.

Well, he had watched and followed her, for here he stood beside her—no, it was the other mask!

Instantly she was frightened again, and again knew not why she was so. The air about her seemed to change, to become thin, dark and cold and charged with something to tell, something terrible, something piteous. He did not speak, whoever he was, any more than he had spoken walking beside her an hour or two ago. She saw the differences, the elflocks, the arms bare to the shoulder, the red smear upon the shirt. She wished that he did not have a mask so that she might better cope with this terror that was invading her, terror and yet also something achingly deep and compassionate and unafraid. She had no sooner formed the wish than instantly she saw that he was not masked . . . . She did not know him, no, of course not—a ravaged face, a tragic, pathetic, dreadful and beautiful face—and not unlike Bracknell, if Bracknell had ever lived like the picture he copied. Cold terror rose about her as though the sea had come up over the side. She sprang to her feet; the figure barred her way. In a moment she was in flight, running blindly along the deck.

Coming from the companion was Bracknell. He caught her. "What is it, Rosamond? What is it?"

She clung to him breathless. "The other one—the other one —the one you are dressed like!"

"Where? What do you mean?"

"Look, look!" She caught his hand in both hers. "Look!"

The figure stood before them in a desolate and lost way and yet with pride. It seemed to say, "My seas—these seas are mine." Then in an instant it was gone, gone as though it had passed through all obstruction and sunk into the sea it claimed. It was here no longer, there was only the moonlighted deck.

They sat down upon some raised bit of wood in the shadow of a boat. She was trembling violently. "You copied from one who once was—was like you."

"I chose because of the name."

"Bracknell?"

"Yes. Philip Bracknell."

And she clung to him weeping, "Oh, Philip----"

He was stubborn. "I don't understand. These are pirate seas of course. Pirates and buccaneers, buccaneers and pirates, and of course there is a difference, as the buccanner would have you know! You mustn't confuse the two, Rosamond, you mustn't confuse them. And tonight with that witch's path over the sea, and a kind of excitement everywhere—all right, say we've seen a ghost, but now it's gone, it's gone, and it won't come again. But on the whole I don't believe we saw it. Everything's wrought up tonight. It was a trick of the light and these masks----"

She took off her mask and when he saw her do so he removed his also. "Say it was a ghost, Rosamond. But it is gone now, gone! And I love you, I love you, I love you!"

The ship held on where other ships had sailed. On the deck below the masks and the music whirled together, embraced, parted, kept their distance, whirled together again. The moon shone, approaching the midheaven. The sea glistered, and now and then it looked as though dolphins or schools of flying fish leaped and played.

Black Lace

Old Miss's twin brother had sent her the black lace shawl, a very fine one, from Spain fifty years ago, when she was a brilliant young married beauty and went each summer to the Virginia Springs. Then, two years afterward, he died in Spain of fever and was buried there; and she never saw him again who was to her her other self. She was wearing the shawl over a rose tarlatan dress the evening they brought her the news. She never wore it again but put it away with damask rose leaves in an ebony box on the top shelf of the huge mahogany wardrobe in her chamber at Deep River. Twice a year, upon his birthday and on the anniversary of his death, she took it out and sat with it unfolded over her lap and over the wing chair. Her little girls stood around her and she told how handsome and how gifted their uncle had been.

The girls—there were four—grew into young ladyhood. Often enough they ransacked the old wardrobe and a highboy and a chest and made free for their youth with the fineries preserved from her youth. But not with the black lace shawl. When Fanny went to New Orleans for Mardi gras she begged for it. "Oh, mother, over my blue—it would be so Spanish and right!"

But her mother shook her head. "No, child, no! I should not sleep if it were gone. I've made your father promise that it shall be put about me when I am dead. Melissa, you remember if you're by me when I die!"

Melissa was her maid—"Mis Anne's" maid. She was not Old Miss then, her mother-in-law being the reigning Old Miss at Deep River. To all the colored folk it was Miss Anne or sometimes Young Miss, and Old Miss. Melissa was a young ebony slip, twenty years younger than her mistress, born at Deep River—and her father and grandfather before her. Melissa said "Yaas, ma'am," and immediately saw as in a picture Miss Anne lying in her coffin, black lace from head to foot, black lace over a white dress. Melissa made a mark to remember. "Folks that don't get buried as they want ha'nts you." Besides, she was fond of Miss

Anne.

One by one the girls married excepting Betty, who stayed with her mother. Miss Anne's husband died, his mother died; her son Robert married and brought his wife to Deep River. Now she was Young Miss. Miss Anne was Old Miss. In time there were grandchildren; time flowing on in an amiable Southern fashion, the grandchildren passed, several of them, into their teens.

Old Miss's health failed. She lay a great part of her days in her chamber in the four-poster, under the valance with the ball fringe, nursed by her daughter Betty, who was now an old maid, and by Melissa. Especially by Melissa, to whom Old Miss clung.

This rainy spring day, the rain coming down with a steady pouring sound like a million million minute footfalls and whispers, with the great cedar outside the window like a dark sponge, and the water running in cataracts off the stiff magnolia leaves, and the cherry and plum and peach trees in blossom like ghosts in a twilight, and in Old Miss's room a fire fed with pine knots and making the walls and the big dark old furniture all waving as though they were under a red and amber sea—on this especial day Old Miss took a fancy that she wanted the black lace shawl spread over her where she lay in the big white bed.

Melissa brought the ebony box from the wardrobe shelf and, opening it, unfolded the shawl, the dried rose leaves raining back into the box. "Just look at the size of it! Big as all out-of-doors and as soft in yo' hands as rain water, and all black branches and wreaths---"

"Spread it over me," said Old Miss.

"Dar, now! You look as though you're goin' to a party!"

"A great big party," said Old Miss.

It rained all day, it rained all night. Melissa had a narrow bed in a dressing room opening from the chamber. Once or twice in the night she rose to replenish the fire behind the strong fender, Old Miss when she was wakeful liking the light upon the walls. But tonight she slept, drunk with the sound of the rain and the river. Melissa stood at the window. "That old river's sure rampaging."

The next morning Robert and Sally came in to see Old Miss. "Yes, I feel better. How are the children?"

"Molly has the toothache. But it's raining too hard to take her to Hilltop."

"The river's very loud."

"Yes, it is. Too loud," said Robert.

It rained all day. Betty had a spring cold, so sopping wet was the world, and shivered and grew hoarse and at last went off to drink hot lemonade and creep beneath her own blankets. The rain came down steadily, and the river rose as steadily.

High water—those were two words that always brought Deep River alert. The children came into Old Miss's room and talked about the river, but they knew nothing really. "Is it out in the low meadow?" Yes, it was; but being out in the low meadow was not in itself alarming.

Mailtime came, and Old Miss sent for the newspaper. The newspaper was filled to overflowing with high water. Very high water, the highest for many springs. If this continued, if the rains held, if the upcountry streams, swollen with rain, swollen from still other and farther streams fed by melting snows—if all these had still to bring and discharge their burden into the main channel, then no one knew what might happen, how great a flood. Banks might give anywhere, any hour. In places already the river was out; folk were moving away in time or being rescued in boats.

Old Miss read and sent for Robert. He was away from the house, out about the cabins or the barns. Sally came instead.

"Don't ever try to keep things from me!" said Old Miss energetically. "We're going to have to move out; we'll have to go to Catherine's or to Fanny's, as we did twenty-five years ago! And all the house in such a mess when we came back! And they had to do the same thing thirty years before that, and again seventy-five years ago. Robert's great-grandfather ought never to have built Deep River so near!"

That night it ceased to rain, and the moon shone. Old Miss called Melissa. "Look out now, Melissa!—look out again, Melissa!"

"Moon's shining, Miss Anne. The flower garden's just as plain!"

"I'm thinking about the river. What does it look like?"

"It looks all white and solemn. I kin scarcely see the other side. It looks like Jordan."

"Open the window, so I can hear. When it sounds like that it is saying 'I'll take you with me!' "

Melissa shut the window and came back to the bed. "Miss

Anne, I'm going give you yo' beef tea now instead of later. . . .
There, now!" She made up the fire till the room was all light
and cheerful.

"Give me my black lace shawl," said Old Miss. "Put it over
me. Melissa, it's to be around me, just as a lady would wear
it, when I'm in my coffin. Don't you ever forget!"

The moon shone through the night, but with dawn began
the rain again. As for the river, with every hour it seemed more
lifted, loud and hoarse. Past Deep River House, on a moving
yellow field, went parts of cabins, parts of barns, parts of bridges,
fences, chicken coops, trunks and boughs of trees. A log went
by with a dog atop of it, howling.

The house was built upon a point of land, and that gave the
river on two sides. It had been a mistake to build it there. But
it had stood eighty years, though thrice in that period the river
had entered it, rising five feet, six feet in the lower rooms, leaving, when it went away, a miserableness of mud and ruined wall
papers and warped woodwork. But each time the waters went
back, and the house, the house itself, rested.

Each generation of children thought it very exciting to
move out, to go en masse to visit kinsfolk, to watch the river
rise and rise, to come in clamoring, "It's past the sycamores!—it's
under the gate!—it's on the lawn!" When it touched the lawn it
was time to go.

The young folk now at Deep River were seeing all that
for the first time. Now the river was at the sycamores. Maybe
it would pass them, maybe it wouldn't. They were tremendously excited. The girls ran every ten minutes to the windows; the
boys were out on the place.

And every hour or so arrived some messenger from folk in
Hilltop, from folk in country houses, from Catherine, from
Fanny, urging Deep River to move out. There came news of
other families preparing to leave their homes, though in truth
none was so exposed as Deep River. The Allens above them were
going, the Lydgates below them.

In the middle of the afternoon Old Miss became anxious
about Amy and her children, ten miles down river. Amy was
her youngest daughter, there were three children—Lisle was away
in the East—the house stood half a mile from the river. No one
had ever before dreamed of trouble there, but who could tell
what would or would not happen, with all the newspapers ringing

an alarm bell? As if in answer Old Sam, riding old Selim, arrived from Amy.

They were not in the least danger, and there was no earthly reason for them to move, but Deep River—please, please!—must go at once to Catherine and Fanny. Amy could not sleep nor rest for thinking of their trying to stay it out, when everyone knew the river might come six feet into the house.

Deep River determined to leave. Robert and Sally and the children would go to Catherine; Old Miss, Betty and Melissa to Fanny; the servants to their own color in Hilltop; the stock from the point of land to the old barns.

Old Miss lay and listened to the rain and the river and then to sounds in the house. "They're beginning to move things. Yes, they are! They're moving the piano and taking up the carpets. They're bringing the chairs and sofas and tables and whatnots and paintings upstairs. Melissa, go tell Mr. Robert or Miss Sally to come here!"

"Here's Miss Betty, Miss Anne."

". . .and we're going to take you just as easy in the big wagon, mother. Lift the mattress with you, just as easy!" ended Betty. "Melissa, get her things together and put them in her middle-sized trunk. It can't be more than a week or so. You'll be back, mother, before the lilacs bloom."

"It was six weeks before the house was fit to live in, twenty-five years ago."

"Maybe, after all, the river won't get any higher. It's just at the sycamores now. Maybe it won't come a step farther. It all depends, Robert says, on whether the worst of the streams have come down. . . . Yes, Melissa, everything she could possibly need."

"I want my Bible and Prayer Book and the pictures of the children. And I want my black lace shawl, Melissa."

"Yaas, Miss Anne," answered Melissa, gathering linen from drawers. But then there came one of the children, telling that Melissa was wanted in the kitchen by her old father. "Go, Melissa!" said Betty. "I'll finish the trunk."

Melissa left the room. Negro men were filling the upper hall with furniture from the rooms below. Up the stairs was being borne the long parlor sofa with double claw feet, and after it the tall clock from the hall. Next came, carried high, the portrait of Old Miss's brother who had given her the black lace shawl and died in Spain. The handsome, strong, romantic countenance faced her.

"Yaas, sir!" said Melissa inwardly to the portrait; "she sho does hold by that gift. She gwine be buried in it. Yaas! Judgment morn you just look for Miss Anne with it round her shoulders and hanging long down on her white dress!"

She stopped before the window at the head of the back stairs. "Look at that river!" It was a sight, yellow and ridged, with all the débris of its banks coming down it. Melissa, her hands on either side the sash, gazed with great eyes. "Do you think that river gwine stop outside the big gate? No, my Lawd, that river comin' in this house!"

But it did not come that day. At sunset the sky was clear and a red shaft like a sword prolonged lay across the point of land. And everything living, or whose living amounted, was off the point of land, away from Deep River. The old house, the old trees, the cabins, the road had an unearthly loneliness. The sun went down.

The old house stood dark and vacant in the purple dusk, in the starry night. What it said to the now enormous river and what the river said to it may have been this or may have been that. It was like the Last Eve at Deep River, with the evening star and the flood's hoarse voice.

Old Miss had the big square room at Fanny's. She lay in a four-poster much like the one at home, and a bright fire made leaping shapes on the walls. Melissa slept on a pallet in a corner of the room.

In the latter part of the night Melissa had a dream. Old Miss was walking by the river. She said that she was going to cross it and go to heaven, but she must have her black lace shawl. Melissa waked and lay still in the chill white dawn. Black lace, black lace.

The dream picture faded and in its place rose the hurried departure from Deep River. She, Melissa, was gathering things together for the trunk that stood now against the opposite wall. Old Miss in the big bed had said, "Be sure you put in my black lace shawl." Word came that she was wanted in the kitchen; her father was there, wanting to know where she thought he ought to go.

For a moment Melissa's consciousness turned that way. Old Daddy and the cabin, with the sunflowers and the scarlet runner beans, where she used to play when she was pickaninny and where, when she was older, Junius came courting her. Morning-glories and Junius. . . . Now just Old Daddy there, and he better take his fiddle and go to Miss Catherine's.

Black lace. Melissa returned to the big house and to Old Miss. Must go down to see Old Daddy; and Miss Betty said, "I'll finish putting in her things, Melissa." Old Daddy kept her arguing and arguing about the dog and the chickens, and when she got back to Old Miss the trunk was shut, and then came Marse Robert and the men. Everybody in a hurry and snatching up things.

Melissa raised herself upon her elbow. Old Miss was sleeping soundly. Was or was not the ebony box in the trunk? She left the pallet and, crossing the floor softly, opened as softly the trunk. Not in the tray nor under the tray—it had been left behind.

Melissa stood up. "Somebody's got to get her black lace; got to get it before she finds it's not here!" She moved without sound to the window and looked toward Deep River, less than two miles away, hidden by a twist of the land. "If that river's still where it belongs I kin run and get it." She slipped on her clothes. "I'll go right after Old Miss's breakfast—I won't tell no one."

But it wasn't possible to get away as soon as that. Old Miss wanted the trunk unpacked and its contents bestowed in drawers and presses. "Put the ebony box on that shelf." Melissa appeared to put it there. After that there was some stitching that had to be done. Betty still had a wretched cold. Fanny and her three girls flitted in and out. Robert and Sally's two boys walked over from Catherine's and came up to tell Old Miss the news.

"Somebody ought to send a note to Amy," said Old Miss from the spare room's big four-poster. "Tell her we are well but not very well. I can't stand much more."

No, Melissa had no chance till afternoon. Then she said, "If you don't mind, Miss Anne, I'm going out for a little."

"Yes; go, Melissa. Go and see about Old Daddy. Is he with Sarah?"

"Yaas, ma'am."

So Melissa got away from Miss Fanny's without telling a story, and yet without letting anyone know anything about black lace and Deep River.

Betty coming in, Old Miss said, "Melissa has gone to Hilltop to see about Old Daddy. I told her if she wanted to stay all night to do so."

Melissa went to the point of land, not by the county road that ran along the river, though lifted out of flood reach, but by a path through the woods and between the waves of earth that the region called hills. She met a couple of boys but no one else. "Hi!" they said. "The river's still rising! It's over Merton's meadows."

Melissa walked swiftly, a woman of fifty years, tall and strong and supple and fulfilled with an African comeliness. Her father's grandfather, they said at Deep River, had been an African king. She sang as she walked, though not loudly:

"Swing low, sweet chariot
Coming for to carry me home—
I looked up, an' what did I see there,
Coming for to carry me home----"

Now she was in sight of the river. It ran huge and sullen and ominous, out of borders, sweeping wreckage, sweeping débris into its main current and down through the sodden land. The point of land running into the yellow field had shrunk since yesterday, but the water wasn't across it, water wasn't to the house. But Melissa said "I ain't any too soon."

She was now upon the Deep River road, that took its start from the county road, that ran through Deep River fields, and then out upon the point of land to the house that had been built eighty years ago, so near and too near the river. She was now upon the point of land.

She kept on singing to keep herself in company:

"I got shoes an' you got shoes,
All of God's children got shoes----"

She stood still. The sliver of fat earth running out into river was wider behind her, wider again before her. Why, then, was it narrower just here? On the up-river side she saw a tooth biting in, a yellow fang. She watched it, fascinated. There showed a swirl in the water here; it sucked. Bits of the bank it was making on either hand nodded, crumbled and fell into it.

This wasn't only flood, this was river boring its way.

Out of the deeps of memory rose like a bubble something heard somewhere long ago—white folk talking, but not Deep River white folk: "I wouldn't put it beyond the river sometime to bite off that whole point of land. Bite it off and sink with it and let it never come up again."

Melissa drew a quick breath. "I'm going get that black lace right away and then go to Miss Catherine's and tell Marse Robert. But shucks, it doesn't mean anything! Old river's just making a kind of a gully."

Cedars hid Deep River House until one was almost upon it. It opened before her. Deep River House—Melissa's home as well as another's. The house was frame, with deep verandas; about it stood magnolias, tulip trees and cedars, every tree magnificent. Over the veranda, over two summerhouses placed at equal distance right and left of the house, hung wistaria in bloom, a drooping and cloudy purple. Under the tulip trees were flung great sheets of daffodils.

The sun was now low; a light ineffably cool, pure and still, a light of enchantment infolded the deserted point, the deserted house. All about it the water came creeping, creeping on.

Melissa, standing on the veranda steps, watched it, half afraid, half exalted. "It's coming closer. When it gets a little higher it'll make a rush. Those daffodils won't know what's come to them. Melissa, you'd better go get Old Miss's black lace shawl!"

The front door was locked, but she knew how to enter the house by a long window whose blind had only to be dragged open and the sash lifted. Inside, how forlorn, with everything abovestairs that could be taken there, with the carpets up, the pictures down, the windows darkened. In the upper hall the tall clock struck five.

Melissa mounted the stairs. In the upper hall, as long and wide as the lower, leaned against the walls the portraits brought there out of danger. She paused a moment before Old Miss's twin brother, dead so long ago, young and stately. She had always liked this portrait, though she had never seen its original.

In Old Miss's room she went straight to the wardrobe. There, overlooked upon the shelf, sulked the ebony box. Melissa opened it to make certainty certain. The shawl lay in its pride, so silken, rich and soft, so fine that for all its amplitude it lived, folded, in a little space. She closed the box and with it in her hand passed the four-poster, so strange without Old Miss upon it, and went to one of the four windows to see the flood from there.

The window commanded also the Deep River road across the point of land. Melissa looked at the road, rubbed her eyes and looked again.

Upon it, close now to the house, appeared an old phaëton drawn by a gray horse and driven by a woman, a boy of eleven beside her, and on the back seat two little girls.

"Miss Amy!" breathed Melissa, and ran down the stairs and out of the house. "Miss Amy, what you doing here?"

"Have they gone, Melissa?"

"Yass'm. This time yesterday. Ain't Sam tell you?"

"He wasn't any way certain. He said they might and they might not. He must have got it all crooked. I couldn't stand it, so I just drove up myself to see about mother."

"They're gone. I left yo' ma's black lace shawl and I come to get it. Now we'd better be gone too!"

"Mother, I want a drink of water!"

"Mother, can't I just pick some of the hyacinths to take to grandmother?"

"Mother, just let us look in! You said they'd take everything upstairs----"

"Mother, I do want some water."

"We'll all get out," said Amy, "for just five minutes."

There was water left in a cooler upon the back veranda. The boy, Terry, ran around the house to get it. The two little girls, Fan and Marty, fell to picking Roman hyacinths and then daffodils.

Their mother with Melissa stepped through the long window. "How desolate! Poor old Deep River! I can just remember —the water came up to here."

The two mounted the stairs, Amy wishing just to glance into her mother's room. There was a window on the landing, and the shutters were not closed. They looked out. "Oh, my heavens!" cried Amy, and turning ran down the stairs and out of the house, Melissa at her side.

The little girls were trying to get into the phaëton. The horse was terrified; the boy at his head tried to quiet him so that the phaëton would keep steady.

"Miss Amy, we can't get away thataway! It's cutting us off; it'll be deep in a minute! Get the children into the house!"

The five reached the veranda before the water was upon them, but in a moment it came sweeping and covered the green earth. The horse grew mad with terror, turned and, the phaëton rocking behind him, made up the road. But now the water rose on all sides, the house was islanded, the road disappeared. The flood bore with it logs and interlaced boughs. The phaëton was caught and held. The horse, putting forth all his strength, broke from it and went plunging through the water into the twilight beyond the cedars. "Oh, Selim won't drown, will he mother? He'll get away?"

The water came upon the veranda, the water came by every opening into the house. It began, though very slowly, to eat up the stairs, step by step.

In Hilltop, at Catherine's and Fanny's, up and down the river, by everybody who had had to move and everybody whose houses were safe, it was presently known that upcountry was only now doing its worst and that the final high water was upon them.

By dark those concerned knew that the water was in Deep River House. "Ah," they said at Catherine's and at Fanny's, "it will be six feet in the house again! It will take till summer to get it clean and dry and papered again." They said to each other, "Mother holds up wonderfully!"

Said Fanny, "Where is Melissa?"

Betty answered, "She went to Sarah's to see about Old Daddy. Mother told her to stay all night if he wanted her to do it. I'll stay with mother. She can't seem to get her mind off Amy."

"Then I'll have a cot put in for you," said Fanny. "What do you think she'd like for supper?"

Amy, a slender, fair-haired, dark-eyed woman, the youngest of the flock, and Amy's three children occupied with Melissa the upper floor of Deep River, and indeed Old Miss's room, for that to them all seemed the midmost, the safest, the most reassuring.

Until the light was out of the sky the children and their mother watched the spreading, rising flood. "Six feet in the house," said Amy. "It never in the time of man went over that!

And after a day or so at most it begins to go down.''

"First thing in the morning," said Melissa, "I'm going hang a sheet out of most every window. There's the flag, too, we uses reunions and Memorial Days. We'll hang that so's it can be seen. Somebody'll make it out pretty quick and come in a boat.''

"The cedars hide us so," said Amy.

Terry and the little girls thought that on the whole it was fun. But Amy and Melissa consulted together. "They haven't had anything since early dinner. Who knows if tomorrow anyone will come? I'm frightened, Melissa!"

Melissa considered. "I know there's plenty in the storeroom. That water ain't more than waist-high downstairs. But Miss Sally locked the storeroom door. I couldn't get in." She thought a moment, standing still and straight and strong, the greatest comfort to Amy that she was there. "Miss Sally always keep beaten biscuits and her fruit cake, too, in the linen closet. I don't believe she lock that. You just wait here, honey!"

The linen closet was on this floor. Melissa looked down the well of the stairs and saw the last gleam of day reflected in four feet of water. The same ray touched the portrait of Old Miss's twin leaning against the wall. She stood still, compelled by the strong, significant face.

"The day you bought that black lace you never saw the things that'd turn about it. When you bought it Melissa stood here in Deep River House, with the river rising. Terry's more like you than any of them—Old Miss says so, and it's true. When he grows up he'll be powerful like you. Maybe he'll put in life an' take out of life, what you'd have liked to do. . . ."

Amy exclaimed with relief and the children with joy at the beaten biscuits and half a fruit cake and a dozen oranges. There's more oranges, Miss Amy, and there's water in most of the pitchers, though I could boil that river water. I'm going to make a fire now. Plenty of wood and kindling in Old Miss's wood box, and she got a box of candles too."

The fire made the greatest difference, so warm and bright! They lighted candles, but the fire was the thing. Outside the windows shone the stars and rose a round moon.

It was frightening looking at the waste of waters upon which they shone and the dark things that were trees standing up from the water and the dark things going by on the main stream. The sound, too, inspired sadness and dread.

The river was rising very slowly now in the house; perhaps it was at its height. It was far from their windows and only a certain way up the stairs. When it began to go down it would fall steadily, steadily. Even if on the morrow no one made out their signals—the house being so obscured by the cedars—they would not starve and the river would go down until, day after tomorrow maybe, they could wade out, dirty and horrid as that would be!

So they left the windows and sat about the fire. Once an uprooted tree, borne that way, struck the house like a battering ram, and that was appalling for a moment. But it was just a momentary blow and did not repeat itself.

Fan was a high-strung, nervous child, and her mother sat with her gathered in her lap, the rosy light playing over both, in Old Miss's wing chair. Terry and Marty sat on the hearth rug close beside her, Terry with his knees drawn up, his hands clasped around them and his eyes upon the caverns and bridges in the fire. He was a boy with his own thoughts. Melissa had the chimney corner.

Said Amy, "I forgot how you came to be here, Melissa? It is a blessing for us!" Melissa told. "How things stretch out hands!" said Amy. "Uncle Griffith's black lace—where is it?"

Melissa brought her the ebony box. She opened it and took out the great shawl. "Look, Fan! Have you ever seen it close like this, Marty?"

"Oh, mother, dress me up in it!"

It became Marty, it became Fan. They played ladies within its folds, walking stately up and down the fire-lit room. It was as though Old Miss lay in the big bed and smiled at them. It was as though the portrait of their great-uncle, out there in the upper hall, smiled at them.

"If they could see us at Catherine's and at Fanny's!"

"Old Miss thinks I'm sitting still at Sarah's, listening to Old Daddy and his fiddle. Now he's playing Money Musk and now he's playing Eglantine. . . ."

They had wound Old Miss's clock. When it struck eight Fan and Marty begged to sit up till nine. Terry would do it anyhow— Terry was eleven years old. Terry went with Melissa and a candle to bring wood from the box upon the upper veranda. Out here they could view under the moon the sea in which they were set.

The children called every colored servant who had attained to middle age uncle or aunt. "Aunt Melissa," said Terry, "we wanted to see that grandmother was safe, and you wanted to find her black lace shawl that she missed. That's why I think God will take care of us, even if we drown."

"You ain't going to drown," said Melissa. "Yo're going to live and do a lot."

They lifted their loads of wood and went back into the upper hall, where they had left the candle. It was eerie to look downstairs and see the water. They stopped a moment before Great-uncle Griffith's picture. The great-nephew truly was like the great-uncle; the eyes of the portrait, in the candle's straight white light, seemed to rest upon the boy and to rest there with some kind of grave insistence.

"There, now!" said Melissa. "He say, 'You do what I didn't have time to do!' "

Back in Old Miss's room the children must have their sleep. But Melissa and Amy sat late by the fire. The children, too, were wakeful. Terry lay quietly, making his own pictures or thinking his own thoughts, but Fan was very restless and at last sat up and began to cry. Her mother went and lay down beside her. "Talk, mother; I want to hear you talk! Tell about going to grandmother's!"

"But we are at grandmother's."

"It isn't like it!" Fan cried to break her heart. "I want the river to go away—I'm afraid of the river!"

"I'll tell you a story. Or no—Melissa, you come and tell us a story! Just as you used to, when Fanny and Catherine and Betty and I were children. One of Old Daddy's stories. Tell us about the fox and the rabbit and the squirrel and the mocking-bird!"

Melissa brought a chair to the foot of the bed. In her rich voice with its wonderful intonations she told about the fox and the rabbit and the squirrel and the mockingbird and from that passed to a relation of the deeds of the stag, the otter and the opossum. Fan grew quiet, Marty listened big-eyed, Terry from his bed.

"Now sing," suggested Amy. "They ought to go to sleep."

> *"I got wings, you got wings,*
> *All God's children got wings. . . ."*

The children slept, Terry and Marty and Fan. The two

women watched from the windows and went into the hall and halfway down the stairs almost to the water and stood there watching. It had ceased to rise; it stood at about five feet; presently, they made sure, it would begin to sink, however slowly. But it was doleful to look at by candlelight and they returned with relief to the firelight.

"By every way it's ever done we're safe now. I'm dead tired, and so are you, Melissa. Let's lie down and sleep. I'll take off my dress."

They drew together the embers and put ashes over them. They said good night: "Good night, Miss Amy!" "Good night, Melissa!" They put out the candles. The moonlight streaming through the windows gave them light enough.

Terry lay upon his couch between the great bed and the dressing room. Melissa, passing him, looked down upon the young face. "Yaas, you and that painting out in the hall have got your understanding!"

The wing chair was by the couch, and over the chair hung still the black lace shawl. Melissa made a movement toward lifting and folding it. But the ebony box was upon the other side of the room, and Miss Amy was upon her knees by the bed, saying her prayers; and Melissa went on into her own narrow room and to her own narrow bed.

She, too, said her prayers and lay down in her gingham dress in the moonlight. She was dead tired, and the worst of things was over—tomorrow a boat would come. She drowsed. . . . Old Daddy's fiddle. Sunflowers by the cabin, sunflowers and zinnias. Junius drawing her to the cabin porch, and all the morning-glories freshly out and spangled with the dew, and Old Daddy's fiddle playing like heaven—playing like heaven. . . .

Amy slept in her mother's bed, with Fan on one side and Marty on the other. Terry slept on the couch. Melissa slept.

But the river did not sleep, the river that wasn't content with freshet and flood but meant permanently to alter, just here, its shore line. The river went on driving its wedge.

Old Daddy playing Old Dan Tucker. The carriage horses running away—the carriage swaying from side to side, Marse Robert trying to stop the horses, Old Miss sitting inside very still----

Melissa started up, wide-awake; stepped from the bed.

"What's that? What's that noise?" The noise grew, the house began to shake.

Amy cried from the big room. "What is it, Melissa, what is it?" Water covered the floor, water was about their ankles. It was coming up, it was filling Deep River House, which began to leave its foundations, whose walls began to bow. "Oh my children! Oh, my children!" She gathered Fan and Marty from the bed.

Melissa lifted Terry. "What's the matter, Aunt Melissa? What's the matter, mother?"

"Oh, pray to God, children, and be quiet while we think! What is it, Melissa? What do you think it is?"

"Miss Amy, the river done broke through the point of land! It ain't flood water—it's the river come over!"

"The river! What are we going to do? Drown and be buried in here?"

"Miss Amy, let's get, if we can, to the veranda. Better be outside anyhow."

They took the children and opened the door. The moonlight fell upon the black lace shawl over the wing chair. Melissa took it up, folded it swiftly into small compass and put it into the bosom of her gingham dress. Water in the upper hall, water on the veranda, the level of the terrible river. As they reached it, as they came clear into the moonlight the house moved and broke in two. It was like a ship going down at sea.

The river flowed where had stood Deep River House. Only a great chimney stack rested and an angle of stubborn wall and rafter. Gulfs were made in the water and filled again with a wild swirling and a heavy sound. Wreckage sank, heaping the new floor of the river, and wreckage set adrift entered the current and was borne down the river. Down upon it looked the moon, and in the east stood the morning star.

To Melissa a long time seemed to pass. She heard Old Daddy's fiddle, she saw the cabin and the sunflowers, she saw Junius and heard him call. "Come on, honey! Come over here—here's the bank!" Then nothing.

Then she knew that she was swimming. She could swim; Old Daddy had taught her when she was little. She was swimming, but she thought that she had a hurt in the side where some beam or pillar had struck her. She was helping a boy, who could swim, too, but who was too young and slight in the turmoil of this river, who would have sunk without her.

Knowledge returned: It had been no time—only they had gone, she and Terry, to the gates of Death and been thrust up to Life again. That couldn't last; they were going to drown, and drowning wasn't so bad. Dawn was coming. You couldn't swim any longer in this river.

The river was carrying spoils of the land. Something came by her and she seized it with her free arm. It was the half-submerged branch of a tree. She was a strong woman; she held fast and with all her power lifted Terry. "Catch hold of the bough—catch hold!" He caught. "Pull yourself up into it. Now, honey!"

The boy obeyed. The bough, torn from some great tree, upbore his light form, but had no room for another.

Melissa held to it, but if it was a raft she could not come upon it, nor indeed hold to it long. She now became assured that her side was bleeding. The boy lay curled upon himself, gasping. "Are you hurt, honey? Something hit me—did it hit you too?"

"No. Aunt Melissa, can't you come here out of the water?"

"It ain't big enough, Terry. I'd just sink us both. You mind me and stay just where you are! Dawn's coming."

"Where are mother and Fan and Marty—are they drowned?"

"I don't know, Terry. If it's so, they're in heaven now, and everybody's happy in heaven. Maybe we'll go too. Don't cry. You've got to be a man now, like—like your Great-uncle Griffith. Look here, Terry!"

With her left hand she drew from the bosom of her dress the folded lace. "Dar, now! It's sopping, like the rest of this world. Can you take it? Lean over and take it from me, Terry. Unfold it and spread it on those sticks by you. Kin you see the red in the east? It's coming day, and folk will be watching the river. It's rough and high, but they would make out somehow with a boat. Just as soon as it's good light you begin to wave that shawl. Somebody got to see it. You going mind me, honey?"

"Yes, Aunt Melissa. Oh, mother and Fan and Marty!"

"They're happy, child. They're happy now. One day you'll go to them. But you ain't going now. You going to live!"

Bands of amethyst and gold appeared in the east. Melissa saw Old Daddy up and making the fire in the cabin. Her voice was failing, she knew that she had a deep hurt, she was going presently to loosen her clasp of this driftwood, her ears were ringing, her breath was going.

The boy balanced himself upon his slender perch. Any movement right or left might send him wholly into the water, and truly he saw that she could not climb beside him nor even take his place. He looked at her now, dry-eyed, with a sword in his young heart. "Hold on," he begged her. "Please, please, hold on!"

"Something struck me, Terry. I'm bleeding to death. If I was on my bed in the cabin 'twould be just the same. I'd be going fast, so don't you worry, honey! Now it's getting light."

The east flamed, the east reflected itself in the wide and turbid river. "The shores is growing green," said Melissa. "Folk will be stirring now. You turn your face to the nearest bank, honey, and take that black lace and wave it. Tell Old Miss I saved it for her. Do what I tell you, child! Watch the shore yonder. Tell Old Daddy I hear his fiddle. Tell him Junius coming to meet me---"

The boy on his bit of driftwood raised his arm and waved Great-uncle Griffith's gift of black lace and shouted, his eyes upon the bolder shore, where stood a house and before it a group of men watching the flood. He saw that they saw him and that they put themselves into motion. He turned his head to tell Melissa so, but there was only the surface of the river.

Melissa and Junius had met in a green meadow with a cabin at hand, stood about with sunflowers, with morning-glories over the porch.

The Two Business Men

"I alwuz liked dead people en done all I could for 'em."
—*Huckleberry Finn*

For a tired teacher of mathematics in a small woman's college (small college; the girls were average), without much money and scrimpy with teachers, Fisherman's Luck proved the round hole for the round peg. It wasn't expensive. It used to be a modest log house, but got added to in various directions until it sprawled in a comfortable way. It had called unto itself offspring in the shape of three or four detached cabins: happy, old-time, log ones, buried in hemlock and white pine and mountain linden and such. The guests at Fisherman's Luck, or Berry's, as it was mostly called, were hardly what you call fashionable, though they were solid enough, some of them. Once a man tired of staggering under big business found this place out, and he told three or four others in a like predicament. Year after year they came to Berry's for a few weeks and wiped off the world. As near as might be, that is.

Fisherman's Luck, or Berry's, lived two thousand and odd feet above the sea and in untrammeled mountains, ten miles from a railroad, and with some pecularity in the sunshine. It had a spring of ice-cold sulphur water jetting from a cliff hung with ferns and topped by Judas tree and shad bush and rhododendron. Black bass inhabited Winding River, and mountain trout Old Woman Creek and Calico Creek. Yes, those business men enduringly liked it. So did I who wasn't a business man. So did three or four other teachers, men and women, and a poet from New York, and a mighty fisherman from Kentucky, and old Colonel Corbin and his daughter-in-law and her children, and a botanist who was making a botany, and his offspring, two young rapscallions, boy and girl, and the Reverend Mr. Birdsong, and Miss Watkins the librarian, and a few others who are dimmer in my mind. The food was good. After the second day, no matter how many colleges were behind you, in walked mountain appetite. Thin, sun-packed mountain air, right exercise, and a kind of diffused peace-on-earth sensation—that was Berry's. The proprietors were Mr. and Mrs. Berry, Mr. Berry born on the spot, sixty years earlier, Mrs. Berry his cousin. They had a daughter, Lucinda Berry, the sunny side of forty and a strong, industrious piece of mountain timber. Two nephews, Tom and Luke, pretty good, tall, lank young fellows, completed the family. Each summer half a dozen colored folk came from the nearest town, lived in two or three shacks down by a small, abandoned saw mill, and furnished service of kinds. Fisherman's Luck was a primitive place, all right, but, Lord! how we liked it and looked forward through all the grind of the year to getting up there each summer. I know I looked forward to it, and the business men did, for they told me so.

They were big business, miles away from any ideas that the rest of us at Berry's could entertain. My first three summers there were four of them. Then I missed a year, having to teach mathematics at a summer school. The next June I was back again, and glad enough to be there. But this year I found only three big business men. The other one had died in the winter.

Miss Watkins the librarian and I went walking beside Winding River. I've always been a lonely fish, and I don't usually go walking with young women. It's enough to teach them. Not that I have anything against women. That would be absurd. But I am one of the kind that have the hermit in them. However, Miss Watkins was like a sister or a first cousin raised in the family. The river that was very clear and quiet with great sycamores slanting over it and alder and willow and maple and the rest of it made my heart ache with pleasure after college. A boat passed, a man fishing, a darky rowing. It went over to the other side under the willows, and we walked without Mr. Arnold seeing us.

"He isn't like himself this summer," said Miss Watkins. "I suppose it's Mr. Beckwith's death."

Arnold was Iron and Steel. Beckwith had been Railroads. Arnold came first to Fisherman's Luck but brought Beckwith the next summer. They had always fished together. We watched the boat. It kept on past a certain pool, a little bay in the river, with a huge sycamore leaning over and a tall pine shooting up to the sky and a bed of ledgy slate. For some undecipherable reason black bass had a penchant for this place. That being so, this reach of the river had come to be regarded as sacred to

the big business men, and finally to Mr. Arnold and Mr. Beckwith.

"He hasn't fished here at all this summer," said Miss Watkins. "But Mr. Allworthy and Major Jackson seem to consider
that it would be indelicate for them to step in just yet. Captain
Schloss also seems to have some feeling about it. Come to think
of it, no one does fish here this summer, not even the boys."

My Lord, it was clear and peaceful and sweet! A fish
jumped. A little cloud, stretched like an Arabian Nights' traveling carpet, sailed overhead. Under the sycamore there ran out
into the water a tiny horn of sand and pebbles, and beside it
lay an old scarred broken boat. "The Berrys left it there," said
Miss Watkins. "No one uses it unless it is the colored men after
hours."

The botanist's two children, who were thirteen and fifteen,
and as wild as March hares, carried me off to see a cave they had
discovered up Calico Creek. Mr. Allworthy and Major Jackson
and Captain Schloss the Kentucky fisherman were all up Calico.
We passed them, going on to the cliffs. Said Jane, "Mr. Arnold's
down Winding, just with old old Peter."

Jim said, "He's a lonely cuss!"

"He's got something," said Jane, "on his mind."

"He's got ten millions, father says. Whew, it must be
heavy!"

"Mr. Allworthy and Major Jackson have got most as much, I
reckon. It don't seem to turn them sulky! No. It's about Mr.
Beckwith."

"What about him? He's dead."

I said, "They were old friends. Don't you know what 'old
friends' is, Jim and Jane?"

"I know all about it," said Jane. "Captain Schloss told Mrs.
Berry and I heard. He said that Major Jackson told him. She
said that Mr. Arnold was that gloomy and not a bit like himself,
and he said that Major Jackson said it wasn't just sorrow for a
friend, for friends had to die, and time and the world went on,
certainly in the world of finance it did, and you had to live and
men went out and came in all the time. But Major Jackson told
Captain Schloss that Mr. Beckwith died at the beginning or in
the middle, he didn't know which, of a big misunderstanding or
quarrel or feud between him and Mr. Arnold. Captain Schloss
it was that called it a feud. He didn't say whether it had come to
laying for each other with guns behind corn shocks and worm

fences. But anyhow Major Jackson said Mr. Beckwith died, that quick! before they could settle it. He told Captain Schloss that nobody really understands it, for it wasn't like either of them. He said that there ought to be a provision of nature against dying with things unexplained, but there isn't. It was a quarrel, all right. And he says Mr. Arnold can't digest it or get rid of it and it's that that makes him gloomy."

In a week's time my newness wore off and we all settled into our own ways. Winter school and summer school and other things had worn me down. I wanted just rest in solitude for at least half the time. I walked a good deal, but chiefly at last I came to lie on the banks of Winding River. It seemed to be sufficient.

At last I settled down to the shore of that pool where no one fished this summer.

I liked the sycamore, I liked the pine tree, I liked the little horn of sand and pebbles, I liked the old, cracked boat. On this side the river juts, and lines of slate had gathered earth upon them and become islets and peninsulas, miniature and faëry, with mint on them and some aromatic yellow flower, and tall stems of Joe-Pye with large heads of feathery, smoke-pink bloom.

Mr. Arnold, Mr. Allworthy, and Major Jackson no longer fished up Winding. But there were plenty of places below this boat, down river. They used, on the days they were after bass, to bring in good strings. Other days they fished for trout in the two lovely creeks. That is, Mr. Allworthy and Major Jackson did. Mr. Arnold remained faithful to Winding and his own company. Just he and old black Peter in a boat to themselves, but they always went down river. Captain Schloss tried the old pool. But he had no luck. "I never knew it before!" he called, passing the sycamore and me in his boat. "Never in twenty years! Besides—don't you feel something hanging around here?" So he didn't come any more.

One day I met Peter going from the river to the kitchen with Mr. Arnold's catch. We stood to talk. "Where did you get them?"

"This side Walter's Mill, sah. But the bes' fishing in Winding, sah, is Black Bass Pool where Mr. Arnold won't go no more."

"He won't go because he thinks of Mr. Beckwith there. And Mr. Allworthy and Major Jackson don't take it over because of a feeling of delicacy. But Captain Schloss says. . ."

"Yaas. . ." said Peter. His old eyes, deep in his charcoal

black face, fixed an oriole in a tulip tree.

"What is it, Peter? Do you think Mr. Beckwith likes it still?"

"That oriole sho makes a fine nest. . . . Mr. Grymes, you is a noticin' pusson, sah. I knowed that the minute I fust set eyes on you. The trouble with that pool is it jes' don' want anybody to come er-fishin' there but Mr. Arnold, en' he don' want ter go. He stop likin' Mr. Beckwith befo' he daid, en' he got all the re-minderin' he want. He say he thought he try it, comin' back heah this year, but he ain' gwine come back nex' year. . . . Yaas, ma'am! Yaas, Miss Jinny, I'se coming!"

The following day, down at the sulphur spring, I came upon Mr. Arnold. He was drinking the ice-cold water out of one of the three gourds kept hanging in a row in the arbor over the spring. There never was such water. Mr. Arnold said so now, "There never was such water!"

"No. It's cold and light and there's just enough and not too much sulphur. The ferns about it help it out, and this dark hillside."

"When I first tasted it—the first summer I came—the laurel was in bloom. 'My God,' I said. 'This is good enough for me!' " He hung the gourd carefully in its place. "But I shan't be here, I think, another year."

"I'm sorry for that," I said. "The pleasantest thing about Berry's is that folk come back and back."

He was a big man, tall and large and well made, with a massive, handsome face. "That's just it," he said slowly. "And if you don't like it or them. . . If they broke the whole thing up themselves—broke it for keeps—and you can't get it out of your mind. . . You'd better go to Europe."

He stood looking out of the arbor at the mountains with an unhappy, far-away look, and then departed without any more language.

It was about this time that I quit being over-energetic and took to lying beside Winding instead of tramping to Black Rock or Laurels or where not. At last I fell to spending each day a couple of hours beside Black Bass Pool, under the huge sycamore, upon the little sandy horn with the old boat alongside. I had my plaid, and I had a book, and I suppose I read it. At least the mark got changed from part to part.

I don't remember what day it was but I had been coming here steadily for a week or more when I began to have a curious feeling. I recall when it first struck me. I can't describe it, only things seemed of a sudden very quiet though as busy as ever, and then a conviction visited me, like the dragon fly and those yellow flowers, flitting to and fro like the dragon fly but then settling down and occupying the field. "I'm not the only one here." I wasn't alarmed, though I got a kind of anxiousness in the air.

I was curious to see if, next day, I'd find the same feeling. I did. I couldn't localize it. It seemed as general as the air, around and through the whole sunny pool and the trees and the shore. It was not a disagreeable sense. I did not feel any meaning of injury. At the house and with the others I said nothing about it. Why should I, who was never afraid of such things? Though, indeed, this was the first time I could spot so actual an experience. But I had always thought such things just as possible as anything else.

The third day it was the same, only stronger. Something intelligent was there and, it seemed to me, coming to a focus. It was concentrating, and it was near.

The fourth day I deliberately stayed away.

That evening we had a bonfire and corn roast and other matters. It was the birthday of the Corbin twins. They sat up till all hours with their big eyes and their touzled heads like two wakeful young flickers—Courtenay and Carter. Berry's had a croquet ground, and we built the bonfire and roasted the corn on the edge of this and set off Roman candles and half a dozen rockets from the middle of it, and all the dining-room chairs and the porch benches were brought out for the convenience of the invited party which included every human being at Berry's and the dogs. It was a gorgeous night.

Beside the corn there was ice cream, and Courtenay and Carter had two saucers each. Also, Tom Berry and Mr. Allworthy and I who managed the fireworks let them handle the Roman candles. They jumped up and down and squawked, and with a little more excitement might have flown. The fireworks came at the end of the party, and before them we had a speech from Mr. Arnold. Someone had told Mrs. Corbin that he spoke very well and was in demand for public dinners and so forth; and she had great, soft dark eyes and the most appealing way. Wouldn't he make a little birthday speech, no matter how short— just a little talk to Courtenay and Carter that they might remember? Maybe he would tell the twins how they should grow up to be really successful? I was there when she tackled him, and of course at last he consented. He naturally liked to talk, but he was modest about it too.

So after the corn roast and ere the ice cream and the fireworks, he stood under the stars before the chairs and benches with all of Berry's seated on them, and Courtenay and Carter on a bench in front and exactly in the middle, with their legs swinging, and the old Colonel in a split-bottomed armchair on one side of them, and Mrs. Corbin in a lavender muslin on the other.

Mr. Arnold said that he was a business man and could really talk only about business, but that there was a lot of business, a great variety of it in short, in life. When he looked back to his own boyhood he saw that he was possessed of a business sense very early. He thought he appreciated the main problems even when he was little. He thought that that was the case with many children. It might be so with these little fellows. "At any rate, Courtenay and Carter, I'd like to tell you a few things that real business sense ought to suggest to you."

He made them interesting. We all saw that business sense was a very sensible thing, and Courtenay and Carter kept as awake as young flickers at dawn. He talked about fifteen minutes, and he got a great deal in them. Toward the end he came to business associates, and made it clear that all our associates— all the associates the two young flickers were likely to have— are and would be business associates. He took business in quite a large sense.

Mr. Arnold's voice became more and more vibrant. Something in his own talk was taking him unawares. When he said "business associates" he might have been saying "friends." And when he spoke of honesty and honor and loyalty in business it was as though he were talking of what should obtain between close friends. It seemed as though he were warning Courtenay and Carter, and also himself, "Don't you hide things. Don't you ever go in for any shadiness in business!" (Business had got to be life.) "Don't you ever turn down your associates—your associate! Don't you, when you seem to be on one side of a house, creep through the woods without a sound and come up on the other, with the fruit that was for both in your hands, for your own eating alone! Don't you take advantage of what you know to line your own pocket and increase your own prestige while the other's whistling at the door and thinks he knows all about it and that you're in together, in whatever the thing is. Don't you ever treat associates like that. Don't you ever fool and betray. I know a lot of cases. . . A man thinks his associates are not like that—a man thinks his friend is as loyal as God. And all the time. . ."

Mr. Arnold stood for a moment looking at the stars, then wiped his brow and seemed to catch himself up. His voice came back to normal. "And so, my dear Courtenay and Carter. . ." And presently his speech ended and was much applauded. The ice cream came on and the fireworks, and then goodnight, with the big stars looking at us and the katydids as busy as bees.

Next day was Sunday and, as the Berrys were Presbyterians and objected to it, there was no fishing. Everybody lay around and read or talked or wrote letters, and the children built a dam in Calico Creek, and in the afternoon seven or eight of us climbed Eagle Knob to see the stupendous view and the sunset.

Up on the Knob were all manner of separated perches. Mr. Allworthy and I found ourselves on one together. Major Jackson and Mr. Arnold, massively built, both of them, never undertook the mountain, but Mr. Allworthy moved through life and high finance as lightly as a grasshopper. Now he remarked, "Beckwith was an active man. He used to come up here quite frequently. Poor old Arnold! Of course you noticed, last night? It was of Beckwith he was talking there at the last."

"What came between them?" I asked.

"What comes between most people? A deal. It don't matter just what's its nature. A deal is a deal. Well, whether Beckwith just got there first naturally, or whether he knowingly twisted it, or whether there was an honest mistake is beyond me. I don't know, and I don't suppose anybody does. He died just as the deal became visible. But Arnold thinks he knowingly twisted it and meant all the time to let him down. It seems they had some misunderstanding shortly before about something else, and he thinks it went on to this. He's bitterer than gall about it, is Arnold. He don't talk, except in a sidewise way like last night, but he's bitter. I don't think he'll come here another year. He won't even fish where he used to with Beckwith."

I had missed two days at the pool and now I wanted to know if I should find that very especial feeling again. I did. It was there, all right. I met it stronger than before. It seemed to gather up to meet me, and to take on solidity and a definite place. Any old pioneer forbear would have conceived at once, "That Indian is over there," and have begun to lay his plans accordingly. But it wasn't an Indian, I knew that, and it wasn't anybody just at that moment precisely like the rest of us at Berry's. There was about it something otherwise. . .

I threw myself down upon my old plaid on the sand and pebbles, with the water lapping within reach of my hand if I leaned towards it. It lapped a whole little forest of mint and Joe-Pye and that yellow flower I had meant to ask the botanist about and forgot, and it lapped the side of the old boat. . . . In the boat formed the figure of Mr. Beckwith.

No, I wasn't alarmed, and it didn't occur to me to scramble to my feet and vacate the place. In life he hadn't been terrifying, and in death, whatever else he was, he wasn't terrifying. Instead, he was—what shall I say?—ingratiating. I felt at once that he wanted something badly.

Unlike Mr. Arnold, who presented an extent, vertical and horizontal, of body, Mr. Beckwith was only of middle height and inclined to spareness. Mr. Arnold had a massive, handsome face, cut like a Roman Emperor's. Mr. Beckwith's face was narrower and shrewder, yet not disagreeably shrewd. He had a humorous mouth, hair inclined to red, and on the right cheek bone the scar of some old hurt. . . . He was all there, form and face and the old suit in which he fished. Of course he came thin and sheer, so to speak. He had his differences. His voice, when he spoke, was rather thin and whistling. But it was Mr. Beckwith's and not calculated to induce terror. The point about him generally was just that—that he tended toward the general, and there was evidently some difficulty in bringing about the concrete again. His presence tended to spread around, and also, strangely enough, into me. I say "strangely," but at the time it appeared quite natural. And yet he had succeeded in condensing a vehicle, like his old one, there in the boat. I do not know if I make myself clear.

It took a little while for his figure to come into definiteness and the feeling with it, and the voice to emerge.

Moments dropped by, round and quiet, while Mr. Beckwith grew stronger. His voice, that had begun like a whisper, now filled out to natural, though still with a kind of distance, farther away than should be, considering that the boat lay so near. But that was true, too, of his figure. There it was, but it seemed farther away. Both near and far away—and of course I know a paradox when I see it.

Mr. Beckwith spoke, "How are you, Mr. Grymes?"

I answered, "Quite well, Mr. Beckwith. How are you?"

He said, "Why, I should be well, I think, if I were not worried to death. But I am happy to have managed this at last. It's you, of course, as much as me. Perhaps you know that you are probably the only one at Berry's who would allow just this and help me out with it too."

"Believe me," I said, "it was entirely unconscious."

"Very likely," he answered, "nevertheless, effective. However, I did my part, and I can assure you it takes both will and ingenuity."

With that, as though he had become retrospective, he tended to fade a little.

"Don't go!" I said abruptly.

He promptly strengthened. "I won't since you are so kind. And I am sure that you are going to manage to help me."

"What," I asked, "is wrong? You say you are greatly worried. Aren't you—aren't you in the right place? I beg your pardon! Just my joke. I have heard you make them yourself. Of course you are."

"All those things are relative," he said. "I am where it is natural for me, I find, to be. Just as in what we so amusingly called 'life.' You feel entirely 'natural' do you not? And yet you may be greatly worried—though I hope, I am sure," he said politely, "that you are not. If you have your anxieties you of course endeavor to remove them. That is natural to men everywhere. Now—"

"I had always supposed," I said, "that anxieties and pleasures were confined to, and could only be relieved or gratified upon, the plane to which one was, so to speak, assigned."

"You think too much," he said, "in solids and not enough in gases and what may be finer than gases. Things are so pervasive. There are, so to speak, frontiers, but also relations of commerce and travel."

"It is highly interesting," I said and meant it. "So you preserve certain connections, and your happiness or unhappiness is still affected by us here? In a terminology which you used to use, you continue to draw interest or to have dividends passed?"

"Yes," he said. "A good deal of the latter." He paused and seemed to endeavor to grow vivid. He pressed his hand to his brow, then dropped it and appeared collected. "The way," he said, "that you behave toward us has still its effect. And if you leave, as I left, a misunderstanding and heat and bitterness. . ." He pressed his hand again to his brow. "Mr. Grymes, I have tried to reach Sam Arnold direct and I cannot. He is not receptive. It is like trying to swim up rapids. Moreover, the rapids keep beating on me and—you won't understand this mixture, but it occurs here—they are angry and bitter. He can't let me alone, and what he thinks is of a troubling nature. Moreover, I don't want him to think that way of me. I'm his friend. . . . Yet I can't reach him and show him the confounded mistake!"

"You mean that he thinks you injured him and he can't keep his mind and feelings quiet on the subject?"

"I perceive," said Mr. Beckwith, "and not from your words only, that you know the circumstances. As far, that is, as any living person can know them."

"Mr. Allworthy told me something."

He looked at me vaguely, if he ever could have been said to have looked directly. He faded, came again a little, then faded once more. I could see the opposite bank through him. Then suddenly he grew small and bright and stiff again. "It's unendurable!" he exclaimed. "He was thinking of it then, and I can assure you it is devastating! Besides I hate him to have ideas like that! He should know me better. I can't understand why he doesn't know, despite any and every appearance. I am sure that if our positions were reversed, I should never feel as he is feeling. It's unendurable that Sam Arnold should think that I—I, Edward McTavish Beckwith—meant to fool and cheat and harm him in that deal! Well, I didn't. I didn't in the least. And yet I can't get at him to make him see."

He put his elbows on his knees and his head in his hands. "I can't stop his girding at me, and I can't make him hear. . . ."

I was truly sorry for him. He didn't seem to me greatly changed, though of course he must have known things now that we didn't. "You mean," I said, "that you never meant to shatter yours and Mr. Arnold's friendship?"

His head came up at that. "Over and over again, no!. . . . I had all the lines, in that matter, in my hands. Arnold had piqued me a little, that year, going about with a kind of boasting. It had always been nip and tuck between us—like two boys, you know, emulative and combative and all that, and yet chosen friends—and I thought I'd show him something! But he was to be in on it—on the last word of the deal and the—the loot, so to speak. I only wanted to parade a little. We had had a kind of quarrel a little earlier—not about business, though. I thought that he didn't think quite enough of my abilities. I thought I'd show him. But I meant him at the last to clap me on the shoulder. He always was rather the bigger of us two. Old Sam Arnold. Everything was all ready, and I meant to call him up and get him to the house that night. I had laid in the cigars, etc. And then, as quick as that, I died. Something inside that I didn't know anything about. Didn't have time for a word to anybody. . . . Well, the thing was at that point that it went through automatically. My sisters and their children got a lot of money that's very bad for them, and Sam Arnold, who was my only real friend, had the bag to hold, and thinks to this moment that I meant to fool, betray, and break with him! I *get* his thought. How could I or anyone else settle down, I ask you? I don't want old Sam to be thinking those things of me. I don't want him to be unhappy."

He ceased to speak and sat there, a wavering shade, but otherwise as real as the boat. He seemed to be fixing me with a kind of appeal. "Yes," he said, though I had not spoken. "I have been feeling my way toward you for some time. You have a heart for these things and a head that does not dodge them when they come your way."

I said, "You pay me a handsome compliment."

He said, "Oh, if you will help me, Mr. Grymes, I will do almost anything for you! Anything, that is, in my power."

I would have helped him anyhow, and told him so. Anything that was in my power. Power being So and So, Limited.

"Precisely," he said. "What I want you to do is to get Sam Arnold to open his mind."

"And how under heaven," I exclaimed, "can I do that?"

"I want you to bring him to consider probabilities."

"Probabilities?"

"Probabilities. Or rather, improbabilities."

"That you should really murder, or wish to murder, your friendship?"

He seemed to rub his hands. "Didn't I say that you were quick? It'll come to you out of yourself—how to do it, I mean. But get him to see and feel that it isn't likely. Get him to consider the possibility that it was all accidental. My going off as I did without explanation. That if I had had time he would have known that it was only a practical joke. My Lord! he knows we used, when we were boys, to play them on each other. And sometimes we were sore, but we always knew that it was only horseplay, and that we would have died for each other—though that isn't so much to say as we used to think it was. Get Sam to feel that it must have been something else: that never and never again would Ned Beckwith really and truly, in any kind of dead earnest, have undertaken to fool and cheat and injure him. No, not in that or any other deal!"

"When you are as energetic as that can't you reach him?"

"No! He's just as energetic in the other direction. He's more so. He'd like to call me out if it were possible. He'd like to pay me back with interest. He'd like to tell me a few things. He does so, and he doesn't know that he does it. He's vindictive. He's so hurt that he isn't anything more than a hurt wolf toward me now. He's nursed it and compounded it. I can't get at him at all. If he lets it doze for a moment, I try to get in something like us two in the old swimming hole when we were shavers, or when the boat sank and we pulled each other out, or when his wife died twenty-five years ago and I went abroad with him, or when we built the New England, New York, and Mexican, or even this very pool, and eating together under that sycamore, and the bass we caught—this very boat was ours—and how jolly it was! It seems to me that I am succeeding, and I think. . . And then back it comes flying as from armor plate. By God, that's it! he's turned himself as far as I am concerned into an iron-clad. I can't do anything more. It's making me very unhappy. It's hindering me in ways that I couldn't expect you, Mr. Grymes, to understand. And then, damn it all! I have affection for old Sam, and I can't bear. . ."

It seemed to me, almost, that he wept. I felt sorry for him, and I wanted to help.

"You're giving me a hard job," I said. "I'm not intimate with Mr. Arnold. I don't fish, you remember, and I don't play poker. I don't see how I could ever even get him where I could talk to him."

"There's just one thing," he answered. "He's got that passion for picking up neglected knowledge. He wanted you to give him half an hour a day on the latest in mathematics and physics, and you wouldn't for your own reasons. But now if. . ."

I thought it over with my head between my hands. "He was born stubborn and now he's bitter."

"My God, don't I know it? But there's the chance. I've

thought it out. Mathematics makes you cool and detached. Then little by little get him to talk to you, and then you insinuate—insinuate, man! Probabilities now. He knows a good deal about industrial and financial probabilities. Get him to look at moral probabilities. Bring it down to Sam Arnold and Ned Beckwith. The benefit of the doubt, get that in. And forgiveness. Get him somehow within hailing distance of that, even if he had to forgive me nothing more than a piece of rank stupidity. I knew, God forgive me! that he liked to play practical jokes but not to be played them. Soften him and make him reasonable. Get him to tell you stories of his life, behind this last year. It's got to bring me in. Make him see that a man don't change like that."

"Anything else?"

"Make him start back to his old judgment. It's longer and more thorough than his new."

"And then?"

"Get him to come back here to fish. I've worked at this place till its malleable, so to speak."

"And then?"

"I'll try hard to get at him within. He won't know that it is really me, but he'll listen, perhaps, at last to what he'll call 'ancient affection.' "

He began to fade. "I can't hold it any longer. It has been a great effort. But you'll do it, won't you, Mr. Grymes? It may be that some day I can return it in some way. I've not found anywhere yet where a tip is not useful."

"It's so absurdly easy!" I said. "Bringing a man like that to be friends with me—and he'll certainly be thinking I want something from him—and then making him see around a corner and find you walking in the open and go back to walking with you. That is what you want?"

"Angels couldn't put it clearer," he said.

With that he faded. The boat lay empty, the water lapped its sides. Mr. Beckwith was gone, and yet not wholly so. I felt him in a general way.

I went myself presently, and on the porch of his cabin saw Mr. Arnold sitting, reading a detective story.

He had had an irregular, self-initiated training, but he possessed a good mind.

New mathematical uses and the latest physical theories interested him. I am no expert, the good God knows, but as

I went along in life I abstracted what I might from the torrent of special literature and pondered other men's findings, and then laid it out as best I could to the classes I taught. I conscientiously gave him what he asked for, and he was good enough to say he got profit therefrom. To be meticulous, his statement was, "You make the days less deadly."

"Why should they be deadly?" I asked. "You've got a lot of things that men want."

"Yes," he answered gloomily. "I've got something also that they don't want."

He stared at the tulip tree that shaded his cabin. A thrush was in his green bower there, singing and singing. I opened our book. "Minkowski," I said, "considered Euclidean, three-dimensional geometry to be a description of a cross-section only of Reality, or of our next proximate conception of Reality."

"It will be some bird," said Mr. Arnold, "who finds out really what is true."

The half-hour that first we talked about grew to be an hour and sometimes much more. He suggested the evening; then his fishing wouldn't be interfered with. Mr. Allworthy, Major Jackson, and Captain Schloss were not ready for poker before eight o'clock. Supper at Berry's was at six. So we used to stroll together to his cabin through the lovely late light.

"These ideas are great things to recover tone upon," he said. He sighed. "And yet I cannot get it back, Mr. Grymes."

"How did you lose it? But that," I said, "is an impertinent question. Pray excuse me."

"It might be from some, but not from you, Mr. Grymes. You are not that kind. I lost it," he said, "through the treachery of another. . . . Now this Einstein thing about everything being curved and returning. . ."

It was two evenings after this that he dropped his cigar over the porch railing, leaned forward, and spoke. "There's something else I'm going to ask your opinion about, Mr. Grymes. What would you think if—"

At first it came out with a kind of frozen difficulty, but then with a gush. It was a relief to him, I know. He hadn't talked to anybody like that since last September. Except to Mr. Beckwith, and that had been like turning the sword in his own vitals and didn't relieve him. I let him talk and describe and use names and all. It was not until after a considerable time when he had talked himself down into a kind of calm and peace of shared trouble that I spoke. "I think there's some mistake here, Mr. Arnold. I don't believe that of Mr. Beckwith."

He took offense at that, as people will. They don't want their judgment doubted even if it makes them as unhappy as that. But at least he saw before we said good-night that I thought it improbable.

The next night he played poker. The next we kept to mathematics. The third he again dropped his cigar and said, "A man may keep pretty straight, mayn't he, almost through life and nobody, and perhaps not he himself, know about the rotten spot?"

"The weak spot?" I said. "We've all got them. It doesn't do to throw too many stones. Say that in each of us there's a lot of good, and something too, that isn't good. Then it's scientifically inaccurate, there also, to take the part for the whole. The good remains good; perhaps the weak place may be remedied, or perhaps we think it deeper than it is, or perhaps we may have been deceived in its nature."

"You mean that stuff about forgiveness?" he said violently. I said no, that I meant understanding, and got up and went.

Again he played poker the following evening, and the next he told me at supper that he had letters to write. The next morning I was walking beside Winding. I have forgotten to say that after that hour with Mr. Beckwith I had stopped going to Black Bass Pool. The impulse to do so had left me. But now I walked that far, and there I found Mr. Arnold, standing well back from it, under the pine tree, just looking at it.

He did not see me and I turned aside among the rhododendrons. I thought I felt Mr. Beckwith, but I was not certain.

That evening, in the middle of an exposition, Mr. Arnold said suddenly, "God knows I wish it wasn't so!"

"What? The relation between existents?"

"No, no! That Ned Beckwith and I have to be unfriendly."

I put a marker in the book. "What kind of a boy was he? That tells a lot, you know."

He began at once on that swimming hole. . .and then the old barn. . .and then a long tramp and a week out with other boys.

"He seems to have been fond," I said, "of practical jokes."

"We both were," he answered. "But he didn't truly know

how to play them. He was clumsy. His old jokes always missed fire, while I. . ."

He broke off. Over toward Honeysuckle Ridge a whippoor-will began to call, but that wasn't it. Something seemed to drop into the warm dusk and the situation about us, something sharp and intense. It was a thought. I knew it for a thought. I got the wind of it, but he was the target. I don't think it came from Mr. Beckwith. It came from the level of thought, wherever that is. He sat without speaking, with an effect of being drawn up before a firing squad.

Then he said, "My God, he might have been thinking that way about it!"

I got up and said good-night. He did not answer. He was sitting with his big shoulders hunched, and his eyes upon the Great Bear over Honeysuckle Ridge.

The next day, about twelve o'clock, I found old Peter chopping wood. "What are you doing here?" I asked. "I thought you and Mr. Arnold had gone to Walter's Mill."

He leaned upon his axe. "Mr. Grymes, honey, we ain' gwine fish ter day. Mr. Arnold, he sittin' under the sycamore by Black Bass Pool."

"Ah!" I said.

"Des' so," he answered, and began once more to chop, then leaned again upon the axe. "Yaas, sah! I think we gwine fish there again befo' long. That old boat there kin be made river-worthy. Yaas, sah!" He began to sing:

> "I got the gift en you got the gift,
>   All of God's chillern got the gift."

The Mockingbird

The mockingbird sang in the purplish-pink Judas tree. He sang like the wren and the catbird and the oriole. He sang like himself. He sang like the meadowlark, he sang like the thrush, he sang like himself. He sang like the blackbird, the bluebird and the cardinal. He sang like himself. Oh, what singing! They say that the birds in their evolution will not enter the human family, but that of the devas, the angels. Listening to him, it seems quite possible. Eventually a versatile seraph.

Down river, a hundred miles from this Judas tree and this mocker, a young negro man, William by name, threw with freedom and play of muscle the looped rope that settled over the gray piles and linked the small steamboat to the wharf. William likewise had his song.

> *Up the river and down the river,*
> *O Lawd, let me throw straight!*
> *When the golden shore rise up,*
> *O Lawd!*
> *When the boat gits there,*
> *When the golden shore rise up,*
> *O Lawd, let me throw straight!*

He was all rich umber with shadings of copper, for one of his grandmothers had been Indian. Guinea Coast, say a hundred and fifty years ago, and say seventy-five years ago the Cherokees that had plenty of sense among the Indians.

> *When the golden shore rise up,*
> *O Lawd, let me throw straight. . . .*
> *O yaller gal, back yonder*
> *Tall as er pine----*

The mockingbird flew from the Judas tree to the wild plum thicket that was a mist of pearl and extravagantly sweet. The wild plum grew by the broken-down cabin where lived Maum Ann, who had seen it bloom eighty times and was crack-brained and knew about herbs and voodoo. Maum Ann, smoking a corn-cob pipe, sat alone in her door. "Hi, dat mocker! He sing lak he co'tin' de world."

A young woman, dark brown in color, with a broad, come-ly, passionate face, approached the cabin by a little path, through the thicket. She wore an orange calico with purple disks upon it and she had a purple sunbonnet which, however, was not upon her head but hung from purple strings knotted about her power-ful throat. She walked quite beautifully, like a great cat. "Who dere?" demanded the owner of the cabin.

"It's me, Maum Ann. Vinie."

"Hab you got money?"

"Yaas, I got money. I got the two gold dollars the big house give me Christmas."

Maum Ann put down her pipe. "What you want for all dat money?"

"I want what you sell, Maum Ann. I ain't gwine never tell anybody about it."

"You better not!" said Maum Ann. "Ef you do, I come sit on yo' bed at night. Not as you sees me now, but as I is!"

The mockingbird, gray and white in the misty wild plum, sang like the lark, then mounted to the tulip tree that towered above the cabin and sang like a chipping sparrow. Two squirrels ran up and down the log that choked the little stream, and a moccasin stretched itself among the weeds. Maum Ann re-turned from the depth of the cabin. "All disyer is what I mostly sells, en dere ain' no harm in dem! De preacher needn't yell at me. It's to help folks erlong!"

Lowering herself into her chair, she spread the wares a-round. They were chiefly small dried things, roots and powders. To mark them in their parcels Maum Ann used colored bits of yarn. Vinie sat on the door stone. "That one?"

"You draps dat powder in de go'de wif de well water. He drink it, en den he love you moah'n he did. Moah en moah."

"I want what'll make him begin to love me, what'll take his love from her en put it on me!"

"Hoo!" said Maum Ann. "Dat cost moah!"

"I don't care what it cost!" Vinie's throat swelled; she turned on the doorstep and regarded the small stream and the weeds and briers through which it strove to push. Her barbaric dress suited a barbarian. Her orange and purple dress and the lush weeds and the hidden moccasin went together. She didn't belong to the wild plum nor the tulip tree nor the Judas tree nor the mockingbird. In her blood beat a long-ago, savage drum. "I wants him. I wants that William. I don't want her. I don't want that Cynthia." She struck her hands together. "What I pays you mos' for is somethin' that'll take her clean away. Put her in the swamp or up in the moon. So's he never wants ter remember nor think of her again. So's she won't bother me no more! I pays you high for that!"

The color about Vinie shifted and interflowed, red and orange and dull purple and perilous green. Now the red was dusky and now vivid, but red, red, red, volumes and overflows of it. The green coiled and constricted. Maum Ann sat in a brown, twisted and broken light, all full of patches and quiverings and shadows. She watched her visitor out of pinpoint eyes, then left her upon the step and went deep into the cabin and returned, something held under her checked apron. "What you got there?" asked Vinie.

Maun Ann drew from under the apron and placed upon the floor a small figure made of many matters and made so as to give it a horrible aspect. It was black and yellow and white, with huge eyes and a red mouth and stiffened, out-streaming hair. When she had put it down with the other packets of magic, which it at once blotted out and made harmless, she took up her corncob pipe, blew it alive and smoked.

Vinie had uttered a violent exclamation and started from the step as if to run, then returned and drew her breath and lowered her eyelids. "You got Bogey. How he come to you?"

"He come."

"He wicked."

"Maybe. Maybe he help too."

"What he do ef I took him?"

"What you want him ter do?"

"Could he scare her sick? Could he scare her to death?"

"De way Bogey wu'ks is ter scare dem so dey dies of dey-se'f. Dey oughtn't ter die. Bogey's des er li'l black thing. Ef dey peaks en pines en won' eat ner speak, en lays off dey looks, how come Bogey do it?. . ."N who knows where Bogey lives? He don't live in disyer cabin, dat sure! He des happen heah disyer one time, en ef ever you tells hit won't be Maum Ann but

Bogey'll be after you!. . . Yaas, Lawd, dat preacher. I don' hab no doin's with Bogey. It's des himse'f, hits Bogey's se'f dat walks erroun' en he picks where he wants ter pick. Disyer des he figure, but he come inter he figure when he wan' ter, en den hit come erlive en pow'ful."

"How much he cost, Maum Ann? How much he cost?"

"He cost moah'n two gold dollars."

Vinie took from her pocket an old silk glove knotted at the wrist. It held copper and silver coins, and the two gold dollars, and in the thumb one larger piece. "Old Marster give me that five dollar when I pulled little Jim outer the water."

"De way you does hit is dis."

The mockingbird flew from the tulip tree, over the wild plum thicket, over the purple Judas tree, through the greening wood to a hillside silver with dogwood and a cabin with an ash tree over it. This was old Maria's cabin, where she lived with her daughter, Dilsey, and her orphan granddaughter, Cynthia. The mockingbird perched upon an ash bough and sang of bird love in May, sang like all the birds in May. Cynthia came to the door to hear him, stood there in a blue cotton dress with her hands on either side of the doorway. "William Easter, is you singing on the River Queen?"

Down the river the River Queen moved from side to side, to this long, thin, gray wharf and to that. The sky was blue, the sunshine warm, the green water rippled by. William served the River Queen, quite happily busy, big and strong of body. An acquaintance hailed him. "Hi, you William Easter! When you gwine hab yo' wedding trip?"

"When I makes enough an' the captain lets me go. Wedding trip en cabin en er gyarden." He grinned lovably.

"What dat her name?"

"Cynthia is her name."

April days and nights became the days and nights of May. The mockingbird returned to the ash tree, the dogwood, the crab apples and the yellow jasmine about old Maria's cabin under the hill. Now there were two mockingbirds. The male sang more and more impassionedly, more and more true and sweet. Cynthia listened to him. "I never heard a mockingbird sing like that one!"

Her Aunt Dilsey said, "Sho! You jes' er-listenin' ter William Easter way down the river. That mocker jes like all other mockers."

"Maybe," said Cynthia and touched with a moistened forefinger the iron from the hearth.

Her grandmother spoke from the corner. "Is you i'oned
Old Miss' caps?"

"Most. Las' night, I dream about the River Queen."

"Ef you dream erbout water, trouble crosses it ter you."

"What I dream about was the River Queen and William. I
didn't see the water."

"It had ter be there—water had ter be there. I asks you,
ef you dream erbout er boat don' you have ter take the water
too? Yaas, Lawd!" said her aunt at the other ironing board.
"Water's trouble!"

With the ash stick old Maria raked out a coal for her pipe.

"William Easter's swored ter de River Queen till de close
ob summer. Men is pow'ful fickle. No end ob yaller gals down
de river."

"They may be," said Cynthia. "But I got William's heart."

"Hoo!" answered her grandmother. "Neber was no rope
could hol' er heart. You better take Old Miss' caps ter de big
house by deyse'f. She pow'ful finicky erbout dey crushin'."

Cynthia took them in a willow basket, the better part of
a mile, to the big house. When she left the kitchen there the sun
was setting.

She did not hear the mockingbird. She heard the frogs
croaking in the marshy places. At one point her path went by
big trees and a great tangle of swamp growth, old, giant trees and
young trees and bushes and a clambering and network of vines.
The red sky showed through, and a mist was rising. The mulatto
girl walked easily, her slim body rhythmically swinging. She
had looks, a well-modeled head and features to match her body.
Her skin was fair bronze, her face was happy. As she walked she
had in mind a book that she was reading, a book of stories about
princesses and fairies and witches and ogres and such. Miss
Milly had given it to her. She was the only one of her family
who knew how to read, and she was proud of her accomplish-
ment. Now as she walked she was thinking of the princess and
her gold crown. "I make believe," said Cynthia, "that princess
was a colored person."

As she thought it she held up her head, and William was
beside her and they both had on gold crowns.

Kruk! Kruk! said the swampy place. Kruk! Kruk! And a floor of gray-blue mist began to rise with the intent to become the roof of the tangled place. Cynthia stopped short. "Who that?" If there was anyone among the bushes nothing was answered. If a dark brown woman, wearing for her purposes a dark dress, squatted amid bay and greenbrier and watched with eagerness, only the frogs knew about it and they could say only Kruk! Kruk! "Sho, it's nobody!" said Cynthia and steadied the gold crown on her head.

Five paces farther—and there lay a log across her path. Astride it sat Bogey, all black and naked, with his face of horror. He was so small, but he might as well have been a giant. Everybody—that is, every colored person—about Liveoaks knew what it meant if Bogey appeared to you.

Cynthia ran for her life and her soul. She turned sharp from the swamp and ran over the pathless, rough field. Briers tore her, she fell her length and was up again. Now rose the hill and the smoke from the cabin chimney. She sank down in the doorway. "I seen Bogey! I seen Bogey!"

The mockingbird determined upon the clump of crab apples for their nest. It was close to the cabin and they liked that, and they liked the dogwood and the old, old cedar and the ash. They built low, and while the work was doing, in the intervals of rest, the male bird sang from the ash and from the cedar and from the crab and from the yellow jasmine. He sang to his mate, to the earth and the world and himself, and to whatever there was of higher, to the gods and the angels maybe.

His song was in Cynthia's ears, but she could not be said to hear it. She sat on the doorstep all day through. At first, after seeing Bogey, she kept to her work, standing at the tub beneath the cedar, washing and wringing the white folks' linen, striving to kill care, even striving waveringly to sing, to sing a hymn. "Dat's right! Dat's de only way to twis' his naik en keep him f'om pattering erbout you," counseled her grandmother. "Maybe he des look at you en didn't like you. Hit's terrible when he like you!" But after two days Cynthia quit all work and sat on the doorstep, in the blank sunshine, with her head in her hands. "He come for me last night. I couldn't get no sleep, and I sits up at dawn, and he was there, just out of the little window! Oh, my Lawd! Oh, my Lawd!"

Her aunt went to the preacher, and he came and prayed

and exhorted. It got around that Cynthia Ferris had seen Bogey.
As many of the neighbors as could devise an errand to Maria's
arrived to view the soul and body the devil was trapping. Women
stood with their hands on their hips. The mockingbird sang in
the ash tree. He chattered like a blackbird, he whistled like the
cardinal, he mewed like the catbird, he endeavored to attain the
caw of the crow, he moaned like the dove, then sent up a foun-
tain of unique and joyous sound.

"Cynthy, th'ow dat Bogey off! Wrastle wif him en th'ow
him off!"

"Does you feel him now, Cynthy? Dey say he usually at
de th'oat, or des' between de breasts. Hit don' matter dat you
can't see him! He dere des de same. He mek er little hole ne he
suck. Den it is dat you gets languid."

"Yaas, dey loses weight. Dey gets ter be skin en bones. En
ugly! Dey gets ter look lak Bogey himse'f!"

"Kin you feel him, Cynthy, kin you feel him? Git down on
you' knees en pray, while dere's time! After erwhile dey don'
want ter pray. Dey don' wan ter do nothin' but sit en hang dere
haid down, while he suck en crumble en nibble dere soul erway!
Pray, chile, pray! En all ob you pray wid her! O Lawd, O Lawd,
what hab she done ter mek Bogey like her? Heb she denied you
en done tek her soul in her two hands en hol' it out to be debbil,
en he sen' his son Bogey? O Lawd, what habe she done?"

"I don' know that I done anything! I don' know."

One of the women said, "You was keepin' company wif
William Easter. How he gwine tek it?"

The mockingbird sang so brilliantly, high in the ash tree.
The small company of women found itself augmented by Vinie,
who came up the path under the yellow canopy of the jasmine.
" 'William,' she say? Women dat Bogey takes to got ter get used
ter doing without men!"

At that Cynthia stood up from the step. "Don't you come
here, Vinie Doane! What you know about me and William? You
don't know nothing! No more'n you know about that mockingbird or about God! Maybe you see Bogey yourself one of these
days! You get out! I says, you get out!"

Vinie rocked with laughter. She had on her orange calico
with purple spots and a purple kerchief tied about her head.
Cynthia faced her, copper-hued and slender, in blue cotton.
"Ise goin'! I don' want ter stay! I might see him for sure, seein'

he's the one dat hangs erroun' these days! Ise goin'! You reckon anyone's tol' William?"

She departed down the path winding through the yellow jasmine. The mockingbird sang to earth and to heaven. Cynthia resumed her position upon the step. From a box beside her she took pinches of fine white sand intermixed with blue grains of some foreign substance and made a circle around her.

"Dat right!" cried a woman. "Daddy Joe gib you dat?"

"Yaas," said her aunt. "She walked de ten mile en got it. She walked it in de middle ob de night, like dey says, wif her hymn book in her han's. But de wind blows it erway en de feets breaks it. She got ter be keerful ob it."

"She wouldn't go to Maum Ann?"

"No, she wouldn't."

The mockingbird sang of the south and what it knew of the north, east and west. It sang of the strength of man and of bird. It sang of love in May. It sang at the gate of high realms. A hundred miles away the River Queen going down the river, farther and farther away, crossed the green water from small wharf to wharf. William, having done his part, and the River Queen halting here a bit, left her for the wharf.

> *I laks dat girl en she laks me,*
> *Oh, honey, where you gwine?*
> *You teks my han' en I teks you' han',*
> *Oh, honey, where we gwine?*

A boy met him and gave him a letter. "Heah, William Easter! Lonesome Spring pos'master say dat yours."

There it was, printed out, Fer William Easter Working on the River Queen. William turned it about. He could read and write, though not so well as Cynthia. At last he took it to the edge of the wharf and sitting down, his long legs swinging over the dark water, opened it and read, rudely printed:

> Mr. William Easter. I is a friend of yours from the back country. Yesterday I was in Liveoaks on a little business and I hear some news that maybe you like to hear too. Youse been gone two months and maybe you don't know that the devil has been running in and out and around Liveoaks. Yaas, he sure

has. Three people has seen Bogey, and we all know what kinds
of people sees Bogey. We knows what it is if it's a man, and we
knows what it is if it's a woman. My news is that everybody
was talking about the fact that Cynthia Ferris has seen him.
Sometimes they that Bogey favors keeps it hidden, but she
couldn't, being, I've heard it said, without much sense, though
she kin read and write, and some folks have thought high of
her, but they is mistaken. It's terrible, and as you know it
means terrible to see Bogey. You kin be sorry for a person, but
theyse got to keep the company theyse chose and has chose
them. I thought you'd like to know, Mr. William Easter, and I
is your friend. They that told me say she losing her looks and
that she say she don't care for no man no longer.

"Who's printed this?" asked William. (Vinie had procured
someone else to do it for her.) He sat and stared at the water.
"It's er lie. It's er damn lie!"

The River Queen uttered her deep cry. He folded the
paper and put it in his pocket and sprang aboard.

"What's the matter, William?" asked next day the captain,
who was fond of him. "You seem grumpy."

"Captain, I like you en I like the River Queen, en I like
the work, en I wants money. But I got ter go back ter where I
comes from. I got ter go home."

The captain regarded him, then spat afar into the flood and
said, "No, you ain't. You got to stay right where you are. That's
the law of this boat. You can go the day your paper says you
can, but not sooner. What's the matter with you? Yesterday
you were singing around, happy as a June bug!"

William showed him the letter. "All that's jes a lie!"

"Why, of course it is!" said the captain when he had read.
"I never heard the like! Voodoo! Stuff and nonsense! Your
girl never saw such a thing, or if in the dusk she got fooled for a
minute into thinking she saw something onnatural, that happens
to all of us, and next week we've forgotten it, and so will she.
Forget it! Besides," said the captain, striking the paper with his
hand, "I'll lay a month's pay that this is the work of some
jealous woman! There ain't a word of truth in the whole far-
rago!"

The crab apples beside Maria's cabin stood like brides, rosy
cheeks and white garments. They were so sweet and they had a

delicate fragrance.   The yellow jasmine possessed the most passionate fragrance of all the jasmines. The ash tree was putting forth its leaves and rose fulfilled with grace into the azure heaven.   The air was quiet, the sunshine warm.   The nest building had proceeded satisfactorily.   The mockingbird sang with rapture.

"Listen ter him, Cynthy," said her grandmother.   "Listen ter dat bird en smell de flowers en lif' yo' eyes ter de sky!"

"Can't, grandmother.   This morning at dawn, there in the dogwood, I see Bogey again.   I ain't gwine live long, and then what's gwine become of me?   Ise lost!   Ise a lost soul!"

The preacher came and went down upon his knees. He grew massively excited and jerked as in a fit, then rose and wiped his brow and said to old Maria and to Dilsey, "I got ter go ter the protracted meeting at Silver Hill.   I got ter leave her ter the Lawd.   It do seem that religion can't do nothin', and when that is so—O Lawd, only you kin handle Bogey!   My advice, sister, is that you jes leave her sit fer a while, and let her do what she wants ter with that sand that is jes sand, and keep the folk, that's mostly women folk, from crowding heah, and don't talk ter her if she don't want it.   My sisters, I says good-by ter you for a week."

The preacher went as far as the yellow jasmine, then returned.   "I got a letter from William Easter.   He got the captain ter write for him.   He say some foolish person sent him er letter without signing they name, but he don't believe no such trash about Cynthia, and the captain won't let him off the River Queen 'twel de eend of summer.   He say Cynthia Ferris ain't the kind the devil courts.   He say he comin' back jes as soon as he kin get off the River Queen.   He say he write Cynthia a letter, and he want her ter write ter him.   And the captain put in er word of his own and say he can't let William go before the eend of summer because he's short-handed, and William signed on. "What I'm wonderin' is," said the preacher, "that she ain't had the letter."

"She won't let Dilsey go ter de post office," answered the old woman.   "She say she don' want ter heah from William nor see him.   She say ef she touch William now de devil touch him too.   She say ef he come heah she push him erway en run inter de swamp herse'f."

"I kin do nothin', I sees," said the preacher. "And there's the protracted meeting."

Cynthia sat in the hot sunshine and made a fresh circle of sand about her. She sat in the middle of her island, her knees drawn up, her arms resting upon them and her head bowed to her arms. Through and about her quivered from shade to shade, now lighter, now darker, immaterial gray, the gray and green of fear. She was in its coils like a serpent and its density like a fog. When she had the endowed sand about her she thought, "He gwine erway, now that he see he can't get me." But her confidence never lasted, not even while the grains remained untroubled by the moving air. "He kin jump over en he kin fly down. It don' matter ef I see him or not, he's heah!" Her more careful English was lapsing into the tongue of her aunt and her grandmother. When she tried to pray, Bogey took her words and broke them into bits and threw them to the ants and the bees. He was most there when she tried to pray, and so she stopped. There arose also an awful fascination. "When he show himse'f he small en hideous, but Ise heard that at the last his own think he's tall en beautiful, jes' tall en dark en beautiful. Den dey don't fight no more, nor fear no more. Den dey's mad, but dey's happy."

She grew thinner and thinner. Her face became long and sharp with enormous hollows under tragic eyes. The sunshine could not warm her. She sat hour after hour in silence. The old woman and the elderly woman now let her alone. They grew quickly used to things, and now they were used to Cynthia sitting idle upon the trodden earth before the door, for she had removed there from the doorstep, strewing prepared sand against Bogey. The big barbecue approached, and the revival. The preacher went from protracted meeting to protracted meeting. Maum Ann was found one day by two small boys dead in her cabin. That was the next excitement. Everybody said she was a witch and had doubtless seen Bogey herself, but they gave her a big burial, she was so old and had belonged to the best white folks.

Down the river, that summer, William Easter wrote, laboriously enough, three times to Cynthia. But nothing came to him in return. "Captain, I got to go."

"No, William, you ain't! Lord have mercy, there's no such thing as a Bogey walking bodily around! That girl's just working hard and can't get her letters written, or maybe she's coquetting with you. You'll straighten it out the day you get home. But now you're bound to me and the River Queen. Ain't I keeping money for you? Ain't the passengers tipping you heavy because they like your singing? Ain't you seeing the corn growing back of that cabin?"

William stayed on, though nothing came to him from Cynthia and nothing more from Liveoaks, that was not given to writing letters. Now he was hurt and now he was angry. One day he said to himself, "Vinie Doane wouldn't ha' done me this er way. But she ain't Cynthia, and that's true! She ain't Cynthia."

The mockingbird sang in the ash tree of faith, hope and love. He moved from bough to bough like a flash of moonlight. He liked the vicinity of cabins and of human beings. He was slender, he was all grace, he saw the past, the present and the future in a delightful way. An imitator of all musical sound, he must have had an intuition of all psyches. He must have been a great poet in a small body. The female bird sat brooding and hearkening his song. It trilled, it dropped, it mounted and poised and soared to further heights.

Cynthia sat in the circle of efficacious sand. At the best she sat listless and silent, at the worst silent, but like an aspen leaf endued with aspen gray and green and a dim, enduring quivering. Out of this state she moved into apathy. Dilsey had gone to Daddy Joe on Juniper Creek and brought a big box of that sand of which only he knew the bed. "He say dere ain't no Bogey kin come er-round dat!"

"I see him now whenever I shut my eyes. I see him here and I see him there."

"Dat's you' 'magination, honey. You ain' see him for er long time in he flesh. Where's dat William?" cried Dilsey. "Dat's what I want ter know!"

But Cynthia shivered strongly. "If he come here, I go drown myself in the swamp water!"

Dilsey threw her hands to heaven and went to the washtub. Old Maria smoked her pipe in the doorway, seeing through the purple wreaths her daughter's daughter. The sun cleared the trees, the long hot day began. It passed. The sun set like a platter of brass and at the same time the moon rose like a platter of silver. Cynthia sat up in bed. In the small window, astride the sill, was Bogey. . . . At that moment the mockingbird began to sing in the moonlight. He sang of beauty and of music transcendent.

Cynthia sat without breathing, without daring to breathe. As though a hand had withdrawn him Bogey stiffly and bodily quitted the window. It shone clear pearl, the bird's song streaming in.

The mulatto girl sat like stone. Bogey. . .Bogey. . . . To belong to Bogey. To belong—when you're alive and when you're dead. . . . The moon shone. The bird sang. He sang like the vireo and the wood robin; he made his own song, high, pure and confident. Out of himself, out of his own depths. Cynthia could not but hear the clear voice in the night. The little window shone clear. Something real, something frightful had been there, and might and would come again. But where was she, where was herself, the other power? Something in her that had been bound broke its bonds. She moved in her bed, she saw the bright moon and heard the bird, her lips parted. "Oh, Christ, that is a new song, or I hears it newly!" She stretched out her arm, the hand held palm outward. "He ain't gwine come in. He ain't gwine come any nearer. That bird and You and me is gwine keep him away. I is gwine keep him away!"

But when the hot sunshine came again, terror also returned. She sat on the ground within the sand ring. "Ise too weak en tired. Ise too weak en tired. Ise got ter let go. Ise got ter let go. He's real, that devil, as real as me. He more real than me."

The mockingbird was silent after the ecstatic night. In the afternoon, with a great rolling and clapping of hands and lances of light, burst a thunderstorm, drenching the earth, wildly bending the bushes and trees, and sweeping and washing away the sprinkled sand. Cynthia removed to just within the cabin door. The tempest passed and a bow hung above the hill and the wood and the swamp. Suddenly the bird began again.

Her dreams were not so frightful that night, and once she dreamed quietly and happily. But waking in the dead middle, she thought of Bogey and turned to see him in the window. "Oh, Lawd!" said her lips without sound. Cynthia lay and fought. "Ise no devil, and Ise no devil's missy. Ise myself. Ise myself. Ise myself!"

But the next day it seemed as bad as ever. After the rain the weather grew hot and rank. Yet she felt cold and withered, sick with fear.   Her own attempted rebellion tormented her. "He makes it harder for them that don't mind. . . . Like the old slaves."   She sat in the center of the magic sand, her knees drawn up, her chin on her folded arms, her sinews unstrung. "Bogey. . . ."

Night and the white stillness and the bird brought no seeming help, though she did not see Bogey.   But she dreamed that she was drowning, and then that earth was falling upon her.   She was being buried under, but in the bottom of the grave was Bogey.   She woke with a mad cry, "Unless I kin fly with wing!" But she sat the next day with lackluster eyes and skin grown ashy.

"She gwine die," said old Maria.   "Onless de Lawd come down."

Down country, on the River Queen, the captain, leaning against the rail, opened a bit of brown paper, and read in laborious writing:

> Captain Harris, sir. I is going. I got to go. In the fall I
> come back and work it out. You haven't given me this month's
> money, sir. You keep it. I'd like you to. I is going. I like
> you powerful, and the River Queen, but I got to go. William
> Easter.

The captain frowned portentously, then broke into his enchanting laugh.   "Well, he's gone!   The black rascal!   Won't any of them stay put any longer!"   He read the letter again. "Swam off in the moonlight last night!   Got to go see that girl that saw Bogey.   Never had a better hand, and the passengers will miss that singing of his!   I'll miss him myself—till fall."

Cynthia sat in the middle of the traced sand.   She had begun to look spectral.   In a little while you might have to guess whether she were young or old.   The mockingbird sang like the cardinal, the bluebird and the thrush, then mounted into his own ecstasy.   Cynthia put out a hand.   It rested upon the baked earth, then very slowly it began to brush away the sand.   Very slowly but steadily, her eyes following it.   When the circle was unmade she stood up.   She spoke to the bird.   "You sing against him."   She looked at the very blue sky above the ash tree. "Christ, wherever you be, you help too.   And for you, Cynthia Ferris, you stand upon yo' own feet.   This heah's got to stop."

She moved toward the jasmine thicket and into it by the thread of a path. Before her there was Bogey, looking out of a crisscross of vine and stem. Cynthia stood frozen. Her heart stopped then pounded terribly. She grew cold and sick, gray and green and withered. She turned to run, if run she might. Between her and the cabin, out of the ash tree, sang the bird. She stopped, she stood upright. She raised her arms above her head, the hands closed, the nails pressed into her flesh. "Maybe Ise lost that way, but Ise lost this way." Turning in her tracks, she faced Bogey in the thicket. "What you want of me? You can't have it! I ain't yo' food. Ise myself." Bogey said nothing, but looked with a black face and terrible round eyes out of the thicket. Cynthia's body stood still. All around lay the perfumed thicket, underfoot the fecund earth, overhead rose, stair on stair, the sky. She put her body into motion and took it up, step by step, to Bogey. He was fixed in a crotch of a crab apple. Cynthia shot out a long arm. He fell from the bough to the earth. "My Lawd!" said Cynthia. "My Lawd!" She bent and took up the puppet and held it out before her. Fury passed through her in a salt and tonic wave. She tore the figure's arms from its trunk, and its head from its neck. It hung by a shred of cloth, when she suddenly bethought herself and ceased to tear the thing apart. "Yaas, now, my friend, youse got to show yourself! I'm gwine exhibit you, exhibit Bogey. You sure has got yo' haid on one side! And yo' poor arms!"

The mockingbird sang like the phoebe and the blackbird and the lark. Cynthia sat down on the ground, she was so weak, and then lay down, her arm under her head and her eyes closed. The mockingbird sang like the choir of heaven. "Ise been a bawn fool. Ise been a bawn fool. . . . William Easter, I don't deserve it, but you come back heah!"

She sat up in the sun, with the *disjecta membra* of Bogey about her. Deeper in the jasmine thicket something ever so slightly moved. She turned her head and caught a handbreadth of orange with purple rings. Cynthia rose upon her knees and then to her height. "I see," she said. "I see." She raised her voice. "Vinie! Vinie Doane!" The purple and orange moved again, withdrew. Cynthia put herself into motion and went toward it, but it moved faster than she. There was a breaking sound through the thicket as though a wildcat or a deer had determined to leave. "Vinie Doane! Vinie Doane!" But Vinnie was saying to herself, Vinie was saying as she hasted, "Ef I keeps quiet en goes, she can't prove nothin'. There isn't anybody can prove nothin'.''

Cynthia relinquished the chase. She sank down in the thicket, panting, her hands pressed against her breast. "I been to death's door. I couldn't run a race or do a day's work. . . . And if I caught her what I gwine say? 'You made that Bogey and you put it there, and you thought you gwine trap me and kill me, and you thought William'd turn to you. Well, you thought wrong. He wouldn't. And I ain't gwine pine away and die. I done found I'm bigger than Bogey, even if he were alive. I'm myself. I walked up to him, I did that, because I saw I was myself. . . . You kin go, Vinie Daone. I don't care!' ''

Dilsey came to the cabin door. "Where she gone? Where dat Cynthia gone? Mother!"

Old Maria hobbled out. "She gone? you run down to de swamp en look ef she drown herself!"

But while they still stared Cynthia stepped out of the jasmine thicket. She had in her hands the trunk and limbs of Bogey. She came up to the open-mouthed women. "That's what it was, grandmother! That's what it was, Aunt Dilsey! I gwine put it in that sand box and show it. . . . But I ain't proud of myself neither. . . . And now I want something to eat."

The mockingbird sang like the phoebe, the cardinal, the bluebird, the thrush and the lark and himself. William, coming to Liveoaks walking the last twenty miles, coming through the fields with his eyes upon the hill, heard him before he saw the cabin. "Where he is there's the cabin. Mockers do surely like folks! . . .Cynthia's and my cabin gwine have apple tree and cherry tree and peach tree and Rose of Sharon bushes like my mammy had, and a mocker like that gwine come and build. Yaas, Lawd, we gwine have that cabin!"

The Angel

The old, darkened canvas hung above the horsehair sofa. The sofa faced the windows. The three windows opened upon a narrow strip of garden with Guernsey-lilies, syringa and a Seven Sisters rose; upon three locust trees and the village street. Between two windows stood the show case, displaying ribbons on satin, grosgrain and lute-string, with bunches and sprays of artificial flowers, pins and combs and veiling; between these and the other window, five stands for as many leghorn or chip hats. One end of the room had shelves for small milliner's stores in a small, sleepy, out-of-the-way place. An ancient piano graced the other end.

The angel had been for many years a regarder of this room. The millinery business, it was true, had not been forever there. Mr. Dance, the old Presbyterian minister, had always said that he thought that someone who knew what he was about had created the angel, or more likely copied it, long ago. Mr. Dance thought the painting was really old. When he came to see Mrs. West and Jinny he would stand before the angel and make a quaint gesture of reverence.

But now old Mr. Dance was dead, and neither the new minister nor anyone else in Two Rivers cared particularly for the angel—the canvas was so old and darkened, so dusky and shadowy!

Moreover, though to an extent Two Rivers thought in Biblical forms, they were, generally speaking, the forms mediated to it through the publications of the church or churches. This deviated from those. The Wests' angel had artfully shaped and colored wings and a garland of red and white roses and a strange, sweeping garment with a working in and out of it small flowers. Two Rivers had hardly considered the appearance truly angelic. Two Rivers had known it as long as it had know Mrs. West's family, and that was some time—five generations, in fact. But it neither now nor at any time had esteemed it highly. It was, and somewhat slurringly, "that old picture of the Wests."

The angel continued to regard with supersubtle gaze the sometimes parlor and finally the shop of the mother and daughter.

The ribbons were flowered and the ribbons were plain. The flowers were chiefly in wreaths and clusters—roses, morning-glories, daisies, poppies, lilacs, with purple asters and pansies for the elderly. The hats indicated the opening years of the century and a community miniature and remote, unrecking alike of great shops and of galleries. The angel had had time enough in which to study the room, for the house was old, and a woman in a short-waisted gown had sat at that piano. And before that there had been a spinet and a man with a pigtail. Before that a ship, and an Italian passenger, and the angel very heedfully wrapped. It was all one to the angel—or perhaps he, too, took pleasure in his varying adventures.

In the kitchen off the back porch, under the grapevine, Jinny prepared supper for her mother and herself and then carried it to the room behind the room of the angel. It was slight supper, for Jinny had trained herself not to eat much, and Mrs. West, being an invalid, never did. They had enough, and Jinny had cooked it delicately. They ate together from an old table with three Hermosa roses in a blue bowl. They talked.

"How much today?"

"One dollar and twenty cents. Just a ribbon bow and a round comb for little Mary Jackson, and that jet buckle for Elivra."

". . .I don't want medicine."

"Oh, mother, you must have it! Mr. Jones will wait for the money."

"He's waited too long, and we know it. It'll have to stop. However I resolve against it, I cost too much."

"Oh, mother, I wish I could give you and give you and give you! I wish I could take you to New York to that hospital. Doctor Drew says that doctor could make you walk again and be as well, almost, as anyone. Sometimes when I get up in the morning I think 'Maybe the whole stock will be bought out today! And then I'll get some more and that'll be bought right away, and some more, and that'll go just as quick! And we'll pay Blank & Blank in full, and every other account!' And I feel so gay! And then no one comes, or almost no one."

Jinny swallowed hard. Her mother looked at her pitifully

and lovingly. The bell rang. "There!" exclaimed Mrs. West, who had truly a gay and courageous spirit. "They've come to buy out the stock—including the pelargoniums and the rhinestones!"

But it was only Sally Ashley, wanting a yard of bobbinet. When that was bought she produced an illustrated paper for the crippled woman. Sally was somehow a cousin, and she had the largest dwelling house in Two Rivers. "No, I won't stop to see Cousin Maria this evening. But I know she'll like these pictures. There never was such a woman for wanting to see the world!"

Jinny stared at St. Peter's in Rome. "She always wanted to travel and never could. She's never had much that she wanted."

"Well, I always say----," began Sally Ashley; and then she stopped, for what she had started to say was, "that we get what we deserve." But that did sound cruel, and Heaven knew she wanted instead to be kind to poor Cousin Maria and to Jinny!

Now Jinny was speaking. "Sally----"

"Yes, Jinny?"

"Sally, could you—would it be convenient to you—would you make me a loan? I haven't got any surety, unless you'd take the piano or my angel—or both."

"What do you call a loan?" asked Sally, so good-naturedly that Jinny's heart leaped.

"Oh, Sally, could you let me have five hundred dollars?"

"Why, Jinny!"

"I know it's a lot," hurried on Jinny. "But times have been hard this spring, and people aren't buying. There's the doctor's bill for the whole year, and mother's medicines, and the wood for last winter, and a lot of things besides. And I still owe Blank & Blank a good deal on stock—really a good deal. They've been patient, but I can't keep them waiting much longer. Oh, Sally, if you could, being kin and all----"

Sally, leaning her considerable bulk against the show case, faced the angel. "I wish I could, Jinny; I do wish I could. But you said the truth when you said that times are hard. Because a woman's got a fairly big house and three servants doesn't mean that money comes easily. It only means it goes easily. To keep a girl at school these days means something awful! And the Leroys have asked the twins for August, and that means they've got to have clothes and spending money. And I gave more than I ought to for the new church. I do wish I could, Jinny. . . . But maybe things will pick up. And I never have thought that you bought from the right people in the city, or they'd wait. I've told you so, you know."

"They've waited this year. All right, Sally. Forget that I've asked you. Shall I wrap up the bobbinet?"

Sally departed, voluble to the last as to her own difficulties. Jinny was willing to believe that they existed. She and her mother didn't have growing and demanding children, that was true. She didn't really feel bitterness toward Sally; why should she? Sally and all the Sallys and Johns and the little Johns and little Sallys in Two Rivers were always being good in pleasant little ways to her mother and herself. Only, pleasant little ways were like pleasant little flowers when you needed wheat and corn and a fire and skill.

It was not yet dark. The odor of the roses came in at the windows. . . . There was the angel.

Jinny sat down upon the silk patchwork ottoman. That had been her favorite seat in this room when she was a child— and ever since. Then there had not been the hats and the shelves and the show case; then it was just the parlor. There might be company, and her mother would come in, walking as well and better than anyone else, and seat herself and talk beautifully, in flowing skirts. Or her mother might play the piano. Thirty years; it was thirty years ago. Her mother was only sixty now, having married very early. And she never got old inside. Her body, if it were straightened and healed, would be beautiful still, and active.

Thirty-eight years old, and fifteen of them the Two Rivers milliner.

These summer dusks showed a gold light still. There was light enough to see the angel by—his wings and splashes of gold and his eyes. He had always been in her life. She didn't care how smoky and dusty---"Oh," breathed Jinny, "angels are powerful beings! If you could only come down and help us."

The light made his plumes quite beautiful, and now it touched the chaplet of white and red roses, only those colors were long ago dimmed, and now his face seemed to break up into a smile. There was something about his cheek bones that smiled. It was a strange face; certainly not Sunday-school angelic. Old Mr. Dance had said he might be a seraph—they had more subtlety than the angels.

"Jinny! Oh, Jinny!"

"Yes, mother!"

Later in the evening, by lamplight, they looked at the pictures in the magazine Sally brought, and Jinny read aloud an article upon the hill towns of Italy. Maria West sat with folded hands in the wheel chair that Jinny had bought three years ago. "Ah, yes," ran her thought. "To walk in those places----"

They went to bed, and the moonlight streamed in upon them sleeping.

Also it streamed through all the windows of the front room. It was a round moon, and the room came into living silver. The show case gleamed; there were the hats and the shelves. All the flowers on the hats became moonflowers. The piano held a pool of moonlight; the two conch shells on either side of the hearth opened rosy mouths for the beams; the china figures on the whatnot bathed in the rays; the plain, faded gilt frame of the angel expressed its oblong being. The form of the angel appeared to come into the round.

Angel or seraph, wide-eyed, he seemed to regard the room, regard the moon through the windows, regard the many days and nights he had known this room, animate and inanimate things and persons, regard the very many other days and nights of his existence—all the moonlight that he had known, all the sunlight, in whatever countries and times.

The moon shone all night. Then the moon set and the sun rose.

Jinny and her mother had their breakfast. The garden flowers smelled deliciously; the flowers in the show case and the flowers on the hats assumed their brightest look. Mrs. West remarked it when she wheeled her chair into the front room. "I declare, Jinny, when the morning's fresh like this they look almost real!"

"So they do," agreed Jinny. "I thought I'd trim the blue chip this morning. What would you think of daisies and ragged-robins?"

"I'd think very well of them----It does seem to me a day in which something ought to happen!"

But what happened was a letter from the city. She managed to keep it for this morning from her mother, whose pain had come on again and who lay, rigid and patient, in the darkened back room. The letter said she must pay in thirty days. Of course she must pay—honest folk paid—but she wanted more time than that.

Jinny sat and stared at the letter. What was going to happen to her mother and herself?

Miss Ann Trefusis, who was going with her brother, the lawyer, to Washington and Niagara, had to have a traveling hat—small neat straw, with one flower. "Yes, that's it, Miss Jinny! How lucky that you had it! I'll get my good hat in Washington----How is Mrs. West?"

"She's not feeling well this morning, Miss Trefusis."

"I'm sorry for that. You don't look very well yourself, Miss Jinny."

"Oh, yes, I am well. I think that hat's lovely on you."

"I'll take a veil too. That one with the little dots."

Jinny's hands trembled, measuring off the veil. "Miss Trefusis, I want very much to sell our piano. You know people all through the county. Have you heard of anybody wanting one?"

"Sell the old piano! Why, that's a pity, isn't it, Miss Jinny? It's been here so long that it seems to me to have been born and grown up in that corner."

Jinny hunted her scissors and cut off the veil. "It's still a fine instrument, if it were tuned. You remember that Mr. Marks who was at the Harris House a couple of years ago and who played? He said so. He said there were years of music in it yet."

"Why do you want to sell it?"

"I want the money."

"That was a brilliant question!" thought Miss Ann Trefusis. "Of course she wants the money, with her mother like that year after year, and country millinery, I feel sure, in a depressed condition." She walked to the piano and stood looking at it.

Jinny came after her and opened it. "It had a good maker."

"I don't know of a soul who wants one, Miss Jinny. I'll remember that you would like to sell it." She thought, "if it wasn't for this trip and everything coming on top of it I'd buy it myself and give it back to her. But I *will* buy that chip hat she's trimming."

Two hats made a good day's selling. Jinny knew it and was thankful. Only, nothing—no day's selling—could lift the long-accumulating load of care. The old piano couldn't do it either; it was only a beginning that she was clutching, with whatever wrung heartstrings. And now she saw how impossible it was going to be to sell the piano. She might just as well expect to sell the angel! A little candle of hopeful purpose went out. But she liked Miss Ann Trefusis, and she was glad that she took two hats.

She didn't even rest there; she took another veil and hat pins and two mull ties. Going away, she said, "I'll remember, Miss Jinny. How much would you take for it?"

Jinny's sunken brown eyes regarded the locust trees, the river and the mountain. "I asked Mr. Marks two years ago what he thought it was worth, and he said that if the right person wanted it I might get as much as two hundred dollars. I'd take less than that, Miss Ann—a good deal less."

Miss Trefusis went away. The morning deepened. No one else came. Maria West lay flat on her bed, in the grip of one of her attacks of pain, now simply grimly enduring, now eased for the time and floating with closed eyes in and out of the hill towns of Italy. Jinny came and went between the two rooms. She began, the blue chip sold, to trim a gray straw with gray tulle and purple asters. She was thinking, "It looks like Miss Belle Young. Maybe she'll come by and see it and want it."

Every little while a picture of her mother rose before her— her mother lying there on the bed in the big cool room. What if they had to sell the house? No one would buy the piano, but somebody might be found to buy the house—Tom Watson probably. There was the mortgage. When it was paid, and the debts, what would be left?

And where might she find a shop like this, and a room like that for her mother? Nowhere. Nowhere such use and comfort as they now had.

The letter—she had as well show it to her mother, just so soon as she was over this spell. She was going to have to show it, so it might as well be done and over with it; her mother wasn't a coward. When she knew it would be a relief. She would say, "Well, Jinny, let's face it!"

She did say very much just that: "Well, Jinny, let's stand up to it—figuratively, that is, for me! Cheer up, Jenny Wren! We've got the angel still."

The doctor came to see Mrs. West. In the front room he talked to Jinny. "You haven't any money, hey? And you want me to know that you don't know when you can pay me?

Have you ever noticed, Jinny, that with all the misfitting there's still a lot of fitting in life? It happens that I don't *want* any money. So now we've got harmony, and for goodness' sake let's keep it! When they're ripe you send me a big basket of your grapes, and we'll be quits for this year."

"Oh, doctor, but we send it to you anyhow!"

"Then just keep on sending it year by year, and I'll step in, year by year, when I'm at this end of the street, and the thing's done."

Jinny thought, "How can we send the grapes, if we have to sell the house?" She was standing before the angel, and the doctor was standing before the angel. "As I'm living, Jinny, I believe that two years under Carrick's care would make her almost a well woman! I wish you could do it."

Jinny said, dry-lipped, "I wish so, too, doctor."

When he was gone she sat down upon the faded silken ottoman and put her head upon her knees and clasped her hands behind her neck. The angel, so dimmed by all his years and by unknowing keeping, soared above her. Where did he come from? She did not know, and perhaps he had forgotten. He was that dark old angel of the Wests, and that was all Two Rivers knew. "I wish—I wish a miracle would happen!"

The next day her mother was better, but again there were no customers other than two children for hair ribbons. The day after that Miss Belle Young did see the gray hat placed in the window that was nearest the street and, opening the gate, crossed the ribbon of flowers to the door and the room.

"Good morning. Miss Jinny, I'd like to see that gray chip hat."

"Good morning, Miss Belle. It does favor you. I thought so when I put the asters so."

Miss Belle tried it on before the narrow old pier glass. "I like it, Miss Jinny, and I need it; but I just cannot take it now. If you could hold it back two or three weeks—or if you will trust me for it until I get my November money----"

"Yes, I'll trust you, Miss Belle. It does suit you."

"How is your mother?"

"She is better."

"I was at the Watsons' last night. Tom's crazy to find a house. He don't want to build—you've got a lot of room in this one, Miss Jinny. Did you ever try for summer boarders?"

"Yes, I did. But there isn't anything in Two Rivers to draw them. I tried to get a small family or a young couple to take the upstairs room steady, but there isn't any one hereabouts wanting anything like that."

"No, I reckon it would be difficult. . . . Tom's got a curious liking for this house. He says he took a fancy to it when he was a little shaver—and it's lasted. As for Martha, she likes what Tom likes. If you've got it anywhere in your head, Miss Jinny, that you and Mrs. West would like to sell I do think you ought to talk to Tom. In fact, he said to me that he'd like me to speak to you."

"Do you know what he'd give, Miss Belle?"

"Well, he says it's just sentiment—he don't believe any one else in the world would want it. He'd give you six thousand for the house and the two acres."

Miss Belle Young departed with the gray hat, gray tulle and purple asters, to be paid for in November. She had a final word. "The Gurdeys' cottage at the mouth of Walnut Lane— they're going to move away because the sawmill's going. I should think a small place like that would be so much easier to keep. And cosier, too, for you both. It could be made much better looking than it is now. The Gurdeys didn't know how, but you and Mrs. West would. And I don't see that it isn't just as good a situation as this for a millinery."

Jinny thought, "I reckon Tom'll give her a present."

The Gurdey cottage. Terror came upon her in a wave. Home—to give up home! She had never really envisaged it.

"If we can't help it——" said Maria West at last, when it was deep in the night and they had turned it this way and turned it that. "But let us help it, if we can! Let's go to sleep now, Jinny, and then we'll think and we'll think."

They thought and they thought and they thought, but if anything came of it they did not see it. If they had one thousand, five hundred dollars—But where, in God's name, would they get one thousand, five hundred dollars? And how could they ever pay it back?

Jinny went to the post office. There were two letters. She brought them home, and the two women opened and read them on the shady back porch under the great grapevine. One—a short one—was from Miss Belle Young: "I forgot to say, Jinny, that Tom Watson says he can get the Robertson house if he acts right away. He'd considerably rather have yours, but he couldn't wait too long about it. He knows he can get the other."

"We'd never get another purchaser," said Mrs. West.

Jinny, sitting beside the wheel chair, put her head down on her mother's knee. "Oh, mother, it's for you. I can't stand it!"

"We'll stand it together," said Maria. "What is the other letter?"

"It's from the bank. I'm afraid to open it."

When they did open it it was to the effect that the times were difficult, the bank was in need of funds and they must ask that Mrs. West's long-standing and oft-renewed note for seven hundred dollars be paid off.

The two sat very still in the midst of the sun and shadow and the vine-leaf patterning. The older woman was the first to speak. "You had better go to Tom Watson's office the first thing tomorrow."

And then the wonderful thing began to happen.

The bell rang. Jinny started up, saying, "It's little Patty Atkins, begging ribbon ends for her doll." But it wasn't Patty Atkins; it was Miss Ann Trefusis. With her was a thin, grayish gentleman whom she introduced as Mr. Theobald.

It appeared that Miss Trefusis had met Mr. Theobald several times in New York last winter, and that now he was on a riding trip through this region and had stopped by Two Rivers to spend a day or two with her and her brother. "He's not a musician like your Mr. Marks, Miss Jinny, but he's an artist. I told him about your angel, and he wants to see it."

It all happened so fast. Through the four windows in the front room poured an amber, afternoon light. The show case, the hats, the shelves, the piano, the angel. Mr. Theobald stood before the latter. "It has never been cleaned."

Jinny could not stand for that. "I wipe the canvas off with a little warm water."

"I do not mean that. The varnish is very old and decayed. Altogether, it is so darkened. But——"

He lapsed into silence. Once or twice he altered his station. He looked around, saw the ottoman and, pushing it before the picture, sat down. He leaned forward, his chin in his hands and his eyes upon the figure.

Jinny thought, "Mother oughtn't to miss being here." She left the room and returned pushing her mother's wheel chair.

The three women sat and looked at Mr. Theobald, there on the old silk ottoman before the angel. He had an expressive face; it now expressed absorption and question. From the wall, from between his wings, the seraph opposed his subtle supersensitive face, "smiling with his cheek bones," forever young, forever old.

Mr. Theobald sighed and stirred. He got up and went again to the canvas. He touched it, he touched it again, he stood off a little way. He turned. "Would you let me take it down and unframe it?"

Jinny and Ann Trefusis helped him. The angel in his old worn gilt frame now leaned against the sofa. Mr. Theobald resting a moment, looked at Maria West. "What is the history of it?" he asked. "How did it come to you?"

"My father's grandfather—his mother's father—was an Italian, Antonio Sacchetti. It belonged to him; he brought it from Italy. My father always said there was some story about it. It was bequeathed to his grandfather, or it paid a debt, or maybe it belonged to his family but was claimed by somebody else. My father rather thought the latter, for there was certainly a story about it and some secrecy somewhere. But my great-grandfather lived only a year or two after his emigration here. He married my great-grandmother, Virginia Russell, and was drowned in a storm on the bay, out in her father's sloop, before his daughter, my father's mother, Maria Sacchetti, was born. I can just remember her. She said there was a story about the angel, but she didn't know what it was. It had been through flood and fire, and no one in the house thought much of it. My grandmother gave it to me who was named for her, and I brought it here with me to my husband's house."

"All that's interesting," said Mr. Theobald. "All that's very interesting!"

Jinny saw that he was excited. He was so excited that he was quieter than almost any man she had ever seen. Old Mr. Dance now and then had been quiet like that in the pulpit, and out of it, standing looking at the sky.

Mr. Theobald took out his knife and began to rip away from the frame an ancient linen backing.

"That was put there I don't know when," said Maria West.

"A long, long time ago."

He released the canvas from its gilt borders and set it free upon the floor in the full light, rich and soft. There was a mark for which he was looking, and he found it. Moreover, on the reverse of the painting, hidden by the oblong of linen so old that it now fell into tinder, appeared a line or two of Italian carrying a statement.

"Of course," said Mr. Theobald apologetically and almost tenderly, "a great deal will have to be done to it. And there rests a possibility that experts will differ. Some may claim that it is a pupil's work and a copy only of his lost angel. Even so—— But I don't hold that; I hold it is his very own—his angel."

The seraph looked at them subtly and similingly. They could see now that he was beautiful, always in his own fashion. Mr. Theobald gazed back with homage in his eyes. Indeed, his eyes had tears in them when he turned to Miss Trefusis. "This," he said, "is one of my great days."

The bell rang. Jinny went to the door. It was now little Patty Atkins. "Tomorrow, dear," said Jinny. "Come tomorrow. I can't give them to you just now."

They had waited for her to return. She sat down beside her mother and took her hand.

"What does it mean for them?" said Ann Trefusis softly. "You know what I told you."

"If others say as I say," answered Mr. Theobald, "and it turns out as I think it ought, they should be able to go see—him— any time they wish to in some great gallery. The Metropolitan should have it. One of the great dealers will probably enough buy for some private owner, but it should come to the public as a gift eventually."

Ann Trefusis continued to speak for them, quietly and gracefully. "It ought to mean, then, a considerable sum—enough to put them at ease?"

"Yes," said Mr. Theobald—and named a sum that seemed to Maria and Virginia West, until they received it and became used to it, pure Arabian Nights. "They won't really lose the angel either; to share a wonderful thing with many is not to be reckoned loss."

"And they'll keep this house," said Miss Trefusis, softly still. "But Miss Jinny need not have the millinery shop, unless she wants to. And in New York, in the hospital, that great doctor will make Mrs. West so that she can walk again, will make her almost quite well. So well that they can travel, if they want to—go abroad, see Italy."

The angel regarded them all, smiling his tender and enigmatical smile through the centuries.

The Baptizing

"Come through! Come through, sister!"
"Bress de lord!"
"Sing it again! Start that hymn again, Brother Pickett!"

> *"O my Lord,*
>> *Give me your hand!*
>
> *O my lord,*
>> *Give me your hand!*
>
> *I'm sinking in the river of my sins!*
>> *O Gabriel, blow your trump!*
>> *O Gabriel, blow your trump!*
>
> *For the Lord is coming down,*
>> *Coming down,*
>> *Coming down!*
>
> *O my Lord, give me your hand!"*

"She's standing up on her feet!"
"I see her wrastling—I see her wrastling with Satan!"

> *"For the Lord is coming down,*
>> *Coming down,*
>> *Coming down!*
>
> *O my Lord, give me your hand!"*

"Hol' to him a little harder, Lily! He's the Rose ob Sharon!"
"He'll wash you whiter'n snow!"
"Po' sinner—po' sinner! Come through, po' sinner!"

> *"My sister, want to get religion?*
>> *Go down in the lonesome valley!*
>
> *My sister, want to get salvation?*
>> *Go down in the lonesome valley!"*

"Come on, come on, po' sinner, to de mourners' bench!"

"Let us pray!"

There was the Rev. Thomas Meiklejohn, pastor of Moriah Colored Baptist Church, and there was the Rev. William Howard Boykin, helping him in this revival, lent by Curfew in the next county. The Reverend Mr. Meiklejohn was old, but the Reverend Mr. Boykin was young. Tall and young and black and shining. And strong. He could lift an ox—but now he was lifting sinners.

"O Lord, you've given us seven tonight, now make it eight! O Lord, make it eight! That mourners' bench is long enough for another, and the salvation bench is right near it! O Lord, you've shook the tree tonight, and the lovely fruit is falling, it's falling! O Lord, this poor, stray, erring, lost child, crying and moaning for the promised land, and not seeing the plain way to it! O Lord, step out on the dark, lonely hillside after her! Bring her into the fold, the blessed, blessed fold! O Lord, shake the tree once more! O Lord, shake the fruit from Satan's grip into the angels' palms! O Lord, do it now, for this sinner's been seeking a solid week, and it's time for her to come in, to come in from the lonely and the dark. O Lord—O Lord! Amen!"

"Want to enter yonder in the kingdom?
Go down in the lonesome valley!"

The dozen oil lamps smoked and flared. It was hot. The atmosphere hung fairly visible; it pulsed and tasted and smelled. Small lights ran about with big shadows; the hymns locked arms. Ejaculations and groans, short cries, tensions and despairs, and abandons and ecstasies populated Moriah Colored Baptist Church. Egypt and the Wilderness and the Dead Sea and Pisgah and Canaan and the Jordan! And everybody, everybody, save those kneeling or prostrate beside the mourners' bench, looked at Adelaide Lily Camp.

Adelaide Lily had been "coming through" for the better part of this revival. And yet it seemed that she could not get through—and each night the ministers prayed for her, and the revival, saved and unsaved, looked at her, and the excitement mounted. More than that, one or the other minister came in the daytime and wrestled with Satan for her, inside the cabin or on the little porch covered with scarlet running bean and Madeira vine, or in the grove immediately behind the cabin where it was cool this hot weather. Brother Meiklejohn was elderly and heavy, and the season July. Brother Boykin came oftenest.

Adelaide Lily was getting religion. She did not work that week.

"Yaas, I can do her work as well as mine," said Sarah, her mother, at the washtub by the stream, to the passing neighbor. "Ain't that chile settling her whole future till kingdom come and after? Yaas, I lets her sit there in the door, all doubled up and studying the ground, without any mo' words than a chicken has teeth. Or she'll get up and go prancing round, waving her arms and then falling on her knees. It takes her different ways different times, but she sho ain't missing anything!"

Thomas Jefferson Camp, aged nine, stopped swinging on the gate and pattered up the path between the zinnias. "The preacher's comin', Sis' Lily!"

"You mean Brother Meiklejohn, Thomas Jefferson?"

"No, I means Brother Boykin."

"Yaas'm," said Sarah. "It's kind of cool and pleasant under the trees. He can 'spound the Book to her there and get down on his knees and pray while she rocks and mourns. Lord! I was three years younger'n she when I got religion. Them was the days!"

"Yaas, they was. We don' have no such shoutin' an' testifyin' now. Don' you remember when it went on for a month an' they baptized a hundred?"

"Yaas, I remember. I gwine get him a glass of nice, cold buttermilk and a piece of pie."

"He mighty fine man. They say er lot of Curfew gals are after him."

"I dare say!"

"Right poor stock round Curfew, *I* think."

"I think the same. Well, if you must be going---"

> *"Abraham sitting in the door,*
> *Abraham sitting in the door,*
> *Oh, don't you know when you got a blessing?*
> *O poor sinner, don't you know?*
> *Here come the angel a-string along,*
> *O poor sinner, don't you know?"*

Adelaide Lily stepped into the aisle. She was of medium height and inclined to plumpness, a warm chestnut in hue and comely. She wore a pink lawn with ruffles that Sarah had done up that day, and beautiful blue glass beads. Her hat, a leghorn with morning-glories, she left upon the bench. One couldn't well "come through" in a flapping hat that hid the working of one's countenance. Adelaide Lily's arms went up over her head. "O my Jesus! I cyarn' get no further!"

"O po' sinner, yass, you can! Oh, pray to him with yo' heart, po' sinner!"

Moriah Church was at a tension. It spread to the mourners' bench, though not to all who had sought it. Three out of the seven had knelt here night after night. They could not get through though they had come so far. They agonized—old Abner Shaw, who had grown old in unbelief, whose two sons had drowned in last spring's big flood; Judy Corbin, whose sins were as scarlet, so she said and believed; and big Ransom Moore, who had had a Dream and it would not let him go and yet would not save him. They crouched silent, with their brows against the wood, and Adelaide Lily made no difference in their lives. Nothing mattered but a certain Food, and they did not know how to cross the space between them and it. But the others at the old worn bench had shallower lives and needs, and they looked sidewise and began to make room for Adelaide Lily. All the dusky church held its breath except where it indulged in audible encouragement. The emotions rushed ecstatically upward. "Come through! Come through! Come through the deep waters to the promised lan'! Hab courage, gal! Hab courage!"

The Rev. William Howard Boykin prayed again, standing in the clear space between the mourners' bench and the bench of the saved, standing tall and strong and shining and earnest. Pictures came and went in his head. He did not let them block his communion with the Lord, for he was a sincere believer and worker in the vineyard, honest and zealous as the day was long. Nevertheless they sifted through. The Camps' cabin, a mile from town, and the porch with scarlet running bean and Madeira vine that smelled so sweet. The corn patch and the watermelons and the spring. The grove of trees, so pleasant and cool, with a big log to sit on, and Adelaide Lily begging comfort and hanging on his words. Adelaide Lily. Adelaide Lily. "O Lord," he prayed, "save this special sinner, so's we can all go in a band together. O Lord, if she wasn't baptized with the others

when we go down into the river on Sunday, how hard would that
be! But Your Arm isn't shortened----"

"Glory hallelujah! Glory hallelujah! Glory hallelujah!"

Adelaide Lily in her pink ruffled lawn and blue beads went
dipping and rising up the aisle. "Ise coming! Ise coming! O my
Lord, you and me is joined! Oh, gib me room, Brother Meiklejohn, at that bench! Not the mourners' bench but the saved
bench!"

"Glory hallelujah! Glory hallelujah!"

"Ise going to be in the baptizing! Thank the Lord, thank
the Lord!"

"Glory hallelujah! Glory hallelujah!"

"O Brother Boykin, gib me your hand! Gib me your hands,
all of you! For Ise going to be in the baptizing!"

"Glory hallelujah!"

> *"Over Jordan,*
> 　　*Yaas, my Lord!*
> *Over Jordan,*
> 　　*Yaas, my Lord!*
> *The angels knows what's in the heart.*
> 　　*Yaas, my Lord,*
> *Over Jordan!*
> *The angels knows and they takes a part.*
> 　　*Yaas, my Lord."*

Adelaide Lily sat upon the saved bench.

The hour was waxing late. Outside Moriah Colored Church
the big, round moon climbed up the sky, and katydids discoursed
in the hot, still night. Folk had to work next day. The katydids
began to say that. *"You know we hab to work. You know we
hab to work. You know. You know. Eight sinners tonight.
Dat's all right. You know. You know. Folk hab to work. We
got dat gal what give us a show. Now sing de doxology. Doxology. Doxology."*

The Rev. Thomas Meiklejohn spoke: "We haven't got but
a little while before Sunday and the baptizing. It's mighty little
time! O my friend, don't you want to come now? Now is yo'
chance, and yo' chance is dwindling! Don't you want—don't
you want—to be in the glad day? If you put if off, the days
that come'll be blacker for you than pitch. Yaas, my brother,

yaas, my sister, blacker'n pitch! Yo' heart know, and it say to you, 'Don' you see others going into the kingdom and you losing yo' chance?' You stand to lose, and you knows it, and yo' heart wants what it's losing! Come now—come now, my brother, my sister!"

With that Ailsa Craigie rose. "You ain't none of you expecting it, but I'm going to get religion! I'm going to get religion!"

No, they had not expected it—Moriah Colored Church.

The fact that folk had to work tomorrow left the air, that now palpitated with a most revived interest. For here rose, stalk and blossom, a sensation that promised to overlay that of Adelaide Lily. "Ailsa's getting religion! Ailsa Craigie's getting religion!" Even the children, of whom there were many in the congregation, drew breath and rolled eyes. A kind of whish and stir went everywhere, followed by the most flattering silence.

"O Lord, yo' mercies air not straitened!" cried Brother Meiklejohn, whose scoffing and stubborn niece was Ailsa Craigie. And Brother Boykin stood tall and earnest and solemn and happy, with rapt eyes and inaudibly moving lips. The revival was successful—he was seeing himself baptizing many, standing waist deep in the Moriah, laying them, one by one, under the flood that typified saving grace. And now Ailsa Craigie, that they said nobody could convert. He had heard her laugh one day when he passed her house, laugh and say, "Lord! If I was that big and strong I'd sure go work in the fields!" All his dignity of minister of the gospel had risen up against her. *Now* she saw that he was in the field. He hoped the Lord might show her, good and hard! She was a tall, slender, supple, charcoal-dark woman, about his own age. She had been sometimes to Curfew. Brother Meiklejohn had brought her once with him in his old buggy. Brother Meiklejohn was fond of her. But she was one of those silent mockers and queens, thinking their own thoughts, making you uncomfortable with their eyes. They said she had sense. But what kind of sense was it if you didn't have religion? She was fine to look at, though she wasn't like Miss Adelaide Lily. He had met her three-four times. There was something about her— she'd help a man with her sense through the brier patches and the stony places of this world. She was likely—she was surely likely. He had felt that even through his anger when she had said those hard words. But she had been a scoffer and an unconverted

sinner and that wasn't possible for the pastor of Curfew Church!
No, nor for William Howard Boykin either! But now the Lord
was drawing her, was drawing her into the fold. . .

David Craigie, a deacon and the half brother of the Rev.
Thomas Meiklejohn, had his place in an amen corner, and so
when his daughter quitted his side she stood in the clear space below the pulpit and faced the mourners' bench and the salvation
bench and all the rest of the benches and the congregation.
Everybody could see her. If they couldn't see her sitting they
stood up promptly and saw her so. All their eyes were drawn,
and their lips hung parted. She seemed to them suddenly very
tall and strong, and as though the air quivered about her. It
quivered and it seemed another color. When she spoke the
congregation of Moriah Church at once began to get religion with
her—that is, all but a few.

"O my Lord Jesus, you knows Ise a scoffer!"

"Yaas, Lord!"

"A scoffer and a doubter and a despiser and a mocker!"

"She's got de language—she always had!"

"O Lord, Ise the thief and the leper and the publican and
the Pharisee and the woman who had seven devils----"

"Oh, it's wuhking! The Holy Ghost's wuhking!"

"O Lord, Ise the blind and the dumb and the palsy! O
Lord, Ise the hypocrite! Ise Laz'rus in the grave, and Judas! O
my Lord, Ise Judas!"

A child of twelve clutched a woman. "Oh, mammy, Ise
trimbling up my backbone an' the tears air coming out!"

"Hesh! Ise heard her befo'. When she wants to she's got a
voice like all de fiddle strings, an' she sho wants to now!"

"She's dancing too, mammy!"

"Hesh! That ain't dancing. That's bowing down an' rising
up."

"O Lord, Ise in the dust."

Said Adelaide Lily's heart in her bosom on the saved bench:
"You weren't decided on getting there when you came here tonight in that old blue calico that Miss Sally Mason give you! Git
up out of the dust, gal, and stop drawing attention!"

Ailsa, rising up, seemed to touch the beam above her. She
had genius for position and genius for richly departing from it,
and for shaking things alive. She no more than Moriah had a
name for that, nor thought about it. "That gal, Ailsa, can mek

herse'f felt same as a ha'nt!" That was the extent of Moriah's tribute. The blue calico, straitly made, wrapped her long limbs and her small breasts. Throat and head and half her arms were bare. She was Africa, all right, rhythmically moving there, in the uncertain light, in the emotional tension, with the moon outside and the church as vibratory as a drum. Africa, but likewise, and maybe mainly, Ailsa; just Ailsa.

"O Jesus!"

"O my Jesus!"

"O Jesus, help this sinner home!"

Brother Meiklejohn prayed aloud for his niece, for whom he had an affection, for all that she was an unbeliever. She it was who mended his shirt and brought him the first roasting ears out of the big patch. He liked her better than his other kindred. "O Lord, look down and bring her through! O Lord, who knows the temptations, who knows we're po' things, just chil'ren who wants sweetness and'll snatch at it in the wrong places! O Lord, mind her steps till she can mind them herself! Amen! Let us sing!"

> *"Oh, rock Mount Sinai,*
> *Oh, rock Mount Sinai,*
> *Oh, rock Mount Sinai, in the morning.*
> *Oh, come on, Moses, don' you get lost,*
> *Smite the water and come across!*
> *Oh, rock Mount Sinai----"*

Brother Boykin's lips moved, but no sound came forth. His hands were tightly clasped. His heart ached and swelled. "O Lord, bring her through and down into the waters of baptism!"

Old Abner Shaw got up from the mourners' bench. "Oh, Ise through! O Lord, Ise through! O Lord, Ise coming just as I am!"

"Glory hallelujah! Glory hallelujah!"

Ailsa continued to bow down and rise up. The church was so dusky, with flaring lamps; the moon outside shone so bright. "O the Holy Ghost, come help!"

"I pray the Holy Ghost bring you right through, Ailsa!"

"I sees hell fire! Oh, I sees hell fire!"

"Oh!" went the watchers. "She sees hell fire!"

"I sees Abraham and Sarah and the promised land. But I

tastes the gulf! I tastes the gulf!"

"Oh! She tastes the gulf!"

"Oh! The devil is towering alongside of me!"

"Oo-h! The devil is towering!"

"Let us pray!"

William Howard Boykin prayed with all his might. Moriah Colored Church prayed—that is, most of it prayed. Adelaide Lily prayed, but she prayed against Ailsa. "O Lord, she actin'! She ain't gitting religion! O Lord, she want *him*, and she don't see no other way lef' now. O Lord, she ain't the one for him. She won't make him happy. She'd never help right in the church. She got all kind of opinions. O Lord, don't let her! She do mos' always what she set out to do. Ise 'feared of her. O Lord, I'll work, I'll work for you----"

"Let us sing!"

> *"Oh, don' you hear the big bell ringing?*
> *Come up, sinner, to the pleasant land!*
> *Pleasant land, pleasant land.*
> *Come up, sinner, to the pleasant land!"*

Ailsa began to chant. "Oh, when I gwine see Jerusalem, Jerusalem? Oh, when I gwine see Jerusalem? They come from the north and they come from the south! Oh, when I gwine see Jerusalem? The sun's in the east and the moon's in the west, and the kingdom comes with the seven lamps, and the pathway shine into Jerusalem! But when my feet gwine find the way—oh, when they gwine to find the way?"

Moriah Colored Church hung upon her paces round and round, and upon her thrilling voice. Young Ransom Moore at the mourners' bench came through, rose with a shout and passed to the salvation bench. Adelaide Lily made room for him. Her face was working. "It's scandalous, that's what it is!"

"What is?"

"What she's doing."

Ransom stared vacantly.

Ailsa stood stock still, then brought her long arms together over her head, clasped her hands and parted them. "Glory! Glory hallelujah! I'm through! I'm over the gulf! I got religion!"

"Glory hallelujah! Glory hallelujah!"

"Oh, bless Jesus!"

The moon shone and shone. The katydids began again. *"You know, you know we hab to work. You know we hab to work. You know, you know. We got nine sinners. We got nine sinners. Dey's saved, dey's saved. Judy Corbin, too. You know, you know. You know folk----"* A whippoorwill struck in from the big woods. The Rev. Thomas Meiklejohn pronounced the benediction.

The next day dawned clear with pink in the east and mist over the river and the town and the hills. Ailsa Craigie was up in time to see the morning star all still and pure and silver above Deadman's Hill. "I'm gwine up there. Pappy can get his own breakfast." She went, meeting no one, and lay down upon the short, burned turf and stretched her arm above her eyes.

"What's got in me? That's what I am asking. What's got in me? . . .*William Howard Boykin. William. William.* I reckon I love him. I reckon I think there ain't but one way to turn his head towards me. I reckon I work myself up and *get religion. . . .* But I ain't got any religion. Or is I?"

Adelaide Lily had reddened eyes that morning, and a drooping mouth. "What's the matter with you, gal? In my time when we knew we was saved we sung lak every bird in the wood."

"She's 'fraid of de water," declared Thomas Jefferson.

"I ain't a thinking of the river, mammy."

"Then it's Ailsa. She's owdacious—that gal's owdacious!"

"I think she's bold, myself—getting religion thataway! Oh, mammy, you think she gwine mek him look at her?"

"No, I don't. I think he look at you. She bawn owdacious! But she ain't got the hang of it lak you. She mix something else with it."

When the morning was hot and bright Ailsa came down from the hill to the cabin with its sun-flowers and zinnias and a great oak tree and the Moriah flowing by. The cobbler, her father, who had had to cook his own breakfast, was surly with her. "I hopes getting religion ain't gwine make you a fool!"

"Did I get it, daddy?"

"Did you get it? Well, it *look* lak you got it!"

Baptism Sunday drew on apace. The women had white dresses. All but Ailsa. It transpired that she didn't have a white dress and wasn't going to make one. Nor ask for one from the white folks neither.

"For the land's sake! Goin' down into the Moriah in er

blue calico!"

"I heah she say if the Lawd's the Lawd he'll not be caring!"

Adelaide Lily wanted to wear her blue beads, but Sarah shook her head. "No, chile, you better not do that! You don' want to look *vain* when the river a-washin' away sin comes over you."

Old Aunt Betsy was standing by. " 'Tain't de river. It's de grace ob Gawd dat meks you' heart en mind des' spick-en-span. De Moriah neber clean lak dat!"

"Don't you think I knows anything, Aunt Betsy? No, chile, that white dress with angel sleeves is all you wants."

It was Friday, and that hot and bright! The Rev. Thomas Meiklejohn and the Rev. William Howard Boykin visited the converted, confirming their faith and explaining points of doctrine and the solemnity of Sunday. Adelaide Lily received them on the cabin porch. The roses and the pinks were blooming in the yard, the scarlet bean and the Madeira vine over her head.

When the two went away the pastor from Curfew Church up the river heaved a sigh. "I most envies you your charge here at Moriah, brother! You got fine souls, and they keeps up their places so well. And your young people do seem to me to have cha'm above what they have at Curfew."

"Adelaide Lily's been thought jest to be waiting for the pick of the bunch, brother. That ain't nothing against her. No, sholy not!"

"What counts with me," said William Howard Boykin soberly, "is that she's saved! A woman that isn' saved and in the church and ready to work in the church—such a woman might tempt me, but she couldn't *take* me, brother." He looked at the blue hills and the waving trees. "They's both saved."

With that they arrived at the cabin of David Craigie, who sat at his cobbling upon a bench beneath a giant sunflower. "Morning, brother! We desires to talk with Ailsa."

"She ain't here. She's gone to the big woods."

"The big woods! But everybody knew we was coming around among the candidates. It was given out in meeting----"

"I know it was. I done reminded her. But she's gone all the same."

Blood to the face could not show in William Howard Boykin as in a white man, but it rose. He flushed. There is propriety in all things and this wasn't propriety!

That evening, in Moriah Church, three more were converted. Now there were twelve. "Oh, make it fifteen, my good Lawd! Make it fifteen!"

> *"Oh, what does you say, seekers,*
> *Oh, what does you say, seekers,*
> *About that Gospel war?*
> *And I will die in the field,*
> *And I will die in the field.*
> *I'm on my journey home!"*

Twelve sat on the salvation bench, in front of them all, in front of Moriah congregation; with the preachers just above them Adelaide Lily and Ailsa Craigie sat side by side.

William Howard Boykin was a powerful preacher, and he did desire the salvation of the world, and he loved all people and anguished for them. Also in his heart, in his private and personal heart, ran behind the great things a little talking sweetness like a naked cherub. "They both is saved, and they both has got a desirableness. It's different. Miss Adelaide Lily is not Miss Ailsa Craigie and Miss Ailsa Craigie is not Miss Adelaide Lily. They gifts is different. But they both is saved. Then which, William Howard, then which is you going to take by the hand?"

"O Lawd, save out of the worl' fifteen! You got just to-night and tomorrow night which is Saturday and folks is tired! O Lawd, fifteen befo' Sunday and the baptizing! Fifteen, Lawd, to go under the water, under the water that's the token of their salvation!

> *"I look over yonder on Jerico's walls.*
> *Rocks and mountains, don't fall on me!*
> *I see dem sinners tremble and fall.*
> *Rocks and mountains, don't fall on me!"*

Saturday morning rode in, warmer and sunnier than Friday. The Rev. William Howard Boykin came without Brother Meiklejohn to the cabin under the big oak tree. David Craigie was gone to take a pair of shoes to their owner. Ailsa sat upon the bench under the sunflower.

"Good mahnin', Miss Ailsa!"

"Good mahnin', Mr. Boykin."

"After tomorrow, after you comes up out of the water, it

will be 'sister' in the church, in the fold of the Lamb, Miss Ailsa!"

"I reckon so. I reckon I did get religion."

"Have you got any doubts, Miss Ailsa? Then let us pray----"

He prayed, and Ailsa bowed herself and shut her eyes tight and her hands tight and prayed too. He got up from his knees. "It would distress me powerful, Miss Ailsa, if you had been in anyways mistaken. I wants you for the Lord. Don't you think I knows that doubts will happen, doubts and despairs? But the little light keeps burning in the darkness. You follow that, Miss Ailsa. It'll lead you through the wilderness. You follow what God says to you, in you, and I believe certainly it will lead you down in the river tomorrow. The Lord'll give you that and give me that."

He looked very big and strong and earnest. She was tall, too, and supple and dark and clean of line. The sunflower held its disk and rays just above their heads. He pressed her hand and went away. She looked after him till she could see him no longer, and then she looked at the hand he had pressed, holding it out before her. "He like me. He like me, I think, as much as he like her. But he ain't gwine do nothing that don't mean a helping hand and a church member! What he thinks of most is a helping hand in his church. If I wants him I've got to be baptized tomorrow same as Adelaide Lily. Even if I was putting on the other night—putting on coming through! Even then, maybe she get him----"

That night, in Moriah Church, the three needed to make the fifteen came through.

"Glory hallelujah! Oh, glory hallelujah!"

> *"Oh, the old ark a-movering, a-movering along!*
> *It rain forty days and it rain forty nights.*
> *Oh, the old ark a-movering, a-movering along!"*

Adelaide Lily sat on the salvation bench and sang with all her might and a shining face. And she welcomed warmly the three who joined the saved. "Oh, bress the Lawd, sister! Oh, bress the Lawd, brother!"

> *"The old ark a-movering, a-movering along!"*

It was evident how valuable she could be henceforth in the church.

But Ailsa Craigie did not sit beside her, nor on the salvation bench at all, nor even it seemed in Moriah Church. When Adelaide Lily surreptitiously turned her head she could not find her anywhere in the dusky hollow. "I don't believe she coming. If it takes her like that maybe she won't come to the river neither. She never was the kind could stay in religion however many time she got put there! O Lawd, you don't want her if she ain't ready and wouldn't do you any credit----"

The moon shone very bright that night. Ailsa sat up in her bed, in a diminutive upper room of her father's cabin. The river ran not far away. Sometimes she could hear it. She heard it now. It was middle night. The moon flooded the room. The patchwork quilt upon the bed had almost its colors back again. A whippoorwill metallically called, was silent, called again, was silent. "I cyarn' sleep," said Ailsa. "I got a mind. It's a terrible thing to have!"

When another hour had passed she slipped out of bed, put on her dress and descending the stair without sound left the cabin. It was dead of night, with a cock crowing in the distance. Barefooted, she went out under the nodding sunflowers. She could hear the river plainly now, murmuring through the land. Opening the gate, she took the path that led to the clear, dark stream. The moon brightened it, and it ran dark, and the moon brightened it again, and it ran dark. Ailsa sat down on a stone, her elbows on her knees and her chin in her hands.

"O river, you and I and God has got to have it out!"

Sunday rose out of the east more hot and bright than Saturday. Good baptizing weather, that it was, good baptizing weather! Moriah Church was packed for the short service prior to the solemnity. Those to be baptized sat in front, the women in white and Adelaide Lily with angel sleeves. But Ailsa was not there.

"Where's Ailsa Craigie?"

"I don't know. She ain't here at all."

"Maybe something's happened to her----"

"Reckon she'll be in the ma'ch to the river all right. Reckon she'll join us in the road."

"Reckon she will, but Sarah Camp do say maybe she wan't converted at all."

"Oh, who that coming?
    Tall angel at the bar.
Oh, who that coming?
    Tall angel at the bar.
It looks lak Gabriel.
    Tall angel at the bar."

The big road ran a mile from the church to ford the Moriah and mount the opposite hill. It went, dusty and firm, between cedars and locusts and wild-cherry trees and thorn bushes and pawpaw. Dust lay thick upon the wayside growth, and high in an intense blue sky buzzards were stilly and elegantly sailing. The Moriah ran clear and cold between willows and sycamores and now and then between pebbly strands and grassy banks rising in terraces—predestined spots for baptizings!

Outside the church they formed the procession. In front walked the Rev. Thomas Meiklejohn and the Rev. William Howard Boykin and the deacons. Then stepped the band of those who had seen salvation and would wash their sins away, and after them important and rejoicing relatives. Then streamed, road wide and to a considerable depth, the remaining members of Moriah Colored Baptist Church and mixed with them children and others, churchgoers, but not yet organically joined. The homely, unpainted gray building, weather-worn frame with a steeple and a bell, so hardly bought with such exertion, the bell so proudly listened to when it rang and rang—the gray, beloved church stood empty on this Sunday morn while the congregation moved in column to the flowing river. A dusty mile and a singing company.

"I got a home in the rock.
    Don't you see, don't you see?
I got a home in the rock.
    Halfway between the heaven and the earth,
I got a home in the rock!"

The Rev. Thomas Meiklejohn was thinking, "Where's Ailsa? Where's my niece? Ise scared for that chile!"

The Rev. William Howard Boykin, marching so tall and strong and shining and earnest, was thinking. "There's one isn't here. If she goes back into the world, Lord, can I help it? I've like her powerful, I surely has! But she ain't for me, Lord, if she ain't for you!"

The road ran down to the river and the shore rose most conveniently in low tiers to either hand, and there were few trees.

> ". . .Deep river.
> My home is over Jordan.
>   Deep river, Lord!
> I want to cross over into camp ground,
> Lord, I want to cross over into camp ground!"

The column broke. The van, ministers and deacons and candidates and their families, kept upon the road, right down to the ford, but the large remainder turned right and left to the warm turf of the water side and the gray bowlders whence they could see so well, see the absorbing spectacle.

And yet no Ailsa Craigie.

Adelaide Lily was saying: "Lawd, I'll work for you. I'll work hard in the church. They say Curfew Church sholy need workers. Lord, I'll work and I'll love him forever and take care of him----"

A number who had not marched from the church, and white folk, too, were already gathered upon the river bank.

> "Over Jordan,
>   Yaas, my Lord!
> Over Jordan,
>   Yaas, my Lord!
> The angels know what's in the heart,
>   Yaas, my Lord!
> The angels know and they takes a part,
>   Yaas, my Lord.
> Over Jordan!"

"Ain't Ailsa here at all—ain't she here at the last minute?"

A young girl came along the water edge and spoke to Brother Meiklejohn. "Ailsa, she ain't coming, sir. She done sent me to tell you. She say she beg yo' pardon, Brother Meiklejohn. She say she know now she didn't get religion nohow. She gone to the big woods. She say it ain't any use sending for her. She say tell her daddy she won't be back befo' night."

The families of the candidates clustered at one side of the road, on a smooth green strip sloping gently to the water. They had with them blanket shawls and ancient capes and coats with which to wrap the drenched bodies coming up from the Moriah. The candidates stood in front, upon the road where it dipped into the water. They numbered fourteen, a band of men and women with several children over ten. The unearthly, the set aside, the sacred, misted them about; they were, to at least some of the beholders, in the shadow of a wing and in the curve of an arm.

Thomas Meiklejohn was elderly and heavy, and Doctor Michie had told him that his baptizing days were over; he mustn't strain his heart. So it was William Howard Boykin who entered the river and made his way slowly over the stony bed of the ford. The water did not run deeply enough just here; he turned a little and came to where it lapped above his waist. Here he stopped and stood, a big man with a lifted and enthusiastic spirit. And all the time they were singing upon the shore. The two appointed deacons with Abner Shaw followed him into the water. The singing ceased. He put one hand between Abner's shoulders and the other below his throat. "In the name of the Father and of the Son and of the Holy Ghost, I baptize you----" and laid him with solemnity under the Moriah, then lifted him from the grave of water and wiped his face and said, "Bless you, my brother!" and between the deacons Abner returned to the bank, shouting, and they all sang beside the Moriah, all the colored folk and the white folk joining in. After Abner, King Walker was baptized, and then a child, and then a woman, and then a brother and sister.

> "*Swing low, sweet chariot,*
>   *Coming for to carry me home!*
>   *I look over Jordan and what did I see,*
>   *Coming for to carry me home?*"

Adelaide Lily stepped into the green water. Adelaide Lily's heart was saying, "I loves you, sweet Jesus, I does love you, and I will be a good woman. I vows it, I makes a vow!"

"A band of angels coming after me,
    Coming for to carry me home.
  Oh, swing low, sweet chariot,
    Coming for to carry me home!"

Out of the big woods rose a bare hill, cropped over, all short and tawny turf and blue thistle and sunken bowlder. Ailsa Craigie came up here, to the top that was bare of tree or bush, and sat down upon a great stone raised above the turf. The hilltop gave a view of the woods and the valley, the little town and the Moriah and the country around. She could see the old ford and the dots that were people.

"O God, I'm like them and I'm not like them, and they think I'm wicked. . . . Maybe I was wicked there in the church, trying to deceive myself and all of them and William Boykin, because I wanted him and hated Adelaide Lily. . .because I thought I wanted him and thought I hated Adelaide Lily. . .
    "But what I want—what I do want, O God—is to know You. What I am and what You are. . ."
    She sat very still, on the hilltop, up against the blue. Over by the Moriah Ransom Moore came up out of the water:

"Deep river. . .
My home is over Jordan.
    Deep river, Lord.
I want to cross over into camp ground,
Lord, I want to cross over into camp ground!"

Elephants Through the Country

His perceptions were, in order: That it concerned him, that it concerned him vitally, that it involved his end of life which might, or might not, this time be avoided. These perceptions were so removed, they must cross so much of terrain to his bodily brain, that they succeeded only in alarming the latter and putting it on the alert with a painful and inexplicable interest. His brow wrinkled; his heart thumped, seemed to lose a beat, then resumed its march but more slowly and heavily; the unfolded county newspaper shook a little in his hands.

FORREST BROTHERS CIRCUS
THE OLDEST AND GREATEST
FIRST TIME OF SHOWING IN MOUNTAIN COUNTY
LOCKERBY THE TENTH OF AUGUST
THREE RINGS
ELEPHANTS. LIONS. TIGERS. LEOPARDS. ELEPHANTS
SHIVA THE BIG ELEPHANT
TREMENDOUS HORSEBACK RIDING. TRAPEZE THRILLERS
CLOWNS. TRAINED DOGS. KNIFE THROWERS. ACROBATS
ONE HUNDRED FIRST CLASS FEATURES
COME TO LOCKERBY AND BRING THE WOMEN-FOLK
AND CHILDREN
LOCKERBY AUGUST TENTH

Everybody who could get there would go to Lockerby that was twenty-five miles from Last Creek and Last Mountain. He could get there. He had a horse and wagon and he had a Ford, and it was likely enough that his mother and his sister would wish to go. Sometimes he went to Lockerby; once or twice, maybe, a year, when he had business. It was the only actual town and the county seat, and the real stores and the lawyers were there. A Show could only come there, nowhere else in Mountain County. He remembered Shows there. He had been just as eager to go as the other boys—or almost as eager. He

didn't think. . . . He could remember. . . . After about seven-
teen, he thought, he had kind of lost his taste for them, and for
crowds, and towns anyway. It had stayed lost. . . .

COME TO LOCKERBY AUGUST TENTH

No, he wasn't going to Lockerby, August tenth.

His sister came to the door behind him and stood there
looking out. "What does the Herald say this week, Norman?"

"It says there's going to be good weather—only it don't
know. Chickens air twenty-five cents apiece."

"There's thirty ready, and I've got twelve dozen eggs.
When you going to Little Town? Ma wants you to take her hook
rugs to Mr. Warner's."

"I aimed to go Friday."

Both returned to silence, she in the doorway, leaning against
the jamb, looking out upon Last Mountain and Last Creek and
the smoke tree and the tiger lilies in the door yard, and the
ancient apple trees and the walnut tree; his long gangling figure
in butternut jeans seated on the porch steps under the gourd
vine, the Lockerby Herald open in his hands. But presently she
stepped across the porch and stood behind him, looking down
upon the paper.

FORREST BROTHERS CIRCUS
THE OLDEST AND GREATEST
FIRST TIME OF SHOWING IN MOUNTAIN COUNTY
LOCKERBY THE TENTH OF AUGUST

"There's going to be a Show! Let's go, Norman!"

"You can if you want to. You and Ma. You can have the
Ford. Charley will go with you."

"Why don't you go? I wouldn't be such a hermit as you
for worlds! That's what Mr. Warner called you, but it's just a
fine name for it! I call it plain lazy—or feared!"

"Feared! Feared of what?"

"Don't ask me! I know you'll fight when somebody's
forced it on you for I've seen you do it. And you ain't scared
of the dark or of speaking your mind in meeting, or of a gun
and hunting. And you can break a colt. And you ain't feared of
a kind of patient figuring a thing out, and I couldn't exactly say
you were feared of work. Not of moderate work. No, I don't

suppose you air afeared. But you certainly air a hermit!"

"I never could see the use of straying away from home where you've got your walls and your fire. It's *better* to stay at home except now and then, to see how things air going on."

"Well, *I'd* not live all my life between here and Little Town and back again. *I'd* go to Lockerby every month, and *I'd* go to the City on the train for the State Fair. I ain't you, thank the Lord! Neither is Ma."

"I never did know how I got into this family," said Norman.

There were many things he did not know—he did not know—he did not know. That afternoon he went down to the mill. The mill, a small one, belonged to his mother. She had leased it, when his father died, to Jerry Wilson, and it stayed leased. He, Norman Manners, though he was forty-two, had never wanted to take it over. . . . The lease paid them enough, with chickens and eggs and small fruits, to live upon. Miranda had never married, he had never married. At the mill Jerry and Charley and old Bob Watts were reading the Herald. "Going to be a Show at Lockerby August tenth, Norman. Ain't you going?"

"No. Charley, I thought I'd get you to take Ma and Miranda. You can have the Ford."

"All right, I will. But why don't you go yourself? You are getting to be the solitariest cuss!"

"It don't suit me to go. That's all. A man's got a right to his ways."

"Nobody on Last Mountain ever disputed that! That's why we like it," said old Bob Watts. "I've always said and maintained that you've a right to look and go about as though you'd kind of taken refuge here, but wasn't quite certain how good the hiding was! Of course we know that isn't the case, because you were born and grew up right here, and you've always been straight as this stick, though curious."

" 'Hiding'!" said Norman. "Of all the ridiculous words!"

That evening, after supper, when the two women had read and vividly discussed every item in the Herald, he gathered the paper to himself and carried it with him when he went to bed. He slept in the small, sloping-roofed room that had been his when he was a boy. The Manners weren't changing folk. There was the narrow bed, and a table and a bureau and a washstand and a chair. When he set the lamp upon the table the shadows sprang and stood and leaned. He lifted the window sash and propped it with the stick.   Now you heard Last Creek and the endless murmur of the climbing woods, and insect life in the dry, warm summer.   Moths began to fly into the lamp.   He shut the window and undressed.   The Lockerby Herald lay open upon the table.

FORREST BROTHERS CIRCUS
THE OLDEST AND GREATEST
FIRST TIME OF SHOWING IN MOUNTAIN COUNTY
LOCKERBY THE TENTH OF AUGUST
THREE RINGS
ELEPHANTS. LIONS. TIGERS. LEOPARDS. ELEPHANTS
SHIVA THE BIG ELEPHANT
TREMENDOUS HORSEBACK RIDING. TRAPEZE THRILLERS
CLOWNS. TRAINED DOGS. KNIVE THROWERS. ACROBATS
ONE HUNDRED FIRST CLASS FEATURES
COME TO LOCKERBY AND BRING THE WOMEN-FOLK AND
CHILDREN
LOCKERBY AUGUST THE TENTH

Standing with his hands upon the table he read it over again and with the same wrinkled brow and interest that hurt.   The name of what he felt was anxiety, fear of bodily harm and death. But why he should feel that, he could not tell, nor what threatened him, nor what he could or should do about it.   The one thing that rose out of a sense of mist about him, or rather of a cold and wide void, was that he wasn't going to Lockerby.   So long as he didn't do that—He put out the light, opened the window again, and got into bed.

The next morning, as he dressed, his attention quite suddenly focused upon the word "elephants."

At breakfast, as he drank his scalding coffee, the women were again upon the price of chickens and the bundle of hook rugs.   "Ma," he said, as she stood beside him, helping him to batter bread, "you never got a scare, did you, before I was born, from elephants?"

"My land, Norman!"   She put down the dish and moved back from him a step or two.   "Well, of all and of all!   No!   I didn't have a scare of any kind.   I ain't one of your scary ones." She stopped speaking, but stood looking at him still without moving to take up the dish.   "For the Lord's sake!   What ever put such a question into your head?"

"I don't know."

"I believe you! What's the matter with you?"

"Nothing's the matter with me. How many hook rugs have you got?"—though he knew how many she had.

On the road to Little Town with Whitefoot in the light wagon he thought for some time that he had escaped from that inexplicable, towering shadow and world of deep care. "I've got nothing against elephants, and elephants have nothing against me!" It was a bright high summer day, with stirring air and shimmering leaves. He felt idle and happy, and this lasted to the top of Middle Ridge.

From Middle Ridge, to either hand, spread a panorama of forest and mountain, continuous forest, and mountains in chains or broken into solitary and imposing masses. He checked Whitefoot; he always did so, just here. Below him, at no distance, lay Little Town, a mere hamlet, and small up-and-down farms and mountain clearings. Ahead rose Eagle Mountain and Hawk Mountain. Catamount River, a sunken streak of silver, divided the two. . . . There was the new bridge and the new county road. He had voted against that; roads enough already. . . . Scattered farms and solitary houses, or two or three in a group, but very scattered; so sparsely settled, so backwoods and frontier-seeming still was Mountain County, that had no railroads after you left Lockerby until you came to Caerleon in the next county. . . .Before him, beyond forested waves of earth, through a great notch in the mountains, the mind perceived Caerleon that was twenty miles from Last Creek and almost double that from Lockerby. He turned in his seat and looked toward Lockerby, invisible under the climbing sun. All these mountains and Last Mountain. He was looking back now at Last Mountain. It had vast bulk, a long, high mountain. It stood like a wall between him and Lockerby, between Last Creek and the mill and his mother's house and Lockerby. . . .

He perceived that that feeling was back upon him. "What is the matter with me, in God's name? I reckon I'd better stop and see Dr. West."

When the chickens and the eggs had been left at the general store in Little Town he stopped the wagon before the physician's house, climbed out and found the doctor hoeing corn. "Good morning, Norman! What's wrong with *you*?—Come to the well. I'm thirsty."

Each drank out of the dark, old brimming bucket, then sat

down upon the curb. "I was bringing some chickens and eggs and Ma's hook rugs, and I thought I'd just stop. Doctor, what does it mean when a man's plain afeared for his life and all because of nothing at all?"

"What do you mean by 'nothing at all'?"

"I can't get a clear picture of it at all. I first noticed it day before yesterday when I was sitting reading about the Show at Lockerby August the tenth. But I ain't going, so how could it be that? Then yesterday morning I had an awful feeling growing up around the word 'elephants.' But that's just as foolish! The Show's got elephants, but it's just at Lockerby one day and I ain't going."

"Let me see your tongue.—Now your wrist.—Now I'm going to listen to your heart and then I'll ask you some questions. . . . I'll give you a fair bill of health. Not that you ever were, Norman, a monster of strength!"

"No, I know that, doctor."

"It's your mind just now. Some notion or other came drifting through and you let it get caught on some snag or other that's itself in its turn just a hardened notion, and now there they both are interfering with the natural quick run of things, hooking other notions to them and setting up a kind of dam and swirl and backwater. . . . Best way to break it up is to keep active and think of other things. There isn't any *reality* in it, you know. If I were you, I'd go to that Show at Lockerby."

"No!"

The country doctor looked at him with interest. "Well, it wasn't a death warrant I was offering you! If you've got that much energy I'd certainly turn it to some account! I'd go and face my notion down. . . . Well, goodbye, Norman."

The principal family in this part of the county had an old brick house a mile from Little Town. Here he left the hook rugs. "Mrs. Warner, I'd like to speak to Mr. Warner." Mr. Warner was a bookworm and was found among his books. "Good morning, Norman!"—"Morning, Mr. Warner."—"What can I do for you?"—"I thought maybe, sir, you had a book about elephants you'd be willing to lend me for a while?" There lay the Herald on a chair in the window. "Why yes, Norman, I'll be glad to. Going to the Show at Lockerby?"

"No, I'm not. But I've got a notion I'd like to know more'n I do about some things."

"That's always a laudable notion," said Mr. Warner, and

stood upon a box to take down a big book and a little book.

Re-crossing Middle Ridge he reached the top not far from sunset, which meant that he would be home at dark. Again Whitefoot stood still. The big view rolled and spread. Sitting with the reins loosed in his hands with his head sunken between his shoulders, he regarded in the afternoon Last Mountain and Lockerby that it hid, as in the morning he had faced Eagle and Hawk Mountains and Caerleon. Last Mountain—there was a big one!

FORREST BROTHERS CIRCUS

The words formed for him, gigantic, in the pale blue heavens and the gulf of air. Each letter stood lofty, out there and in himself.

FORREST BROTHERS CIRCUS
THE OLDEST AND GREATEST
FIRST TIME OF SHOWING IN MOUNTAIN COUNTY
LOCKERBY THE TENTH OF AUGUST
THREE RINGS
ELEPHANTS. LIONS. TIGERS. LEOPARDS. ELEPHANTS
SHIVA THE BIG ELEPHANT

The line that he had reached rushed at him with the force of a bullet, passed through him, was gone and yet stayed.

SHIVA THE BIG ELEPHANT

"That's it," he said, "that's it," but a moment later did not know why he had been able to say, "That's it."

It was full dark when he got home. After supper and all the women's questions he mounted heavily to his room, lighted the lamp and when the moths began to fly against it shut the window. He undressed, and in his long, country nightshirt sat beside the table and read in Mr. Warner's books. Elephants. There was a deal about them. They seemed to have quite a history. . .old countries. . .hot old countries, cities and towers, swarming men. . . .

SHIVA THE BIG ELEPHANT
LOCKERBY THE TENTH OF AUGUST

When he went to bed at last it was not to sleep. *Lockerby—Lockerby—Lockerby. The tenth will come and the tenth will go. It will go and the show will go. The show will go on the train from Lockerby to Wrightsville. There's a show train. It has to have a railroad track. The show will go on and Old Danger will pass.*

LOCKERBY THE TENTH OF AUGUST
SHIVA THE BIG ELEPHANT

The moon looked in—the moon looked in between the branches and showed his hiding-place. . . .

Four or five days passed. Forrest Brothers must cast their net over the whole of Mountain County. Pictures of the Hundred First Class Features appeared not only at Lockerby, plastered over convenient and purchasable walls, but at Little Town and Cross Roads and elsewhere. Barbaric and gorgeous pictures. The remote neighbourhoods, the folded away in creases of great mountains, the much out of hearing of the shriek of any locomotive, the served by narrow and faint roads, yet stared at those pictures.

COME TO LOCKERBY THE TENTH OF AUGUST

"Air ye going, Norman Manners?"
"No!"
"I'd like mighty well to see that elephant!"
"Would you? Well, I—"
They stood and stared.

SHIVA THE BIG ELEPHANT

Norman jogged on past the barn adorned; then, having looked back to make sure that Dan Ellis had taken his own road and was hidden by the oak scrub, turned Whitefoot and came back to the apparition.

SHIVA THE BIG ELEPHANT

He talked to himself with dry lips. "They've pictured you in a spirited way. But you air just paper and colours. You can't do anything. You air in a Show, and the Show's on a railroad and has got to stick to it. You air a big slave in a Show. And the Show's going to be in Lockerby just one day and I ain't going there. I don't even have to bother about making certain nobody's going to pick me up and *take* me there. I *know* I'm not going. Then why can't I rest?"

A small boy advanced to the barn. "O my stars!" He stood absorbed, his legs wide, his touzled head flung back. Norman said, "Air you going to Lockerby, Jim Bee?"

"I ain't got the money."

They continued to look at the flaming picture. "You're so little, you can tuck in the Ford with Ma and Miranda and Charley if you want to. It's a pity," said Norman, "that anybody that wants to go can't go. I'll give you a dollar."

"You've always been good to me, Mr. Manners!" said Jim Bee. "And I thanks ye kindly! I'll ask Maum, and I'll take the dollar anyway. You know about part of the Show coming over Last Mountain to Caerleon?"

Norman sat quite still upon Whitefoot while his heart made four heavy beats. Then he said thickly. "What you talking about?" As he spoke he dismounted and leaned against the horse's neck. It seemed to him that Cross Roads and the world were falling from beneath his feet. "What you saying? You're fooling me, Jim Bee!"

"It's in this week's Herald. I been to the postoffice. They was reading it."

"Reading what?"

"The Advertisement. It says, Forrest Brothers going to do what's never been done in Mountain County. It's going to show at Caerleon. Not all the Show, it says, but some of it. What they can bring over Last Mountain. It says they can bring elephants." Jim Bee's eyes shone and he wheeled like a top. "They're going to bring elephants through the country. Over Last Mountain, walking along! This one walking along. Over Last Mountain. After the Show's over at Lockerby, they'll travel that night and in the morning they'll come over Last Mountain. He'll come! This one!"

Norman got back to Last Creek. "Has the Herald come?" Yes, it had. He spread it over his knees, sitting hunched on the step under the gourd vine. There it was. Garrett the Editor had something to say about it—a whole editorial. He read that; then opened upon the old advertisement.

FORREST BROTHERS CIRCUS...
LOCKERBY AUGUST THE TENTH

But now below this ran another line.

CAERLEON AUGUST THE TWELFTH

The paper crackled dryly under his hands. His sister came out upon the porch and was excited about the Show. "Ma and I'll see it at Lockerby, and then we'll see the part of it that's going by to Caerleon. My land! Over Last Mountain. They gold-scrolled wagons and they white horses and they men and women dressed like fairies and they elephants!"

The night fell hot. He walked up and down in his room. He opened Mr. Warner's two books, and stood looking down at the print and at wood cuts, then closed them and stood at the window. The moths streamed in, and the sound of Last Creek, and the hoot of an owl. "A week. . . . Then he'll be at Lockerby and then he'll be at Caerleon, and then he'll be gone. But in between Lockerby and Caerleon he'll cross Last Mountain."

Last Mountain showed its bulk against the stars. "Who would have thought it? As Garrett says. . . ."

The next day he told his mother, "Ma, I think I'll go to Old Church, to Tom Manners for a spell. I think I'll go next week and stay to the middle of the month. I think it'll do me good. I ain't well."

"No, you ain't, Norman."

"They say that iron spring of his does folk a power of good. . . . I'm just plain tired of this part of the country and of Last Mountain."

"Yes, I'd go. Change is good for folks, and you ain't never took much of it, Norman."

"I'll go next week."

"You can't go till Miranda and Charley and me are back from Lockerby. I ain't going to leave the house by itself."

It had been in his mind to go the eighth. But of course if he left by dawn of the eleventh that would be time enough. He'd take the old saddle-bags and ride Whitefoot. Old Church and Tom Manners abode at right angles from Last Mountain and the road to Caerleon—a long way at right angles. But even while he thought this he saw that it wasn't enough and that something would happen. Old Church and Tom Manners were flimsy things. . . .

The next day he rode to Little Town, again over Middle Ridge. Mr. Robertson the lawyer had a little white law office in a grove of pine trees. "Hello, Norman Manners! What can I do for you?"

Norman sat down, planting long, slender feet on the bare floor and resting long slender hands upon his bony knees. "Mr. Robertson, I desire to know. Ain't there an injunction or something can be got out to keep Show People to the railroad track? What right have they got to come *through* country, bringing their wagons and their beasts over our roads that weren't made for such? Bringing them through our streams and by our houses. Over Last Mountain and across Last Creek. I say they ain't got any right, and there ought to be a way to stop them!"

Mr. Robertson stared. "Well, you're a curiosity! Suppose, Norman, you get up a mass meeting of indignation! Speeches on the subject from men, women and children, not to mention rag, tag, and bobtail, between Cross Roads and Caerleon! Of course you are voicing general opinion?"

"I don't care if I'm not! It'd be their opinion if they had any idea about things!"

"They say that the crazy cannot detect satire. So I don't suppose you're crazy. But again they're said to be blind to a joke. So it may be that I am crazy."

"Joking!" said Norman. "I am not joking. And as for your being satiric, I reckon it's the ignorant that are satiric."

"Your mind went up then several pegs," said Mr. Robertson. "I recognize and respect the truth that you utter. But all the same I am afraid that you would make yourself unpopular with the course that you suggest. There are, you know, popular impossibilities and unpopular impossibilities. Don't choose the last if you can avoid it."

"Then it ain't possible to enjoin them?"

"No, it ain't. And why in thunder," asked the lawyer, "do you want to? Is entertainment too frequent on Last Mountain and Last Creek? Think of them on the mountain, plastered against the sky, and rejoice, man, rejoice!"

Re-crossing Middle Ridge he checked Whitefoot at the old place.

FORREST BROTHERS CIRCUS
THE OLDEST AND GREATEST

Last Mountain stood before him. "I don't rejoice, but I got to see it!"

He felt compulsion, though he didn't understand that either. "I don't reckon I'm going to Tom Manners. . . ."

In and out of season he began now inwardly to behold that procession diverging from Lockerby through the country to Caerleon. The Herald had more than two or three items about it. The mass of the show was going on the railroad, on its own train, to Wrightsville. It was not reasonable to expect the mass to show in Caerleon, or to cross Mountain County to do so. From Caerleon what did cross would have to rejoin at Wrightsville, where Forrest Brothers meant to rest a bit. They wouldn't for instance bring the lions and tigers over the mountain. The elephants could come afoot: perhaps not all of their elephants, for they had a lot of them. Horses, too—and the men and women who, all spangled, would ride them. Certainly some of the gilded wagons, and a part of the band, and acrobats and trapeze performers and knife throwers and clowns. . . . All of these coming over Last Mountain. . . . The road was in better condition this summer than ever before. . . . It couldn't well have happened before.

ELEPHANTS THROUGH THE COUNTRY

It was Garret whom that sound and picture and earth-shaking tread fascinated. Over Last Mountain, into Last Creek country—Elephants. It pleased Garrett to take a saunter through geological time. It pleased him to paint them returning.

SHIVA THE BIG ELEPHANT

Garrett, apparently, did not think any more of him than of the others. It was just elephants that made the magic for him. He had no personal stake. . . .

In season and out of season, Norman now beheld the show winding through the country. But it was not blind; it had an eye in the face.

August was here, the first week dropping away.

The preacher, Brother Abraham Wills, riding his round, came to supper and to spend the night with the Manners. The women welcomed him gladly; Norman put up his lean old horse and conducted him to the spare room. The preacher splashed the water into the basin. "That feels good! It's hot weather. I missed you, Norman, at Mount Moriah last Sabbath."

"Brother Wills, I'd like to have a word with you after supper."

"Surely!"

Downstairs, Norman being out of hearing, he said to Mrs. Manners. "Norman's got a kind of haunted look. What's the matter with him?"

She spread her hands. "I'm glad you've come, Brother Wills! Maybe you can kind of straighten him out! It seems to Miranda and me that he's going crazy about elephants. He's got books about them. He'll set and tell you about their ways, and how in them hot countries sometimes love grows up between them and men and sometimes hate. It's that Show at Lockerby that's put them in his head!"

"He missed Church last Sabbath," said Brother Wills austerely. "When a man begins to do that—This Show's a godless thing."

Last Creek was known for its good meals. For supper there were fried chicken and potatoes, light biscuit and honey and scalding coffee. Brother Wills did full justice to all. When it was over and the two women were cleaning up he and Norman walked to the barn and then on to the stile. The west hung purple and red; a species of amber light bathed the top of the opposite wall that was Last Mountain. It was warm and still, the katydids and whippoorwills vieing, and Last Creek forever talking.

"What's the matter with you, Norman?"

"I don't know. . .Brother Wills, I feel all the time an awful sense of danger. . .an awful sense of danger, and deeps and deeps behind me, and yet I don't know anything about the one or the other of them. I don't know how I am connected with them if I could remember, but I can't! Something came into my mind, but it ain't enough. . . . Now it wasn't sufficient to be at Lockerby, but he's coming over Last Mountain. . . . I could escape if I knew how. There must be a way to escape. I've tried before but I never could. I thought for a moment that maybe you knew, but I see now you don't. . . . There's Old Danger treading toward me! the same Old Danger!"

"Don't shout! Air you going crazy?"

The two lank mountain men loomed in the dusk. The preacher seized the other and shook him. "Come to yourself, man, come to yourself! That's a sense of sin that's seized you, sudden and terrible! That's your life you're seeing and all your ways of wickedness! Let's kneel right down here and pray!"

Again at the house, the dusk having closed in and a great moon rising, they prayed again, the two men and the two women. Brother Abraham Wills read from the Family Bible, and then he wrestled long and fervently in prayer. *Lead us not into temptation. Deliver us from evil.* At intervals the women said, Amen! Amen! At last they all rose from their knees and returned to their chairs and Miranda, who had a sweet voice, raised a hymn. Then they went to bed; and in the morning Brother Abraham Wills rode on to Gurney's over the shoulder of Last Mountain. His final words to Mrs. Manners and Miranda were, "You get him to come to church Sunday—and I'm not of the mind that I'd encourage him to go to Tom Manners. He's a born scoffer, Tom Manners!"

It left the women unsettled again. "I reckon maybe we'd better not go to Lockerby after all. We'd better stay here and make him stay. I've always heard if you give in to fancies it's the worse thing for them."

Fifty small things arose to keep him from going to Tom Manners. But they weren't needed; he wasn't going anyway. Suddenly he saw that Last Mountain had turned into a magnet and was keeping him by its side.

At the mill, too, the men gloated over the coming show. They had already passed Lockerby in their minds, and were on the road to Caerleon. They were on Last Mountain. . . . His mother and Miranda used to come to the door and look at the bulk in the light and say, "My sakes! to think of the show coming along the top yonder!" They seemed to have been doing it for years. Time seemed as long as that, and yet night and day shifted like the spokes in a fan when you opened and shut it.

He returned to the barn at Cross Roads and looked on the picture there. Yes, that was him, that was the eye in the face.

He saw him now all the time, coming, coming. . . .

"Yet what does it mean to me? I don't have to go up on Last Mountain any more than I have to go to Lockerby. He isn't going to drop in for supper!"

At the mill old Bob Watts said that the whole neighborhood, he reckoned, would find business that day on Last. "I won't," said Norman. "I'll keep the mill for you, so all of you can go."

"That's kind."

"You mean you ain't going even to squat by the roadside and watch them go by, over Last to Caerleon? My Lord! To be just quietly and soberly crossing Last for the five hundredth time, going along lonely on a lonely mountain road, where maybe from time to time you may have seen a wild turkey or a fox or a deer, or even, for something to talk about, a bear, not to speak of snakes and rabbits, just to be riding or walking, thinking, or just going without thinking climbing and climbing that on a hot day or a cold day never seems to end, or going along the long top that shows you the world with a few buzzards or hawks or just maybe an eagle or beginning to drop down and drop down, loose and easy. . .to be just going along, dreaming maybe, and everything just as it was for ever, and there, turning a big rock, coming up the road to you, an elephant. . . . You not knowing anything about it. . . . My Lord, you'd get a shudder up your spine! . . ." So old Bob Watts.

Norman looked at him desolately, then walked away softly over the black earth. Said Jerry, "If he isn't the queerest cuss!"

The tenth of August came wheeling up, seconds, minutes, hours, the total day. His mother and Miranda went to Lockerby with Charley in the Ford. He made them go; he wanted the place to himself. They weren't difficult to compel or persuade. Old Bob Watts stayed at the mill. A long, still solitude of a day, the heart of Mountain County departed for Lockerby.

FORREST BROTHERS CIRCUS. . .

THREE RINGS. . .

ONE HUNDRED FIRST CLASS FEATURES

He spread upon the porch floor the several Heralds and from the step under the gourd vine studied them.

SHIVA THE BIG ELEPHANT

"Nothing else matters," he said.

The gourds and the gourd leaves made strange shadows about and over the spread papers. It was hot and dry, and still, the air a blue haze. He looked up and saw Last Mountain. Something came to him out of the Bible. First and last, he had been taught a good deal out of the Bible. "I see men as trees walking."

In the evening the Ford came back with the three. They had had a full, magnificent day. Everybody was at Lockerby that could get there; they had met friends and kindred whom they had not met for a year. As for the show, the papers and the pictures had not lied. Mountain County had never seen a show like that before. The Three Rings and the Hundred Features were there. Miranda had liked one thing best, her mother another, Charley a third.

"Did you see the elephants?"

They described them, especially the big one. They had forgotten his strange scunner at them and their coming through the country. They were still excited and tired as well, and as soon as supper was over and they could make the house straight they went to bed. They wanted to know if anything had happened in their absence. "No. Nothing you could count as happening," said Norman. "Of course a lot is happening all the time that we take no note of."

His mother paused in her aimless wandering up and down in the room. "Ain't you going tomorrow to Tom Manners? Maybe you'd better—"

"No, I ain't going. It can't get itself done."

"Everybody on Last Creek almost is going to line up on the Caerleon road. Miranda and me thought we'd get the work done early and go with Charley to Covered Bridge. They say they won't be hereabouts before ten o'clock."

"Do what you please, Ma."

"Why don't you come along?"

"If I go I'll go by myself. But I ain't going. I ain't going near the Caerleon road or Last Mountain."

Miranda shut the front door and took up a candle. "Well, all I can say is if I was as interested as you are in elephants I'd go see them!"

When he knew that the women were asleep he took his shoes in his hand and stole down stairs and out of the house. He stepped into starshine and the sound of Last Creek. Stooping he put on his shoes, then crossed the dry grass to the gate and the road that carried you two miles into the Last Mountain road that was the road to Caerleon. "Roads now," he thought. "There's a saying that I've heard Mr. Warner say. 'All roads lead to Rome'—or to the place you've got to go to. All roads lead to the place you've got to reach." His brain felt very clear. "Something happened to me once and has kept on happening. It isn't impossible that it would stop. But I don't know how to make it possible. Maybe it'll happen now or maybe it won't happen, and I don't know which."

The word "placate" formed before him. " 'Placate'—that means to make at peace with you. If I could placate him."

He wandered about through the dry, warm, star-lighted night. His feet knew the old paths. Sometimes he sat down or lay upon the earth. Placate—placate—placate—placate—placate . . . . It formed itself into a deliberate and ponderous tread. . . out of the big tent now, red, and on the road. . . .

When the coldest light was in the east he went back to the house. The others, too, were stirring early. Miranda, coming out upon the porch in the full sunrise, exclaimed, "You've saddled Whitefoot! You're going then up the mountain?"

"I don't know where I am going. I just thought I would ride."

"I guess you will see it," said Miranda. "You won't be able to help it."

"Maybe not."

To himself he said, "She spoke a true word then. I know about a candle and I know about a magnet and I know about a will."

They ate their breakfast and left the table. He put some matters from the store-room into a small bag. "Air you going to be away all day?"

"I may be. Yes, all day."

In himself again he said, "You are telling the truth there. A long day. Yet it is possible. He might be placated. If you knew the secret, and didn't indulge forever in mere fooleries."

Who was talking he hardly knew. He was at a moment similar to that moment two weeks ago when he first unfolded the Herald upon that Advertisement. There was perception, but so removed, so faint, so nerveless and supine in the thick brain . . . . It died again. He drew a long sigh and shook his head and went out and got upon Whitefoot and rode away.

He passed the mill. "Where are you going, Norman? You going away from Last Mountain?"

"No, I don't suppose I am. I'm just riding round and round."

An hour later, having gone aimlessly for a while at a tangent from the mountain, he turned Whitefoot and they retraced their way. At the foot of Last he met Jim Bee. "Where are you going, Jim Bee?"

"I'm going to Top Rock. You kin see them coming, three turns below you."

"It's a long climb up Last. Get up behind me."

"I sure will, and thank ye!"

Jim Bee sat behind him on Whitefoot, and they began to climb Last Mountain. "Folks ain't settling so thick on the mountain side as they are by the Creek. There's a few I hear say they are coming up so's they can get a good look down on the roads as well as when they tramps right by. But most is gathering by Covered Bridge."

No, they were not settling thick, for it was not a populous region. Norman and Jim Bee were not overtaken, nor did they overtake any, but from way up Last, looking back, they made out folk on the road. By now they could view Last Creek that in size was like a small river, and Covered Bridge, and the region people gathering on either side the creek. Norman could see the mill and his mother's house. One by one came into sight Middle Ridge and Mount Moriah Church and Little Town. The sun was well up and strong, a light haze over everything, the day promising heat and drouth. The extent of country seen increased. Whitefoot's hoof struck musically enough the stones in the road. The road had been widened this year and worked. Forrest Brothers must have been apprised of that, else they never could have granted the feasibility of crossing this way to Caerleon. Jim Bee had the talking chiefly to himself, though now and then Norman spoke. Last was a big mountain. The road looped and looped, now through ancient timber, now through second-growth, burned-over tracts and scrub. The view widened. The face of Last became cliffy; on the one side of the road, gray, wild and broken masses running up to the top and the August heaven; on the other, rock still, plunging downward into ravines and rolling forest. Whitefoot plodded on. As the road wound and climbed, it was four good miles from Last Creek to the narrow and long plateau that formed the crest of Last Mountain. "They must be over First Mountain by now," said Jim Bee. "It's a little mountain, ain't it? set by Last Mountain. . . . They say a man's going ahead on horseback to tell everybody so that the roads will be clear and horses and such won't get scared. My fathers! to think of they big things in Mountain County!"

They climbed. "I reckon there's a hundred people down by Covered Bridge. More'n a hundred. And there's some folk on the road below us. And there's Top Rock away up yon."

When they got to Top Rock, that was a vast boulder poised above the road, the latter being visible from it in a great double S, up and down. On the far side of the way occurred a downward plunge of sheer cliff and broken cliff, going a hundred feet down into a deep ravine with sides of oak and pine. From Top Rock on every hand spread Mountain County. They lowered themselves from Whitefoot and took him into the scrub behind the boulder and fastened him there securely. "Horses is sure tarrified at them!" said Jim Bee. "I was most tarrified myself, over yon at Lockerby! That big one—"

They swarmed up the boulder that was as big as a small house and standing on the roof looked down upon the road up Last. The morning was now advanced and the sun grown hot. Below them came toiling up three men afoot. "That's Luke and Rob Corbin and Dave Smith," said Jim Bee. "I reckon there ain't any more but just us now."

The three joined them. "Well, I vow and declare, Norman Manners, after all your saying you wasn't coming!"

"Couldn't resist it, could ye, Norman?"

"Whew, it's hot! You might think it was the tropics!"

They sat, swinging their legs, upon a jut of the boulder.

"This is the place; there ain't any doubt about that!"

At the foot of the mountain, approaching Covered Bridge, so far away that they seemed puppets, marionettes, too small for state or significance, could now be made out those parts of the great show that Forrest Brothers had elected to send through the country to Caerleon. It was no great procession, but it included painted and gilded wagons and in one of them musicians with horns and drums, and there were show horses, and bedecked men and women, acrobats and riders and trapeze specialists and clowns, and there were zebras and several camels and three elephants. "Yon they are! Yon's the elephants!" It drew from out the woods upon the visible road, there by Covered Bridge, so very much below Top Rock. The imagination caught faint, thin cheering.

All passed into Covered Bridge and all emerged upon the hither side, and all drew into the thick wood on the lower slopes of Last and vanished. "They've seen it!" crowed Jim Bee. "But we're going to see it two-three times, and then right by us!"

Dave Smith grumbled. "Thar ain't much of it, and they

weren't so big."

"You jist wait till they come nearer! You just wait till that one's *thar!*"

In twenty minutes they saw it on the Old Cabin slope—just caught glints of it where the road intermittently showed. Then it was gone again and Dave Smith said he was going to sleep, and to call him when it got to the Cold Spring turn. They called him, and he said it was getting larger, wasn't it? and it was a sight now, wasn't it?

Then again it was gone, as though it had gone into the mountain.

"Norman, you got book-learning. Tell us about they things!"

"I haven't got any book-learning. I haven't any learning at all."

"Well, it'll be a good long time before they get here now. Call me, boys, and don't you forget it!"

The boulder reared itself part in sun, part in shadow. Dave Smith and the Corbins sprawled upon the shaded surface. There was a great view, with blue sky, and small clouds gathering and parting. Norman did not sprawl with the others but sat with his long, gangling figure drawn together, the old saddle bag beside him, and his eyes upon the road and upon the drop of cliff and the tree tops far below in the ravine. Down there, though hidden, brawled a stream. He heard it faintly, and it brought to him the night sounds from his window at home, when the lamp was lighted and the moths came to it. Jim Bee was as active as a cricket and did his own exploring. Presently Rob Corbin began to sing in a tuneful and powerful voice,

> "Fire in the mountain!
> Run, boy, run!"

When he had ended that one he tried another Mountain County song, and then another. Dave Smith sat up. "Thar they come! I dreamt it so I know 'tis so!"

"There's the man that rides ahead!"

A man on a brick horse, a man dressed like a cowboy, appeared below the boulder. "Hey, you! Have you horses and are they well tied?"

"Only one. He's fast tied, ain't he, Norman?"

"Yes, he's fast tied."

"Because elephants don't go through the country every day! And this morning the big one has got some bee in his bonnet...."

He rode on, upward to the plateau that was the top of Last Mountain. Behind him stretched empty road, a little unstable to the eye in the August heat. Item by item, this became filled with the show that was going to Caerleon. Item by item, it arrived before and passed Top Rock. Last of all came the elephants, the lesser ones first, and then, the big one.

"Ooooh! Look at the big one!"

Jim Bee was the only one who noticed Norman leave Top Rock. "Where you going?" he cried after him. But Norman only shook his head and with the old saddle-bag scrambled down to the road.... The deliberate and ponderous tread. The deliberate and ponderous tread. Placate—placate—placate—placate....

The elephant tenders shouted to him. "Don't get in the way there!"

But he took brown maple sugar and yellow apples from the saddle-bag, and came out upon the road. The elephant turned a vast head and saw him. Into each of the small eyes leaped a red spark. The showmen shouted. "You fool there! get out of the road! Don't you see he's wicked today?" The Corbins and Dave Smith and Jim Bee shouted from the safety of the boulder, "Come back here, Norman! Come back here!"

But Norman with widened and glazed eyes stepped farther into the road and held out the sweet stuff and the fruit.... But though he had the word he did not have the thing. He did not know how to placate.... The great beast, as though he had expected the incident, lifted his trunk and seizing Norman swung him aloft and out and amid objurgations and shouts of horror tossed him over the cliff a hundred feet into the depth of the ravine.

Buried Silver

Dauphin, under Mr. Backus' eye, dug the great hole in which to bury the Minden silver. He dug it close under the south face of the brick wall inclosing the Minden graveyard. Honeysuckle draped the wall and ran thick and strong over the earth below. Drag the network of it aside and dig the place. Bury the chest, scatter the remaining earth, restore the thick network and neither the Yankees nor any one else—but those in the secret —would ever know. Said Mr. Backus, "There's the locust and there's the cedar, and here's a brick in the wall that's a little whiter than the others."

Dauphin was twenty years old and as strong as a mule. His skin was shining dark, his head a good one, his features well enough. His father, King, had been the Minden coachman for long years, but not so many months ago Death had played coachman for King, since when Dauphin had driven when the horses were driven. That did not often befall; they had to be taken nowadays for farm horses. Star and Needle accepted their fall in the world without outward murmur, but it may be said to have hastened the death of King; not to have caused his death, of course, but to have made him that much less able to struggle. On Sundays, Dauphin and Star and Needle and the big, old, high-swung carriage—as capacious, almost, as the ark—conveyed Old Miss and Young Miss and Miss Mag and Manny, with the present number of refugeeing cousins sheltering at Minden, to church in Auburn—named from the poem—five miles away. Lately Young Miss did not go. Young Miss was looking for a baby in June.

King had taught Dauphin how to drive. He was going, everybody said, to be such another coachman as his father. When the war was over and Richmond never, never, never taken, and General Lee and the rest of the generals and Old Marster and Marse Jermyn had finally—it had been a long time and they had won many battles, but then the others won other battles—had finally won, then Dauphin would have the third-best cabin in the quarter—he and Sally—and all his life he'd be Minden coachman. . .and a prop of the church like his father.

Old Miss had decided on the spot. In the flower garden? Too near the house. Under one of the trees? It's hard to cover traces in a moment. Young Miss—that is, Gay—had thought of under the summerhouse floor. Mr. Backus in consultation considered that that would be a good place.

"They camp," said Old Miss in her deep voice, "they camp all over the place and they tear to pieces, for their fires, fences and sheds and arbors. They might do that to the summerhouse when they would see that the earth had been disturbed." Old Miss was walking to and fro in the chamber—in a stately way, not with agitation. Now she paused by the big window. It showed her always the Minden graveyard, on the lower slope of Hugh Hill, among high trees. "Somewhere by the wall, under the honeysuckle," said Old Miss. "By the graveyard wall, Mr. Backus."

"Dauphin and I will make the excavation, Ma'am," said Mr. Backus. "It's just as well to keep it all quiet."

"I trust every soul on the plantation," said Old Miss. "But in view of the enemy's ability to terrify it's better as you say, Mr. Backus. Miss Gay and I will walk over now and mark the place. Then as soon as it is dark----"

Dauphin's spade rhythmically lifted earth, rhythmically deposited earth in a growing hillock. Mr. Backus sat and chewed tobacco or walked about and looked at the Minden gravestones. Mr. McNulty was the Minden overseer. Mr. Backus was only his assistant. But Mr. McNulty was fighting somewhere in Tennessee. Mr. Backus didn't have the grip on things that had Mr. McNulty. Besides it was Old Miss that really overseered.

Minden had two thousand acres, two hundred negroes. It was deep in the war—much more than halfway through—but no one knew that, though they might guess. The big house, brick with wings and a portico, needed repair. The garden had ceased to be trim, the grass grew long, the box went unpruned. The quarters, on the other side of the house hill, were down at heel with whitewash spared. Barns and stables and out-buildings began to show decrepitude. Fences wanted mending; many fields sprawled uncultivated. The stock was greatly lessened. No farm implements had been purchased for a long time. All things suffered depletion, retarding. . . . Difficulties of agriculture in a land where armies marched and countermarched and your hands became filled with bank notes of no value. Difficulties of more than agriculture. But until now the county in which was set Minden had not been actually, immediately, overrun by the Yankees. It was to be so no longer. They were on their way. Hawke's raid was in motion.

Dauphin dug a fairly wide and deep pit, Mr. Backus giving the measurements. Then he scattered the idle earth far and wide in the tangle of honeysuckle and myrtle, and together he and Mr. Backus dragged the ancient net of interlacing vines across the opening. It was like covering a grave, and now there was no visible grave. "Mrs. Royall has got a headpiece," said Mr. Backus. "All the looters going ain't going to think of this place! It could stay here till kingdom come."

Dauphin agreed. He considered Old Miss to be a wonderful woman—like a Bible woman. He shook his big, healthy, young man's body and together he and the overseer left the graveyard. As he went by the house on his way to the stables Araminta summoned him from the dining-room porch: "You Dauphin! Old Miss say come and help Cassius carry all dis to the chamber." Dauphin washed his hands and brushed earth from his clothes and went to the dining-room. Something in his head went about saying, "Old Miss trust me—Old Miss trust me good and hard—just like she done King."

Cassius, the Minden butler, and Araminta, Old Miss's maid, were collecting Minden silver.

Minden owned the silver given to Old Miss and Old Marster when they were wed, and to Jermyn and Gay when they were wed, with a part of grandparents' and great-grandparents' silver, and all of Great-great Aunt Aurelia's silver, and some silver beyond that that had come from England long, long, long ago. Cassius and Araminta crowded upon big silver salvers and little silver salvers, coffee urns and teapots, sugar and cream bowls and jugs, silver pitchers, silver goblets, silver dishes, spoons and ladles, forks and salt cellars, and what not. Miss Mag entered the dining room—a tall, gaunt maiden lady domiciled since youth at Minden: "Have you everything, Cassius?"

"I lef' out enough just to set the table wif. Minden got to have something on the table, Miss Mag!"

"Let me see. Well. . .that much will divert their suspicion,

maybe. If they take it they'll take it, that's all! You and Old
Miss settle it between you, Cassius. Carry it all, Dauphin,
through the back passage, so that the children won't see. Cassius
and Araminta, Old Miss wants you both." She turned to leave
the room.

Araminta, stepping behind her, stepped faster and came
close: "Mis Mag, are you scared?"

"No," said Miss Mag austerely. "But I find myself impatient with God."

In the chamber—that being the local word for Old Miss and
Old Marster's room—a mahogany chest stood open in the middle
of the floor. Around it stretched the cool, big room, with
mahogany furniture and a vast four-poster bed, blue counter-
pane and white curtains with knotted fringe. The big table
stood cleared, as did Old Marster's desk. The wing chair held
cloth for wrapping, such cloth as could be spared where all
cloth grew more and more precious. One of the refugeeing
cousins enveloped silver candlesticks in an ancient apron. Dauphin set down the salvers, one by one, upon the table. Cassius,
Araminta, Miss Mag and Mrs. Royall, the cousin, wrapped the
pieces and laid them in the chest. Young Miss sat in a window
seat and gazed out upon the hyacinths in bloom. Old Miss
stood looking at the silver. She was tall and stately—Old Miss—
not tall and unstately, like Miss Mag. Full sweeping skirts, full
sleeves, worked-muslin collar showing her strong throat, black
lace upon her head only half hiding the smoothly banded, silver-
ing hair—all about Old Miss aided her stateliness. She stood
looking at the workers and at the Minden silver disappearing
piece by piece from sight, and then she glanced at Gay in the
window seat. Gay's head was down upon her arm, and her eyes
were now for the great trees and all their opening buds. Her
fingers played music upon the window sill. Old Miss stepped in
her stately fashion across the floor and, bending, put an arm
about her daughter-in-law. "I want Jermyn," said Gay. "I
want Jermyn."

"Yes, dear. Yes, dear."

"There is something," pursued Gay, "that sounds so fatal
to me, and I say it over and over: 'The Army of Northern Virginia. The Army of Northern Virginia.'"

"I've determined," said Old Miss, "to hide the jewelry with
the silver. One safe place is better than dividing things."

"Then I'll go get mine," said Gay, and left the window seat

and the chamber. When she returned, in her hands a rosewood-and-mother-of-pearl box, the silver was in its resting place, almost filling the chest. On the table stood a row of small ornamental caskets, and Old Miss and Miss Mag and the other cousin and Araminta were gathered round. "Look, too, Cassius," said Old Miss, "and you, too, Dauphin. "It's all of gold and gems that Minden has."

Even with Gay's added they made no great display. Old Miss's wedding pearls and Gay's wedding pearls. Certain other necklaces of amethysts and topaz, of garnets and jet; and bracelets, plain and heavy, or chased, or of fine, soft, plaited gold with settings of carbuncles, or of cameos. And earrings, long and slender, or hoops of gold with small precious stones. Brooches and finger rings, quite a number, and two gold watches. In Gay's inlaid box, beside her pearls and her amethysts, lay in their own cases two rings whose stones were of quite considerable value—a beautiful emerald, a beautiful ruby.

They put everything into two receptacles—Gay's rosewood-and-mother-of-pearl box and the lacquer cabinet that stood atop the highboy. These went into the chest; the chest stood ready to close; they closed the chest. Old Miss turned from it, stately and authoritative: "If they pass us by—and I pray to God they do!—then, Dauphin, you and Mr. Backus will dig the chest up again, and, Cassius, you'll have your silver back, so don't look as though you'd lost your last friend, and, Gay, you shall have your pretty box and your emerald and your ruby, and the lacquer cabinet will be again on the top of the highboy----"

The refugeeing cousin who was embittered cried, "Why should you be spared, Henrietta? You won't be spared." She struck her hands together. "And I and my children will have to wander again."

Araminta broke out, "Old Miss, is they gwine burn the house?"

"No!" said Old Miss. "No! Go on, all of you, about your business! And remember that right will prevail. Right will prevail though every house in the world lay in ashes!"

That night there shone a young moon. That night when the children—they all belonged to the refugeeing cousins—were in bed, Mr. Backus and Dauphin between them lifted the mahogany chest and bore it out of the house and through the garden and across under the oaks to Minden graveyard. There they buried it under the honeysuckle by the wall and drew the net of vines across all signs, after which they returned and told Old Miss. They were together, Old Miss and Young Miss.

While Old Miss and Mr. Backus spoke together Dauphin, all respectfully, like a good dog, regarded Young Miss. She had wrapped herself in a cloak and sat, a part of the spring night, on the step of the garden porch. A white pillar rose behind her— she leaned her head against it and watched the fireflies and the stars. Dauphin, so to speak, worshiped Young Miss.

Gay turned her head and spoke to him: "Before you dig the silver and my emerald and my ruby up again, Dauphin, what will have happened and where will we all be? I think and I think that God may mean a lot of things that we know nothing about." She had used to talk that way to King, King being the most religious man, black or white, upon the plantation. Now it seemed that she thought she could speak so to Dauphin as well. But Dauphin could not answer out like King. He did not know how. So he only made a murmur in his strong young throat.

Hawke's Raid befell Minden, befell Auburn and all that countryside; the hamlets, the crossroads, the plantations, the little farms, the cabins, the fences and the fields, the mills, the barns, the bridges, and if anything else was in the world then it befell it, too. It befell horses that were corralled and swept away, it befell cattle, sheep, swine and poultry that went into Hawke's commissariat, it befell dogs that were killed defending this place, this thing or this person.

Hawke fifty miles away. Hawke thirty miles away. Hawke fifteen miles. . . . Should they flee, and where should they flee? Better stay by Minden, said Old Miss, better stay by Minden, and Old Miss' word was law.

Hawke ten miles away, Hawke at Auburn. . . . Old Miss called the household together. She and Gay stood side by side in the big parlor. "We shall meet them," said Old Miss in the deep voice, "as gentlefolk and those devoted to the Confederacy should."

From the windows, silent enough, even the children silent, they watched a company of Hawke's ride through Minden gates. . . .

Minden was burned, burned to the ground. They saved nothing material, the women and children who were let to shelter themselves in the overseer's house that was spared. From it they watched home vanish; the barns went, the out-buildings, the stables. Hawke's men were camping, camping, there was singing in the night and shouting. The quarters were not burned, the negroes were told they were as free as the wind, had better indeed go while the traveling was good. A dozen went with the wave when it retired; the rest stayed. But what were they to do now that they stayed? Minden—Minden was no more. . . .

But Cassius and the rest of the house servants and two-thirds of the others said that they were going to do what Old Miss told them to do.

Hawke moved rapidly. Strike and weaken a region. Depart. Hawke and his troops departed, leaving a blackened country-side, which yet would recover, as a whole, that is. Some things were hurt beyond recovery in this world.

Three nights after the burning, in the overseer's house, the grandson of Old Miss and Old Marster, the son of Jermyn and Gay, was born in April who should not have been born till June. He lived, but his mother died—Gay died. They buried her in Minden graveyard that Hawke had not touched.

The refugeeing cousins refugeed still farther, and the very day that Old Miss was left in the overseer's house with Miss Mag and the thirteen-year-old Manny and Araminta and the babe came the tidings of Old Marster's death. Killed in a skirmish, shot through the heart.

Old Miss and Miss Mag and Manny and the baby, with Araminta and Cassius, stayed on in the overseer's house. Hawke's Raid to a little world at war became but a backward flying incident of a war of many incidents. The countryside and Auburn were doing what they could. Kinsfolk and country neighbors whose houses stood begged Old Miss to come to them. But Old Miss would not; she would stay with her own, however little of her own was left. When Jermyn returned he should find his mother there, and the little Jermyn. . .Jermyn the fifth or sixth, was it? Old Miss oversaw the plantation, now at the quarters, now in the fields, now at the acre of ashes and débris that had been the home place. Many of the negroes were gone. What else could they do, she asked, and was not bitter.

Cassius took to his bed, Araminta was a power, David and Anthony became right and left hands, but the one was a little palsied, and the other had rheumatism. King was dead. As for

Dauphin, no one knew where he was. No one had seen him since that black, gigantic day and night. He must be dead, too.

Dauphin was not dead but badly hurt and that in the head. He saw the torch set to Minden.

Dauphin left with the others the big house that was now set in red light. He walked behind the company of women and children. He was walking with the thirteen-year-old Manny. Old Miss had said, "Take care of him, Dauphin!" A soldier who had been in the dining room and found there the decanter with the peach brandy, lurching up said something to Manny offensive and taunting. The boy, who was beside himself, struck out at the man, a huge man, brutally strong. The soldier seized him. "You're just the age for—for—for a beating!" In the moments that all this occupied, in the shadow with red dancing light, for it was now night, there occurred a break between the little forward company and the boy and his captor and Dauphin. Manny would not cry out, he only fought like a young tiger cat. But Dauphin came between. "Don't you tech him, soldier! He's a child!"

But the drunken man had arrived at fury. He lifted his rifle, Dauphin being bent over Manny, who had been flung to the ground, and brought the butt down upon the negro's pate. It was the blow of a giant and Dauphin dropped. By now had risen a racket and a sergeant was on the ground.

"Drunk again! You'll get what's coming to you, Sawney! Let that boy alone! Run, boy, to your ma!"

"He's killed Dauphin!" cried Manny, stamping.

"No, he hasn't," answered the sergeant. "We'll look after Dauphin. See, he's sitting up! He's all right. It takes a lot to hurt his hard head. You run along, bud! Yes, you got to go."

Dauphin was indeed lifting himself from the ground in the red light of Minden. But there lay a huge gash across his head and he was bleeding and seemed entirely confused. "Here you, Jenks!" called the sergeant to a soldier. "You look after this darky!"

Hawke's company departed. Swift come, swift go. The plantation horses, the cattle, went with them. Star and Needle went along. A young negro with a bandaged head, with his senses quite astray, fevered and babbling, went with them.

"Carry him along," said Hawke's captain. "He'll get over his head and I'll take him on as a boy. I need one."

Hawke left that region. The army that he rejoined also swung aside. Presently it was far enough from all these parts.

The summer went by. Autumn appeared, then late autumn with rain and wind and falling leaves, falling leaves and mist and shortened days. The fall of the Confederacy was not six months off. Old Miss walked too far and too long in the cold and the wet; when she came home to the overseer's house, fire and dry clothing and the hot drink that Araminta brought her could not warm her. In the night she waked Miss Mag. "I've got a chill." She shook and shook.

They sent David to Auburn for the doctor. "Pneumonia," he said to Miss Mag. "Well, it'll be happier for her, I fancy----"

In a week the heart failed and Old Miss died.

They buried her beside Old Marster, with Gay lying close at hand. Jermyn, master now of ruined Minden, fought in the trenches at Petersburg. Back in the overseer's house, when all the folk were gone, sat Miss Mag and Manny and Cassius and Araminta, with Gay and Jermyn's babe asleep in the cradle. The fire burned and they sat there and mourned.

The next day Cassius came to Miss Mag. "Miss Mag, did Old Miss eber tell you jes' where dey buried my silver?"

"No! I thought of asking that last night, but I couldn't. Mr. Backus knows. We couldn't use it if we had it up, Cassius. There might be another raid. When Mr. Backus gets free. . .or we could surely find it if we looked hard enough! Cousin Henrietta knew and Gay and Mr. Backus and Dauphin. Manny, she never told you?"

No, Manny had not been told. And Mr. Backus never came back, and they saw and heard no more of Dauphin. Miss Mag and Araminta thought he had run away, going off with Hawke. But Cassius shook his old head and said, "No. He daid." And Manny believed that he was dead. "They took him away and killed him!" That was Manny's passionate conviction. Old Miss, too, had believed that he was dead. Manny kept a monument to Dauphin in his heart. "They'd have killed me if he hadn't been there!"

Somehow or other they got through the winter. In April, the Confederacy fell. In June, Jermyn came home. Father, mother and wife lay in the Minden graveyard. Weeds were springing up where had stood his house. Miss Mag sobbed in his arms. Manny clung to him, then Araminta brought his son

Jermyn, laughing, crowing and springing.

The year went by. A second and a third went by, and so on and on. Jermyn took up his task and did his part well, Manny was growing up, too, to help him. The negroes were free and mostly gone. Minden was not rebuilt. That was not among the things possible in this particular marble of space-time. And the plantation itself did not, could not, recover. There was no money with which to medicine ills. The skies lowered and the wind blew cold for ten years and more. Then Jermyn sold Minden, reserving only the field in which was set the graveyard, took what it brought him, which was not much, paid his debts and with the little enough that was left, went West—he and Miss Mag and Manny and the eleven-year-old Jermyn and Araminta. Cassius had died at eighty.

And all this time no one knew where the Minden silver had been buried.

Jermyn and Manny went away without knowing. At different times they had searched. As a boy it was a favorite occupation of Manny's and he had taught young Jermyn to look on it much in the light of Captain Kidd's treasure. It was very exciting, thought young Jermyn, his treasure hunts with Uncle Manny. But they never thought, and no one ever thought, of lifting the immemorial thick carpet of honeysuckle and myrtle from the earth beneath the graveyard wall.

In the meantime where was Dauphin? Well, for several years he quite forgot his own past. Something had happened to the brain under the rifle butt swung by a drunken giant. The skull recovered, but not the brain. During the remainder of the war Dauphin rested, a healthy and strong and capable enough dispatcher of physical tasks. He was sunny, he was obedient. The captain who had assumed his ownership became fond of him.

The captain lived in a Northern town, far Northern. After two years Dauphin came nearer to himself. He was Dauphin all right, only with a dream and a confusion about all things beyond this pleasant elm-shaded white town and the captain's big old frame house and five or six acres of ground. Star and Needle were long dead, but the captain had two horses and a carriage and Dauphin drove the captain and his wife. After four years he began to romance to a boy of twelve, the captain's son. "Yaas, chile, I cert'ny was alive before!"

Then, when five years had gone by, one night in April, he came fully to himself and ran away. "Fully" means that he clearly saw Minden burning and a giant of a soldier making for Manny with drunken fury. He found that he knew perfectly the way about this town and the goings-on of the railroad. The right train to take was the nine P.M. He boarded it without a ticket but paid his fare to the conductor and sat bolt upright in the day coach through the darkness staring at Minden. With the dawn he was deposited in a big city, this train was going no farther. He asked intelligent questions, found another station and another train and went still farther south to another city, but a city still in the North. Here he must change again. (All this was long ago.) And somewhere in that transition from station to station the door closed in his tired head. He lost Minden, lost Old Miss and Young Miss and Manny and Mr. Backus, he lost Star and Needle, he lost King. . . . He was only Dauphin, Dauphin who must find some place to sleep and eat and must get work.

For ten years a negro named Dauphin lived and worked in this city. He found and kept a job as porter in a hotel. He handled baggage, he met trains, going with the omnibus twice a day. He wore a coat and a cap with a bit of gold braid. He had a big frame and an honest, dark, shining face. Patrons of the hotel grew to look for him as they came out of the station upon the line of shouting hackmen. At first they called him "Dolphin," thinking that must be his name. At last to every one he became "Dolph." He forgot all lives before this life, but thought this a very good life. He married a chambermaid in the hotel. It turned out to be a mistake. After three years she left him for a light-weight yellow waiter in the dining room. When he was thirty-seven, though he did not know his birthday, he and another man were carrying one day a heavy Saratoga trunk. His foot slipped at the top of the marble stair and he had an ugly fall. His hip was broken. The hotel sent him to a hospital.

Dauphin lay there a long while and the hip never thoroughly mended. When at last he left his bed, he was lame and had a crutch; he would always be lame, they said, and walk with a crutch. He began to sell papers at a certain street corner, seated in a recess made by two buildings, his crutch beside him. Time passing, he became a known figure, a darky, rather a picturesque darky, hale and strong but very lame, selling papers and pencils and matches. Years went by.

One of the two buildings was a large store where silver-ware was sold and jewelry was sold. A window displayed silver service, silver baskets, silver candlesticks and candelabra; another showed gems set in rings and earrings and necklaces and brooch-es. Often enough on sunshiny days, Dolph paused before these windows and supported by his crutch surveyed the wealth of the Indies spread there behind glass. He saw purchasers go in and out, he saw clerks take this or that away and put another beauty in its place. Sometimes he saw prices in the window. . . . On the farther side of his basement, down a dark little side street, stood a very small and retiring shop where old silver and such things were bought.

Summer and winter, summer and winter, summer and winter, he sold newspapers, matches and pencils. He was forty-six, though he did not know it. The war was a quarter of a cen-tury past. Spring, summer, autumn, winter, spring. . . . He stood one morning, leaning on his crutch, before the window with its silver show. It was early. The air moved fresh and far. The small wagon of a flower seller passed, bearing pots of hya-cinths.

Minden silver. . .The chamber at Minden, and Old Miss standing by the table and Young Miss seated in the window. . . . Gems on the table. Pearls, amethyst, topaz, ruby, emerald. Somebody said the names—maybe it was Miss Mag. . .Minden silver, and the jewelry of Minden women. Buried under the graveyard wall, beneath all the honeysuckle. . .Mr. Backus. Hawke's Raid. Minden.

With the ease of an oiled hinge the shut door opened, noiselessly and fully, and this time not to close again. Dolph vanished. Here was Dauphin.

This was April. In June a lame negro got off the train at Auburn, for now the railroad ran by Auburn. The conductor helped him and his crutch and his large, old-fashioned carpet-bag to the platform. Dauphin looked around bewildered. He seemed so at sea that a good-natured young darky accosted him: "Who you looking for, uncle?"

"I don' know," said Dauphin. "I don' know who I'm look-ing for. I ain't been here for twenty-five years."

"That's just about the time I's been here," said his helper. "What's your name?"

"Dauphin. Dauphin Royall."

"My name Jack—Jack Field. You used to belong to the Royalls?"

"Yaas."

"They's all gone. There ain't none of them in these parts any longer."

"Is Minden gone?"

"The house was burned in the war and mos' of the land is sold and it's running down. Ain't nobody much to care for it."

"Is the quarters there?"

"The quarters is all broke up, as they is everywhere. Mos' of the cabins is ruined down. But Caesar, he lives in one, and old Aunt Sarinda and her daughter has one."

"Who's the overseer?"

"There ain't any overseer now. Mr. Jeremiah Martin owns a third of the land, and he lives down by the burned mill."

Sarinda's daughter would never see fifty again, so Sarinda herself was quite an old woman. From their cabin door Sarinda and Sarinda's daughter watched a lame man with his crutch come up the locust-shaded lane from Minden road. Behind him a little ragged darky tugged a big carpetbag all over roses. "Howdy, Sarinda!" he said. "Ise Dauphin."

"Dauphin! Gawd-amighty, Dauphin, you's daid!"

"No, I ain't. . . . Is there anybody in King's cabin?"

"King's cabin mos' ruin down."

"Then I gwine build it up. I gwine ask if I kin live there."

The women stared and stared. "Where you been all this time, Dauphin? Where you been?"

"I been asleep and dreaming," said Dauphin. "Ef you'll let me sit down I'll tell you about it."

Mr. Jeremiah Martin said that he could live in King's cabin. Dauphin paid a man to restore the roof and rebuild the chimney and rehang the door and mend the fence and plow and harrow the garden patch. In the meantime he lived with Sarinda, and every day she told him what she knew about Minden.

Old Miss and Old Marster and Young Miss dead and buried in Minden graveyard. Where now was Young Marster, where was Manny, where was Miss Mag? And Young Miss had a baby. Sarinda could tell him nothing of them after they had all left the old overseer's house that now itself was grown ruinous. Dauphin got a lift into Auburn and went to Major Worthington's law office. Major Worthington had an empty sleeve, got at Cold Harbor. Dauphin explained who he was and Major Worthington stared at him. "Well, well, come back to life!"

Yes, the lawyer could tell him. Jermyn Royall was dead; died of fever in the West, a dozen years ago. He had an idea that Mr. Manny Royall also was dead; at any rate nothing had been heard of him for a long time. He remembered Miss Mag; she must surely have passed away; she was an old woman when they went West. But young Jermyn Royall was living, unless he had died since last year, when Major Worthington had seen his name in the papers. He was an artist, across the ocean, in Paris. He had gotten some kind of a prize. Maybe he meant to live and die abroad. Or maybe he'd come back some day to see where he was born and his mother's grave. That was all the Royalls had kept of Minden—the graveyard and an acre or two around it.

The money from the sale of his stand was dwindling. Dauphin cast about for some means of making a little. At last, by process of exclusion, Dauphin arrived at cobbling. Long ago Daddy Jack, the Minden cobbler, had taught him. Again he went into Auburn and bought with almost his last wealth tools for his new work, and the next day he nailed his sign up on a locust:

COBBLER UP THE LANE.
GOOD WORK DONE RIZZONABLY.

While he awaited custom he went one day to Minden graveyard. It was a slow progress, but he and his crutch managed it. The brick wall yet stood, though with here and there a breach. The tall trees waved, the birds were singing, but the waving and the singing did not disturb the unearthly quiet. Dauphin took off his hat and went in. All was overgrown. "I'll clean this place," thought Dauphin. The gravestones were half buried. He came to Old Miss and Old Marster and Young Miss, and they were plain and simple stones that Jermyn and Manny had been able to put up, and honeysuckle ran over them all.

Dauphin hired one of Caesar's sons, a gangling youth of fifteen, and together they rid the graveyard of the weeds and rid the stones of their veil of vines so that the inscriptions might be read. Then one autumn day he came alone and sat beside Old Miss's grave, sat there a long time, and his mind that was clear before seemed to grow clearer. He was back to the time when he was a pickaninny at Minden, and then a boy and then a young man.

When it was time for him to go and he was out of the mended gate, he stood a moment, still looking at pictures. Then he turned and went around the corner of the wall to the south side of the graveyard. The poplar and the locust, and near the top of the wall a brick that some reason of clay or of drying had vaguely whitened. Not conspicuous, only if you happened to be attending to the evenness of color in an old brick vine-draped wall. Dauphin leaned upon his crutch and gazed, then slowly he drew nearer. In a twisted cataract the honeysuckle overgrew the wall and descending flowed out far over the earth into the thick grass. Dauphin, lowering himself to his knees, with hands and arms and crutch parted and pushed aside the mat of leaves and stems.

"Lawd!" he whispered. "I don't believe they ever dug that chist up!"

That night he returned with the spade that Sarinda and he shared, and made certain. The moon shone round and brilliant through the night. The chest, the old, mahogany chest that had been standing forever in the chamber at Minden. It was corded; he and Mr. Backus had tied it thrice around with rope. Dauphin felt it with his fingers. "That knot old sea Jack taught me—it ain't never been untied."

He restored the earth and the matted stems of honeysuckle. The moon shone like silver, the stars in their loopings glittered like jewels. "Dauphin, you's the only person living that knows where that chist is. They's all dead. All but the last Jermyn, and he's across the ocean."

Out upon the doorstep the next morning Dauphin spoke to the sun. "You knows about it and I knows about it. . . . If he didn't go away twel he was ten he'll be coming back to Minden one of these here days sho's you's rising and Ise standing here! Then I'll take him and show him and we'll dig it up together, and Young Miss's son will have the jewels and the silver."

Later in the day, as he sat mending a shoe, something occurred to him. "Dauphin, you ol' fool, you might die any time and then not a living soul would know. He'd never get the silver and the necklaces and the ruby and the emerild."

That night he printed out upon a bit of paper, directions for finding the Minden silver, then copied this upon another piece.

One he folded and put in the Bible the preacher at the crossroads had given him. The other he placed in an envelope procured through Sarinda's daughter, sealed it and printed upon it,

> If Dauphin Royall die before he see him
> this is to be got to the hand of Mr. Jermyn Royall.

A passing wagon took him into Auburn and he watched the lawyer put, without question, the envelope in his safe.

"How are you getting on, Dauphin?" Major Worthington asked. "Can you live by cobbling?"

"I don't live much, Major, and that's a fac'. But I reckon I can manage."

He got back to his cabin, and the apples in the old apple tree were ripe and falling in a high autumn wind. "No, I ain't gwine tell no one twel he comes. Then I gwine tek him and show him and watch him open the chist."

The years began to drop by like the apples from the tree. Sometimes, not often, but sometimes, someone came up the lane with work for him to do. He cobbled shoes for the folk at the crossroads, but altogether it was little. Major Worthington gave him an old suit and now and then sent him a dollar. He and Sarinda's daughter together worked the garden patch and he kept a few chickens. Sometimes he fished in the river that ran by Minden. At Christmas Mrs. Jeremiah Martin sent him a bag of meal and a side of bacon. He didn't starve, and he had wood to burn, but altogether he was far poorer than he had ever been, poorer than when he sold papers and pencils and matches.

Sarinda died. Sarinda's daughter didn't know what to do. Dauphin thought for her and for himself too, and then he went over to her cabin and told her about Marilla. So they couldn't marry and live in one cabin, and after a while Sarinda's daughter got a situation as cook in Auburn, and that cabin stood empty. He did not care for the one other inhabited cabin, Caesar's cabin around the bend of the hill. "That stock's wuthless," thought Dauphin, and "that stock," though it was good-natured enough, saw nothing that it would gain from Dauphin and let him and his cabin be. The spur of the hill came between. Caesar's family had visitors, but these did not always come on to see Dauphin. Sometimes the preacher came, but the preacher was not greatly to his liking either. He sorely missed Sarinda and Sarinda's daughter.

Dauphin arrived at being nearer sixty than fifty. Yet his body except for that heavy lameness was strong. His face was not wrinkled, he was not gray. He missed activity and he saw days when he was savagely lonely. And he got poorer and poorer. Another cobbler set himself up, nearer Auburn and right upon the main road. Moreover a wave of hard times came upon the heels of old hard times. People moved away from, rather than into, this region. Crops failed, purse strings tightened, folk postponed generosity. At last it was only infrequently that Dauphin had work. Often enough he went hungry.

One night—it was wintertime and cold and he had no work— he saw all, suddenly, as he lay in his bed that was getting to be more like a lair than a bed, he saw that shabby, downward plunging side street near his old basement, where a withered merchant, black-eyed and low-voiced, bought old silver and old jewelry. Likewise there spoke a voice in Dauphin, "Somebody told you once that he didn't care where he got the silver and the jewelry. He'd buy from crooks if things were rizzonably safe."

It snowed that day. He sat bent over his fire, without work and with little to eat. The next day, drawing himself painfully through the still falling snow, he had to go borrow from Caesar. It seemed bursting with life, that cabin, and sleek and jolly. Caesar had a good job driving a team, and his sister and his daughters seemed to pick up things. They were kind enough to lame Dauphin, come at last to begging. They gave him a meal and a bit of bacon and invited him to sit and warm himself and talk. But he would get back to his own cabin after thanking them quite humbly. Going home, Minden land rolled before him quiet and frozen. "Daid. It's daid. Ise just staying here watching by a corpse." The trees of the graveyard stood over there unnaturally tall. "Young Miss's son ain't never coming. . .and he's rich anyway, maybe."

When he got home the fire was almost dead. Raking the embers together he sat bowed above them. He had a good headpiece and he had to work it out correctly. "Just the jewelry. I

couldn't carry the other. Maybe two-three the smaller pieces.
Who gwine open old negro's carpetbag? No one gwine open it.
The night train. I get on the night train at the flag station.
This time tomorrow Ise up Norf. I gets back to my city. It's
my city mos' as much as this is. I was happy there. I knows
the ways of it lak my hand. They take me in at my old base-
ment. The next day I goes feel my way with that old man. . .
Sell one piece and then another and then another. Gawd knows
how much I'd get! Dauphin wouldn't have to sell papers.
Though he couldn't be idle neither! He'd sell them for fun, with
a bang-up stand! And everybody saying, 'Good morning, Dolph.
Glad to see you back!' and the traffic going by."

He threw a pine knot upon the coals. "I have to have
money to leave these parts with. Well, I borrow that money
from Major Worthington. He give me that much. I send it back
to him, somehow. I tell him I hear from Marilla, and I got to go
see about her. I ask him, and he give me back that paper I give
him to put in the safe. I burn it and I burn that piece in the
book yonder."

The glow from the pine knot filled the cabin. He was excited and he got to his feet and with his crutch limped about
the place. Out-of-doors the snow had ceased. The moon shone;
it was warmer. Dauphin knew weather. "Gwine turn into a
thaw. All this white stuff'll be off presently. Night after tomorrow night I kin do it and cover it up all right."

He turned from the door, the pine knot still lighting the
cabin. "Old Miss, you knows how it is. . .Young Miss----"

She was standing there by the tall white pillar, with a cloak
wrapped about her. Young Miss. She had a rosewood-and-
mother-of-pearl box and she took from it necklaces of amethyst
and necklaces of topaz and of pearl, and a ring set with a ruby
and a ring set with an emerald, and brooches and earrings and
bracelets. They ran through her fingers and flowed upon the
cabin floor. She had dark eyes, had Young Miss, beautiful, com-
pelling dark eyes. Dauphin's eyes met her eyes. "No, I ain't,
Young Miss," he whispered. "No, I ain't. Dauphin gwine keep
them right there for you and your baby."

The vision was gone. He turned again to the door and set it
open. Beyond the white ground and the naked apple tree and
the winter moon in the winter sky he saw Minden, he saw Minden in bloom. "And for Minden and for Old Miss and Old

Marster and for King and for Dauphin—for Dauphin and for
Sally—for them all. . . . I keep them. Ise Minden."

"No," said the lawyer. "There are very few of the old lot
living around here now. But Minden Quarter keeps its name
and two or three cabins are standing. Caesar and his family have
one and Dauphin has one."

"Dauphin!"

"A lame negro, almost a pauper," said the lawyer. "He has
a story, too---"

Mr. Manny Royall left his chair and walked to the window,
then turned. "Do you mean to say"—and his voice was vibrating
—"do you mean to say that Dauphin has come back?"

The much younger man, his companion, Mr. Jermyn Royall,
the artist, also displayed excitement. "Then he wasn't killed by
Hawke's men after he saved you from Goliath, Uncle Manny!
And, by George, maybe he knows where they buried the silver!"

The apple boughs above King's cabin sent down a rosy drift
of petals. The bees kept a-humming like a turning wheel. Dauphin had that day a shoe to mend. He sat in the sunshine, on
the gray bench, mending it. In at the gate, by the thousand-
leaved rose, came two men—gentlemen, like Minden men. Dauphin sat turned to stone. One of them paused; the other—that
was Manny—came on. He was crying. He had his hands out.
"Dauphin, you old sinner!"

A thrush was singing, oh, a thrush was singing so sweetly.
On the hillside, brush was burning and the scented smoke came
across in curls. "Of course I'm not dead!" said Manny. "But I've
been in Mexico. And Jermyn here has been years and years
learning how to paint a house! But he and I made a pact to
come back to Minden just as soon as we had money enough. . . .
Yes, Major Worthington told us all about you. . . . And we've
got money now, you old savior of my life or pretty near my life!
And Jermyn's marrying some lady who knows, too, how to paint
a house, and we're going to buy this land back and rebuild Minden."

The honeysuckle and the myrtle overran the brick wall of
the graveyard and the graves too, and the gravestones. Manny
and Jermyn had been here. First they had stood where Minden
house had stood, and then they had gone to the graveyard, and
then to the quarters. But now they went there again with Dauphin. The birds sang, the birds sang in the trees that grew so tall.

The poplar had young shining leaves, the locust was swinging clusters of fragrance. "The white brick!" cried Manny. "Underneath the white brick! Why, I have looked at it a thousand times---"

The Church Festival

Each spring the Presbyterian ladies had a festival, and likewise the Episcopal ladies and likewise the Baptist ladies. Greenway being only a village and the surrounding country no more populous than other surrounding countries, it meant a strain alike upon the preparatory and the purchasing powers, even though in this case these powers became religious and, therefore, should stand strain. Old Mr. Aldwick regularly suggested that the three churches pool their festivals and divide the profits. But who ever heard of such a thing? It is necessary in this life to stand out a little, it is necessary to have distinction! Immemorially so! And if there weren't something to work for and be interested in, and to sacrifice for over and above personal necessity—well, the world would be in a bad way!

Lydia and Fran and Norwood were awfully glad that the ladies didn't do any such foolish thing. Three festivals were *much* better than one festival. Three festivals were one festival just delightfully happening three times, with each time a different variety of wonderful experience in a pristine, marvellous world! For Lydia, the world was ten-and-a-half years old, for Fran nine, and for Norwood eleven. Worlds at these ages can stand three festivals all in the month of May. It had to be May because of the strawberries. Churches, too, the country over, seemed to have a predilection for May, or at least springtime, though naturally festivals were held in other seasons, money always being needed. The Presbyterian ladies, just now, wanted it for India.

> From Greenland's icy mountains,
> From India's coral strand. . .

Lydia said the words over and over in a kind of intoxication. Coral strand. Coral strand. "From India's coral strand" . . . The coral strings with gold clasps that Mrs. Duncan used for her baby's sleeves—dear, little short, puffy, nainsook sleeves fastened with coral strands. Little bits of rosy coral, three and four strings together.

> From Greenland's icy mountains,
> From India's coral strand. . .

Lydia knew the meaning of "strand" for Miss Sally had told her. Miss Sally taught her in Sunday School. Moreover, she had read a book about India. Elephants—terrible idols big as mountains—warm all the time—coral strands with waves of the sea chasing one another up them, waves like those that swallowed Pharaoh. . .when they weren't little, darling waves.—Idols and heathen, heathen and idols.—Palm trees. I wish I might see palm trees.—Spice. . .all-spice, nutmeg, cinnamon and cloves.

The Presbyterian church stood on the Presbyterian Hill. Oaks grew about it, just now with the divinest, fresh, young leaves. The grass was blue grass and violets mixed themselves with it. There was room, being warm May, for tables under the trees. Likewise for them in the Sunday School room if it set in to rain. But it wasn't going to rain. No, not it! This spring the Presbyterian ladies found themselves especially ambitious, for India's needs were great. Moreover, there were strangers in town, important persons staying at the Harper House, big men come to look things over in the interest of a Railroad. Railroad—Railroad at last through this region! After years of agitation. Such agitation as Greenway and Walnut Hill and Stebbins could make . . . . The first train roars in, roars through! We might hang the locomotive with roses. Produce to market, cattle and horses to market. People getting off and strolling about Greenway and saying "We'll stay here." Silver dollars and a thin golden stream and greenbacks fluttering around. The capital only five hours away, the capital and its joys. The world and Greenway in touch. . . The guests at the Harper House—and they had their wives and they had their daughters—would certainly come. They had been invited and had accepted. But not in the afternoon— driving then to River Point. Both afternoon and evening then. Not that they had not done that, too, before, the Presbyterian ladies—India's needs running perpetual and great. Tables under the oaks with Japanese lanterns, and in the Sunday School room as well. If it rained, all in the Sunday School room. But surely it wasn't in God's interest to let it rain. Several pointed this out to Him. "O Lord, the heathen—. We need a good sum for the heathen."

Lydia and Fran were going to be flower sellers. They always were, or at least they had been as far back as they could remember, for three years anyhow! Lydia's dress was a smoky blue dimity with a small pink flower whose species she could never decide. Maybe it was a rosebud, but then certainly not! Maybe it was a clove pink, but no, there were reasons against that. Maybe it was larkspur—maybe it was wake-robin. All of them or none of them. "I believe," thought Lydia, "it is a fairy flower," and at once she was off with Thomas the Rhymer.

> "O no, O no, Thomas!" she said,
>   "That name does not belang to me;
> I'm but the Queen o' fair Elfland,
>   That am hither come to visit thee."

Fran had a white dress with a million little ruffles and a blue sash. Mother had done the ruffles. Fran was mother's girl. "I don't really care," thought Lydia. "I can look at her being it. I can look at myself, too, in a blue dress with little pink flowers." But that detachment didn't always prevail. Sometimes she was green-eyed jealousy itself in regard to mother and Fran. " 'Mother's baby'! Well, I'm not a baby anyhow!"

When it came to selling flowers to Greenway in May truly "coals to Newcastle" was not in it! But the buying would be for Foreign Missions, not for any novelty in flowers. Small, bright bunches on a silver salver. "Will you buy flowers, Mr. Everard? Will you buy flowers, sir?" Japanese lanterns—Japanese lanterns like colored moons with mountains and reedy seas and flights of birds. Small, bright bunches of flowers on old, thin, silver salvers—Grandmother Curran's salver, Grandmother Bankhead's salver. Fran carried hers *so;* Lydia carried hers *so.* There were other little girls selling flowers, but they all had only lacquer trays. Indeed, Sarah Ann Berry had just a common tin waiter. It was pleasant, thought Lydia, to belong to the aristocracy.

The Episcopal and the Baptist ladies contributed to the list of the salables and the success of the occasion. When it came the turn of their festivals they would expect as much of the Presbyterian ladies. They couldn't imagine, any of them, how the others could think of religious things as they did. Each denomination pitied the other and on occasion shrugged. But they were all Christian, they all had salvation, they were inside! The heathen were outside. The heathen were for all—their problem and their opportunity. "Lord," prayed Peter Barclay, the Presbyterian minister, on his knees in his study, or walking up and down underneath his old cedars. "Lord, let Thy kingdom come! Let Rama, let Buddha, let Mohammed know Thee for Who Thou art, and themselves the shadows! Let their images fall and their temples and mosques crumble! Let the gongs and the muezzin be silent and only Thy church bells ring forever more! And only the true metal, Lord, not the popish bells!"

Fran, before the pantry table with her hands behind her back, gloated upon the three cakes that mother was sending, that Betty was preparing to wrap in white cloths, that Big Sam stood waiting to take. A white fruit cake, a marble cake, a spice cake, and she had watched each one when it was mixed, and Betty had made her a little white fruit cake[1] of her very own, and she had watched mother ice them, bunches of grapes and pretty leaves and stems all made of white icing, and the icing that dropped to the paper beneath mother let you scrape away with your little finger, so that it didn't touch the cake, and eat. There had been enough icing left in the bowl for her own little white fruit cake .... Dolls' tea-parties. On the Little Porch or under the syringa. Blue and white doll-dishes. Princess Alice and Rosabelle and Melinda. Rosabelle's pink tarlatan had a rent in it. Get a needle and thread.

Betty wrapped the cakes and Big Sam took them to the Festival in a basket.... Tables under the oaks and in the Sunday School room and twenty ladies, setting and decorating the tables and India in the background, dark and white-clad and benighted. Mother, too, was going now to the Festival to help, going early. Fran begged to go with her. Mother had a lavender dress and bonnet and a thin black shawl. Mother was so beautiful. Fran wanted to go with her always and everywhere.

Lavender dress and thin black shawl. "He gave me this shawl. James gave it to me. James, where are you? James, do you see me? James, I love you, love you always! ... It is going to be a pretty day after all.

> Be still, sad heart! and cease repining;. . .
> Into each life some rain must fall. . .

Ivy and box. Look, Fran, at the little, fresh ivy sprays!"

The festival would begin at three though no crowd might be looked for before four. The white-covered tables, artistically placed, each under its oak tree, had their tablecloths looped with garlands, and on the white plains what Greenway could do when it came to festivals and the salvation of the world. Strawberries in rosy mountains, and strawberry ice cream, in so many freezers behind the tables, packed in ice, awaiting invasion. And jelly in moulds of melon and pineapple, calves'-foot jelly, wine jelly, amber and red. And cakes galore, Greenway ladies being famous for their cakes. Fruit cake, pound cake, jelly cake, cocoanut cake, angel cake, snowballs, citron cake, marble cake, spice cake, sponge cake, lady fingers, Great-Aunt's cake, Adam and Eve cake. And naturally there were other things beside all these. . . . And the Japanese lanterns were being hung. Mr. Campbell, the Sunday School Superintendent, was seeing to this, directing Joe the sexton, and Abraham, the son of Joe. Hang the big one there, Joe, from that bough. . .*A man dangling from an oak bough—among higher mountains and narrow, rapid streams, long ago, long ago, and the pipes skirling, skirling, skirling, and the pipes skirling. . . .*

Norwood put his tousled red head around a thorn bush. "Hi, Abraham!"

"I sees you but I's occupied."

Norwood deposited with Aunt Viola the **angel** cake he was bringing from home. She took it and gave him a snowball—two, a big one and a little one—for she was extremely fond of Norwood and indeed the whole connection expected him to grow up and go to the Seminary and become a minister. There had always been one, father to son, in his branch of the family. Norwood took the cakes with a wide-mouthed smile and sea-blue eyes drawn almost shut. Fran, importantly pinning ivy leaves upon the white table-cloth, paused in her labors to regard him. "You working for the heathen?" demanded Norwood. "Yes. Don't you want to? They want some more ivy."—"Where do you get it?"—"Off the back of the church."

At the back of the church the sole chatter came from the birds. Norwood sat on the grass and ate his cake, then lay on the grass, upon his back, with his knees up and his rather grimy hands behind his head. "There's a ship—a ship up in the sky. She's a five-master—every bit of sail is out—she's going round the Horn."

Greenway town clock had a musical voice, deep and musi-

cal. *One. . .One, Two. . .One, Two, Three.* "Clocks now—how
wonderful are clocks!" thought Miss Dorinda Clarke. "The
one at Strasbourg with all the Apostles coming out and the cock
crowing. I should so like to travel!"

Miss Dorinda, with several other ladies, had the fancy-
work table under the big oak with a string of Japanese lanterns.
Fran, having given up the ivy, wandered over here and stood
in ecstasy. What of all things she coveted for mother was Miss
Jane Fortescue's wax flowers under glass—or the old, tall, candle
shade with little *décalcomanie* pictures—or the ivory fan that
someone had given. *One, Two, Three,* said afar, like a musical
giant, the town clock. The festival began. Naturally there were
few in the first hour; 'twas always so; but then they began to
stream. When the sun was in the top oak branches and thereafter.

> From Greenland's icy mountains,
>   From India's coral strand,
>   Where Afric's sunny fountains. . .

The Baptist ladies over a wide region had a missionary in
the Congo. Mumbo-Jumbo, cannibals, witch-doctors, hippo-
potami. . . . The Baptist minister, Hugh Price, and the Presbyterian minister, Peter Barclay, ate strawberry ice cream and
white fruit cake in company. There followed always the same
drama. The ministers wished to pay for their refreshments;
the serving ladies would not hear to it. They insisted among
lyric refusals. At last Peter Barclay paid for Hugh Price and
Hugh Price paid for Peter Barclay. The idols of India were a
dollar the nearer destruction.

> Roll down their golden sand!

Hugh Price sat on the church steps and looked things over.
"It isn't intellect—it's the heart. In June the Baptist festival. . . .
That's a pretty girl yonder, but not so pretty as Catherine
Derry. . . . Thank God, I am what I am. I couldn't be a Presby-
terian, I could sooner become a Roman Catholic. If I weren't a
Baptist, I think I would be a Roman Catholic. . . . Jesus of
Nazareth, Jesus of Nazareth, increase my love of my neigh-
bor! . . . In Africa today, in Africa today. Heat and a great yel-
low river, moving like a serpent, moving like a cat. The huts

of that village under palm trees and breadfruit, and the little mission church with palm thatch and a bell, the bell they brought up the river. . . . And my brother, my brother John, giving his life there, giving his health, giving his youth, giving his life. . . . John, can't you hear me, can't you sit here beside me, out of that torrid hell? . . . 'Greater love hath no man. . . .' "

Joe the sexton and his son Abraham and Big Sam fore-gathered in the clump of ailanthus, thorn and pawpaw where stood in row the ice cream freezers. Joe was highly venerable, with gray hair, a straight spine and a powerful frame. Joe Harris. . . . Joe Harris who had belonged to the old General. . . . Joe who had dug so many graves in the neighboring graveyard. "They going have a good day, iss, they is! Folk at the Harper House going buy out all that's left when the lanterns is lit."— "What you gwine do when the Railroad comes? Gwine ride on it, Mr. Harris?"—"Iss, I is. I ride on a train twicet. I ride on a ship and on a canal boat and on a street car and on a stagecoach and on a train, and sometime I gwine ride in the air."—"When the Lawd come, you mean, Mr. Harris?"—"The Lawd comes all the time. I asks you, ain't life and ain't death coming all the time? The Lawd stands between. He lift he right hand and it's life. He drap he left hand and it's death. But I meant a train or a ship or a stage coach that goes in the air. I dreamed it oncet—and I was on it—and I know it's coming. Jest like dishyer Railroad that we thought never was coming by Greenway." Abraham his son was thinking—moonlight on the gum tree, and that still excrescence upon the limb is an opossum. Three hounds, and they talk to him, and they'll bring him down by and by.

One, Two, Three, Four, Five!!! cried the town clock and the festival spread its skirts and wore its crown. "Won't you have a bouquet, sir?—Won't you have a bouquet, ma'am?" The bouquets were small, they must be small or they wouldn't be bought, and each had a rose geranium leaf or a sprig of lemon verbena. Silver dimes tinkling on a silver salver. In India pigeon-blood rubies and great, deep emeralds. In India great gongs beating, and burning-ghats, and many-armed idols.

All Greenway was coming to the festival, now and later; most of Walnut Hill, most of Stebbins. All of the pleasant country houses round about were coming. The aristocracy were coming, and the commonalty down to a certain point. They were here—all the hill was buzzing—a wonderful hive making wonder-

ful honey for a wonderful Queen named Foreign Missions. The
flower sellers reaped dimes, for people were in a buying mood.
(The Railroad was certainly coming.) The big men at the Harper
House were coming (in the evening) to the festival and their women-folk with them. They had money, a million apiece no
doubt. A sense of money was gathering and spreading—a subtle
aroma—not geranium nor citronella but powerful.

The ice cream was holding out, the cakes were holding out,
some wonderful prevision having told the Presbyterian ladies that
this was the day of a neap-tide. . . . Norwood now had a clean
shirt and his Sunday jacket, but his red hair couldn't get combed.
He went and talked to Miss Dorinda Clarke. "I've got a dollar.
I want to buy two presents. What would you say I ought to
get?"—"For whom are they, Norwood?"—"For Grandmother
and for Lydia. Have you got a book?"—"No, I haven't, Norwood,
but here are some lovely book-marks."—"That shell. Where'd you
get it?"—"It was old Miss Hull's. Haven't you seen it on her parlor mantelpiece? She said she didn't have anything else, so she'd
give that."—"It's beautiful, I think. I'd like it for Lydia."

Lydia and Fran and other flower sellers, including Sarah
Ann Berry, reaped dimes. A tremendous exhilarating extrava-
gance wrapped Presbyterian Hill. Likewise it was the period of
buttonhole bouquets and of clusters of flowers below the throat,
between the breasts of women. Pansies, the early yellow rose,
lilies of the valley, veronica.

Mr. Campbell bought pansies. Pansies, that's for thoughts.
Heather and the wild rose. Yes, indeed, Mrs. Nicholson, I'll
lift it for you. A very successful occasion! But you ladies always
make it so. . . . We are doing very well, Mr. Barclay! Yes, yes,
we are doing our best. No, of course, that is so. None but God
does his best. I thought if you'd make a little talk to the Sunday
School about the Mission? . . . *The pipes, the pipes skirling. The
tree and the crag.* Ha, Mr. Price, if I can help you next month
with Africa, call on me! Have you heard from your brother
lately? A great work he is doing—a great work. . . . I'll make the
round of the tables. . . . *Hanging and swinging, hanging and
swinging. But I've had his blood. I've burned his house. My
knife's in her heart whether she lives or dies.* From where does
that come, O Lord, from where does that come? Miss Dorinda,
are you selling your stores? Bead work and shell work and wax
work and crocheting—

"I've set aside," said Miss Dorinda, "a stamp box for you.

This one with the painted scene. I said, 'There! That's for Mr. Campbell. The Highlands of Scotland. Ben Cruachan and a hunted stag swimming the loch.' I knew you'd like it. You know, I'm mad for things that bring up other things. I suppose they all do, if we'd pay attention!"

"I was never in Scotland. I've never seen a loch, nor yet the ocean."

"How absurd!" said Miss Dorinda and took his money for the box. The festival shimmered at its height, or almost at its height; evening with the Japanese lanterns and music from the Greenway String Band would be the pinnacle. . .and all the tables rearranged and additional cakes set out and new freezers of cream, and all the fancy work left from the afternoon. . .table mats and lamp mats and baby sacques and afghans, macramé lambrequins and baskets, spatter work and pin cushions and painted plaques, tidies and emery bags and starch bags and cat-tails gilded in strangely painted jars, texts worked in colored silks upon perforated cardboard, sachet bags and turkey-feather fans, hemstitching, tatting and embroidery, and on and on and on. . . . Fresh small bouquets on silver salvers. . . . And the hands of the clock were drawing toward six, and at six would occur interregnum. *One. Two. Three. Four. Five. Six.* Inter-regnum.

Seven to ten. What do figures mean anyhow? thought Lydia.

One, two,
Buckle my shoe;
Three, four,
Open the door;
Five, six,
Pick up sticks;
Seven, eight,
Lay them straight.

Seven in May equalled a soft rose dusk, and the frogs down by Greenway Creek creaking and croaking. Presbyterian church-yard hadn't many people in it now, and the tables were tired. That would all change when the lanterns were lighted and the moon came up. The moon was a lantern; each lantern was a moon. "Why don't ghosts carry lanterns? They never do. If I saw a ghost I'd die. Sarah Ann Berry, I'd die! . . . I'm tired of

the smell of these flowers and of taking in dimes. I'm going away
by myself and sit under that tree."

Joe and Abraham and Big Sam lighted the lanterns, Mr.
Campbell directing. . .*Dangling and dangling from that oak, and
a wind comes up from the sea.*

The Baptist minister, walking about by himself, his hands
behind his back, met Mr. Carmichael, the rector of Saint Anne's,
coming in at the gate. They greeted. "I couldn't get here earlier.
Old Mr. Aldwick died."

"Greenway will find it strange to be without him."

"Yes. . .Death. . .I hear it's a highly successful festival,
and India will profit. You and Africa next month, and then we
and China take the road."

The lanterns were lighted now, in wreaths, in single moons.
Greenway's string band, under the tulip tree, began to tune its
fiddles. Through the arched gateway returned, or appeared,
who had not appeared before, the attenders of festivals, pre-
destinate helpers of strayed continents. Death, thought Mr.
Carmichael. Greenway will find it strange to be without him.
I wonder now if it is without him, now, this minute. I wonder
. . . . O God, I wonder and I wonder.

Fran had a saucer of ice cream, and Mother bought one
also for Sarah Ann Berry. They ate them together, under the
Rose of Sharon bush by the church steps. About the church-
yard were scattered benches, and ladies in soft full skirts,
flounced and billowing, sat upon these, and gentlemen brought
them refreshments, or stood and talked to them, bent from the
waist, gallantly conversing. And now the moon was up, round
and neither silver nor golden but between, and she and the
Japanese lanterns and a manner of light that yet shone from the
west gave the whole an appropriate illumination. The string band
played "Know'st thou the land?"

Fran said, "I think I'll have a tea-party tomorrow. Princess
Alice and Rosabelle and Melinda will want to talk it all over."

"I'm going to tell Evangeline all about it before I go to
bed," said Sarah Ann Berry.

Fran thought, "She hasn't got but that old Evangeline with
a mended arm. . ." and as if she answered that, Sarah Ann Berry
thought, "I'd as soon have one as many! Anyhow my Evangeline's got sense, which is more than her three have!" Fran
thought, "And she hasn't got a mother like mine, no she hasn't!"
Her heart softened. She looked at Sarah Ann's tin waiter beside

her silver salver. "S'pose you come to the tea-party, Sarah Ann, and bring Evangeline. Mother will let me ask you, I know. It'll be at ten o'clock, under the syringa."

Mother came by in her soft, flowing lavender dress with her black lace shawl, like a Rose of Sharon. "Are you girls having a good time? Fran, darling, tell Sarah Ann to come to see you." She went on by. ". . .for charity—for the greatest of these is charity. . . . It's coming night and isn't it beautiful with the moon and the stars and the lanterns? I remember. . .I was eighteen and James was twenty-four." Here was Miss Dorinda's table and she thought she would buy an embroidered handerchief. Mr. Campbell came up to her. "Oh, Mr. Campbell, how do you do? Don't you think we're doing well by India?"—"Mrs. Curran, mayn't I buy you a bouquet? Pansies and veronica". . . *Violets and a fern leaf and the pipers piping around a house, piping in the moonlight.*

Norwood bore about with him the mother-of-pearl shell for Lydia. He didn't intend to give it to her until the festival was over and they were all going home together. He had found a piece of tissue paper to wrap it in. It had three moon-like spirals and when you held it to your ear there sounded the sea. It enraptured him. He went behind the cedar tree on the north side of the church and finding no one there sat down upon the grass and taking out the shell listened to those waves, wave upon wave from the other side of the world, from around the earth. He put it down. There rose the moon at his right and he swung himself to face her. A shell, a round shell, and what was her species?—though Norwood, at eleven, can hardly have thought that consciously. But he stared at her, and questions and answers and answers and questions floated far away in his mind.

The string band played "Old Folks at Home," and then it played "Maxwelton braes are bonny," and then it played "Nita—Juanita! Ask thy soul if we must part." The churchyard grew thronged. Everything was being sold. The colored lanterns glowed so beautifully among the trees and the moon shone in the higher branches, and the perfume of May powdered the world, and the voices of men and women, words and laughter, sounded as though they would sound forever. . . .

A stir, a piece of information running excitedly around, a thrill and access of power. Was that a locomotive—was that a train of cars thundering up? The Harper House folk—the Harper House folk were at hand! They were coming through the arched

gateway, and the string band played "Believe me, if all those en-
dearing young charms"—and now certainly Foreign Missions
would greatly profit!   In India, at the antipodes, Shiva the Destroyer saw his own Destruction. . . .   Lydia, under the big tree,
scrambled to her feet with her silver salver. Geranium leaf and
citronella, tulips and scented flags and yellow roses. . . .

Note

[1]*The Bookman*, p. 68 gives rake.

That Cold

"You are a little late, Petunia." That was Mrs. Amyas Raleigh, the white lady who employed Petunia. She stood upon the back porch, between the pillars, and spoke to Petunia coming in the seven-in-the-morning glow up the brick-paved yard from the alley gate. Petunia continued to approach, between the high brick walls, past the big sycamore and the brick outside kitchen. Everything was warm, old, red brick that wasn't white pillars and green blinds and bronze sycamore and wine-colored oaks. Petunia moved languidly, with her hand upon her breast. Mrs. Amyas Raleigh foreboded. The small, silver, interior voice that kept her informed said quite clearly, "Armistice Day."

Petunia now stood upon the lowest of the three porch steps. "I got a terrible cold, Miss Kate! It's heah, and heah. I can just drag myself along. And I coughs."

She coughed. "Hollow," remarked the silver voice inside Miss Kate.

Petunia resumed explanations. "It just seemed I couldn't leave mah bed, but then I said to myself, I says, 'I got to go tell Miss Kate, even if it most kills me, so's she can get Nelly----' "

"Petunia, you know I've company coming today."

"Miss Kate, I downright sorry, but I got to go back to mah bed. Nelly'll help you out just like me, or as much like me as she can." Petunia clasped her hands above her forehead. "I 'clar to goodness my haid's just distractin' me!"

"Do you want some aspirin?"

"Yaas, Miss Kate, maybe that would help."

"Laura!"

Laura, who was Mrs. Amyas Raleigh's grown daughter, brought the aspirin and shook three tablets into Petunia's trembling hand. She also shook her bright head. "Petunia, you're leaving us in the lurch."

" 'Fo' the Lawd, Miss Laura, you'd have to do just the same if you was me!"

And Laura, who was a candid young one, thought, "Maybe

I would, maybe I would!"

The magnolia by the porch rustled in the morning air its strong, dark green and glossy leaves. The sun made torches of the autumn trees and intensified the white pillars. Beyond the alley, from Ludwell Street, sounded the cry of an early vendor. "Sweet--sweet—sweet potatoes—potatoes!" Down the river some craft uttered its deep-throated word. . .perhaps an excursion steamer, it being Armistice Day and Indian summer.

"I reckon," said Petunia, "I'd better be creeping along, for I've got such a swimming in mah haid. . . . You let Erasmus get Nelly, Miss Kate, and I'll be back first thing in the mahning."

Slowly and waveringly she departed, down the brick-paved yard, to the alley gate. It shut behind her in the definite way the alley gate had of shutting. Mother and daughter looked at each other. "Well," said Laura, "that's that!" and put back a branch of the microphylla rose that had loosened itself from a pillar.

The alley through its length might be considered to be commanded by the upper windows. Petunia traversed that channel, sun-lighted, brick-paved and garaged, with a few remaining, abutting, small brick houses in which yet dwelt servants of the habitations to which they belonged, with overhanging trees that cast bright leaves, and overhanging ivy casting no leaves, contemning the red and yellow. Petunia arrived at the mouth of the alley, pausing ever and anon to cough, and with her hand going periodically to her head.

Out in Ludwell Street she began to straighten and to step more lightly. This increased until you would never have thought she had a cold. Once again she coughed, deeply and hollowly, and then she grinned. "Miss Laura always talking about 'saving energy'! Reckon that's my last racking of my po' frame till I has to have another holiday!" She began to swing herself as she walked, and her hand forget the way to her head.

"Sweet po-ta-toes! Sweet po-ta-toes!" George Washington Harris checked his old white horse and his ancient wagon and himself, ancient too. "Mahnin', gal! Does you want----"

"No!"

"You's vigorous erbout it. Seem to me you finish yo' work mighty early."

"Sho! I got a holiday."

"I heah say it Armistice Day. I been figuring' what dat wuhd mean."

"Sho! It's the name of the general who stopped the war by getting in between the armies."

"That so? Well, Bob and I must be perambulating. Sweet po-ta-toes! Sweet po-ta-toes! Where you gwine now?"

"To my sistah's, to get on my best clothes."

"There's room in the wagon, ef you's gwine my way."

"I'm going your way, but I'm going faster than you're going. So long!"

Elvira lived in an alley, in a very good upstairs room. She was not at home because she cooked for Mrs. Edward Paulett and was now in the kitchen. Petunia's new dress and hat lay where she herself had deposited them an hour ago. The dress was red and brown, the hat was brown and red. She had in her pocket a new pair of stockings, and her Sunday shoes stood at the edge of the patchwork quilt upon Elvira's bed. Rapidly enough she divested herself of the dress in which at this moment she should have been sweeping Mrs. Amyas Raleigh's front steps—if she had not had that cold. She stood in a clean slip, her bronze skin smooth and warm, and her body like a young Juno's. Through Elvira's window came the strains of a hand organ, an early, a holiday hand organ.

"It's that Trovatore thing," quoth Petunia, and as she moved about the room hummed to the organ.

Elvira's small mirror. She set it on the washstand, then on a chair, then on the floor. "Ise complete," said Petunia. "It's a great pity I got to wear this old coat. Vow to the Lawd I won't wear it! I'll make Percy or Breckinridge carry it. It's a warm November."

Her peregrinations brought her to Elvira's small table. Elvira's Bible lay open upon it. Elvira was a tremendous church member. A match box kept the leaves as they were, and a silver pen, one of Elvira's treasures, pointed out a verse. Petunia glanced that way. "Humph! I know she lay a trap for me! I'll step over there and read yo' verse, Elvira, when this holiday is over. I earn this heah holiday, and don't you think I didn't!"

This alley led to John Rolfe Street, which led to High Street. Above the fiery maples a clock struck half-past eight with a single startling sound. She met an acquaintance. "Hello!" "Hello!" "You got holiday?" "Jes' the same as you!" They both smiled widely. "I'm on my way," said Petunia, "to Crab Hill, to the Jones'."

"Then what specially going to happen?"

"I don't exactly know yet. But something always happens," said Petunia, "when I has a holiday. It happens and it
keeps on happening and it happens right away!"

The street car turned the corner and clanged at the square
above. "Heah's the chariot," said Petunia. "So long, and a good
time, Charlotte!"

At the rear of the car, reserved for her color, she found only
three or four passengers and none that she knew. "Too early
for the crowd. I've got a long day, a good long day, because I
was foreseeing! I'm more foreseeing than others," thought
Petunia.

An old, very large, charcoal-hued woman had a bushel
basket and a peck basket and an armful of chrysanthemums and
marigolds. She had come from over the river and she would sell,
seated on a box, at such a street corner. She eyed Petunia,
sitting beside her. "Dese heah christian-anthems en ma'igolds
favor you mightily, honey, in yo' fine new dress!"

"I'm going to a friend where they have them by the million.
Christian-anthems and marigolds and cosmos and zinnias and
asters and prince's-feather and dahlias."

"Does she sell them?"

"No. She gives them to her friends. She and her brother.
She got brothers."

A well-made, warm-bronze young man seated across from
Petunia exhibited interest. "That must be the Jones'. They got
a yard packed full like that. I am a friend of Percy's."

"They are the Jones."

"My name is George—Walter George. Is it possible I am
speaking to one of the Miss Sandys?"

"I am Petunia Sandys."

"I already guessed you were the youngest and the fairest."

What really could be said to that except to draw a full
breath and smile and continue the conversation? The old flower
woman faded out.

Walter George was dressed for toil, not holiday. But he
explained: "I've a half holiday. I've got my clothes at the works.
My mind's been projecting about what it wanted to do, but now
it knows! It wants to come to the Jones' this afternoon."

"We are going to the new amusement park."

"Then it wants to go right there."

Petunia sighed. "I got to get off the next corner for the Crab Hill car."

"I wish to goodness the works wasn't sending me to Argall Avenue about something mighty important!"

Petunia stood by the curb waiting for the Crab Hill car. Flags—there were a lot of flags—fluttering before the big red business houses, over the red-brick, sunlit street, streaming against the genial, blue, autumnal sky. Music. . . . "Fo' the Lawd, I heah a band!" There was now a morning crowd, coming and going, in spirits and talkative. All of them heard the music. They swarmed like bees to this corner. "That's the Ninety-ninth, coming from the station!" The band played Dixie. Petunia in her excitement let a Crab Hill street car go by.

Dixie—Dixie—Dixie. Borne flags, proud, streaming flags. . . the band; the horns and fifes and the drums. . .marching men.

> Look away! Look away!
> In Dixie Land I take my stand,
> To live and die in Dixie!

The sidewalks, the attentive houses cheered and cheered. Petunia felt herself inwardly rising and falling, like an excited wave—like shouting in church, though her generation never shouted in church. "My Lawd! I wish Armistice Day come every week! I wish there was er crowd of generals like that general!"

White folk were talking beside her. "They didn't stay in Dixie. They went overseas."

"Lot of colored men went, too," thought Petunia.

The Ninety-ninth marched by, marching up High Street, the flags dwindling, the music dwindling.

> 'Way down south in the land of cotton,
> 'Simmon sees and sandy bottom.

The ranks along the curb broke, dissolved, flew or sauntered about their business. Some had holiday, but not all. The Crab Hill car approached, stopped. Petunia boarded it. Crab Hill had ten minutes in which to arrive. She sat in meditation. "Walter George. That's an unusual name. . . . Percy. Breckinridge. Walter. . . . He right handsome and educated. 'Is it possible I am speaking to Miss Sandys—the youngest and the fairest?' . . . Walter George. I heah say there are Georges in Gloriana County. . . . He's at the works, and they's sending him on something important. He looks like he's trustworthy. So's Breckinridge. Percy ain't trustworthy, but he's dashing. . . . Mr. George looks dashing, too, but he's solid. This is a nice car. I think Crab Hill is beautiful! Those trees are lovely. That sky's lovely. . . . Sure as I'm bawn, yonder's an airship!"

The small yard of the Jones' bloomed profusely. There seemed, in this warmly lingering autumn, every fall flower. The older women of the large family had brought them from every house in which they had been in service. There were scarlet sage and late-blooming dahlias, marigolds of every shade of gold, cosmos in white and mauve clouds, chrysanthemums red and tawny and yellow and white, cockscomb and straw-flowers. A gum tree that had not yet cast all its polished and deeply crimson leaves contributed to the splendor.

The family received the visitor with *empressement.* Percy and Breckinridge were not there at this hour, their holiday, like that of Walter George, being but a partial one. But Mrs. Jones and grandma and Maria and Constance and Rosalia and the children were there. Mrs. Jones and Maria and Constance washed and ironed for three white families; the back yard fluttered now all white with many articles. But washing was yesterday, and ironing tomorrow. Today was happily falling interim holiday. Rosalia worked as waitress in a tea room in the city, but she also had achieved a holiday. The family was out in the yard, looking up at the airship. It was a small dirigible, and now it passed above Crab Hill, not so far up in the blue sea, looking for all the world like a big, silver fish disporting itself or voyaging upon its own needs. It showed a flag—swimming there with its flag.

The Jones family and Petunia watched it absorbed, their heads thrown back, their eyes rounded, their lips parted. It passed right overhead. There dropped overboard a bit of paper— it was waggish today. The paper described a spiral like a snowy leaf. The silver fish sailed on, its bulk and its sonorous droning lessening. The paper spiraled down into the gum tree and thence to the roof of the small porch of the Jones residence. Ephraim, aged twelve, burst into action. "I gwine get it!" He swarmed up by the grapevine and the slim wooden pillar and retrieved a sheet on which was penciled in bold capitals, HEAVEN IS OUR

HOME.

The Jones family became voluble. "Will you think of that!" Mrs. Jones laughed and laughed. "What you think they mean? They think they going fool colored folk?"

"They didn't know we's colored. They didn't know where that was going to drap, fast as they were going! They just out to fool the world."

"Just someone fool up there!"

But Ephraim, who was going to turn out a preacher and a saint, looked with large eyes and a dreamy face. "Maybe it's so---"

They returned to the house, that was a very good old log one.

Going, Petunia appreciated the blooming yard. "I never see such a hand as you-all are with flowers! . . . You-all know Mr. Walter George?"

Yes, it seemed, they did, though not to say intimately, but he had come once or twice to Crab Hill with Percy, and everybody like him. "That man's a cut above mos' folk around heah!"

"He's a high yaller."

"Percy say he got a powerful good place and money in the bank. Moah'n that, he got education and he got family. His folks was raised with the best white folks."

"How come you know him, Petunia?"

"He heah me talk about you-all to someone I met on the street cyar, and he introduced himself. I got it in my bones that he coming this way this day."

"Then," said Mrs. Jones, "we'd better put his name in the pot."

They had to prepare dinner, a real holiday dinner, but Petunia, as company, and grandma, as having done her part in life, sat on the porch. The small children played in the yard, among the chrysanthemums and the asters and the zinnias. Grandma was old and small and withered. Petunia, who was largely made, though not a young giant, could have carried her about. Grandma smoked a pipe. After a time she took it from between her lips to ask, "How yo' mother?"

"She's dead, grandma. Long ago. Don't you remember?"

Grandma said placidly, "You're a liar," and smoked again.

Petunia nursed her rayon knees. The sun mounted to the

zenith. "I reckon by this time Nelly's got the house clean. . . . 'Is it possible I am speaking to Miss Sandys?' Things sho do hap-hen on my holidays!"

Rosalia called her to come help set the table.

When the table was set Maria and Constance and Rosalia went to change their dresses. Petunia sat beside the corner table and looked for the hundredth time at the Joneses' photo-graph album.

The girls reappeared, dressed in their best. Marianna Alicia burst indoors: "They's coming! Percy and Breckenridge and Mr. Walter George!"

The dinner was such a good dinner. The company around the table had such a good time. Armistice Day was such a suc-cess. Petunia thought, "I ain't caring what her old text was! I likes him. O Gawd, make him like me, way up in C! . . . Appears that he likes Rosalia, too, but he ain't precisely co'ting her. Be-sides, she got Jim Reedy, down the river."

After dinner was no time to waste. Like a golden balloon rose before Petunia, Maria, Constance and Rosalia, and Percy, Breckenridge and Walter George the golden afternoon at the golden, new amusement park; with to follow, when the stars came out, a tremendous moving picture. . . . Ephraim and Mari-anna Alicia, who belonged to Mrs. Jones, and the three smaller children, who belonged to Constance, who was a young widow, had their own lesser golden balloons. Mrs. Jones had hers of rest in the porch and Brother Armstrong and Susan coming in at gate to sit with her and converse of Crab Hill and the church. Grandma had her silver balloon of her chair and warmth and her pipe and a pretty procession miles in the past.

Percy lived, as they said, dashingly—a limber, yellow fel-low. Breckinridge had the soundness of a big, dark tree. He was grandson, son, brother and uncle to the Jones family, and his boughs protected them all, but Percy was no blood kin that they knew of, only they had known him always. The delightful, the stranger element was provided by Walter George. Petunia's large eyes grew immense, staring at her great golden balloon floating so richly in a blue heaven.

"He's a tiptopper. Never in mah bawn days did I meet such a man befo'! . . . He likes Rosalia, but he's maybe coming to like me bettah, and she's got Jim Reedy."

It was high afternoon when they reached the new amuse-ment park, for they had a good way to go, over various lines of transit, and all crowded on Armistice Day. But the very going proved vastly entertaining. Percy amused them so! Breckinridge had a great, honest laugh. The girls laughed too. "Ain't he killing?" Percy cut more and more monkeyshines.

Here at last the amusement park, and the men bought the tickets. Everybody going in. A lot of white folks and quite a number of colored folks. Everybody well-behaved, in a well-behaved part of the world. What a paradise of fantastic buildings and tents and structures out of dreams and buzzing talk and laughter and sunniness and blaring music! Petunia thought, "And Elvira's there, cooking away." Walter George was speaking critically. "It isn't much of a place. If you could only see Coney Island!" Petunia admired him so, the profound traveler! "What'll we do right away?" asked Rosalia. "Let's do everything right away," recommended Percy. "Like this!" He turned rapidly upon his heel, then came to a stop. "Lawd have mercy, I see the Ferris wheel!"

Constance would not go up. It made her dizzy to look at the thing. That left Maria and Percy for one seat, and somehow or other Rosalia and Walter George were placed in the next. "I don't find myself mindin' moah than is necessary," thought Petunia. "He was the Joneses' guest to dinner. He has to beau her. His manners is perfection." She and Breckinridge took the third seat. . . . It was thrilling when they were all fastened in and cautioned and the engine worked and the immense wheel began to turn, and they were now creakily and now smoothly leaving the earth behind. Now the amusement park began to be below them, like a coat of many colors. "We're even with the tree tops," said Breckinridge. "I like it quiet up here. There isn't anything to be afraid of, Petunia."

"I'm not afraid," gasped Petunia. "Not with all you men along!"

"I'm always thinking God's along," said Breckinridge.

That was like Breckinridge, to say a thing like that and yet not to let it interfere. Breckinridge was likable, though he was so much slower than the others. Petunia felt suddenly how much she had always liked Breckinridge. He was the kind of person you could always—not just sometimes—feel confidence in. Always! Breckinridge would always be like a rock in the midst of any dizzy adventure. She thought, "He's the kind of person

Gawd listens to. And he wouldn't be always showing you texts either."

Up and up and up, and there spread the city and the river and the fields, and the distant woods all dressed in amber and maroon and the jade of pine trees. They poised up there, they tilted, they began to go down. She seemed to perceive that Rosalia was uttering squeals of terror. At any rate she wouldn't squeal. She thought, "If I'm killed Elvira'll say. . . . But I just ain't going to be killed. Gawd never did mind a little pleasure."

They came to earth without accident and rose again on the outward curve. Down again, up again, down again, up again, down again. Released from the wheel, Maria said, "My Lawd, who ever thought that out?" Rosalia affected speechlessness and clung to Walter George's arm. Petunia thought, "Straighten up, Miss Rosalia! You ain't really scared, you's flirting." Walter George smiled upon them all. "That wasn't anything, ladies! If you could see the devices they've devised at Coney Island!" Petunia was visited by an intuition as swift and conclusive as an arrow. "He's a high yellow and educated and though he's got dash he ain't wild like Percy, but he's patronizing. He's patronizing us that ain't on the limb with him. O Lord, I ain't never liked a patronizing person!" Percy was grinning. "Let's go shoot the chute." "No," said Breckinridge. "Constance don't want to and it's her party too. Let's just walk about a little and look at things. There's a band concert at four o'clock." Petunia, gazing at Breckinridge, suddenly saw that besides being big and strong he was handsome. "Ain't it funny, but I never saw him that way before. . . ."

Just to move round about in so gayly crowded and talkative a place, with all the shows and all the booths, was enough to make Old Misery, had he been along, joyful. He was not along. A gypsy was sitting in the door of a tent. "I'll tell your fortune—tell your fortune—dark skin or light skin. Everybody's got a fortune. It imports you to know it. Tell your fortune, gentleman! Tell your fortune, lady!"

"Let's stop right here," said Walter George. "What's the harm in knowing what's going to happen. Maybe then you can do something about it."

They all had fine fortunes, though with certain perils darkly indicated, enough to keep up the excitement. But their barks steered past secret enemies, loss of worldly goods and

public ills into havens of wealth and love and station. Constance
was elated. Life was not over for her, the gypsy said. Percy
could not make out something that the kerchiefed and bese-
quined woman had told him. "Look here! I got a friend, she
say, and I got an enemy, and they both of my height and shade,
but I better lay the one low, she say, and hold fast to the other,
and the sign of them is----"

"I don't hold with fortune tellers," said Maria. "But they
is exciting." They had a pink lemonade and kept on talking
while they sipped. "How you think she know? She told me
things was the gospel truth!"

They were walking now, and Walter George with Petunia.
"She told me, Miss Petunia, that my life would be affected by
somebody named for a flower."

"That must be Rosalia. She have roses in her name."

"Petunias ought to be in every garden. Big, dark, velvety
ones."

"He is mos' awfully handsome," thought Petunia. "And
he know so much!" And at that moment they came to the
scenic railway.

On the scenic railway they were all pleasantly together.
The car in which they were seated plunged into a tunnel. A
hand pressed Petunia's, but the darkness was of the shortest
and she did not know whose it had been, whether Percy's or
Walter George's or----No, it wouldn't have been Breckinridge's.
He didn't do things like that. Out they shot into colored light
and a miniature mountain pass with a wild waterfall and twisted
fir trees and a castled crag. "Oh, we're traveling!" breathed
Petunia. The gorge narrowed and the spray of a second waterfall
made a real moisture. Some strange creature, jumping from a
tree, shouted at them. They passed into a spangled grotto where
gnomes, big-headed and goggle-eyed, looked from behind
stalactites and stalagmites. "Are they real?" quavered Constance.
"No, goosie!" answered Rosalia, looking superior. "Somewhere
in the Bible," said Maria, there's talk about 'many inventions'."
Breckinridge was laughing. "When I was little I used to have a
little being lak that to play with. I could see him just as plain
with his long beard and his pack on his back. I reckon I saw a
picture book and it put it in my head. But I outgrowed him. . . .
I wish we had brought Ephraim and Marianna Alicia along."

They were out of the grotto, and had arrived in the midst

of a picture of tropical forest and elephants feeding. "That's meant for Africa," quoth Percy. "Do you-all feel at home?"

"My home is America," said Walter George sententiously. "It's been my home a long time." The five others nodded their heads. "Of course it's America," thought Petunia and thrilled and scarcely saw the next fantastic bit. An inner string of picture and voice presented itself. The airship seen from the Jones' flowery yard. . .the Ninety-ninth marching up High Street, playing Dixie. . .the old flower woman. . ."Sweet po-ta-toes! Sweet po-ta-toes!" . . . The white columns of Mrs. Raleigh's house and a microphylla rose that she admired. . .Elivra's room with the little white curtains and her Bible by her bed. . ."I wonder what was that text!"

The scenic railway returned them through the tunnel to its first station. Petunia kept her hands locked under her coat. "I don't encourage no flirting in the dark—I ain't a flirter, anyhow!"

Here they were, out again in the broad light, upon the highly decorative street through the amusement park. "I liked that," said Breckinridge. "Now let's go hear the band concert. It's four o'clock."

The band played marches and patriotic airs, and played dances and lullabies and love music, and played Way Down on the Swanee River and Auld Lang Syne. It was growing cool, and long, thin shadows overstretched the bright earth. The band crashed into the Anvil Chorus. The concert ended. With a mighty rustling as of all autumnal birds rising from a field, the crowd left the seats and began to scatter. Percy cut a pigeon wing. "Now let's go shoot the chute!"

That was an experience reckless, dare-devil and awe-inspiring! Petunia felt exaltation. "Maybe it's kingdom come—maybe it's kingdom come!" But she would not for worlds have screamed like Constance or clung like Rosalia. "When I gwine die I gwine die straight—straight inside anyhow!" The music still pounded in her ears and here they were doing this awful thing! "But I won't show the white feather! I ain't ever gwine show the white feather!"

At last it was over, and well over—shooting the chute. As they tore themselves away from it Breckinridge and Petunia found themselves again together. "I liked the music better," said Breckinridge.

"I've always thought I was bawn for excitement," said Petunia. "But they's excitement and excitement. I don't know as I wants to see the world go to pieces."

The others were ahead among the glittering booths. "He's mighty attractive."

"Percy."

"No, Walter George. He's got a good place too. He calls it a 'position,' and I don't know but he's right. And he ain't wild like Percy pretends to be. He's a dashing fellow, but he's reasonable."

"You're reasonable, Breckinridge. You always has been."

"I'm reasonable, but I'm slow. I've had to look after things so, I ain't never had any time to be fancy. It ain't my meaning that Walter George is fancy like Percy tries to be. He ain't—not like Percy. But he's got a feel of—of broadcloth about him all the time. Broadcloth ain't sleazy. It's mighty good to have."

"I wonder what you talking about anyhow," said Petunia, and put her hand to her eyes.

"What you crying about?"

"I don't know."

"Is you tired, honey? You work pretty hard."

"I don't work any harder than Elvira or Rosalia or anybody. You work pretty hard yourself, Breckinridge."

"I got to. Anyone that came with me would have to take pot luck——"

Percy was calling them. "Merry-go-round. We're going on the merry-go-round!"

The merry-go-round went round and round in a brilliant, circular procession. Children and grown people sat fantastic beasts—beasts out of heraldry and children's painted books. The music undulated in a twinkling, smiling stream. It was now dusk and the lights of the amusement park shone out like suns and wreaths of suns. Percy rode a donkey and Rosalia a hippogriff and Walter George an Arabian steed with flowing mane, and Maria and Constance beautiful ponies, and Breckinridge and Petunia lions.

"A lion and a lioness," thought Petunia. "I love Breckinridge. I gwine marry Breckinridge."

Elvira, though she was tired with her day's work, kept

awake for Petunia, who was to spend the night with her. Not later than eleven Petunia arrived, supper and the moving picture and the street cars accounting for her evening. "I'm thankful you's heah at last!" said Elvira, sitting up in bed. "What did you do, all this living-and-dying day?"

"I had a good time. I had the best time, Elvira, I ever had in mah life! Most come of it, I tell you, most come of it! Something come of it that gwine last me through to heaven. Breckinridge and me gwine marry!"

"Well, you might have done worse," said Elvira. "Did you read that text I marked for you?"

"No, I didn't," said Petunia, taking off her shoes. "And I ain't gwine read it neither. It was you picked it out; Gawd didn't pick it out."

"It was what He said——"

"Well, He don't mean that there ain't exceptions." Petunia put on her nightgown and slipped into bed beside Elivra. "Elivra, ain't you glad Breckinridge and me is happy?"

Elvira put her arm around her sister. "Yaas, honey, Ise glad."

Seven-in-the-morning glow struck the alley gate and the brick kitchen and the brick-paved yard and the big sycamore and the magnolia and the white pillars of Mrs. Amyas Raleigh's back porch. A bird was singing just like spring. Out on Ludwell Street old George Washington Harris lifted his voice. "Sweet po-ta-toes! Sweet po-ta-toes!" An early hand organ burst into something ancient and sweet. Mrs. Amyas Raleigh, looking out of her window, thought, "It's sweet—the world does manage sweetness oftener than you'd think."

Petunia came through the alley gate and up the walk. Mrs. Amyas Raleigh leaned from the window. "Good morning, Petunia! How is your cold?"

"Good mahning, Miss Kate. Mah cold's bettah."

"I'm glad of that! Rest in bed will help most colds. Well, the house is ready for you, for I'll tell you what you already know, and that is that there are greater treasures than Nelly! I'm glad to see you back!"

Petunia in her blue gingham, going into the parlor with her broom, put her hand into her pocket and found there three aspirin tablets. She regarded them contemplatively and then the three vases of flowers, one upon the piano, one upon the table and one before the pier glass. "I heah say aspirin make flowers hold up they heads just lak they was back in the gyarden." With which she dropped the tablets into the vases.

The End of the World

"Yaas," ended Dilsey with unction, "that was the way of it! I lay under that sunflower kiver all dem two days befo' I got back to wukh and thought of a name for him, and he lay there looking back at me jes' so long, and solemn as a possum, with the moon shining down and the dawgs making remarks erround the tree! Yaas, Lawd! He had the big eyes and he seemed to be considerrating even that early. So I jes' said sudden, the old rooster crowing and the sun coming up, I gwine name him Vowed-to-the-Lawd. Ef it too long to say, we kin call him Vowed. And I 'clar to goodness he look it, right away!"

"Yaas, he do, Sister Dilsey! Yaas, he do! He look it little and he look it er grown man."

"That was befo' the war, and we all belong to the Jordans, and I say to myself, 'I reckon he gwine be Marse Athelstan's body boy.' Then the bugles blew and the world was all bruk up into little bits, and we come free, and he growed up, and one day he say, 'I gwine make application to old Mr. O'Flaherty to larn me how to be a mason.' And he larn how, and he been the best mason in these parts ever sence!"

"Dat so! Dat so! They all wants him when they builds a house."

"And then he got somehow taught how to read. And then he taught himself out of a book how to write and how to figger. Yaas, Lawd! Old Mr. O'Flaherty himself tol' me befo' he die, 'That boy Vowed is er master figgerer!' And the years went on and the years went on and he tuk to the Bible----"

"Yaas, Lawd. Yaas, Lawd. He tuk to the Book."

"And he got made the preacher to Dandelion Creek Church."

"Vowed Jordan. He got the right name. Vowed Jordan."

"Yaas, my Lawd! He got the right name."

Saba began to intone and to sway: "He named Vowed and he nature Vowed. And the Lawd hab allowed him, and the Lawd hab showed him. And I believes his word and I believes what he say. He say a mighty thing, and is that against him? Somebody is a got to say the mighty things! You was told to name him what you name him!"

Dilsey hastened to disallow. "Neveh have I say I was told! It jes' came into mah haid, lying under the sunflower kiver----"

But the three visiting women would not have that: "You was told—you was told to name him what you name him!"

Saba's rhythms became more marked: "Yaas, he is Vowed. Glory hallelujah! And the end of the world, the end of the world is coming! He has seen it in the Book and he has seen it in the arithmetic. The end of the world, the end of the world is coming!"

The cabin sat by Dandelion Creek. Dandelion Creek flowed from Thunder Mountain until it joined the Winding River, a mile from the village of Windingville. Around Windingville rested three or four pleasant old plantations, with some life in them, such and such a number of years after the war. Up Dandelion Creek wound a string of cabins and colored families and Dandelion Creek Church. Vowed Jordan's cabin stood nearest to Thunder Mountain, on a green rise above the creek.

Vowed Jordan had been building a chimney and laying a hearth. He came home at sunset in his blue overalls, a tall negro who might be thirty-five with a strongly built, spare body and a well-shaped head. His color stood a clear brown; he had long, narrow, sinewy hands and feet. His lips were not thick, his nose was high, he had deep-set eyes and a short, thin black beard. It is likely enough that in his veins ran Indian blood, and possibly from very long ago, before ever Virginia, before ever the slaver, Arab blood. He managed to combine being a preacher, an artisan and a thinker.

Saba and her companions had departed. Dilsey prepared her son's supper. They ate together, at the deal table, in the cabin that was not the cabin in which he had been born, for that event had taken place on the Mt. Pleasant plantation, across the Winding.

But they had often enough been hungry in this cabin; or sometimes they had had food but the question had been of clothes, of shoes in winter, of blankets for her bed and his pallet. War times, hard times, easy times, they had traveled them through together—they and the cabin. Now the three seemed much of a piece and conversed without sound. They ate their corn bread and drank their coffee and the little they said started from the house that was building and employing Vowed as mason. Mr. Tom Jeremy was building it. He had been walking about the place that day and had stopped and talked to Vowed. "What did he say?" Vowed, having finished supper stood up from the table. "He say somebody told him I say the world is coming to an end. He wanted to know if I thought 'twould last out his time, or if he'd better stop building the house?"

"What you say, Vowed? What you say?"

"He weren't noways serious. So I say I didn't really know, and asked him if he wanted the bricks in the hearth set this way or that way? But he wouldn't let me be, so I tell him that I hadn't been shown the day and the hour. But the main signs surely laid around us mighty plain, and he had education and he ought to go read them for himself. 'Twas coming to an end, but I didn't know just how many years. There weren't any too many to get ready in!"

With that he went out of the door and stood on the greening earth before the cabin, with his eyes upon the west. The great shoulder of Thunder Mountain jutted bold and black. Behind that shoulder and the long head of Thunder streamed the shorn rays of the departed sun. It was early springtime. The bare trees yet showed velvety with their swollen buds; up and down Dandelion Creek the frogs were at their old, old singing, their thin, distant, rapid choiring. Vowed stood and gazed. "It's beautiful. . .things are beautiful just before they end."

Behind him light sprang up in the cabin. Dilsey placed the lamp upon the table and brought his books from the shelf. He went indoors. His mammy took her chimney corner, at her hand a pile of chips and pine knots for the fire when it burned too low. She had her old corncob pipe and her memories. Vowed sat down beside the table and opened the Bible and the arithmetic in the ring of yellow light.

Sitting so, all the lines of his long figure became austere and intense. The exaltation of which he was capable was as much of the mind as of the emotions. There, too, perhaps, some faraway, multitudinous ancestry. . . . Had it come his way he could have received a high degree of education, but circumstances had given him only reading, writing and arithmetic. As for books, all that he had ever owned might be carried, with room to spare, upon his mason's hod.

The Bible. The arithmetic, with a continution into algebra. A book of general history and a geography. A poetical collection. An almanac. Vowed opened the first three where pressed leaves marked them. He had a slate and a slate pencil, and a cheap school tablet and a lead pencil. He read intently, and he turned from that to figuring upon the slate, figuring and wiping out with a bit of rag dipped in a cup of water. Now and then he left the slate and with the lead pencil recorded results upon the tablet. Texts and texts. So well he knew the Bible that he was his own concordance. This one, that one, back and forth. He left the Word of God, and took the history book, and then the almanac. He read with the slate pencil in his fingers, poised above the gray plain. The lamplight showed his dark, nervous hands, the book and the slate. Dilsey, rousing from a doze, tossed a pine knot upon the fire. His shadow expanded along the cabin wall.

The clock on the wall struck, and in an hour struck again, and in an hour struck again. Dilsey, her small withered figure all bowed together, had a dream. It was before the war again, and everything was mighty peaceful. Then the big plantation bell began to ring, and an army was coming this way and another army was coming that way. You knew they were coming by the pillar of cloud and the pillar of fire. . . . This cabin—she was in this cabin now—this cabin had got between the armies. Vowed was taking her out of it. Vowed was saying, "Come, Mammy, let's go up on Thunder Mountain. Clean to the top, Mammy!" They were on the top, and the pillar of cloud and the pillar of fire swirled up on either side of them and Dilsey felt terror. Then the armies struck the mountain, and it shivered and broke . . .and the old bell said one word—two words—three words—big and deep!

Dilsey woke upon them, and the old clock was striking, the old clock that Old Miss had given her. Dilsey stared about her and shivered and shook. "My Lawd!" she said. "That falling mountain!" It was late. The old clock struck eleven. The lamp had burned low. She threw pine upon the fire. Vowed was not sitting there. He had risen quickly, pushing back the chair, and the chair had fallen. He had gone out of the door. Straightening her small, aching frame, Dilsey followed.

The April moon peered at herself in Dandelion Creek. Everywhere shimmered a light of smoked pearl. Thunder Mountain looked remote and not so high. *Chir, chir, chir*, went the frogs. An owl in the little wood made his lonely remark. A slow, dreamy wind played touch and go. Vowed stood on the bank above the creek, and he was gazing at the sky with his arms up and out.

Dilsey went to him over the moon-soaked earth. "What's the matter, Vowed? In the Lawd's name, what's the matter?"

Vowed spoke in a whisper without turning. "Mammy, it's coming right away! It's coming this summer!"

"The end of the world?"

"The end of the world."

His voice became raised, clear and awed. "I found it that sudden! There's been comets before. But the Message wasn't for us and they went on by. But the one this summer is The Messenger. I didn't fool myself, Mammy, for I wasn't thinking much of the comet for all the talk I've heard about it. Things hadn't seemed to point to it. Right straight along I've seen the End for fifteen, twenty years from now. . . . Then it opened up, one text and another and another twel I thought the line of them would never end! And the history of the world stepping with them, step by step, step, step, step! And the arithmetic singing its song in and out. . . . The almanac shot out a long arm and pointed. . . . And then I saw the Angel of the Lord, Mammy, I saw the Angel of the Lord!"

Vowed Jordan sank down upon the bank and cried, "Oh, the poor world, Mammy—oh, the poor world!"

Sunday by Sunday Dandelion Creek Colored Church grew more and more crowded until it overflowed into the wildly sweet and unkempt half acre about the wooden building. Sunday after Sunday Vowed Jordan prophesied, at first within the church, but as April advanced, without, from the church steps where he stood, his long arm making his rare, impressive gestures, his thin intent face raised to the blue vault of day, the deep words rolling forth.

"My brethren and my sistren, I have got to tell you, and it is a sore task, and I have got to tell the people of the earth and it is a sore task, what has come of my studying and my studying and my wrastling in the mind that is given us to wrastle with and overcome ignorance and set up a knowledge of what is going to come about. . .and I have wrastled and I have wrastled and I have come out with a truth in my hand, a great and terrible truth! And it is, my brethren and sistren, it is that this world of ours is about to end!"

Crowding and crowding into Dandelion Church and church-yard, shouting and praying and singing.

The deacons, Simon Peter Dandridge and Third William Harris, kept at hand. The first was a master hand at prayer; he got his innings here. Third William exhorted at every chance. Cato Baron started most of the hymns, but sometimes Drusie Wood started them—Drusie Wood whose voice really could make folk cry, cry and laugh, it was so sweet and rich and deep, with all the floods of feeling in it.

> *Swing low, sweet chariot,*
> *Coming for to carry me home!* . . .
> *Oh, I look up and what I see there,*
> *Coming for to carry me home!*

On other days they resorted to the cabin, at first singly, then in groups, then in streams. All the Thunder Mountain and upper Winding region, if you were colored, wanted to speak with Vowed, wanted to ask Vowed. White folk, some of them, came to see Vowed. They came to be amused, or for love of sensation, or sheer curiosity. A prophet was as valuable to the countryside as a ghost or a witch! But whatever they came for, some at least went away with something different and disturbing. For Vowed Jordan was not ridiculous, nor luridly emotional, nor this, nor that. He was quiet, and he wanted to show them mathematically. He wanted them convinced, he wanted them not to admire him but to take advantage of his knowledge. . . . The old colored woman, his mother, brought them silently well water if they were thirsty. If other colored folk were present they sat or stood around with a hushed aspect, waiting for Vowed to make the white folks believe. All going together, white and black, all going together when the comet struck and the sky shook and the earth was not! . . . The preachers from Windingville came to see and to reason with Vowed, and they knew their Bible, and other books as well and everything that the schools and the newspapers said. They reasoned with Vowed and prayed with and for him. They told him about comets. But Vowed looked them through with his deep eyes and figured it out for them on paper. It must be stated that they went away somewhat uneasy, though as summer sauntered up the ways they preached Sunday by Sunday upon piteous ignorance.

The sun strengthened, rising earlier, staying up later. All this end of Elderflower County came, as far as the colored population was concerned, into commotion. Results of kinds began to show. The county paper took notice. Later on a big daily at the capital city reported upon the resurgence in Elderflower County of comet and end-of-the-world superstitions. A colored prophet had arisen and the colored people were in a ferment. Labor was getting dislocated. Of course it was a particularly big comet that was rushing this year into visibility.

Vowed sat in the cabin under Thunder Mountain deep into the night with his lighted lamp and his books and his slate. By now he had other books. The white folks had seen to it that he had books and newspaper articles and magazine articles. It was a Great Comet that was approaching the sun and the earth and that would become visible in high summer. The head should be extraordinarily bright, the tail very long. Much was said about comets in the papers. Scientific men wrote about them. Vowed Jordan read what was sent to him to read, stumbling at certain of the words. He read the marked pieces, but they altered nothing—they altered nothing.

He worked on, under the lamp, with his books and the slate and tablet, slate pencil and lead pencil, and his own powers of calculation and of taking apart and running together, of foresight and throughsight to find the precise day. . . .

Dilsey watched with him or lightly slumbered by the hearth where the embers were grateful in the nighttime, under Thunder Mountain, even if the night were June. Then she waked, and Vowed's long figure bending over touched her on the shoulder.

"Mammy!"

"You, Vowed, ain't you in bed yit?"

"Mammy, it will end at dawn, the twenty-third of August!"

Sunday came in two days. From the church steps, to the colored population of these parts and to any white folk whom some manner of interest had brought there, under the locust trees in bloom, in enormous, white, fragrant bloom: "My brethren and sistren, now I know the exact day. The world will end at daybreak, the twenty-third of August. Let us pray!"

Vowed's prayer was short. "O God of every kind of life, give us that great new life! O God that gives us Mind, help us still to use it and go over safely! Amen!"

The Elderflower Gazette called Vowed Jordan a public menace. For it was getting out of hand, the excitement was getting out of hand. Vowed, no less than the Gazette, felt this and tried to draw upon the reins. But he, too, as the days grew longer, hotter, drier, began to sway and waver and answer to the heat in the blood, the floods of feeling and the restlessness. The summer grew older, stronger, heated and parched, with threads of red and gold, and the brown of burned fields. The papers talked about the unusual weather and the troubles of the times and the prognostications of experts and the approaching comet.

The number of negroes preparing to meet the end of the world increased and increased. At first Vowed had preached, "Stick to your work!" But at last it became difficult and then impossible to make them stick. Had he not found that he himself could not do so? He finished chimney and hearth for Mr. Tom Jeremy, but he did not find and perhaps did not seek another job. He said to himself that he must impart and instruct, also he must wrestle and dream. So he must, but all the others said to themselves that they must flock together and be instructed. Being instructed at all hours grew incompatible with work. Also they developed a need to talk and talk and talk among themselves, or to wander in a strange way from place to place, or merely to set and regard the fact that they were all going, going, going, at the trump, at the trump of Gabriel. Saved money was used up, and then why be concerned about owning? Many began freely to disencumber themselves of their worldly goods. Though of course none of them had much worldly gear. The Elderflower Gazette fulminated. Labor lacked, and the county was going to suffer. The situation was becoming fanatic.

The form of Thunder Mountain was a bold one. It stood up alone from the rolling valley. It was not sky-shouldering. But its aloofness and its shape gave it all kinds of worth. It had a way of bathing itself in a sullen storm light and in a magic sweet light. For all its strong lines against the sky it was easy to climb, and the top spread into a plateau where a thousand could stand. To this top came late in July Vowed Jordan.

The night before, with little sleep and little eating, there had come upon him a dizziness. He had risen from the Bible, open at the Apocalypse, and moving like a drunken man made for the door and the reviving air. All the sward was burned and dry and the trees rustled dryly and the fireflies waved up and down in their million million. Vowed sank upon the door stone. By littles his eyes cleared and his ears ceased their drumming. Then he saw Thunder Mountain, lifted and calm among the stars, above the fireflies. He thought, "To wait for it up there—I should like to wait for it up there. . . . Why shouldn't we, all of us, wait for it up there?"

As soon as the dawn was in the east he left Dandelion Creek and climbed Thunder. He had done it before, many and many a time. So wonderful up here—cooler than below—and a great view on both sides, and the pure blue sky so solemnly untroubled. Yes, indeed, yes, indeed! This was the place to come to meet the end of the world.

He sat himself down upon the dome of Thunder Mountain. All the world about him and the skies above and he himself, Vowed. He thought of Dilsey, his mammy. Her light, shriveled frame—he would half carry it up this mountain—his mammy who had named him Vowed. . . . Vowed lay his length upon the short mountain grass with outcropping rock. A soft wind blew across, tempering heat, tempering light. There ran the Winding, away down there, and Dandelion Creek and all. Bees around the blue thistle, and bronze butterflies. . . . Vowed drifted afar into childhood and boyhood. Before the war—enduring the war —after the war. Little things and little things, rich and lasting little things. He made a boat of them and the boat moved upon a sea of them. Vowed relaxed, Vowed rested.

Gathering sticks in the wood for mammy. Hoeing corn. . . . And I will make a covenant with you and seedtime and harvest shall not fail. . . . He lay there an hour and more. He almost determined that he would not go down that day at all. Then he had a vision of his mammy looking for him. Yes, he would carry her up the mountain the night of the twenty-second of August. Many a time had she carried him when he was little. Mammy, Mammy!

He went down the mountain, and there were his books again and his calculations. What if they were mistaken? But they couldn't be!

Dandelion Creek Church and churchyard on the hot, dry Sunday; with the wind blowing, but so hot and dry. "What night'll we see the comet? Tell us dat! What night'll we see the comet?"

Vowed Jordan, standing upon the steps of Dandelion Creek

Church, that and his height giving him range, remarked the surge of men, women and children that his knowledge and his learning and his insight into words and figures and into the ways of things had brought around him, under the locust trees and the heaven trees and the oak trees. Even though companies of them broke away to those others and their poor mixing and poor masonry, he, Vowed, had told the thing!

He began to speak and his own voice sounded to him thin and far away. "My brethren and sistren, turn your eyes and look at Thunder Mountain. Most of us have climbed it. Maybe we've climbed it many a time when we were boys and girls. Look and see the great top up there, with room for us all. I been there yesterday. Yonder is the place for us that last night. Yonder is the camp ground for us that is pilgrims of the forever and the forever! Let us travel, the twenty-second of August, to the mountain top, to watch our old cabin going and our new cabin building larger and taller----"

It took Vowed to originate. All the lines of cleavage blurred themselves over.

"Praise God! Praise God!"

> *"Oh, Rock Mount Sinai.*
> *Oh, Rock Mount Sinai.*
> *Oh, Rock Mount Sinai in the morning!"*

August drew on and August drew on. The Great Comet careered always closer and closer.

Dilsey went out of the cabin, leaving Vowed reading the poetry book. Cobwebs might be said to have gathered for months past over the poetry book, but now there sat Vowed reading it. Dilsey returned. "Vowed! Vowed-to-the-Lawd! It's there—it's there!"

He got up and put his arm around her and they went out to the burned grass above Dandelion Creek. The sky clear and vast, and brushed across it the Great Comet, the Pale Steed. . . . It was not late; the small lights shone in the cabins sparsely threaded along Dandelion Creek. The oak scrub rustled, then parted, and Drusie Wood stood beside them. "I saw it, and I had to come. . . . I thought it would be ugly and terrible, but it's grand and beautiful!"

"Yes, it's grand. Yes, it's beautiful," said Vowed. The three sat down upon the turf. They looked up in silence. As the night deepened it came plainer and plainer, the Great Comet. It had a bright and wondrous head, and a pale and long and wonderful veil streaming backward across the heaven. It was a marvel, an awful loveliness. . . . Now someone else down Dandelion Creek saw it. There began an excitement and hurry of human voices. Many who could not read had believed in the comet solely because Vowed Jordan had said it was coming. Now there it flared across the sky!

"It don't look fiery," said Drusie. "It look ez peaceful ez a dream."

Vowed passed his long, sinewy hand over his eyes. "I can't tell you how I feels. I feels different from what I thought I would feel. It looks so solemn I want to weep, and it looks so innocent I want to laugh."

The August days dropped away hot and dry, fever hot, cinder dry, and the August nights dry and warm and superbly clear, with that vast portent sailing overhead. The twenty-third drew nearer and nearer.

The women of Dandelion Creek Colored Church were making white cotton dresses for the great day in the morning when the Ark should swing low for them and they would go aboard. Only Drusie Wood, it seemed, was not making a dress. She said she didn't have the money for the cotton.

"Mr. Paul Turner Brothers will trus' you, Drusie. It's right for them to trus' you, right at the end----"

Drusie thought that over. She had a wish to look well and was not too fond of being singular. But in the end she did up an old lavender calico dress that she had. Ironing it, she sang at the board:

> *"When I lay my body down,*
> *Yaas, Lawd, in the graveyard,*
> *When I lay my body down,*
> *Yaas, Lawd, in the graveyard,*
> *Then you hear my coffin sound,*
> *My voice a-singing under the ground.*
> *Toll the bell, Angel, I have got over!"*

And all the time she sang she saw Vowed. God was fond of

Vowed and He ought to be!

Dilsey was not troubling about her dress. Her brown linsey was good enough to go to heaven in. But she bothered about Vowed. He looked distracted and he worked and worked with those texts and figures and the history book. And then again he put it all down and went out and lay in the grass with his face to the skies, and when he came back to the cabin he looked big and peaceful. But that would fade and his master figuring catch him again. Once in the big peaceful spell he said to Dilsey: "Mammy, I was double sure it was coming to an end! I am double sure. Most all the time I am. But what if it isn't so? What if, work and study and think as hard as I have, I was plain mistaken? What if I ain't anywhere like strong enough yet to catch and hold Knowledge by the mane? No more than I can swing myself up there and take hold of that comet! What if it don't end, Mammy, what if it don't end?"

Dilsey, who was washing potatoes for their dinner, said in her small, quiet voice: "It'd make an awful ruction, Vowed!"

Each night now flared the comet. It would be visible, the wise men said, up to the end of the month. The twenty-third bore down upon Elderflower County.

The twenty-second was the day of the great and final Pilgrimage. All the colored folk who could get there were at Dandelion Creek Church as early in the morning as might be. Nearly five hundred were going to the top of Thunder Mountain, going as high as they might to meet the end of the world. All that believed and yet could not go to the mountain wept, shouted and said farewell, looking to shout "Howdy! Howdy! so soon in another and better order. Just as many of the white folk as could get there lined the road to the foot of Thunder.

They marched in column, men, women and children, singing and shouting. Some of the women carried babies. Men had sacks of cooked food or food that could be cooked before a fire on Thunder Mountain's level top. The spring just under the big cliff would give them water. Vowed Jordan and Dilsey . . .and Simon Peter Dandridge and Third William Harris and Magnus Carter—and Cato Baron—and Drusie Wood with her old father, and all the rest, the host of them.

"Way up on the mountain, Lord!
Mountain top!

Lord! I heard God talking, Lord!
Children, the chariot stop.
Lord!"

When the mountain was reached the road became lonely. Lonely and narrow and stony and twisting upward like a ram's horn. Hot; it was so hot!

They halted for the feebler sort, the old people, the women with babies and the children; halted and went on, halted and went on. After all, there was a breath about it of a great, a gorgeous holiday. All the excitement culminating, and the opposition flung off, remaining below.

It was afternoon when they reached the crest.

They cooked and ate their supper. Then came sunset. Fiery gold, pale gold, purple isles, meadows of green. They watched and were silenced. It grew darker; there showed no color at all in the west, and no particular light. The stars appeared, the big ones and the little ones, thick, thick, in the clear, high, summer night. The Great Comet streamed overhead. To their excited fancy it seemed greater to them tonight, it seemed nearer.

A giant with a pale robe, and what was coming? And they had no definite idea of what was coming, beyond angels and chariots, and the figures of Jesus out of the illustrated Bible, and destruction for the people of the plain.

At daybreak—at daybreak the trump would blow, and they would see their salvation.

"I've been traveling all the day,
Ride on, Moses! . . .
They prayed so long I could not wait.
Ride on, Moses!

I knew the Lord would pass that way.
I want to go home in the morning.
Ride on, Moses!
Ride on, King Emanuel!
I want to go home in the morning."

They were folk used to early bedtime and sound sleep and also to early rising. They thought they would sleep a while—

being worn out with excitement and the climbing and the un-
usualness of it up here—and then awake.

Toward the middle of the place a lift of the three or four
great bowlders made as it were the boss of the shield. To these
came Vowed Jordan and seated himself upon a ledge of the rock.
Now he had the sky and the earth, the sleeping multitude, and
that swift Presence, whatever it might truly be, up there in the
sky. Vowed sat hunched up, his chin sunk in his hands. He
would recapture that rich, that awed, that tremendous, authentic
sense of the problem solved. That which he felt in the winter
and the spring, when he was first assured, when he saw God's
Mind as to earth, and God's hand indicating to him, Vowed
Jordan, his proper trowel and hod and mortar. . .Vowed sat there
and he sat there, and the stars moved from east to west and the
comet changed its place. Vowed thought and Vowed thought.
At the very end to be not assured, and that not because he
doubted he had gone too far, but by reason of a doubt that he
had not gone far enough.

And always the night streamed away from Thunder Mountain rather than ran toward the dayspring.

Down by the Winding a cock crew and was answered by
his fellow. Just the turn of the night, but the company led here
by Vowed stirred, stretched, opened its eyes and began to rise
from the earth. Down among the vales and hills flowing from
the foot of Thunder cocks were crowing, telling the day. It
could not be long now—any moment, any moment, Lord!

Excitement mounted. They demanded that Vowed speak
to them. He spoke from that central bowlder. "Oh, people! I
worked and worked, all you here know I worked, to understand
the world and the ways and the beginning and the end of it!
And last year I was certain and this spring I was certain, and
June and July I was certain, and what could a man with a heart
in his bosom do but tell his neighbors and his friends and the
whole world if it would listen? Like Noah, like Noah long ago!
Oh, folk, I don't see—I can't see—but I got it right. By the books
and by figures what is true. But now I've a strange feeling, a
strange feeling. I'm but a child—I've felt that more and more—
Ise but a child. . . . The dawn is breaking. There's a streak of
light yonder in the sky. We've got to wait and see, Vowed
Jordan just the same as all of you. Vowed Jordan has got to wait
and see!"

His voice reached them all. But it is to be doubted if they perceived his doubt.

They sang, they prayed, they shouted and some of them danced. And always the cocks crew down below and the pale light strengthened. And the eastern stars began to fade, and then the midheaven and the western stars, and the comet that was now low in the sky. Across the east started a band of lilac and then a band of saffron.

"It's time, it's time! The blast of the horn, Lawd, the blast of the horn!"

"The end of the world—it's the hour and the minute for the end of the world!"

But the minute and the hour went by. The end of the world did not happen. Unless it was always ending and always beginning.

The sun came up amid a silence as of exhaustion. The stars were gone, the comet was gone, the day had broken, the same old day. The difference was that it found them high upon Thunder Mountain, lifted for a laughingstock, a laughingstock for the white folk, for Windingville, for Elderflower County, for everybody, for themselves. . . . Out of work, out of food, out of money, everything run down, belongings given away. . . .

Third William Harris made himself their mouthpiece. "What we wants to know is, what do you think of yo'self, Vowed Jordan?"

And Vowed, from the boss of the shield, answered, "I think lowly of myself, I think lowly. I was honest mistaken. I thought I was serving you all and bearing you with me into the truth. I got a sorrowful heart toward you all, and I asks yo' forgiveness. I thought I was given to understand the height and the depth and the ways of things. . .and I was just a baby, I was just a dog. . . . Yet will I grow up to understand, though it take me a million years! And I see that it may take me a million years. . .maybe longer. I never fooled you meaningly. And now we're going down Thunder Mountain."

The August heat and drought broke in a torrent of rain. When, finally, the weather cleared a half-moon rounded and rounded and whitened the night with her beams. And always the Great Comet grew fainter. When the full moon had come and gone, and again shone the host of the stars, the comet had quit this corner of space and time.

September sun, September color, September ripening and garnering. Drusie Wood came up Dandelion Creek. Drusie was a strong, rather tall woman, still young, in a blue cotton with a kerchief about her head, with a dark wide, comely face. The zinnias were in bloom, rows of them, before Vowed Jordan's cabin. Dilsey sat out-of-doors, in a low chair, peeling apples. "That you, Drusie? Ise glad to see you. Sit down and rest yo'self."

Drusie sat down upon the door stone.

"I was in Windingville and I see Vowed making the brick steps for Miss Mary Marchant's garden."

"Yaas."

"Ise honest-Indian glad he's found work!"

"Yaas; it saves a man."

"But," said Drusie with pride, "before he looked for himself he went to all the white folks and begged work for the others."

"Yaas," said the little old woman peeling apples, "dat boy Vowed's a good man!"

"I thought I'd just rest here awhile, if you don't mind."

"I don't mind a bit," said Dilsey. "Ise glad to have you. You and me's the kind kin get on well together."

They sat in silence. Then said Drusie, "Is he studying, just as he used to do?"

"I don't know erbout it being as he used to, but he's studying. He wouldn't be Vowed," said Dilsey, "ef he wasn't studying."

Drusie said, "No, it wouldn't be Vowed. I like his studying."

"I hear him coming," said Dilsey. She looked at Drusie and she looked at Dandelion Creek, then she got up from her chair with her pan of apples. "You stay heah. I gwine put these heah apples away."

Vowed in his blue overalls came by the creek path and up the hill. He came slowly and he looked bowed. Drusie rose from the step and went to meet him.

"That you, Drusie?"

"Yaas, Vowed."

The water ran like molten gold. They stood and watched it. A red-shouldered blackbird flew down to drink. "Ise glad you's got work, Vowed."

"Yaas, I'm glad."

"Ise glad you's studying on, Vowed. Ise glad you's a thinking and a studying man."

"I can't help it, Drusie. I'm made that way."

"I wouldn't want you any other way. . . . Vowed!"

"Yaas, Drusie?"

"Vowed, couldn't I help you?" She stretched out to him a brown arm, and her voice had all the power of song. "Ef you'd see it that way, Vowed, I could help you. . . . I could, I know I could! . . . Vowed, Vowed, I want to help you. I want to, Vowed!"

Vowed returned her look. His eyes dazzled. A thrill went through him. The world kept on coming to an end and beginning afresh.

After the Storm

Cherry Hill and Merryville were a couple of miles apart. Cherry Hill was a Crewe place. Major Jernigan Crewe lived there with his wife and his three children, all daughters—Sybil, Sylvia, and Susan, eleven, nine, and six—and with his distant kinswoman, Miss Margaret Jernigan, a gentlewoman of sixty and decidely odd.

Cherry Hill had many blackheart cherry trees and a serpentine brick wall, and a flower garden, exceedingly sweet. Old Miss Margaret walked in it, early and late, when no one else was there. Sybil, Sylvia, and Susan had one day heard a visitor whisper that she was cracked. Henceforth, each time they were in the company of Cousin Margaret they looked shyly, though with great curiosity, for the crack, but could never find it.

Cousin Margaret lived in a large, cool room in the garden wing, with a little tacked-on room that they said had been an old powdering room. Now it held ancient matters, chests and an immense wardrobe and a highboy, all filled with curious and interesting things. The three little girls loved going to Cousin Margaret's room, but they did not often do it, for their mother did not like their father's old kinswoman nor for them to be with her.

There seemed the less reason in that her cracking did not make her disagreeable nor irresponsible, though it did make her quaint, and so Major Crewe represented to his wife. But that lady simply did not like her. She was rather haughty, was Mrs. Crewe. A handsome, quick, dark woman from another part of the country she was, who knew how to bring up children and to keep people and things in order. She resented wanderings and vagaries and Kindness with its arm around Justice.

Major Jernigan Crewe, who himself was a very simple, kindly person, said, "Don't be too stern, Octavia!" But Mrs. Crewe answered sharply, "I'm not! And I simply won't have Sylvia and Sybil and Susan up there with her!"

"There's in her a deal of poetry and truth," said Jernigan.

"I used to love to go to Cousin Margaret's."

" 'Poetry and truth,' fiddlesticks!" answered his wife. "I know that you used to go to her queer old house. For my part, I wish you had left her where she was! She was doing very well."

"I couldn't do that, you know, Octavia. Not after her sister died."

" 'Poetry and truth!' " repeated the lady of the house with scorn. "A crack-brained absurdity! If I'd allow it, she'd haunt the children and spoil every servant on the place. Well, I won't. It's got to be hands off entirely!"

So it was hands off. Cousin Margaret rarely interfered with anything. The servants knew that she was not to interfere. Mammy Julia, the children's mammy, and Pallas, her young helper, knew it. Old Miss Margaret Jernigan lived in her two up-stairs rooms in the garden wing like a little old fairy.

Pallas had been at Cherry Hill no long while. Pallas had had her nineteenth birthday. Marietta, the chambermaid, ten years her senior, was the one to whom, chiefly, she turned for in-formation. For counsel there was always Mammy Julia. Marietta belonged to the Daughters of Culture. In the big house among her fellows, and in the brick kitchen and in the quarters, she ex-pressed culture, being a cousin and a loyal henchwoman of Esterella Walters, founder of the order. Especially this June, it being Esterella's great effort.

The Daughters of Culture (Colored) esteemed themselves and were esteemed by their community an important organiza-tion. Their own little community named itself Greenmount, but Merryville white folk had immemorially called it Clothes Line Creek.

The Daughters of Culture numbered a hundred women aged from twenty to threescore, and worked for the best white families. Esterella Walters had organized the society four years before and rested its president. When it met twice a month in the First Baptist Church (Colored), "Madam President" ran and sang like sweet music in the ears of Esterella. Esterella had great notions, having visited in Washington and Baltimore. Twice a year she "brought" someone—though never from far away and always with the stalwart aid of contributions and a general col-lection—to entertain, instruct, and increase the prestige of the Daughters of Culture. This June, Esterella's presidency being threatened by a young upstart, she was "bringing" Mr. James Monroe. Her rival subsided.

"Who is he?" asked Pallas, lifting her big eyes.

"This ignorance!" Marietta made answer in just the tone of Esterella. "Don't you know anything, Pallas? But, my land!" She laughed good-naturedly. "I know you couldn't, chile, not away yonder in Grassy Hollow with Uncle Abram and Aunt Melinda all you' bawn days! You better thank the Lawd you's come to where you can get knowledge! Mr. James Monroe is a *writer.* He writes poetry and thinking books, and all the white folks buy them."

"Oh!" said Pallas. "Ah like poetry."

She said that in a rich, sweet deep voice, slowly and reflectively. "Poetry and stories."

The servants' table in the big brick kitchen under the huge walnut tree received all the information that Marietta could give. Mr. James Monroe was a young man. He was a graduate of Dorset Institute—he had taught there—and then he wrote a book. A poetry book, and one of the white folks behind Dorset got it published. *And since then Mr. James Monroe could do what he pleased.*

Pallas thought: "*Do what you please. Even to going to Heaven.*"

Marietta continued her discourse. He had written another book, a book of stories in poetry. Its name was *Old Gold.* All cultured white folk read it. Besides writing, he had become a lecturer. He wasn't one of these here spoiled colored folks. He loved his own kin and kind and lectured to them. He was going to speak twice, and he had chosen his own subjects—Thursday night, *The Value of Reading,* and Friday night, *Fairy Stories.*

Pallas left the table and slipped away to the nursery, bearing upon a tray Mammy Julia's breakfast. Mammy Julia had developed a misery in the knee and couldn't come downstairs.

Mammy ended her breakfast. "Heah, take it away, honey! And give me yo' hand. Ef I don't get up and walk about I'll go stiff lak a tree."

She hobbled across the floor, with her big, warm hand upon Pallas' slight shoulder. "It's gashly," she said, "to go lame when you got colts and lambs and children to follow!"

"You ain't going lame, Mammy. You been praying—"

"Yaas, Lawd, I been praying—"

"My granddaddy says if you want a thing powerful and you pray right for it, you sho' going get it. If you pray right and don't miss the opening—"

"That's it," said Mammy.   "But you mustn't miss the opening!"

She was back in her chair, and Pallas worked on. Pallas thought, "I wish I could hear Mr. James Monroe. I lak fairy stories mighty well. But I won't ever hear him. I can't go. I don't never go anywhere."

Meanwhile, Esterella Walters pondered the length of Mr. James Monroe's stay in Merryville. His letter had stated that his great-grandmother had come from this county, and that he was glad of an opportunity to visit a region that must always be of interest to him. If it could be arranged, he would be happy to stay in Merryville from Thursday until Tuesday. And could he rent an old car, or perhaps a horse and buggy?

And then her cup of satisfaction overflowed. Through a committee of two, the white ladies and gentlemen of the Pierian Reading Circle, very old, very well established in Merryville, requested the Daughters of Culture to lend them, so to speak the author of *Old Gold* for Saturday evening!

All of his evenings were arranged for, and also the reception Thursday evening, after the lecture at the First Baptist Church. As for going out into the country, there was Daniel's flivver and also Uncle Ezra Buchanan's horse and buggy. But there must be something else, just one thing to be certain of and the rest left to happy chance! It was gorgeous weather, gorgeous June. And it was never terribly hard, in Merryville, to get off for a day, if you had a good reason.

There grew up in Esterella's fertile mind a picture of Spangler's Wood and a picnic at which all the Muses should be present. High June, and the beauteous wood, and all the respectable colored people who could get there. Games and jollity and singing, and the banjo and the fiddle, and the visiting star, the king's son out of another country.

Esterella pondered all this until she could image it quite clearly and splendidly, with all the perfection it should have if there were a perfect or even a faëry world. Then, because she had a kind of magnetic power, she proceeded to make others image it too.

She managed best of all with Marietta, who was her echo, anyhow, and Marietta was able to transfer the vision to one, at least, at Cherry Hill. All the colored folk there listened to

Marietta, but Pallas listened in a dream, in a story, in a great burning wish to go to the picnic in Spangler's Wood.

Pallas was not a Daughter of Culture. But she could read and she could write—and she liked to read.

Mr. James Monroe was only a name to her, but the picnic in Spangler's Wood took possession of her imagination. She dreamed of it, she went about dreaming of it. She saw the big trees, and the short grass in bright lawns, and then again the brown earth beneath the hemlocks and the pines, and the delightful, sliding, murmuring stream, and the cold, cold, big spring under the ferny rock. She heard the birds of June and the fiddle and the banjo. Everybody dressed up, everybody laughing and singing and talking and playing, and maybe dancing—just maybe dancing.

But of course she couldn't go. She was no Daughter of Culture, she was only Pallas from Grassy Hollow. She had no one to take her, and she had no dress, and she couldn't get away from Cherry Hill, anyway, for there was Mammy Julia's knee and she had to go about with the children all the time.

Usually, in June, Cherry Hill enjoyed an influx of visitors. But this year Fortune, it seemed, shut the big gate after folk going out, not coming in. A matter of business took Major Jernigan Crewe to the capital, and Mrs. Crewe reigned alone.

Mammy Julia's knee grew better, but not much better. She could hobble, but not walk. She could oversee the children just so long as they stayed at hand where her voice might reach them, but she could not follow them about. They were as active as birds with as many boughs to light upon. It was Pallas who must be with them from morn till eve, watching that they did not get into mischief.

Mrs. Crewe regarded Mammy coldly but justly. "No, you can't help your knee, Mammy. I hope it won't grow any worse. Just sit here by the window and let out these tucks. Children, you mind Mammy, whether she's up or down. And Pallas, don't you leave them, wherever they go. They're not to go wading, and they're not to eat green apples nor blackberries, and they're not to climb into the hayloft, and they're not—do you hear, Pallas?—to go to Miss Margaret's room nor to the attic."

The children were the most active children ever, but Pallas was active too. She liked them and they liked her. They played together finely, and when they were healthfully tired, she told them stories, sitting back on her heels before them. When she was little, herself, Old Abram had told her a thousand stories. Now at Cherry Hill she rehearsed them to Sybil, Sylvia, and Susan. Stories of animals and birds that were just living folks with four legs or with wings. Stories of trees and the big woods and of spirits.

There was one person only whose stories were more enthralling than Pallas', and that was Cousin Margaret. They would gather in her room (where she had all the treasures), or in the summerhouse in the garden when Father was at home and he said, "Why, yes, you may go. Tell her to tell you Aladdin." And Cousin Margaret, with her thin, high features, and her parchment skin, and her eyes so sharp and pointed and burning, and her gestures—her long, extended forefinger—and her words like diamonds and rubies, created for them fairies, giants, talking birds, genii in bottles, magic bean stalks and glass slippers, younger sons and sleeping princesses.

Spangler's Wood. The picnic in Spanger's Wood. Pallas dreamed about it that night. She was going. A flight of birds were taking care of the children, then they changed into Christ Jesus, who said that He would look after them. But she, Pallas, said, "I haven't got a dress. I couldn't go in this brown calico." Mrs. Crewe came into the dream and remarked, "I should think not!" and she grew tall and dark, like a thunderstorm, and the children began to cry.

Pallas woke up and there was a great owl hooting in the tulip tree, and Susan sitting up in the little bed crying, and Pallas had to tell her about the partridge and the mocking bird. When she was asleep again, Pallas went and stood at the nursery window. Heavenly sweet and bright out there in the moonlight! The honeysuckle floated up, the roses. The cool air refreshed her.

Nineteen years old. . .the cabin in Grassy Hollow. Granddaddy and Grandmammy and all the good things they had taught her. . . . Cherry Hill was a good place, but mighty few holidays! Miss Octavia didn't believe in holidays. . . . "Granddaddy, Granddaddy, I want to go to the picnic! I want to go so bad! I don't know why, but it jes' seem I couldn't stay away!"

And in Greenmount, Esterella Walters was writing a final letter to Mr. James Monroe. So and so, and so and so, were the arrangements, and they were certainly rejoiced to have him and they hoped—the Daughters of Culture hoped—that he would have some happiness out of it himself.

Monroe reread this letter in the railway coach approaching, after a considerable journey, the seat of his lecture engagement. About him, without the window, was growing the quite lovely country from which his great-grandmother had been sold as a child. Her parents had dwelt on such and such a plantation, and their parents before them. He had a sentiment for this country that he had never seen before. All manner of hues and tints and sounds, aromas and flavors, made an iridescence, a honey. It wasn't memory, and yet it must be, he thought, the long memory. He sat with his hands clasped before him and his eyes upon the unfolding landscape. They were good, strong hands, thoughtful and kindly eyes. He was a slender, dark-brown man, modest and friendly. He was conscious of intertwining, inter-fusing worlds; he was a poet born.

It was a lovely country. Hills; blue, distant mountains; a river; high, singing woods; and happy fields. Merryville the next station. He saw on a hill, with rich fields and orchards about it, a white-pillared old house. "In the quarters of such a place as that, maybe, lived my great-grandmother. . . .a little, black, bare-legged girl. . . ." The whistle blew, there began a stir in the car. Here was the county seat. Here was Merryville. He rose and took down his bag from the rack above him. Here was the platform, the train stopping. He saw, evidently, a committee, three or four colored ladies. . . .

It was the greatest success, his appearance that evening in the First Baptist Church, *The Value of Reading,* and the reception which followed. Everybody felt so edified, everybody liked him so much, everybody congratulated Esterella. When she lay in bed that night, her body tired with much exertion but her spirit peaceful, she saw it golden down the years until she should be too old to care—the presidency of the Daughters of Culture.

And everything was arranged for tomorrow. Uncle Ezra Buchanan's old horse and buggy—he had said that he would much rather have the horse and buggy—and he could drive himself. He didn't want to go far afield, just here and there in the country around Merryville. In the afternoon there would be visitors, in the evening *Fairy Stories.* Esterella slept.

Henry Clay Buchanan, aged ten, brought the horse and buggy. "Would you like me to go along, suh?" And James Monroe, looking at his eyes and his grin, said that he would, and they drove away from Esterella on the little porch under the Madeira vine. Soon they were out of Greenmount, or, if you like that better, Clothes Line Creek, out of Merryville.

"Do you know a place around here named Cherry Hill?"

Henry Clay knew it and presently pointed it out. "There's Cherry Hill, suh. The Crewe place."

"Crewe? Jernigan was the name I've heard."

"That's right, suh. The Jernigans owned it once. Now it's Major Jernigan Crewe's. Old Miss Margaret Jernigan she live there still."

Mr. James Monroe stopped the buggy under a wayside cedar and sat looking and looking. "Where would have been, in old times, the quarters?"

"The old quarters? They's jes' ruins now, suh. Over yonder, below that hill." Mr. Monroe sat and looked, with his elbow on his knee and his chin in his hand, for so long that Henry Clay Buchanan grew weary. Then he picked up the reins and spoke to the horse, and they drove on by other country houses and Tall Mountain and Covered Bridge and Indian Fields, and so into Merryville again.

Afternoon and visitors. Sunset over Merryville; the dew fell, birds and small children went to bed. Colored folk streamed to the First Baptist Church—all the Daughters of Culture and their kindred and friendship, male and female. James Monroe talked out of a real and great gift upon *Fairy Stories*.

Lecture was over. Colored folk, with a happy, childlike feeling and likewise with an awakened, deeper sense, streamed back home. It was bedtime. Lights went out. The short June night passed; it was day again—Saturday. James Monroe, Henry Clay Buchanan, the horse and the buggy once again journeyed through the sweet country. A narrow, winding road took them past a small vale among hills, all wild flowers and ancient trees of the forest, and one cabin with a garden path about it. "Grassy Hollow," said Henry Clay. "Uncle Abram Day live in that cabin. He so old he kin remember when he belonged to the Jernigans. Aunt Melinda's daid. His granddaughter's Pallas. . . . She's got a place at Cherry Hill."

"Pallas," said James Monroe. "That's a fine name to have! Pallas."

Saturday evening he talked in the Town Hall to the white folk, talking about what made him write *Old Gold*. The colored folk filled the gallery. The occasion was highly successful. *The Merryville Clarion* told all about it the next week.

Sunday morning and evening there was church.

Colored folk streamed home in the warm perfumed darkness. It was bedtime. Lights went out. The short June night, the round June moon, reigned. It was, though only Mr. James Monroe caught it, the Eve of Saint John.

The short night passed. The cocks crew, the birds roused to matins, the dawn deepened, the sun colored the great earth, children woke. Pallas began her care of Sybil, Sylvia, and Susan. Mammy's knee was no better. Pallas brought her her early breakfast and helped her to the big chair. Mammy needed a big chair, she was so capacious. For all her lameness, she found herself cheerful this morning. She said, "Chile, it's a day when something gwine happen. I knows those days when I taste them. You mark my wuhd, something gwine happen!"

"Ah," thought Pallas, "the picnic's going to happen. But not for me. I'll not go to Spangler's Wood. Nothing is going to happen for me." And then in an hour it began to happen.

A colored man on a horse appeared with a note, all three dispatched at sunrise from By River, an estate eight miles away. The By River ladies wished ardently for dear Octavia Crewe's company. A common friend had most unexpectedly arrived, but must take the train again tomorrow morning. Couldn't Octavia come over directly after breakfast in the car, and stay the whole day?

Mrs. Crewe left Cherry Hill as early as nine o'clock, William driving her in the car. Before going, she gave her orders all around—kitchen, dining-room, house, nursery, out-of-doors. "Sybil, Sylvia, and Susan, you are to be as good as possible and not get into mischief. Mind Mammy and mind Pallas. Pallas, keep them in the garden or on the porch, and don't let them eat anything they shouldn't." She started to say also, "Don't let them go up to Miss Margaret's room," but Mammy began to speak of Susan's dresses and it went by. In the car she thought, "I should have told that girl not to let them be with her, or rather I should have spoken to the old witch herself—"

But she drove away without doing so, and the three little girls watched her, capering. They loved their mother, of course, but still they capered. "You got to be good," said Pallas. "If you don't Miss Octavia'll do something terrible to you! Come let's get some rose leaves and make cologne for the dolls."

Rose leaves for dolls' cologne, and a flower party on the brick walk below the serpentine wall! And here came Miss Margaret's stick, tapping, tapping. Miss Margaret wasn't a bit lame, but she always bore this ebony stick with the ivory head. The old butler said that she got it from her own grandmother. They were all glad to see her. She took her seat upon the summerhouse step and watched the party.

"And what did you sigh for then, Pallas?" Miss Margaret asked presently. "And why have you tears in your eyes?"

Pallas winked them back. "For nothing, Miss Margaret. I just was seeing something else. Yaas'm, that's all. . . . Sylvia, here come the red rose and she's the belle of the party! Jes' look at Mr. Ragged Robin jump up to meet her!"

The party did not last. Nothing lasted very long with the three limbs of Satan. Up they scrambled to rush away and play croquet. Pallas moved to follow them.

"It's the picnic in Spangler's Wood," said Miss Margaret. "I've been talking to Mammy. You want to go mighty bad."

"Yaas'm. But I can't."

"Why not?"

"I got to look after the children."

"If there was somebody else perfectly safe to do it? You needn't stay more than three or four hours."

Three or four hours. . .years of bliss. . .Spangler's Wood sprang and waved and sang about Pallas. Once or twice she had been there. It lived in her inner world, a wood of dream and depth and romance, filled with a strange whisper of things to come. And now—the picnic would be entering directly, in a brilliant stream, with the fiddle and the banjo, with Marietta and Mrs. Esterella Walters, and all of them. . .with Mr. James Monroe, who was a miracle, who was a prince out of a far country. . . . She wanted just to see him, just to hear him say, "How do you do? I'm sorry you couldn't be at the lecture." No more than three or four hours. Maybe she could have gone, if Mammy's knee hadn't been bad.

"No'm, I couldn't have gone, anyhow," said Pallas, and shook her head sorrowfully. "I haven't got any dress. I couldn't go this-a-way. My other dress is jes' a calico too, and is most worn out, beside."

Miss Margaret was looking at her, measuring her up and

down with sunken eyes that yet were bright. She picked a spray of coral honeysuckle and put it to her thin, beaked nose, then laid it on the step beside her and rose with her quick, birdlike movement. "Well, Pallas; well, child," she said, "it is a pity! I remember a ball once that I thought I'd die if I didn't go to."

She went away, a strange figure, in a full-skirted, ashes-of-roses muslin adorned with little quillings of ribbon, with small, square-toed, rosetted shoes, with her high tortoise-shell comb and bit of lace over it, her black fan, and her stick, tapping, tapping, upon the brick walk. Pallas betook herself to the croquet ground under the three tulip trees.

Mammy Julia's voice called down from the nursery window. "Pallas! Come heah, Pallas!"

Pallas ran up to the nursery, and there with Mammy sat Miss Margaret.

"Pallas," said the latter, "you are going to Spangler's Wood to the picnic. Issac shall put Star and Lady to the old carriage and take you. I shall look after the children, I and Mammy together. You know that they are perfectly safe and perfectly good with me. I'll answer for you to Miss Octavia. You need not have it upon your conscience at all. Issac will return for you before four o'clock. That will put you home in plenty of time."

The authority of white folks, of Jernigans, the weird authority of old Miss Margaret herself when she chose to exercise it! Colored folks were used to letting white folks decide. A Jernigan was speaking, and they trusted her, anyhow, just naturally.

Mammy took the word. "Yaas, chile, you kin go. Lawd knows, I don' see what kin happen! Miss Margaret always was a master hand with children. En' ef she say she'll answer for you to Miss Octavia, I reckon that's all right too. I reckon it is. I'll tell her, too, though I wish the Major was at home. . . . Yaas, you go erlong, Pallas. You ain't never had much fun, and you's a good chile. It's my belief yo' granddaddy would say so too, and ev'ybody knows he kin heah the Lawd a-talking! I's gwine look after Sybil and Sylvia and Susan with everything but this heah knee."

Upon a chair beside Miss Margaret rested matters out of fairyland. "Here is your dress. God knows I've old things enough in camphor and tobacco! We are pretty near a make and height. This blue dress—I've an old association with it. Once I was happy in it—very, very happy. Now I'm going to give it to

you, Pallas. It's old, but isn't really out of style. There's everything that goes with it. Take it all into Mammy's room and put
it on. Hurry, child! No, you don't need to say a word. There's
a current that it's right to take when it sweeps our way."

The blue dress was of a fine, silky poplin, sheer and cool,
the color a heavenly one, deeper than forget-me-not, though
not so deep as ragged robin, the skirt full and flounced and to
the ankle, which also was the length of the skirts of the day.
The bodice was cut to show the column of the throat, the
half sleeves had a fall of lace. There were clocked blue stockings
and low shoes that Pallas could wear, being if anything, of a
slenderer, smaller frame even than was Miss Margaret. The wide
hat was blue chip with blue morning-glories; there were a fan
and silken mitts, a small bag of flowered brocade, an embroidered handkerchief. . . .

"There now!" ejaculated Mammy. "Wunst I was young,
honey, and you look lak all I ever thought of it! You's gwine
be the lily of the valley and the bride of the ball!"

The three little girls cried—for now they were in the nursery: "Pallas is going to the picnic! Pallas is going to the picnic!"

Spangler's Wood, a little before high noon on a June day,
shone warm, but not too warm, fresh and bright exceedingly,
every hue of green and blue and every depth and shallow of light
and shade.

Esterella Walters was a happy woman. Hour by hour
James Monroe was proving himself the right kind, young and
strong and good-looking, friendly and plain as possible, and yet
so evidently possessed of the treasures and royalty of culture!
Culture and a good heart. "Yaas, Lawd Jesus," thought Esterella, "that's what makes a king's son!"

For an hour Spangler's Wood had been vocal with rich
African voices. Also, there were three fiddlers. More and more
arrivals, until at last all seemed on the ground.

And then, just then, someone exclaimed and pointed,
"What come yonder? Uncle Issac Jernigan driving the old
Cherry Hill carriage! Who that sitting in the carriage?"

The equipage rolled down the gold-flecked wood road; it
was dilapidated, and the horses were old and the coachman
old, but it had the *cachet* of the plantation, and all was faëry,
anyhow, today, or so thought James Monroe, who was poet
by true election of the spirit. He was standing beside Esterella

in a kind of major grouping, upon a little grassy knoll. The carriage approached. "Of all and of all and of all!" cried Marietta. "Yonder's Pallas!"

The carriage stopped. It was so venerable. Uncle Issac, the coachman upon the box, was so venerable. In the depth of the carriage Pallas sat alone, in waves of blue. She was frightened. She had begun to be frightened as soon as she had passed through the big gate at Cherry Hill. "O Jesus, if I'm doing wrong, I'm sorry, Lawd! O Lawd, make it come right. Make Sybil and Sylvia and Susan be just as safe and not do anything to worry anybody. O Jesus, make it come right!"

"Why, Pallas!" cried Marietta.

James Monroe stepped forward and gave his hand to assist the descending and latest guest. Pallas put her hand in his. Her dark eyes looked into his dark eyes, and all her terror went away. "I thank you, sir," she said in her deep, sweet voice. A thrill went through James Monroe. It seemed to him that his whole being—body, soul, and spirit—shook and unfolded wings, and before him was another winged creature whom he had always sought without knowing it.

Green glade in Spangler's Wood buzzed over this arrival.

"Will you look what she got on?"

"She got on a party dress for sure!"

"Fo' the Lawd! She lak those *Fairy Stories* he was telling about!"

The morning began to sing itself away. When it had sung a stave or two, James Monroe and Pallas Day found themselves walking in a brief, divine solitude beside the stream, under trees that had known half a thousand Junes. "You weren't at the church any evening?"

"No, I was telling Sybil and Sylvia and Susan about the 'possum and the humming birds. I couldn't go. But Marietta told me it was mighty fine."

"Do you know I had a great-grandmother who belonged to the Jernigans? She was sold from Cherry Hill a long, long time ago."

"All we Grassy Hollow folk belonged too. . . .I'm glad you've come back."

"So am I! How glad, you do not know."

James Monroe knew love at first sight.

The Daughters of Culture continued their picnic.

Up till three in the afternoon there was never a sunnier June day. Nor was the heat too great. Why, then, the worst thunderstorm of the year should have chosen that afternoon remains unexplained. Anyhow, it arrived and with suddenness, the clouds rolling up, the lightning beginning to manifest, though yet in the distance, the thunder to mutter, even while Mr. Monroe was in the middle of his short discourse upon *Poetry*. He had a strong, musical, vibrant voice; it was carrying; everybody was grouped around under the trees of Spangler's Wood. He was repeating poetry; he was telling them about Ballads:

> "The King sits in Dunfermline Town
> Drinking the blood-red wine."

And above Love Poetry:

> "Oh, my love's like a red, red rose
> That's newly sprung in June;
> Oh, my love's like the melody
> That's sweetly played in tune."

And above the poetry of Nature:

> "Hail to thee, blithe Spirit!
> Bird thou never wert,
> That from Heaven, or near it,
> Pourest thy full heart—"

All the Daughters of Culture, all the men and women without that proud name who yet were happy in Spangler's Wood, listened intently, perceiving that it was well, it was certainly well, to have Culture.

Pallas, her body seated beside Marietta under an oak tree, dwelt in a rich and deep heaven—yet she heard the thunder and she thought, "It's time the carriage was coming!"

But Uncle Isaac and the carriage did not appear. She ought to be away, she knew that, if she was going to reach Cherry Hill by four o'clock. Maybe, with it clouding up and all, Miss Margaret couldn't send him; he didn't like bad weather. She ought, she thought, to slip away; it was but four miles, which was nothing for Pallas to walk. . . . But, ah, how charming to listen to this poetry—and maybe the storm would go by—and maybe

Uncle Isaac and the carriage would come.

A brighter flash, a louder, longer roll. The wind began to moan. James Monroe ended his discourse. "There is a storm coming, but it leads to rainbows—Mrs. Walters, where's the nearest shelter for us all?"

The nearest shelter was indeed and in truth the houses of Clothes Line Creek. The picnic broke in all suddenness, in a scurry out of the high woods into the several roads and the paths of the fields. Exhilaration accompanied the going. "My land! Will you look at the clouds!"—

"I wish I was a bird!"—"Lan's sakes, it's getting dark!"

Hitched among the trees were ancient buggies and surreys, and half a dozen flivvers kept a line like beetles upon the dusky road. The owners piled into these and took friends upon their knees and upon the running boards.

"Get in here, Marietta; get in quick!" That was Esterella in the surrey that had brought her and Patsy West and Mr. James Monroe.

"I thought I'd go with Pallas," cried Marietta. "Has Uncle Isaac come with the carriage? I can't see for the trees whipping about so! Pallas!"

"Pallas's gone," cried Esterella. "She went with Jane Corbin. I told her she better not wait for Uncle Isaac. I told her she better go right along and not get that dress ruined nor be late neither. They'll let her out at the big gate. . . . Get in quick. Get in, Mr. Monroe. O-o—h! That lightning's like the Judgment Day!"

"You're sure she's gone?" asked James Monroe.

Yes, Esterella was sure. The Corbins' car was ahead of them. The surrey, Monroe driving, departed the place. All the wheels were turning, all the feet hurrying away. Spangler's Wood was left dark and swaying.

But Pallas was not in the car with Jane Corbin. It must have happened in one of those ways that are inexplicable and yet certain, infallible, supernaturally frictionless. Jane Corbin perhaps heard her say, "I'll crowd you, ma'am," and thought she said further, "I'll go with Marietta," or perhaps esteemed that she saw Isaac and the Cherry Hill carriage. It was now so shadowy in the wood! The car, already well filled, started to move, move faster, was gone. Pallas fought with a great gust of wind; a lightning flash dazzled her and a thunder clap brought her hands to her ears. Everyone was streaming from the wood. She had better go too, if was dangerous to stay under the trees.

She hurried, in her fluttering blue gown, with some boys and women whom she did not know well, but no Cherry Hill carriage met her, and the storm grew louder and longer and the rain began to fall in slow, enormous drops. Spangler's Wood and then the narrow Spangler's Road fell behind the hastening cluster; here was the highroad, in thunder, lightning, and now sheets of rain; here was the forking road to Cherry Hill. By now each individual was individually fighting the storm; those also hurrying homeward hardly saw Pallas when she turned aside for Cherry Hill. Merryville—Clothes Line Creek—was much nearer. It would have been easier to go there, or to strike across the fields to Grassy Hollow.

But she had promised Mammy and Miss Margaret. . . . She must get to Cherry Hill. The storm—and it was a terrible, big storm—was making it like night, and she had three miles and more to go, and the wind and rain against her. The blue dress was ruined and clinging about her. She ran as for her life through the thunder, lightning, wind and rain.

Uncle Isaac and the carriage never appeared because Mrs. Crewe had refused to let them go. Mrs. Crewe had arrived at Cherry Hill well in advance of the storm. Yes, she was home much earlier than she had expected, though not because of the storm! Simply, she had had a premonition. She had said to her friends, "I know that things are going wrong in my absence."

"The mice were playing?" said Miss Margaret. "No, I didn't mean that, Octavia! But nothing is wrong."

Mrs. Crewe's lips made a hard, thin line, then opened: "With Sybil's face swelled twice its natural size by a hornet's sting, and Susan confessing to have eaten berries that may as well as not have been nightshade, and Sylvia fallen into the creek—"

"Sylvia periodically falls into the creek," said Miss Margaret. "This is the fourth time, Mammy says, this month. It's nowhere deeper than her knee, and we changed her clothes immediately. The berries were not nightshade, but early huckleberries. I'll have to grant the hornet. It stung Sybil as she was sitting on the porch reading aloud to us from Miss Edgeworth."

"As for Pallas," said Mrs. Crewe, "she goes tomorrow morning! I'll have nobody with the children who is not trustworthy."

The wind blew, the rain fell, an hour and more passed. Upstairs the children were in bed and Susan was crying. Mammy, who was afraid of lightning and whose knee, Mrs. Crewe said, was much worse, cowered in her own small room. Mrs. Crewe sat beside Susan in a clear, loud soprano sang "Happy Land." The lightning flashed vividly. A little blue figure was running up the drive. "Here she comes, poor Cinderella!" said Miss Margaret.

"No'm," a few minutes later said Pallas to Mrs. Crewe. "No'm, it wasn't wrong. If it had been wrong, Miss Margaret and Mammy Julia wouldn't have let me do it. And I wouldn't have done it myself, Miss Octavia. No'm. I ought to have got back earlier because I said I would. I take sin to myself for not leaving before I did, because—because it was so pleasant, ma'am. But I thought maybe the carriage was coming and—and I was so happy. But when I did come, I came as fast as I could, Miss Octavia."

It all made no difference. "Go and get out of that wretched, unsuitable, dripping and streaming blue dress! Everyone must have laughed at you in it! I will tell someone to make you a hot lemonade. You deserve an illness, but probably you will not have it."

"No'm, I won't. Miss Octavia," said Pallas. "And I must tell you, ma'am, that they didn't laugh at me."

Whereupon Mrs. Crewe said that she was impertinent, and that wet did not hurt weeds. "And tomorrow morning you will go back to Grassy Hollow. I will pay you for two weeks and let you go. I have been thinking for some time that you would not suit me."

It broke the most beautiful morning after the picnic in Spangler's Wood. The storm had washed everything clear; never were such greens and blues, never such sunny freshness of air. No one had been hurt by the tempest.

Mr. James Monroe must leave upon the afternoon train. There existed an engagement that he must keep. But that mattered the less because he was coming back. He had been going to give himself, he told Esterella, a month's holiday this summer. Now he knew where on the earth it was going to be spent.

In the meantime, this morning, he wished to drive again about the country, and might he have that horse and buggy? Yes, indeed, he might, and Henry Clay Buchanan, happily grinning, brought it to the Walters' door. But today, Mr. Monroe, leaving a silver half-dollar with Henry Clay, drove off alone.

He drove toward Cherry Hill. The road mounted, and here was the best view. Checking the horse, he sat in a dream, his eyes upon the white-pillared place. In his mind he planned: "I must go today because of that engagement. But I can get back by the middle of July. . .Pallas—Pallas—Pallas! . . . And how do you know that she is crying for you as you are crying for her?"

A figure coming from that old plantation was climbing the hill toward him. As it approached, he saw that it was a woman, and then he saw that it was Pallas. . .no longer in that beautiful blue dress, but in a brown calico, with a kerchief around her head and carrying a basket and an ancient carpetbag. He sprang from the buggy and went toward her.

"Where are you going?"

"I am going to Grassy Hollow. . . ."

"I will drive you there," said James Monroe.

Never was anything so lovely as the June morning! The waving trees and singing birds, the earth and the water and air and fire, and light and love and power and glory!

Lion Loose!

Moriarty's Circus would be at Rivermead on Friday. The excitement of that small village and its neighborhood mounted a degree a day. The flaming pictures upon board fences and the sides of barn and stable fed it. MORIARTY'S CIRCUS. Golden Chariots Discoursing Music. Thrilling Trapeze Events. Clowns. Knife Swallowers. Snake Charmers. Elephants. Camels. Giraffes. Bengal Tigers. Lions. Beautiful Women Riding Milk-white Horses. Ring-masters. Lion Tamers. Moriarty's Favorite Lion, by name Big Tim.

Anticipation has its joys. All felt it—little town, sparsely settled country, white folks, colored folks. The children most, but their elders also. The elders, as of old, were going because they must take the children. But young people of a marriageable age were going because they might go together.

Colored folks were dotted about in Rivermead and the region around like pepper with salt, or soot on snow. A whole pepper pod resided in the miniature delta formed by the Grapevine Creek and a bend in the River Mead. Grapevine Town, with just the creek between it and the white folks' big houses and gardens and High Street and the three stores and three churches and the old tavern and all the rest of Rivermead. Grapevine cabins and garden patches, ailanthus and locust trees, and perennial flowers, hardy and bright. Above Grapevine the creek withdrew into papaw bushes, witch-hazel, greenbrier, wild plum, sycamore and sundry. It was a tangle and persisted for a long way, the creek pushing like a corkscrew deep into Old Wood. Old Wood that had lived on from pioneer, from Indian, days. Old Wood, loping shaggy and strong, through Mead's Gap and up the steeply sloping sides of Great Mead Mountain.

But on Rivermead side of the creek, before you came to the Gap proper, on the edge of Old Clearing, a mile and more from Rivermead and Grapevine Town, stood, with a corn patch and a dooryard, the cabin of Old Aunt Jinny. Old Aunt Jinny was at least a hundred. No one could remember when she was born. When any asked her she answered, "Lawd, chile! I don' remember no moh'n the res' of you. Maybe I was nevah bawn. Maybe I just is."

All her family had died from her or journeyed away from the cabin and these parts, saving only her grandson Elijah and Elijah's daughter, Rhoda. Elijah worked in Rivermead; Rhoda stayed at home with her great-grandmother. Old Aunt Jinny couldn't walk any longer. She sat in a rockingchair with a Rising Sun quilt wrapped about her, and she smoked a pipe and saw pictures of very long ago. Rhoda was twenty, a slender girl dark and smooth of skin as a chinquapin, with the big and liquid eyes of her race and its rich voice. She loved Old Aunt Jinny and took good care of her.

The circus of Moriarty. Moriarty had begun in a humble capacity as a tender of animals, long ago with old Jones' circus. Moriarty had all Ireland in him and he rose. He determined to rise by means of the animals, a born gift that way helping him. Few were the beasts that Moriarty could not handle. When he couldn't use affection he used terror, and when terror failed to pay, again he took up affection. He honestly preferred affection, and came largely to depend upon his grin and his blue eyes and the stroking movement of his big hand, and upon something else, impalpable, but in which he believed. He became—upon the bills—MORIARTY THE LION TAMER. Then he married old Jones' daughter but kept on with his great cats. By now there was hardly any big circus that would not have jumped at Moriarty. Old Jones died. The circus became Moriarty's Circus. His wife, whom Moriarty loved quite tenderly, died. There were no children. At forty-five, Moriarty stood owner of a prosperous concern with which he had been identified since boyhood. He no longer tamed lions, nor in parade rode in the cage with them, nor went through—apparently—terrifying adventures with them. Most of the animals only knew him now for the King of the Show. The exception with whom he still maintained, as it were, a personal relation was Big Tim.

The connection between the two was of long standing. Moriarty had tamed him and named him long ago. He was a huge fellow. Moriarty said he was an Irish lion. Jim, the clown, on that long-past day, had remarked that there were no lions in Ireland. "Nayther are there snakes since the blessed Saint Patrick," said Moriarty. "Yit there are Irish snakes and by the same token Irish lions. This big one is me own counthryman."

Once in so often Moriarty rode in the parade in the cage with Big Tim. When he did not, no one else did. Long James, the lion tamer engaged before the death of Mrs. Moriarty, handled the other lion and the lioness and the leopard. But not Big Tim.

All Rivermead and Grapevine and the country around were going to the circus; everybody who wasn't too young or too old or too sick or too ghastly poor or too utterly utter religious, or who wasn't tethered by a responsibility.

Juniper worked at Flower Hill, a plantation five miles from Rivermead and Grapevine Town, six and a half from Old Aunt Jinny's cabin. He kept thinking and dreaming. "Rhoda and me'll go together lak we did last summer. . .and the summer before that." But when at last Sunday came and he saw her, Creed had forestalled him.

"I kept thinking you'd wait for me, Rhoda. I kept thinking you'd know."

"You move lak a terrapin in the road, and Creed move lak a bird."

He got no more than that. She liked her figure of speech. "Yaas, Lawd! You move lak a terrapin in the road, and Creed move lak a bird."

"You mean you gwine fly away with Creed for good?"

"What you got to take," said Rhoda, "is that Ise going with him to Moriarty's Circus. I don't have to explanify further." She retied the blue kerchief upon her head. "Maybe there isn't anything else to explanify."

Juniper struck his hands together. "I been dreaming and dreaming of us going----"

"That's just it. Dreaming and not doing."

"I had to work."

"Of course you had to. I said every evening, 'Juniper had to wuhk'. . . . Why don't you ask Evie to go to the circus? Seem to me she kind of bawn yo' kind."

"Bawn slow, you mean?"

"I certainly thought I heard grandma calling. Yaas, she is . . . . Yaas'm, Ise coming! . . . Creed asked me last Sunday. You'd had a week since they put bills up."

"I thought you'd know----"

" 'Thought—thought!' You sho is lak that terrapin! Ef this

cabin was afire you'd nevah get heah in time to pull me and grandma out! . . . Yaas'm. Ise coming!"

The gate had on one side a Rose-of-Sharon bush and on the other a sweetshrub. Juniper waited. Time went by. Rhoda appeared in the cabin door. "She got one of her spells. You might as well go along. I ain't coming out any more. So long, Juniper!"

She vanished. The cabin went out like a candle.

"I'm going along," said Juniper. "I'm going along. But I ain't going ask Evie in yo' place. You sits in yo' own place with me. You's the Queen on the Throne. Whatever you do, you's the Princess in the Tower. . . . Even if I die, even if you takes Creed for all the time, not just for that circus, Friday! . . . Creed! He ain't much!"

He left behind him the lonely cabin, set as it was away from everybody else, far up Grapevine Creek. An old white folks' cabin. An old pioneer cabin, a hundred years ago. But now, for many a long year, Old Aunt Jinny's. The path down the creek had thick growth left and right. Juniper strode along, a young black man, strongly made, charcoal-black, slow speaking, slow thinking, but sound when it was thought, with the type of countenance that when it is old will be venerable, but now is taken for simple. He had those figures of a queen on a throne and a princess in a tower out of a fairy-tale book that Miss Everarda West at Flower Hill had given him. He might have taken, too, the figure of the disappointed knight.

Rivermead High Street. Creed coming toward him—Creed, brown and limber, lively as a cricket. "Mawning!"

"Mawning!"

"Circus coming."

"Yaas."

"Who you going to take, Juniper?"

"I lay out to work that day. I got er rail fence to make at Flower Hill."

"You're earning a lot of money."

"Yaas."

"I read something once in a paper, 'Spending's as important as earning.' Rhoda and I are going together."

"Yaas, I asked her," said Juniper. "She said she was going with you."

"Yaas, she is."

Juniper looked him up and down. " 'Terrapin,' " he said. " 'Terrapin.' and 'bird.' Bird, is you a crow or a humming bird or a mockingbird or a whippoorwill or a hoot owl or an English sparrow, or what?"

"What's got in you? Only I reckon I knows?" said Creed, and laughed.

Juniper prayed within himself: "Lawd, make me remember I belongs to the church! Lawd, make me remember I belongs to the church! Ef Ise a terrapin, make me remember who I is and draw in mah head and feetses."

Creed laughed again. Said Juniper, "Lawd knows, I'd lak to fight you right heah and now, or any place you'd lak to appoint! But I ain't gwine do it--I ain't gwine do it. And now Ise due to Flower Hill. Fare you well—fare you well, Mr. Bird!"

He went on up the street with his head hanging. Creed made a skip in the dust. "Poor ol' Juniper! He is that slow and peaceful."

Thursday night there shone a great round moon. It looked down upon Moriarty's Circus, coming, in the gulf of the night, into Rivermead. So mysterious, so shadowy, so huge, the paraphernalia, the wagons, the walking animals; so exotic the sounds. A not inconsiderable part of Rivermead waked with the moon. Just at the edge of town, between Grapevine Creek and the river, spread a great open green, or common, immemorially used for anything of this nature. Here the shadowy army, here the twinkling lights, here Moriarty's great voice, "Hurry up now, or be jabbers----"

An elephant trumpeted in the night. A lion roared. Young boys of Rivermead, down at the meadow, under the moon, on the fringe of things, shivered with strangeness and delight. "Oo-oh! Did you hear that lion?"

The moon slid down the western sky. In Rivermead, in Grapevine Town, in the country round about, cocks were crowing, dogs were barking. The morning wind rose from its own lair, birds began to peep, heraldic colors flared into the east. In its own good time sprang the sun. The great day had begun. Up went Moriarty's big tent and the lesser offspring tents. The parade was to begin at ten. That gave time for the country folk to come in.

The sun shone upon Great Mead Mountain and Little Mead Mountain. The sun splashed into Grapevine Creek and gilded

Old Wood. The sun touched with golden fingers Old Aunt Jinny's solitary cabin, and the smoke tree and the sweetshrub and the Rose-of-Sharon. Old Aunt Jinny's grandson, Elijah, had not meant to go to the circus, because he was a preacher, though a lovable preacher, and also because his eyes were bad and he could not see much anyhow. He had meant to stay with grandma and let that chile Rhoda go. But so late as Thursday morning he had a letter about his sister Eliza at Lockwood, thirty miles down the river. Eliza was mighty sick; she had had a stroke. Elijah had better come right away and see about her. Elijah took twenty dollars out of bank and the noon boat. He spoke to his daughter. "Honey, I don' want you to miss that circus. Yo' grandma seem pretty spry. I reckon Ellen Shirley won't be going, seeing the grass ain't sprouting yet on Jim's mound. You get her to come sit with yo' grandma." And so Rhoda went to Ellen.

But Ellen Shirley was going. She was going with the Browns, because Jim had come to her in a dream and told her to be sure to go.

Rhoda went to Sarah Jones. But Sarah had to go to take her dead sister's children. Rhoda went to Aunt Ailsy Semmes. "Aunt Ailsy, would you spend the day tomorrow with grandma? I'll leave a good dinner in the safe."

"Lawd, chile, I would jes' for love, layin' aside yo' good dinner! But my white folks done ask me to watch the parade with them, and afterward to spend the day and look after the baby so that Miss Julia and that yaller nurse, too, kin go. Miss Julia give me er shawl jes' as good as new!"

Rhoda went to Alice Lagg. But Alice, too, was going, crutch and all. All Grapevine Town was going.

Rhoda returned to the cabin, walking sorrowfully in the late afternoon light. Old Aunt Jinny sat nodding and nodding in her chair. Her pipe was in her hand, the ashes fell out upon her checked apron. "I jes' couldn't leave her all day long by herself," thought the girl. "She might set herself afire. Oh, Lawd, I want to go that circus! . . . Maybe you'll send someone to stay."

But no one came. "I reckon the Lawd's sending me what I deserves. . .treating Juniper thataway and taking up with Creed . . . . Oh, Juniper, Ise sorry!"

When Old Aunt Jinny woke up it was to put her foot down.

"In co'se youse gwine to the circus! Don' you reckon, gal, I wants to heah about it? What gwine happen to me? Ise smoked by this ha'th for er hundred yeahs and hasn't burned myself up yit! You kin go see the parade en you kin come back heah en give me my dinnah right quick en then go back to the circus. Do that yaller nigger Creed good to stretch he legs! As fer yo' grandma, she des' as safe as the Bible."

But in the middle of the night Old Aunt Jinny took another of her spells. As soon as it was dawn she would get up and be helped on with her clothes and sit in her rocker between the door and the hearth and be given her pipe. "Ise all right en I'll be all right when the rest of you is being druv to de burying ground." But before the sun was well up she had turned forgetful again and was sitting smiling toothlessly, or nearly toothlessly, to herself and maundering of Grapevine Creek and Rivermead when they first began. "Mah ol' massa. You never saw such a man as mah ol' massa. He was a man! Dey don' mek them thataway any moah!"

Creed came up Grapevine Creek, dressed in his best, limber and gay. The nine o'clock sun washed the cabin and the garden patch, the slight fence and the blooming dooryard. Rhoda came to the door. "Hey!" cried Creed. "You ain't dressed yet to go? Hurry up, gal!"

"Creed, I can't go. Father's in Lockwood and grandma's took one of her spells of wandering in her mind. I dasn't leave her and I can't get a soul to stay. I could cry about it, but I can't go."

Creed grew excited and persuasive. "Pshaw! The old woman's all right. Ain't a thing going to happen to her! World knows Old Aunt Jinny's set a thousand days in this cabin all by herself! You put things so's she can get them and come along! It's the finest circus ever!"

"No, I can't."

"Yaas, you can! You ain't got no call to throw me over and disappoint me. Bareback riders and trapeze folk and clowns and a great gold band wagon and the drums beating and the horns blowing and elephants and lions. . . . The tents are all up in Big Meadow."

"Of course I want to go. But it ain't right for me to go. Ise dreadful sorry, Creed."

"You let me speak to Old Aunt Jinny! I know she'll want

you to have yo' pleasure."

"No, I don't want you to! It makes her wander more when she's talked to. I can't go, Creed."

Creed stamped his foot and swung his arms. "Then I holds that you's treating me shabby! I has the money and I has the will to make you have the best time you ever did have, and I counted on you! Every fellow in Grapevine Town has got his girl—unless it's that po' lazy Juniper. I tol' everybody I was going to take you and now I'm out in the cold."

"Take somebody else, Creed. I done tol' you I was sorry."

"There ain't anybody else this time of day."

"Did Juniper ask Evie?"

"I reckon he did. Anyhow, I ain't a-going to. Ah, come along, Rhoda!"

"No." Rhoda shook her head with the tears in her eyes. She wanted to see the parade. She wanted to go to the wonderful circus. She didn't have so many pleasures, away up here, away from everybody. She saw a shining small picture of Juniper and Evie, shining and sorrowful. She did not see Creed, either with or without another. She was sorry that she was disappointing Creed, but that was all, as far as Creed was concerned. Creed wasn't behaving well either. . . . Creed wasn't Juniper.

Creed, losing his temper completely, began to say unpleasant things. Rhoda went into the cabin and slammed the door in his face. She thought, "Juniper wouldn't act thataway, for all he is slow to come when you want him."

Old Aunt Jinny caught her by the sleeve. "Is you Rhoda or is you Dilsey? Dilsey, ain't we gwine to the barbacue? Dilsey!"

"She calling her sister," thought Rhoda with awe. "She calling her sister who been daid seventy years."

Old Aunt Jinny began to sing, and it was an awesome sound.

"De mountain rock an' de river flow."

Creed departed down Grapevine Creek. He almost ran, he was in such a hurry. Evie Marshall would be second choice or even third choice with all the fellows. It would be right likely that Evie was going just with her family. He might catch her in time. She would go—yaas, Lawd, she would go and jump at it! But when he got to the Marshall's in Grapevine Town, Evie was gone with Baxter.

It was not in Juniper's heart to go to Rivermead at all that day. He meant to stay at Flower Hill and finish that rail fence. Then something spoke to him and spoke right plainly. "You go, Juniper. You go." He obeyed, though still his heart ached, and High Street and all its humming and commotion, so pleasurable to others, could not at first lighten it.

At the Big Meadow end of town, where High Street, trailing its glories, became dusty and poor and joined Grapevine Town, he met Creed. "Where's Rhoda?"

Creed was quick to let him know. "Old Aunt Jinny took a spell. Yaas, I know you are surprised. But Old Aunt Jinny took a mighty bad spell, and she just had to stay, though she was weeping over it."

"Ise sorry," said Juniper in his slow way. "Ise sorry she's lost her pleasure."

Out of Big Meadow and its tents sprang music. The parade —the parade was beginning! The parade would go High Street and return Winding Street, a mile in all. All Rivermead was out on the old brick sidewalks of High Street. When the parade had passed a certain station that station would rush by lanes, and no matter how, down to Winding Street, and so have the parade twice. All Rivermead and all Grapevine Town and all the country folks.

Grapevine Town would have the glories first, would get from High Street to Winding Street first. "Oh, well," stated Creed, "I ain't going lose the taste of this day for no girl living, Rhoda nor anybody! There's plenty on the bushes!"

The music grew louder. A surge of excited folk brought by Todd and Leana, Ragland and Althea, Baxter and Evie. "That you, Creed? Thought you going have Rhoda——"

"Old Aunt Jinny——"

Juniper thought, "She's missing this heah parade, then I gwine miss it too." He left High Street and went by Green Path down to Winding Street. Here it was quiet enough, but he did not stop; he went on down to the river. The river bank was as quiet as a desert, and the long clean top of Great Mead Mountain rested still and solemn against a sky like a blue morning-glory. The parade was moving up High Street; he heard the band.

"Honey, I wish you could hear it too. I wish you could hab yo' pleasure!"

Moriarty's Circus paraded. High Street stood rapt, save when it bent itself double, clapped, laughed, shouted with delight. Grapevine Town and the country thrilled and thrilled and thrilled.

"Ah, look at they bears!"

"Ah, look at that boa constrictor!"

"What he name? Dat's jes' plain snake! But he sure is monstrous."

"Old Mr. Tiger----"

"Ha-ha! Ho-ho! Ha-ha! Look at that clown flirting with a dressed-up monkey!"

"Oh, the ponies! Oh, the trick horses!"

"Look at the short-skirt ladies! My Lawd!"

"Dere come the men! Look at the spangles and the tights and the leopard skins! My land! Those girls haven't got a chance!"

"Yonder comes another band wagon!"

Moriarty believed in music and provided it liberally.

"Look at that float with the Fairy Queen!"

"Look at them acrobats!"

"Here come more cages. . . ."

"That's a jaguar. Those are hyenas. Black leopard. Will you look at those birds and the wings of them!"

"That clown on that trick mule will kill me sure!"

"What's that stepping next all by his lonesome? That's a giraffe! Remembered him out of the geography book."

"Zebras and camels! My land! I think I see the Ark up there on Great Mead."

Music blared and thundered from a mounted band. After it came Moriarty himself, for such was his fancy, driving in the parade, sitting back in a shining tall hat, in a barouche drawn by bay horses, with coachman and footmen. Behind the barouche in a cage all green and gold where it was not iron bars followed Big Tim.

"Moriarty and his lion! Moriarty and his lion!"

"He always rides that way. And he tamed that lion—though the Lawd knows it don't look anyways in particular tame!"

Along the top of the cage ran in gold letters, BIG TIM THE IRISH LION. Moriarty, smiling and tipping his hat to overjoyed

Rivermead, had in the back of his head a remark that he wished to make to Big Tim. Something about Big Tim that morning had struck a fine little warning note. "Begorrah, it's afther dhraming ag'in ye are, Tim, me bhoy! Cut it out! This ain't lion country, for all there's a foine mountain and wood."

Big Tim lay down in his cage and put his vast tawny head upon his paws. Brooding and brooding and brooding.

Moriarty went by and Big Tim went by. More clowns went by, more features—then, swinging along, elephants.

Elephants. Five of them.

Juniper down on the river bank ate the bread and meat he had brought from Flower Hill. When it was eaten he walked along the shore, over the little grassy spits and the pebbly beaches. The Mead was a gallant river, running swift and strong through Mead's Gap, between Little Mead and Great Mead Mountains, covered yet with untroubled forest. Grapevine Creek flowed into it, bright and shallow, bordered by all manner of growth. All was close together—the wood, the mountains, the creek, the river, Rivermead and Grapevine Town. Big Meadow and the circus tents, too, were at hand. Juniper might hear the music and all the many voices, brute and human. When he turned from the river, the mountains, the wood and the creek he saw the folk hurrying, hurrying to the circus. Juniper liked a circus as well as anyone. He thought, "Reckon I'll go! Rhoda wouldn't go with me. Taking up with Creed. . . ."

He walked a little way toward the tents, but then stood still, lifting his arms above his head. "No, I won't go if you're not going, Rhoda, my lady! Take up with who you please—Ise yours. Ise yours!"

The river ran by; Old Wood across Grapevine Creek, pushing up the mountainsides to the mountaintop, dreamed under the zenith sun. The top of Great Mead had a long line of broken cliff, juts and insets, broken stony areas presenting many a fortunate den and pleasant lurking place. The sun gliding all made a remoteness and a nearness. Juniper threw himself down on the river bank. An hour passed, two hours. The circus music, the circus genial uproar came to him in waves; he lay idly listening to these, or he lay asleep, or he lay in thought of Rhoda and of a cabin by Flower Hill, a cabin by Flower Hill when Old Aunt Jinny died at last. . . . But now maybe it would never be, now maybe Creed was thinking of a cabin.

With a final coruscation the performance in the big tent ended. Rivermead, Grapevine and the country began to stream forth. Juniper got to his feet, stretched himself and entering Big Meadow crossed to the tents.

The world emerged, happily talking. Moriarty had lived up to the glory of his bills. Moriarty took joy in the simplicity and huge labor of doing well. Everybody had had the time of the summer. Everybody was sorry for the relatively few of the region who had not been packed under the big canvas, watching from the safety of the heaven-soaring benches life in unfamiliar and apparently dangerous situations. Nobody was in a hurry to leave the inclosure. Here were still the side shows, the menagerie tent, the pink-lemonade stands, the balloon man, the striped candy, a whole scattering fire of joys, to say nothing of the exchange of gratulation and valuable opinions. White and colored, young and old, high and low, Rivermead, Grapevine and the country round about swarmed like bees in a small compass.

Juniper found Todd and Leana. Ragland and Althea and Evie and Baxter joined them. Then up came Creed, limber and carefree, over his pique with Rhoda, only pitying her now, and having had a very good time. "Didn't see you, Juniper? Where was you?"

"Down on the river bank, looking at the sky," said Juniper.

"Not at the circus at all! Will you heah that! Old Juniper jes' been mooning erlong the river bank!"

"Mooning erlong the river bank. My Lawd!"

"Such a shoving and a pushing----" began Leana.

"What that shouting?"

"Oh, my Lawd! Oh, my Lawd!"

"LION LOOSE! LION LOOSE! LION LOOSE!"

That was a moment—that was a moment in Big Tim's existence when the bars gave way before him! Something was wrong with them—weaker, hey, than they thought for? "Then out, me bhoy, have a try for your freedom!" What dream had brought him standing, turned all that was latent into open, shouted? And he answered—answered with a sudden great plunge forward and out. Astoundingly out!

Out, and there stretched the trampled earth between the cages in the menagerie tent and shone the opening! Inpouring light, the scent of water, of forest, of mountain! Within Big Tim the Irish lion a myriad languid and sunken voices rose into one great cry. Forth from the tent that likewise now was shouting forth like a tawny bowlder out of a giant's sling----

"LION LOOSE! LION LOOSE!"

Folk tumbled over one another, clearing his path. Had Moriarty been there—but Moriarty was yet in the big tent. Men, women and children went this way and went that, like chickens in a barnyard with the hawk above them. But not vengeance, only freedom, hallooed to Big Tim. Bound on bound, forth from the tent. One moment of pause, out in the light, standing like rock in the shouting and running world. There before him, there before him at no distance, he saw brown, shallow, narrow water and a beautiful bordering thicket, and the thicket ran into tall forest and the tall forest, persisting, became a mountain-side. He saw it and smelled it, smelled freedom. Bound on bound, the lion left behind him Moriarty's tents, cleared the inclosure, burst through the papaw, greenbrier, hazel and sycamore on the margin of Grapevine Creek, crossed that shallow brown water and entered Old Wood, going toward Mead's Gap and the deep flank of Great Mead. Men by the creek saw him to, could report his direction.

In the meantime what a clamor around the tents, in Big Meadow, from Rivermead, Grapevine and the country! "Lion—lion!" "That big lion?" "Lawd-a-mighty, you reckon he coming back heah?" "No, he ain't, not by the looks of him! He's making for the rocks atop of Great Mead----"

Moriarty with a picked dozen and the paraphernalia wherewith to take an escaped lion passed through the throng. The big Irishman shouted, "There's no nade, I'm telling ye, for alarm! He's me favorite and will come running when he hears me voice. We'll bring him back with ropes that Samson couldn't break, and when he sees his cage in he'll jump jist as aisy and glad to be at home again!" He paused a moment and used upon Rivermead and Grapevine and the country his grin and his blue eyes and his general bigness and easiness. "It's to go on home and be at peace I'm advising you. But if the road of any of you is afther lying that way"—he gave a general sweep of his arm toward Old Wood and Great Mead—my advice to you is that ye jist stay talking a bit with your frinds in the town that's one of the most beauteous and altogether frindly I've iver met! Ye'll be hearing before long that Moriarty—that's mesilf—and Big Tim have met again. When that's so everything's as safe for you as the little flower garden of the blessed saints!"

With which Moriarty and his men, with their ropes, net and irons, vanished into the growth about Grapevine Creek, splashed through the brown water, scrambled up the farther bank and departed out of hearing.

At any rate the lion was not in Rivermead nor in Grapevine. The lion would be loping through Old Wood, up the great flank of the mountain, to the rocky dens and ledges, gathered in a long dream up there, against the deep blue afternoon sky. Or he might choose crouching, lying perdu, in some hollow of Old Wood. Nobody lived just at the foot or on the side of Great Mead. He'd never get through Mead's Gap, to the farms beyond. Moriarty would have him long before that! The crowd in Big Meadow buzzed, buzzed, excited and now pleasurably so by this last colorful titbit. The circus folk around told all who applied to them for information that they might await with confidence the event between Moriarty and Big Tim.

Juniper had stood open-mouthed, thrilled, exclaiming, with those around him, with Baxter and Ragland and Todd, with Creed, with the girls, with the generality of Grapevine, with Big Sarah Harrison whom he found beside him. Big Sarah, now that they were all so reassured, clapped her hands and doubled herself as best she might. "Jes' to think of that lion loping along with his mane cutting the wind—or a-crouching in the wild plum with his big yaller eyes, as big as my fist! I reckon he look lak that back in Africa."

Juniper experienced a dropping away of circus grounds and circus throng, of Rivermead and Grapevine Town and every voice of either. . . . Away up Grapevine Creek, how quiet it was in the afternoon light! The cabin of Rhoda and Old Aunt Jinny. All by itself, and Elijah gone done the river. Just Rhoda and the old woman. Lonely cabin, the first to be built up Grapevine, the logs laid and daubed long, long ago. An old white folks' cabin long ago. But now Rhoda and Elijah and Old Aunt Jinny. The cabin and the corn patch and the dooryard with the smoke tree and the Rose-of-Sharon and the sweetshrub and the old daylilies, and the slender rickety fence and the open door this warm weather. . . . What if that lion went that way? Everybody, including Moriarty, knew that he was bounding away from Grapevine Creek, set for the Gap or for Great Mead, but it came to Juniper that you never could tell about lions. This one might take it into his head to turn in Old Wood and come back to

Grapevine Creek and go loping south along it. He might go padding by Old Aunt Jinny's, terrifying a girl if she were looking out. He might come padding up to Old Aunt Jinny's and make one bound over the fence that was slight and low enough, or the gate might be open. He might come slinking up to the door that likely enough would be ajar. He might try to get inside.

All this rose in one lantern slide before Juniper's mind. It didn't take any time to see it. Of course the lion wasn't doing any such thing. The lion at this very moment was halfway up Great Mead. Moriarty knew his thoughts and that was the way Moriarty was going. Up there, high upon Great Mead, where a lion might find dens and fortresses and hunting grounds and solitude. All the same. . . .

All the same Rhoda might somehow hear about it and be scared. Juniper slipped away.

The sunshine grew slant. Old Aunt Jinny, tired for very wandering, happy though the wandering was, fell asleep in her chair. Rhoda took the water bucket from its shelf by the door and went to the spring to fill it.

The spring lay thrice a stone's throw from the cabin. Rhoda, carrying the bucket on her head, went out of the gate, leaving it swinging open, between the sweetshrub and the Rose-of-Sharon.

The spring shone in its rocky cup beneath a high, grassy bank. Around grew mint, fern, boneset and beebalm, and a birch tree shook down shadow. The spring was so near to Grapevine Creek that the latter might be heard murmuring over its ledges. Heard but not seen, for the bordering growth hereabouts was thick and deep.

Rhoda, bending, filled the bucket, set it by, and bending lower, drank from her cupped hands. So cool was this water, so light and pure! When its surface had smoothed itself over, still upon her knees, still bending over, she studied the image it returned to her. "That's my face, that's my head, my arms and shoulders. . . . Young I is, but Ise been playing, playing—and calling names—'terrapin,' and the like. . . ."

In the birch tree a redbird was whistling and singing. Now suddenly it quit its singing. It made a dead pause, then whistled loud and sharp and flew away.

Moriarty surely knew his lion's thoughts and that he was making for the mountainside, for the cliffy brow of Great Mead, where he might find true lurking places and a fort for himself, and a wide, wide view of any coming, together with opportunities for some kind of prey, with solitariness until he could look about him, with maybe some fantastic hope, hope dying late with beasts and men. Surely Moriarty knew, since Moriarty and his men were at this moment going that way. Probably enough they had come upon the lion's tracks. . . . All that was so, Juniper felt. But yet he had a picture of Old Aunt Jinny's cabin and the blue smoke coming out of its chimney like a pretty feather, and the pinky smoke tree and the Rose-of-Sharon and the sweetshurb and the yellow lilies, and the old, worn fence and the open door. . . . Anyhow, he might say to Rhoda, "I just thought you might hear about it and be scared."

The path up Grapevine Creek was narrow. Juniper had a mile and a half of Grapevine old path to cover. The wild grape hanging in festoons and curtains from the trees brushed him at times as he went. He wasn't going in the least like a terrapin.

The redbird in the birch tree gave its strident note and flew away. Rhoda left bending over the water, rose from her knees and putting her hands to the bucket prepared to lift it to her head. The witchhazels stirred. She looked that way. Her hands came to her breast, held each other there. "What's that anyway?" Big Tim moved so that he might be more fully seen. What had motivated Big Tim who can say? Certainly he had escaped into Old Wood and toward Mead's Gap and the rocky face of Great Mead. What alarm, what guess that this was the way they would follow, what whim, what diversion, what pounce toward some small, living, fleeing, four-footed thing, what sense for water and grasp that this creekhead, too, might usher him into wilderness? Whatever and however it may have been, the fact rests that he had swerved and come this way, and he hoped that the men of whom he had grown tired would come to some bad end upon the mountainside. He had come up the creek through the bushes, he had drunk and had been refreshed and made some slight delay gazing at himself in the water; in the exciting, joyful, delirious company of his dreams he had pushed on. Wilderness evidently before him, leagues of it! Perhaps at last grassy desert, and he would know what to do there. . . . Perhaps companions. There ran away from the course he had been taking a thread of a path. The lion followed it into a mess of hazel bushes, old trees and swinging vines. This came to an end in a low growth of fragrant stuff, into which descended a grassy bank. At the foot of this bubbled a spring, and beside the spring kneeled a woman.

The lion halted, stood as though turned to bronze, then crouched. Hunger. Prey. He began to move his tail to and fro, awaking his strength. It was Africa about him—Africa! The woman rose and turned. She stood frozen. Still he crouched, with that moving tail, with eyes growing red and baleful.

Rhoda was praying, though without sound. There wasn't any sound anywhere, now the redbird had flown away and all other birds had ceased. "Jesus, Jesus, save me! Jesus, Jesus!"

But when she saw Juniper coming she screamed to him. "Don't come any further, Juniper! There's a lion here!"

Juniper was coming from the cabin, having been there and found that Rhoda and the water bucket were gone to the spring. So he was on the other side of her from the hazel thicket. And he had Elijah's scythe, having found it leaning against the smoke tree and put out his hand for it. He began to run. He burst through the alder, the fern and the mint, he arrived beside Rhoda. "Honey, honey! I'll stand befo' you lak this. Now you step backward twel you get to that elder bush. Then you run, run hard, for all you's worth, and shut the cabin door. I gwine kill that lion."

"I isn't a-going!" cried Rhoda. "No, I isn't! When he comes I dash this bucket of water—I wish it was scalding!"

"Go, Rhoda, go!"

"No!"

Big Tim's mane began to rise, out of this throat came a sound like distant thunder. A lion had to live. He meant to spring and every sinew now came to time. That scythe was formidable, but it began to enrage him too. It seemed to cry, "They are on your tracts—they are on your tracks!"

He left the hazels, he began to move toward Rhoda and Juniper, slowly yet, attaining his distance, his eyes murky red. Juniper held the scythe ready. "Don't you fear, honey, don't you fear! We gwine frighten him off----"

Up the creek, through the hazel and alder came a loud whistle and a shout. "Big Tim, ye rascal! Big Tim, ye rascal! Big Tim, me foine bhoy!"

And that was Moriarty. He also arrived at a run. "Tim,

Tim, ye Irishman---"

Big Tim gave it up. The world was too much for him, or at least his Irish brother was so. And having laid down he took up again his Irishness and all that it involved. Moriarty grinned at him, blue-eyed, and approaching twisted his hand in his mane. He did not need his revolver, hardly needed the men who came breathless after him. "Ye old giant!" said Moriarty. "What was ye afther, ye old dhramer, running your head into perdition? And if I hadn't felt in me bones just where ye turned and turned with ye. . . . Yis, yis, ye got to have the chains for a bit."

He turned to Rhoda and Juniper. "Ye was going to employ a scythe and a bucket of wather? Moreover and besides, ye wasn't afther screeching and sobbing and turning tail, which would have brought him on your shouldhers. Ye're a foine, up-standing pair, Irish I'm thinkin', in a black skin! The best of all things is Irish. Are yez brother and sister, or man and wife, or jist pure lovers?"

Juniper looked at Rhoda and Rhoda looked back at him. "Jes' pure lovers, sah," said Juniper, and, dropping the scythe, put his arm around Rhoda.

Doctor Barbary's Vision

Dr. Barbary went to the telephone. "Yes? Who is it? George Ross?"

"Doctor! It's come. She had a fall yesterday, and she was taken this morning. I managed to get over to Wilson's, to his phone. It's ever so much too soon, ain't it, Doctor? She's suffering horrid. There ain't anybody with us but old Mrs. Jackson. She says it don't seem to her to be going right. Will you come, Doctor, right away?"

Dr. Barbary, standing at the telephone, had a window beside him, a gray oblong with slow, infrequent snowflakes impacting the pane. He stood, a tall and strongly framed man, in riding boots and an old caped overcoat that he had had Heaven knows how long. Both were mud-splattered.

The telephone had rung as he entered his house. He was tired; he had been out through the morning and up a good part of the night before. It was cold and growing colder, the December roads wretched, George Ross's twelve miles if it was one, and across Danger Ridge.

Ross spoke again, alarmed at the pause. "Doctor, we just got to have you! Doctor, I keep athinking maybe she won't pull through----"

"All right, George," said Barbary. "I'll just get a morsel to eat and start directly. I'll stay the night. Tell Mrs. Jackson----"

He gave his directions and hung up the receiver. Mary his daughter, standing at the foot of the stairs, began to exclaim, "You're never going away the other side of Danger Ridge to George Ross's, Father! It's coming on to snow----"

"I can't help it, Mary. Is dinner ready? I'll ride Lady."

"The roads never were worse! Nobody's come over Danger Ridge lately."

"It'll be a seven months' baby. The first child, and she's had a fall. She's a frail, little thing anyhow. Tell Jim to feed Lady and bring her around. I want a big cup of strong coffee."

"You didn't get to bed till five and you've been out ever since eight!"

"It can't be helped, Mary. A doctor's a doctor."

"A country doctor is—I don't know what he is! A fine Christmas present you'll be giving us if you kill yourself.

"I won't," said Barbary. "I'm whipcord and hickory wood."

In the room that served him for an office he filled his saddlebags with all that he might need. Mary had a good fire burning for him. His big chair, and his slippers beside it, and the tobacco jar and the county paper. It was sad to leave rest and comfort, and he grumbled, to be sure, but such was life.

She rang the dinner bell for him, and he went into the dining room and sat down at the foot of the table and she at the head, and she gave him hot soup and then beef and a roast potato, hominy and greens, corn pone, and his big cup of strong coffee. "I expect to be back by noon to-morrow. If I'm kept I'll send George Ross or go myself to Wilson's and telephone you."

"Father, won't you be careful going over Danger Ridge? Couldn't you go around by Lonely Mill?"

"It takes too long. Pshaw, child! if I've ridden over that ridge once I have five hundred times, and I'm the most careful man living!"

"It's snowing harder."

"If it doesn't turn to sleet," he said, "but I don't reckon it will."

He got up from the table, shook himself into his thick and long coat, wrapped a comforter around his throat and pulled down his wide-brimmed, slouch hat over his brow. Rugged brow, rugged face were all tanned, seamed, and weather-bitten by thirty years of being a country doctor. Sometimes he saw himself as an old rock or gnarled pine tree; but rock and pine stood still, and he was forever going, forever getting into or out of saddle. Now he drew on his gauntlets and took his saddlebags and kissed his daughter, who stood in the doorway to see him mount.

It was all gray and brown or red brick, the small village, and it was seen now through a thin, steely air, with the flakes coming down, though not yet fast, not yet many. Dr. John Barbary spoke to Lady, swung himself into the saddle, and gathered up the reins. Jim, the colored man, stood back. "Going far, Doctor? Going be bad weather or I misses my mark!"

Out of town, descending the hill to the river, he came up

with James Ware and his wife in their old buggy, wheels and body and hood almost as much frozen mud as wood, metal and cloth. Their big gray horse drew them. The bottom of the buggy and Mrs. Ware's lap were cumbered with parcels. "Good day, Doctor!"

"Good day! Been shopping for Christmas?"

"Something pretty for every last child. Going far, Doctor?"

"To George Ross's."

"George Ross's! If it comes on to sleet," said Ware, "I wouldn't just choose to be rounding Indian Head. And it gets dark all-fired quick these days. But it isn't so bad riding as driving."

"Is it Jenny Ross, Doctor?"

"Yes, Mrs. Ware. She had a fall yesterday."

"You mean the baby's coming?"

"Yes."

"Poor little Jenny! Poor little Christmas present!" Once across the bridge, their ways parted. The buggy and the gray horse kept on up the valley upon the main road. Dr. Barbary and Lady turned due west toward the mountain ranges.

The snow fell more thickly and it was cold. Twelve miles of a road not well kept, not excessively traveled, even in summer. One might as well say three hours and he done with it. Two o'clock now, and dark enough by five.

Until three days ago heavy rains, and then gray skies and freezing, and now snow. The river that he was following ran swollen and hoarse. Sometimes the road just escaped the dark and rough water, sometimes it climbed, and he looked down, thirty, fifty feet upon the flood. Sometimes he left the river, but always came back to it. The region grew more and more barren of house and farm; he was leaving human marks, keeping only the road for sign. Presently he would be among the many hills and spurs, outermost defenses of the mountain wall, going on and on, north and south, cleft only every ten miles or so by a deep gap or gorge. His road was going to take him through the nearest of these.

Before him he saw plainly enough stark, purple-gray, seven miles off, Danger Ridge, with Danger Gorge, where the river broke through, running five hundred feet below the road, the road narrower than it should be, just niched out of the solid rock. Beyond Danger Ridge all dropped rather easily down to a high knife-blade vale and George Ross's small, old ancestral farm. When one got by Indian Head the road widened and the proposition grew simple.

John Barbary did not maintain roads and bitter weather in his head longer than was reasonable; he would have pronounced that it were a crazy thing to do so when that was your road to business. The mail carrier and the doctor and sometimes the preacher had as well forget roads and weather. Hardly a road for fifteen miles around that he and Lady couldn't go blindfold. After fifteen miles Berkeley, over in Upland, had to know roads and weather. Berkeley sometimes called him in; then he and Lady had to travel farther. He didn't so often call Berkeley in; did it now and then as a kind of compliment. He was older than Berkeley, had been in medicine longer. It was beginning to snow in good earnest. He pulled out his big gold watch. A quarter to three.

The watch had been his father's, and his father also was a country doctor. The county had given him the watch on his marriage sixty years ago. The watch had been a doctor's watch for sixty years. First Thomas Barbary's, and then John Barbary's. As he slipped it back into its pocket he had a picture of his father jogging this road. Sixty years ago in this county— sixty years before that—before his father's day—there was no road here at all, though maybe an Indian trail. That long ago you might meet Indians. A picture passed before him out of a book. He did not believe he had ever really seen an Indian.

How the snow fell! A white Christmas. In his bureau drawer, in a morocco case, lay a breastpin for Mary; a handsome one, a soft gold twist with an amethyst in the middle. He had written to the city, commissioning his old schoolmate, who was so famous nowadays, to get it for him. A white Christmas. The snow was covering the road.

In another half hour the snow ceased and sleet began.

He was now among hills and abrupt, craggy juts and shoulders, covered, where rock was not, by pine and hemlock, naked oak, beech, elm, birch and basswood, maple, hickory and tulip, with an undergrowth of laurel. When the wind began to blow all these moved and sighed. The sleet borne upon the rising wind came painfully against Barbary's face, and he knew from her movement under him what Lady thought of it. "Take it as it comes, old girl!" he said. "We are half through."

Distract one's mind from these humdrum woes; bring something else about one!

Lambert in the city. Lambert had done everything that Barbary hadn't done. Old "Rhymer" Lambert, with his picture in the Journals! Lambert drew people to his light shining in that wonderful hospital of his; drew them under his hand, and his hand sent them forth again cured. Old "Rhymer" Lambert a famous man! Sometimes Barbary likewise helped nature or the Lord or the patient's self to a cure. Right often, Barbary might say, and still kept his modesty. But he wasn't competing with Lambert! Lambert had the stuff.

A hard winter. This was going to be a hard winter. Such a winter rode in about once in so often. In and out like that—open, shut—open, shut—since Noah.

Jenny Ross. He didn't know if he or nature—he inclined to nature—could pull her through. Poor child! Poor world! And the babe coming before its hour in a sleety night; probably enough, its thread might be cut before it was spun.

The hills were closing in; the river was below him again. Half past three. It would be dark in this weather by half past four. Barbary spoke to the mare. "We haven't all day in which to get around Indian Head. Let's see if we can't be brisker!"

That lasted a quarter of a mile; then, "If you're going to take to slipping—"

The way was growing always wilder and sterner.

Barbary turned a childhood leaf. They were playing in the village street.

> "How many miles to Miley Bright?
>   Three score and ten.
>   You'll get there by candlelight
>   If your feet are nimble and your heels are light.
>   Look out that the old witch doesn't get you!"

After leaving the Wares he had, in the first two or three miles toward Danger Ridge, changed the time of day with half a dozen persons, riding or driving or walking. But for the last hour no one. Now almost at the foot of Danger Ridge, the road branched. Over the ridge went the one way; the other, skirting the mighty base, took in Lonely Mill and wound on to the next gap.

He drew up beside a road wagon with two horses coming from the mill. Wat MacClellan and his son sat among the meal sacks. "Hey, Doctor!" called the first. "This ain't no kind of weather for sick folk to be wailing to you in!"

"How's the road over Danger, Mac? I've got to go to George Ross's."

"Who's taken? Is it Jenny? Well, Doctor, I don't know about that road. Nobody's been around Indian Head that I know of since the weather changed. I couldn't just advise you, 'cepting I'd say that, given what it's doing and going to do worse as like as not, I'd travel to Ross's by the mill and Warner's Gap. That's bad enough, but it ain't Indian Head."

"It's six miles out of my way. As it is, I won't get to Ross's till after night. Are you going to town?"

"No. Only to Tom Jamison's. That's far enough. Doctor, I'm kinder advising you not to try to get to Ross's to-night. Can't she wait?"

"No," said Barbary. "She'll die, maybe, if she isn't helped. I'll go on. Jamison's got a telephone. Will you ring up my daughter and tell her you met me and I'm all right."

He parted with the big wagon as he had parted with the others on the road. Almost immediately he and Lady began slowly to climb Danger Ridge. Before him, around him, rose and crowded whitened earth and rock and sleet-hung trees.

The road broken and stony, little traveled at best, most folk going round by Warner's Gap, was now fast putting on an icy mail. First long rains, then freezing, and now mixed snow and sleet. "Take it carefully, Lady, and get on! That sounds, somehow," said Barbary, "like the old lady who wanted a very small Bible with very large print."

By four o'clock they were fairly high upon the mountain side. The road, with short and sharp turnings, wound from level to level. In the half light he could make it out above him and then again above that, and overhanging the last visible string of it, the huge, rounded, cliffy mass, that meant the top of Danger Ridge, that had been called since old time Indian Head.

They plodded on. Careful, careful must be every step where all things were steadily growing worse. A great pine lay athwart the road and Barbary had difficulty in getting the mare over the massy trunk and through the heaped branches. Indian Head loomed before them. He heard the river rushing below it; he was now in the gorge itself. And now the gradually heightening storm rose to a wild and sustained energy. The wind and the driving sleet, the approaching night, and the bitter cold made life troublesome.

Impossible to turn! Save for that one strip ahead it were as bad to go back as forward, as bad and far longer. "We have no choice, Lady! We've got to get on and get out of this. Dogged does it. Dogged does it."

Dogged did it for a short while. With a forlorn and mighty crash a tree crossed the road before them. They got somehow around this great, melancholy fallen oak. The day was withdrawing, the earth an icy gleam beneath them. Pass Indian Head before it is quite dark! Pass Indian Head before it is quite dark! Barbary ceased to have any other thought or will but this!

"Cold and tired mustn't count, Lady, mustn't count! If we were fools we were fools, but we meant well."

The river roared among its boulders upon the left hand, farther and farther below him in the gorge. The earth dropped toward it more and more precipitously. Precisely up there, at Indian Head, the road became, for a hundred yards or so, naught but a shelf of rock, none too wide, with upon the right hand a towering cliff to hug and upon the left a fall, if you tried it, into eternity.

"Get on, get on, Lady!" said Barbary. He stroked her with his stiffened glove. "I'm sorry for you. I'm sorry for us both in this storm we couldn't exactly foresee. But get on, old friend, carry us through!"

She did the best she could, but in another five minutes slipped and came to her knees. Barbary swung clear of her, coaxed her, and helped her up. She had not broken a leg, but she stood and trembled. He began to lead her.

The cold was desperate and the storm bewildering. Barbary felt a terrible fatigue and sleepiness. The mare stumbled and stumbled. They might have been years upon Danger Ridge. George Ross's valley lay much higher than the greater valley they had quit. Once around Indian Head the ridge would fall quickly to the little valley, and the farmhouse be not so far. But to get there, to come fully to Indian Head and make the long curve, with the icy road narrowing and the deep drop and the wind that was now maniacal---

The mare had another ugly stumble. She staggered up with a frightened and distressful sound. "Lady, Lady! we cannot stay here. We've got to go on."

In another fifty paces another uprooted tree, this time a vast hemlock. When they got by it there was little more of light to spare. All trees now sank away to right and left. To the right of the road naked earth and rock rising wall on wall to the top of Danger Ridge; to the left rock and earth descending sheer. Indian Head.

"Now, Lady," said John Barbary. "Steady! Steady!" They had the curve to make, desolate and dangerous. Lady stood still, shivering and turning her head.

"What is it?" demanded Barbary.

What it proved to be was a landslip before them—the road blocked and cut away, no road any longer, precipice from top to bottom, from the crown of Indian Head to the base in the river.

Horse and man stood daunted. Even while Barbary strained his eyes the daylight began to vanish. The road was lost, the night at hand, the cold intense. He moistened his lips. "Aye, Mary, I'm sorry!" Turning, he led the mare the way they had come, back from the bare and impossible wall. Foot by foot they quit the great, exposed face of Danger Ridge until they had attained the fallen hemlock. Here, halting, he looked again toward the huge, rounded, pathless, rocky head of the mountain confronting him. To get over it, to get over and so down to Ross's.

He believed that there still existed an old, narrow, worn path, running over the mountain top, not around it as the road had gone. It was the heir, maybe, of an ancient trail made by the ancient inhabitants of the land; maybe it was that trail itself.

Most roads in these parts once had been Indian trails. He thought that boys used this path sometimes, huckleberrying up here. He had done it himself once, long ago. It would leave the road somewhere hereabouts, climb at its leisure the thousand feet to the crest, go over that and down again, and join the road at a point no great distance from Ross's. But at both ends it was masked by laurel and scrub.

He had forgotten just where it went in or came out. Impossible in the nighttime, in the icy tempest, to find it or to keep it and pursue it if found. As hopeless to try to retrace the miles he had come. Eight miles that way to Lonely Mill. As he saw all this, night blotted out the road.

He felt greatly fatigued and now at last extreme sleepiness. He knew well enough what the latter meant. And he forced himself to rouse all the reasons why he and Lady should not lie down among these boughs and go to sleep. "If we do that, Lady, we shall never wake—not on this earth!"

He saw his home, his daughter standing at the window. He saw Ross's valley not so far away now if he could only get over the ridge, back upon the road on that side, beyond the landslip. "It's hardly more than two miles. Try it—try it up over the mountain."

He and Lady tried it. Neither road nor path, but branch and bush, steeply mounting, uneven earth, roots of trees and stones of all sizes, masked by dead leaves and snow or ice, and all in the winter nighttime, with driving sleet. A few minutes of that, then, "Impossible!" said Barbary.

He stood indecisive, with wavering thought and sense. All seemed a borderland, the mass of the hemlock, the mountain that he wished to cross, the storm, and himself. He had never been one to give up, but here was no going. "Yet I must, I must!" The sleepiness passed; he felt a strangeness. There grew about him, within and apparently without, a light and color and an intensity of stillness. He saw by this illumination the hemlock boughs and before them the figure of an Indian standing looking at him.

"You want old path," said the Indian. "I show it to you."

"Yes, I want it badly," answered Barbary.

"Come, then!" said the Indian.

He moved from the hemlock, entering the laurels, and Barbary with Lady followed. They were now again upon the mountain side from which Barbary had retreated. Barbary caught his foot in root and fell heavily, and he wished not to move, but to lie there and to sink into sleep. But the Indian bent over him. "Up! Up!"

"It is not possible," said Barbary. "It is easier simply to die."

But "Up!" said the Indian. "Up!"

He gave his hand. Barbary felt the strength of it run into his own and up his arm and into his body. He got to his feet. "I'm with you if you're with me!" he said to the Indian. "The matter is that the road around the Head is broken off clean, gone down into the river. I've got to get over the mountain, to Ross's farm. I'm a doctor, Dr. John Barbary. I know there's the old trail, but I can't find it."

"We go this way," said the Indian, and pushed aside the laurels.

He moved ahead. Barbary followed, leading the mare. Suddenly, the path—he felt it with his feet; moreover, he saw it.

He remembered. Of course, it did go in just here and so, windingly, up to and over the top of Danger Ridge and down to the road again a mile or so from Ross's. He saw it now quite clearly, across forty-seven years, the measure of the last time he himself had used it. He said as much to the Indian.

"I see it clearly now. Three or four of us boys were after huckleberries which used to grow famously up on top. We took this old path—Cherokee Trail, I remember, the old folks then called it."

"Yes," said the Indian. "Cherokee Trail. Much berries always."

"Your people must have used it for hundreds of years," said Barbary. "Then when my people came they made the road."

"Yes. Thousands of years," said the Indian.

"How—" began Barbary, but had just then to engage hands and arms with the crowding bushes. The strange thing was that the path also showed and the bushes on either hand.

It showed, mellowly, the old Indian path, and though he was sufficiently aware that away from it the wind thrust and the sleet drove as before, here they were traveling without that buffeting.

"I suppose," he said, "I suppose you stayed on when your people went—or maybe you've come back from some reservation."

"Maybe both," said the Indian, and that too seemed to Barbary quite natural.

They were great wanderers—Indians—and seemingly independent of any weather. He remembered his grandfather telling him there had been Cherokees in these parts. Cherokee was rather a high type of Indian. He remembered the chief, Young Eagle.

They were climbing the remaining upward slope of Danger Ridge, the path winding and tacking just as he remembered its doing. The big rock—yes! Wild bees had a hive there. They had shouted around it and wished for the honey, but could not get it, those lads of long ago. He spoke:

"I was here once beside this rock. But it was long ago, and a country doctor has so many things to think of that he forgets what hasn't to do with his work. Mine takes me, of course, in and out among our mountains. I'd say I knew them pretty well. But you, I dare say, know them to the inch."

"Yes, to the inch," said the Indian.

"We are getting along pretty well," said Barbary as the path went steadily upward. The Indian kept in front, then came Barbary, and Lady followed him. Moreover the still and mellow light still held and even deepened, as did the release from the storm.

Moreover, in the strangest way, summer would seem to have returned. Or perhaps it was autumn. A sumac by the path had red leaves again. A tall hickory was golden to the top. The earth that they were treading felt softly brown and warm.

Barbary remembered that it was Christmas. If trees became alight at Christmas, why might not the Appalachian forest turn serene at heart and remember its autumn splendors? At any rate it had done so. That, too, was fact.

"Sometimes, riding to and fro, from sick person to sick person," said Barbary, "I've pictured your old life among these mountains, your villages and cornfields, your huntings and warrings. There was good for you, just as for us or for any."

"Yes," said the Indian, " 'good' for all."

"We are coming to the top," said Barbary. "Danger Ridge! Nobody need mind danger when there's strength to meet it. I was all done up down there by the tree. But now I feel—I feel----"

They reached the top of the mountain, long and narrow, with gulfs of space above, around. The path ran golden still, quiet and sure, along the top of Danger Ridge. "I see it as it were yesterday," said Barbary. "Tom Watson, Walter and Ned Young, and myself up here for huckleberries. We had buckets and we filled them and sold the berries. They did; I took mine to Mary Davidson."

"You must not forget," said the Indian, "where you are going."

"No, I won't," answered John Barbary. "Ross's farm, to save Jenny Ross."

He and Lady and the Indian went on. The light appeared deeper, the path sweeter. The Indian himself began to pre-occupy Barbary. He seemed a young and a strong man, with a countenance certainly not without beauty. "I feel," said Barbary----

"Look to the path," said the Indian. "Now you are over the mountain."

The trail indeed, having crowned the top, began to descend

in short and steep windings. It was yet an autumn path. "That ledge of rock—I remember that ledge," said Barbary, "halfway down to the road. I will get to Ross's."

"Yes," said the Indian. "You will make it."

"I have seen men live when all the odds were against them. It's a reality, second wind," said Barbary. "But is this that?"

"I will leave it to you," said the Indian.

"The path ends, I remember," said Barbary, "in the scrub and laurel to the right of the road near the three tall pines."

They descended the steep northern face, going still easily and swiftly, in the light of autumn. "I am sure I am more grateful to you than I know how to say," said Dr. John Barbary, and he spoke gruffly because of a certain dizziness of strength and delight.

"You need not say," said the Indian. "I know."

They came, still in the light, to a great stretch of laurel bushes, stiff and green, and of scrub oak, and through this to three gigantic pine trees set closely together, and thence down a low bank to a level underfoot. "Your road," said the Indian.

With suddenness the Cherokee, if he was a Cherokee, vanished. He took with him the mellow light, the autumn leaves, and coloring. Darkness, storm, and cold closed in upon the country doctor and his horse. Before them, a mile away, set in its small, high vale, burned a light. "George Ross's," said Barbary.

At George Ross's the afternoon had gone in pulses of pain and terror. No, she was afraid Jenny was not doing well, said old Mrs. Jackson each time that Ross made his appeal. She wished the doctor would come, but there! everybody who knew Dr. Barbary might know that he was coming as fast as he could.

Ross went for the tenth time to the big gate whence one could see the road emerging from the woods, descending from Danger Ridge. But the snow too was descending, and then began the sleet and the violent winter wind. Ross wrung his hands.

He went back to the house, to hear Jenny's sharp cry. "Oh, let me die!"

It began to be dark, and it seemed hopeless. Ross lighted three lanterns, the big one, the middle-sized one, and the little one. He and his Negro man, Andrew, swung the big one above the big gate, the second one halfway up the lane, the third at the house gate. The house itself had lamps enough, and Andrew kept up the fires. The wind rose; the sleet drove like tiny arrows.

Time passed, the night deepened, the cold and the tempest increased. The doctor did not come. "Jenny! Jenny!" anguished Ross. The storm heightened from stair to stair, the worst in five winters. Black night, driving sleet. Ross sat before his father's old desk in the upstairs hall, outside of Jenny's room. He buried his head in his arms, he stopped his ears, he got down upon his knees and prayed. Hours, hours.

Andrew, the Negro man, stumbling at the foot of the stairs. "Marse George! Marse George! the lower gate's swung open! I see the lantern move across! Bress the Lawd, it's Christmas!"

Ross sprang to his feet, rushed downstairs and to the door. A horse coming from the lane, through the house gate. Dr. John Barbary out of the night.

If a Weasel Crosses Your Path Turn Back

"And William—"

"Yaas, Marse Dick—"

"There used to be horses enough on this plantation for everything. It's no longer the case. I want Firefly myself, so you'll have to walk."

"Yaas, sah. Hit's ten miles from Wild Cherry to Cedar Hill. Is I comin' back tonight?"

"No, you gump! tomorrow. You'll stay at Cedar Hill Quarter tonight."

William showed flashing white teeth in a charcoal countenance. "Den dat's all, Marse Dick? I give yo' letter right to Captain Tony en nobody else—"

"You give that letter right to Captain Tony and nobody else. I wish, William, to impress upon you speed and perseverance. You are to regard it, in short, as an errand of life or death."

The young gentleman, a visiting nephew of Wild Cherry plantation, elongated his elegant figure. "Life or death, William! Now you go like a house afire! If he doesn't have that letter before night, ROME WILL FALL."

So saying, he partly drew from his waistcoat pocket a silver half dollar, then let it slip back. William again smiled widely. "Ain't anything gwine slow *me* up, Marse Dick, whether I comes or whether I goes—"

"That, William, is your reputation. Who steals my purse steals trash, but who steals any reputation, William!"

An hour past noon, high summer, gorgeous toploftical clouds pushing over the hill tops behind Wild Cherry. Old brick house, hurt a good deal in the war, about it box and rose garden. Big trees, home quarter with many fewer occupants than of old; field quarter the same; fields, rail fences mended and unmended; the big road. The big road for a mile, then the little old road that turned off. Full summer fulfilled with rich sights and sounds, taste and smell and touch. Intense blue sky except where those pearly clouds pushed up spectacular heads. In part their hue was of a smoked pearl. William regarded their height and bulk with an experienced eye. "Maybe you gwine put up a sizable thunder storm, en maybe you ain't. Ef yo' mind ain't made up, jes' don't hurry yo'self!"

The little old road, turning off from the big road, struck across country toward Cedar Hill, and its way lay through lonely woods and by abandoned fields. The big road had life strung along it, three plantations, a crossroads store, occasional cabins, a smithy, a mill, wagons and horesemen and folk afoot. But the Cedar Hill road ran narrow and twisty as a frayed string, thrown aside and forgot, just lying relaxed, with few to use it. Two or three cabins far apart, a deserted house, an ancient graveyard, remnant of an iron forge long forsaken, old fields long untilled, a creek, and big woods and big woods—so ran the ten mile road. But it was ever nice and shady on a hot summer day, cool underfoot, with a plenty of small life to amuse in a small way. William possessed a contented disposition and thought that the road did well enough though it hadn't been worked for a long time.

The first mile was passed. William thought he would sing a little.

> "Marse Cain he was er limber fellow,
> Marse Abel was er lamb—"

He had a big, happy baritone.

> "Nobody knows the trouble I see, Lawd,
> Nobody knows the trouble I see—"

The weasel crossed the road.

A weasel is a small, carnivorous mammal, a cousin of the stoat, the ferret, and the polecat. Its body from tip of tail to pointed snout measures about a foot, and is ruddy brown above and white beneath. In winter, in the far north, like its cousin the ermine, it will turn white all over. Its body is elegantly shaped and incredibly slim, though not as thin to its length as that of an eel. Of a different creation than the last named, it possesses truly an eel-like sinuosity whereby it works itself into cracks and holes that would seem beneath its compass. It is superlatively quick, active, sharp, and cunning. It has never been caught asleep. No more than a grandmother can it be taught to suck eggs, for it sucks them by nature. Frogs, mice, moles, and small birds fall on their knees before it. It slits the throats of chickens and climbs trees to the nests of small frightened birds. Wickedly clever as it is and marked by Satan, it is not of enormous frequency in any landscape. It likes to keep small and hidden and habitually chooses the night for its operations. Sometimes, even if you live in the country, you may not have seen more than two or three weasels in all your born days, and then chiefly at night or dawn or eve, near the chicken yard, a flash of him going by on his nefarious concerns.

Those before whom, in broad day, he crosses a made road, taking his time too, looking sideways at you with a keen eye, must in the nature of things be few.

When it happens, Turn Back! Give up your errand, whatever its seeming importance. Relinquish your need at the least for that day. Turn back—choose another road! He has made this one his. Conjured it, in short. If you don't—

This particular balefulness of the weasel has been long known. The solemn direction, *If a weasel crosses the road, Turn Back,* is attributed to Pythagoras.

William didn't know who first warned the careless race of men. But colored folk had a faculty for gathering up and carrying down time such warnings, strengthening them as they went along with continuing observation. He knew quarter stories of that particular trick of Mr. Weasel. At every other point do what you would. Shoot him down, if you could, at the chicken yard—make folk-sayings to blacken his face—take your own way with smart Mr. Weasel. But just here old Satan gave him power, and wise men had left warning. If a weasel crosses your road, Turn Back.

The weasel crossed the Wild Cherry-Cedar Hill road.

William stopped dead. "What dat? Er weasel cross mah road!"

The weasel was gone, quicker than a darting lean gray squirrel. But his bright eye had fixed William. "His eye done fix me—dat conjure weasel!

"What gwine happen now?"

"I got ter turn back—stop dishyer processionin' ter Cedar Hill!"

Sweat started upon William's brow and the back of his hands. "Reckon I better hurry erway, hurry back to Wild

Cherry and tell Marse Dick—"

And the little old road stretched before him so sweet and shady. He sat down on a stone, the weasel being gone. "Marse Dick, he laugh en laugh en say, 'Go 'way, you coward!' En like enough he get on Firefly en come heself. . .wid dat silver fifty cents staying' in he pocket. Damn dat weasel!"

He wiped his forehead with the bandanna of which he was proud. "En Cedar Hill quarter—en I been lookin' forward ter after supper en de banjo pickin'—en dat yallah gal Sarah wid her arms erkimbo en her haid on one side, layin' out comparisons between Cedar Hill en Wild Cherry—

"How I get dere by ernother road? Dere ain't any 'nother road."

"Dat weasel mighty little man. Reckon I frighten him jes' erbout lak he frighten me.

"Reckon he right far erway by now."

The narrow, little-used old road stretched before him in sun and shade, on one hand a broken, lichened rail fence; on the other, big trees and a stream brawling down from the hills over smooth ledges and around ferny boulders. A mulberry growing in a lock of the ancient fence hung down a convenient branch thick with ripe fruit. The sun, very hot and strong between the heaped clouds, splashed upon the earth a hundred silver half dollars bright from the mint. That yellow girl at Cedar Hill—there she stood, just as plain, at the other end of the road, and he heard the banjo faintly. She was laughing, Sarah. Laughing at him, William Carlisle. . . . Wild Cherry porch with the almighty big tall pillars and Mr. Dick handing him that letter for Captain Tony. Mr. Dick seemed mighty serious, though sometimes he wasn't as serious as he seemed. "Matter of life and death, William!" was what he had said. "Matter of life and death! If Captain Tony doesn't get this letter by candle light, ROME WILL FALL."

"I reckon I'll get on," said William aloud. "Ef hits between dat damn weasel en William Carlisle I'll put my money on de last."

With which he rose from the stone and, drawing a full breath, crossed the diminutive tracks left by the weasel. "De deed's done," he said, and ten feet further down the road stopped—and this was bravado—to gather and eat a handful of the ripe, dark, sweet mulberries. As he ate the last berry he heard it thunder.

"What dat? Dat old storm comin' up anyway! I ain't got no time ter be loafin' en loungin' erlong dishyer road, sittin' on her rock en eatin' mulberries—"

Almost immediately the road led him into a small open place, cleared field and felled wood, whence one could see the ring of the sky. The sky had changed. Over Wild Cherry way the toploftical, fantastical mass was grown and altered, the thunder heads running together into an enormous leaden wall in movement. He saw the lightning play, the whole thing was coming overhead. More than that, from another quarter, unbeknownst and unawares, had risen fast and faster, to meet the first, a like phenomenon. The two were going to join forces. As he stared, one put forth an arm and took the sun from the sky. A wind began to blow. Against a dead gray wall, chain lightning drew the letter W. The thunder answered without much waiting.

"Golly!" remarked William. "Dere's gwine be a storm what is!"

Wild Cherry lay not more than a mile and a half in the rear. If he put his long legs in motion in that direction. . . . The lightning zigzagged once more into the letter W. William knew his letters—Old Miss had taught him—he new that W stands for Weasel. "I ain't! I ain't!" he stated. "I ain't gwine let you outdo me!"

He began to go at a jog trot out of the cleared place into the wood. The road left the old field and the rail fence but kept the stream that now flowed across the way, then turned and raced with the road again but on the left. William crossed on stepping-stones. "Now I got water, too, dat you likes jes' as well as you does land, you old swimmin' weasel! I got water between me en Wild Cherry—"

Lightning tore the sky and immediate thunder rocked the world. "Lawd-er-mighty! You done got yo' big drum—"

The wind heightened—the trees swayed and groaned. It grew very dark, though it was not two in the afternoon. The cloud giants, rushing each upon the other, met in lightning and thunder and a rain like the flood. "Lawd Jesus! dat weasel done bust two clouds together en spilled de sky river!—I got ter find shelter."

Boulders grew like mushrooms in and along the bed of the stream. Two, with a third caught atop and furnishing a sort of roof, answered for a burrow. William burrowed. "I get er hole,

Brer Weasel, same as you! Yo' old lightnin' en yo' old drum, en yo' old waterin' pot don't make no 'pression on de 'tarnal rock.''

He hugged into his small cave. "Warm enough heah in de dark. I jes' rest en think o' dat yallah gal. Dishyer storm too fierce ter last.''

But up the stream, too, there chose to be a cloudburst. The rain fell like the forty days and nights in one downpour. In a jiffy rose the stream and began to eat its banks. "What dat?" said William. "Dat water runnin' in heah!''

He came out of his refuge. "I ain't *smoked* out anyhow, you old weasel!—Lawd hab mercy!''

The stream bellowed like a bull and rushed at him in a tawny, débris-bearing wave. He got out of the way of it, into the woods. The pine trees were tall, the pine trees did not keep out the lightning glare. An intense light fell around William, a crash split his ears, a neighbour tree stood blackened and began to blaze at the top. William cowered to the earth. "Lawd Gawd —Lawd Gawd A'mighty—" All through him ran a curious tingling and buzzing. "Lawd, I got er back stroke—I got er back stroke—''

He raised himself cautiously and felt himself gingerly from crown to sole. "It's gwine off—but it was sho'ly on." He lifted his eyes to the blazing mighty pine. "Sho' I's gwine call you hencefo'th my friend! Ef you hadn't caught it dishyer world en me would ha' said goo'bye!

"Dat weasel done borrowed it or stole it. But he ain't so almighty sure with his teeth en claws as he thinks he is! Besides which he got ter pay one day!''

Stumbling through the alternately dark and strongly lighted wood he curved to the road again where it covered a rise of earth and left twenty feet below it the roaring stream. "Jes make er fuss down dere all you please! You got ter let up presently less'n all the clouds in the world done bust! Old Mr. Rain-en-Wind is er-holdin' off er little too.''

So it was. The extremity of lightning and thunder began to lessen. Further and further away drove their chariots. The rain stopped, the wind hushed, like a god from a thicket outsprang the sun. The stream began to think of its own borders, the little, narrow old road ceased to be something of a stream itself. Tree and bush and vine shook off sparkles from every leaf. The firmament turned azure. The world became quick and light and gay. "I ain't but eight miles from Cedar Hill. So long, old Mr.

Weasel!"

The sun grew hot, the earth dried off as quick as it could. William, too, felt warm and comforted. "Yaas, Brer Weasel, you sho' did try to make er splurge! but I reckon you gone off ter rest now en talk ter yo' family erbout mos' closin' dishyer road forever ter dat William Carlisle.

"Sun feel good! I sho' is obliged to dat pine tree what took de butt o' de lightnin'!"

He walked on, spry as they make them. The sun shone hotter and hotter, the earth dried as though there never had been a rain. "Dat yallah gal—dat yallah gal. . . . Fifty-cent piece. Maybe he make it er dollar. . . .

"Seven miles. Dat blackberry path en de rail fence marks it three miles from Wild Cherry en seven miles from Cedar Hill."

The trees stood back, the sun shone hot, everything was in the sun. William liked heat. He didn't mind midsummer sun at a quarter to three in the afternoon, though he didn't know it was a quarter to three, as he had no watch.

The blackberry patch came close to the road. The berries were ripening, some of them hung ripe. William stepped aside three feet into the patch and came eye to eye with old Mr. Copperhead in coil and meaning business.

"Jesus—Jesus!"

Wasn't any time to be thinking or dreaming. William leaped back and missed the stroke. The copperhead recoiled instantly. William's hand closed upon the stem of a young maple, snapped it with its bushy head and met the copperhead in career. There followed a battle. The man won. The snake, a mighty one, lay limp and dead. William backed from the patch into the road and sat down in the dust, his head in his arms. "Dat was a close one," he whispered. "Dat was a close one!"

He sat in the dust, gathering himself together. "But I ain't turnin' back—I ain't turnin' back."

A stir in the patch brought him up standing. "Old woman—old woman Copperhead mought be er-comin'."

He pursued the Wild Cherry-Cedar Hill road. Now he heard, increasing toward him, the sound of wheels, the striking on chance rock of horses' hooves and the voice of a man encouraging his steeds. "Get up there, Poky! Stop yo' dozing, Slow Coach!"

"Dat Mr. George Pepper haulin' wood," said William. "I

sho' powerful glad ter see him or any one.''

Mr. George Pepper, Poky and Slow Coach and the wagon hauling white oak and hickory, came into proximity. "This is a mortal lonely road,'' said Mr. Pepper, walking beside his horses. "You're the only man I've met today. What's the matter? You look kind of ashy!''

"Dat's a fac' it's lonely of men. It ain't lonely of other critters. No sah, not of Another Critter!''

"You look,'' said Mr. Pepper, "as though a weasel had crossed your road.''

William experienced a catch of the breath. "You done set up for a prophet, Mr. Pepper, sah? Dat jes' the occasion what occurred.''

" *'If a weasel crosses your road turn back'*—I remember my grandmother telling me that and it's always proved itself mighty good doctrine,'' said Mr. Pepper. "In these parts, anyway.—Hi, Poky, what you starting at? Slow Coach, ain't nothing in that bush!''

"Maybe—maybe it's old Mrs. Copperhead—''

"No, 'tain't. 'Tain't nothing. Did you meet a copperhead?''

"Yaas. I killed it, en 'twas hard work. I never see such er big en er determined one. En befo' dat, er storm dat most ended William Carlisle. Yaas, sah, dat lightnin' most ended me. You didn't have dat storm at all?''

"No, but I saw it and heard it over Wild Cherry. When did the weasel cross the road?''

"Three mile back.''

"And you ain't turned and give up the road for a while anyhow? That's mighty onlucky, William!''

William had turned stubborn. "I got an arrand I jes' got ter go. But I wishes you'd emptied yo' load, Mr. Pepper, en was bound back ter Cedar Hill. Dat weasel do make er man like company!''

"I ain't ready yet a while,'' said Mr. Pepper. "Besides, William, you might bring me bad luck.— Whoa, there! This load's slipping!''

So it was—as though of a piece—out at, down from, the end of the long wagon. "Now what do you think of that?'' demanded Mr. Pepper when the mass of the logs lay in the road. "Any rate, William, you got to help up with them!''

"I think it was dat weasel jes' er mutterin' ter himself.—

Whoa there! dat wheel gone over my foot!"

They reloaded the wagon. The logs were heavy and it was hot and Mr. Pepper, at least, already fatigued. He became grumpy. "Weasel or no weasel, this is a kind of cursed road! People don't use it much more, and I ain't a wondering!"

They reloaded the wagon. "Maybe I's used up the bad luck," suggested William out of a native hopefulness.

"Maybe. Well, so long, William! Git up thar, Slow Coach! What you studying about anyhow, Poky?"

Wagon, horses, and Mr. Pepper vanished toward Wild Cherry. William felt a wave of deep forlornness. "He good company. Dishyer road sho' want company of yo' own choosin'."

Yet it was such a pretty little road, though neglected. On walked William, quickly, too, having spent not far from half an hour with Mr. George Pepper. It was shady, it was sweet. "Maybe he done broke old Mr. Weasel's back with dem wagon wheels!" He thought he would sing a little.

> "Way down on de Piankatank,
>   Where de bull frogs jump from bank ter bank—"

The road had left the creek and was winding like a grape tendril through the woods. William's breast expanded.

> "Who build de Ark?
>   Norah!
>   Who build de Ark?
>   Norah build de Ark.
>
>   De dove en de raven set on a beam
>   You mayn't believe it but dey was a team—"

The road bent by an ash tree. A bough crooked an elbow; from it, like a lady's piece bag, hung a very big hornets' nest. How the stick that was carried over William's shoulder managed to strike, or at least to demonstrate against, the hornets' nest, who shall say? Maybe it wasn't the stick. . . . The hornets sallied forth.

"Lawd-a-golly!"

William ran, ducking his head, beating the air with his hands. They stung here, they stung there—one, two, three, half a dozen—the angry hornets. He got to the creek again, he plunged down and dashed in, burying his head and shoulders. The hornets left him, but wow! he was stung.

Eight places. He knew the right weed to apply. When he had found it and had chewed the leaves to a pulp he stripped his blue shirt from his powerful black body and began to poultice neck, shoulders, and arms, sighing and groaning as he worked. "Life too hard for dis niggah. Life too hard—"

"When de weasel crosses yo' path, en you don't turn back—"

"Dat's de p'int of it—*when you don't turn back.*"

He plastered and plastered. "It ain't worth de fifty cents . . . . But dat yallah gal—I like her tell her erbout it."

He measured the sun with his eyes. "I ain't half way. . . . You, William, you bettah be gettin' up from dishyer cool restin' place en be goin' erlong.

"I don't feel like singin' no moah. Dem hornets is hard ter put up with—though they's gettin' bettah."

When he had finished his medicaments it might be four o'clock in the afternoon. He pursued the winding road. "Pain ain't so seveah—but I feels er little giddy."

The sun's rays now fell slant and lovely. "I sho' don't feel like singin', but I wish I had mah banjo. I play de banjo. Mr. Dick, he play de piano. Captain Tony play de flute. Miss Sally play de guitar. Dat yallah gal she play mah heart string. . . . Don't I heah 'em all er-playin', er little way off dare? . . . Psha, niggah: dat's de katydids en de frogs! I gwine make good time now!"

Again appeared the zigzagging fence and a ragged field all bugloss and mullein and an outcrop of rock. The field, mounting in a wave, lay washed in copper light, and was the loneliest of the lonely. Only there grazed half way up the slope an old white horse. "Now whose is you? I don't remember you."

It seemed old, very old—and gaunt, very gaunt—yet a big horse. William leaned his weight on the ancient rail fence and stared. "You's bigger than usual—" The rotted rails gave beneath him; he and they came to earth together. "Now dat weasel's done made er gap ter let somebody's old hoss out of pasture!—I better fix it up."

The old horse moved leisurely toward him where he was working. "What's de matter wid you? I don't like yo' looks."

He restored the last rail and straightened his black body,

over and along which were going little dry quivers of heat. Dr. Jones, who doctored the plantation of Wild Cherry, might have said of them, "A degree or so of fever. Let's see those hornet stings—"

The old white horse was no longer there—no longer in the field at all! William's eyes rolled. "Where you gone ter, I say? Where you gone ter?"

On either hand the empty, lonesome, sun-washed field ran into copse and broken woodland. "Maybe you kick up yo' heels en lose yo'self in de big wood. You sho' must hab put yo'self in motion ter do dat! Maybe—"

He stepped backward from the rail fence and the copper-tinted and lonesome field. "Maybe you ain't been heah at all-'ceptin' as er sign. . . . Dat weasel gwine tuhn on somethin' *new*!"

William took to the road. It was now well on in the afternoon. The shadows threw themselves across and athwart; the katydids put up a fearful shrilling. William made good haste. "I gwine—I gwine ter get dere; I gwine—I gwine ter get dere."

The house rose among pine trees, the fence with half the palings gone just back from the road, and the gate fallen from its hinges and sunken in a trumpet vine in red flower. The old Dollins house—empty for twenty years—gone to ruin and decay —with windows gaping and a broken porch—inexpressibly silent and solitary. It had a story about old Dollins the miser and his well-hidden gold, so well-hidden that no search had ever found it. "You come mighty quick, you old Dollins house!" said William. "Everything comes as quick as er weasel on dishyer road!"

It was the hornets surely, unless it was the weasel! William had a sudden picture of Mr. Dick's silver half dollar multiplied by a thousand, varied into quarters and dollars and gold pieces and greenbacks, all stuffed into an old half-bushel basket with a red table cloth tied about it. It would be hid away somewhere, in some dark place no one had ever looked into, but he saw it, he saw it! Old Mr. Dollins died long ago—folk had 'most torn the place up looking and had never found anything. All the same he, William Carlisle, *saw* that basket. "Jes' er minute," said William. "Jes' er minute spared from dishyer travellin'. Ef I lays mah hands on dat basket dat yallah gal en I sho' get married—"

Passing through the gap where had been the gate, he caught

his feet in the trumpet vine. The late sun striking against the bleached exterior of the house turned it into vague tarnished silver. It stood, broken doors and windows and sagging porch, more lonely than lonely, quite unearthly lonely. William, still seeing that cloth-covered bushel basket, went with super-steadiness up the ragged path and across the porch that sagged in the last stage of dilapidation, to the front door. This was closed, but had no fastening, and he pushed it open and entered the house. "Old Mr. Dollins' money store—*somebody* got ter find it! I sho' seen it in dat basket—"

The inside of the house, for all the windows were out, stood dim enough. It was getting late, and the house having been built long ago, the windows were anyhow small and few.

"Now where dat basket?"

He still saw it quite clearly in some inner field, but no evidence of it presented itself from where he stood in the forlorn hall, before the forlorn staircase. . . . He heard something scuttling. "Er rat, dat's all!" The place was furnitureless, twilight and creepy, but he had that slight rise of fever to buck him up. He went through the four lower rooms and the heat and pugnacity of the hornets seemed to turn to a benefit. He might have been a big hornet himself, buzzing here and there. At last he buzzed upstairs. Here, at the end of the passage, opened a window that gave a little more light, and near it he saw, placed on the floor, the basket.

It came out of the inside light and stood in the dim light of the Dollins house, a veritable enough ancient bushel basket wrapped in an old cloth.

"Land ob Goshen!" remarked William. "Dat's it—dat's old Mr. Miser Dollins' money! Done walk itself out of wherever he hide it en set itself here for me en dat yallah gal en er cabin en er corn patch en er mule—"

There was a cross passage in shadow. Outside the window a pine tree scraped the house with a dark bough. William buzzed across the opening of the lesser passage. Here was the basket for him to settle upon.—The pine bough, he thought, sprang into the Dollins house and turned into the stock of a gun, a lifted gunstock. Down it came upon William's pate—the sun and the basket and old miser Dollins' deserted house all went out together.

William Carlisle was a strong man with a nice, thick skull. It took a lot of killing to kill William; a heavy stick to lay him low for more than a reasonable time. The gunstock, being applied only once, did nothing beyond blotting him out for three minutes, in which space the basket was lifted and hugged under an arm, the stair descended, and the house vacated. Henceforth the old Dollins house might be taken literally to pieces, the ground around mined for gold, the hollows of every tree examined, and nothing, nothing doing! A more or less good-natured giant the other side of the county added to his farm a desirable five acres, bought himself two plough horses, a Sunday suit of broadcloth, a piano for his wife, put up a new spring house, gave ten dollars to missions, went to Richmond for the State Fair, and opened a savings account. But he said he had a legacy. . . .

William stirred and put a bewildered hand to a bewildered brow, encountering a lump as big as a guinea egg, after which he slowly brought himself to a sitting posture. "What dat struck me?" He sat with his wits clearing. "Was it dat pine tree or er ghost. . . . Where dat basket?"

His head swam, but he got to his feet. "Nobody heah— nobody been heah but jes' dishyer niggah. . . . Where dat basket?"

The sun had ceased to enter the upper floor of Dollins' long-left house. "Was it dat pine tree, or was it old Mr. Dollins' ghost. . .or was it dat weasel?

"He whistle up dat old white horse—he whistle ter Mr. Miser Dollins—he put dat basket dere en he take it erway. . . . I gwine erway too!"

Panic beset him. He fled down the stairs, through the lower hall, out of the door, across the sagging porch, down the path that was now just a track between weeds and tall grass, out of the broken gate. The trumpet vine caught again at his ankles. He tore loose from it and stumbled down into the road. "Gawd-er-mighty! I got ter get ter Cedar Hill!"

As he left behind him the Dollins house, the sun approached the horizon. It grew big and red, seen through a grating of pine trees. "Less'n three miles. I git dere by candle light."

A white folks' children's play began to run in his head, which still went somewhat giddily around. It sang itself with variations.

"How many miles to Miley Bright?"
'Two miles en a little mo.

You'll git dere befo' it's night
Ef yo' legs is long en yo' heels is light!
   Look out de old witch don't git you!"

"De old witch--dat's de old weasel!"

The sun became half an orb, then a quarter, then a red rim, then departed William's sky. Colour flared high, red and gold behind the darkening woods. The katydids continued their comment, and now from a marsh between him and the creek the frogs began evening service. "Dat bullfrog, he keep on er-sayin', 'Look out! Look out!' I feels," said William, "powerful strange in my spirits. Yet I is coverin' dishyer road, en dat's er fact!"

The road was running up and down a series of low hills, running between rail fences, edged or draped with bee balm and sumach, and traveller's-joy. Behind the fences again appeared old, lonely fields marked with solitary big trees. William hastened along with the gathering dusk. The red and gold changed into purple and lemon and cool, remote skyey green. He padded up a long hill and heard a whippoorwill, down into and across a hollow and was deafened by the frogs. *Look out! Look out!*

The western sky began to take a cold spectacular light. "I's got de graveyard ter pass. I knows, I knows, I's got de turned-out old McCarthy graveyard ter pass. Top of hill, dere—en dere it is. I wishes I had mah banjo. . . . I wishes Mr. Dick was er-keepin' me company. . . . What he mean anyhow erbout 'life en death' en 'ROME WILL FALL'?—Who Rome?"

The road and William climbed the hill. Whipporwills now were answering one another, and the firefly population lighted their lanterns. Dusk shook hands with night, but as yet the illumination was sufficient. Moreover, a big round moon pushed up in the east. Atop of the hill, cedars like spires announced the McCarthy graveyard. Its brick wall was broken, its memorial stones were fallen, it was choked with weeds and briars and old rose-bushes and myrtle and ivy and honeysuckle.

"I gwine pass you—I gwine pass you quick. . . . I bettah sing," thought William.

"Nobody knows the trouble I see, Lawd!
   Nobody knows the trouble I see—"

But his own voice scared him so he desisted. A hoot owl in an oak-tree began, *Who. . .you? Whoo. . .you?*

"I's William Carlisle," said William. "O Lawd, jes' let me get by—"

Ivy ran over the arch of the graveyard gate. Something sat atop of it like an armorial figure, a heraldic beast. Too dark to see it distinctly, at first it might seem a piece of stone work . . .but then it moved, it enlarged! In the dimness, the shot black and silver, two eyes glared. "What dat? What dat?"

He made haste. The creature leaped and landed upon his tracks. He ran. It ran too, coming padding after him. He looked back. Moon and dusk showed him something, but mixedly. To William the eyes seemed bale fires growing farther apart and larger. The body increased in size. Down came a great moon flood. "O Lawd—O Lawdy! it got er weasel shape!" Whether it had or whether it hadn't, that was what it had to William. "He done come himself! He come with *de power. De debbil* done give it to him!" William ran. William tore through the moonlight night along the road to Cedar Hill. He must look where he was going, or he would get a fall, but now and again he twisted his head over his shoulder. "Gawd-er-moughty! he gettin' bigger all de time! Dose eyes is de deb-bil's saucers! . . . De Giant Weasel. . . . Run, niggah, run!"

He ran and the Weasel ran. The road descended into a hol-low. *Look out! Look out!* shrilled all the frogs. The fireflies turned into a million little glittering eyes. *Whip poor Will! Whip poor Will!* cried all the whippoorwills. The father of all the weasels came on behind him, all the time bigger. . . . Maybe it was a wild cat, maybe it was a fox, maybe it was a dog. But to William Carlisle it was the weasel that had crossed the road.

He ran now without looking back. "Jes' let me get dar, Lawd! Jes' let me get dar—"

The creek, left for several miles, now suddenly reappeared and divided the road into this side of it and that side of it. William dashed through the water then, panting, looked back, and missed the eyes and the shifting shape. They had refused the water, and had turned off into the wood upon the left. The road ran straight, the moon shone strong. Cedars stood up stiffly to either hand. Not a mile and a half now to Cedar Hill. . . .

He was of such a hopeful disposition, was William! "May-be he jes' get tired pesterin' me—"

Ahead of him a tree, a slender thing, an ash or birch maybe, curved in a high arch out over the road. Quite over indeed, its head touching the opposite bank.

"My Gawd!" said William. "Dat's er ha'nt tree!"

A ha'nt crossed a road—some underworld law being opposed to its crossing roads—only by such a tree.

"Er ha'nt tree! I got ter go under it—"

He went under it singing and praying and shouting inside, for that was the way to pass ha'nt trees. But when he had passed it, and that at top speed, something large dropped behind him. He heard the thud with which it struck the road and he looked back. "What dat? What dat?"

It straightened itself in the moonlight into a tall figure of a man, a tall, skeleton thin, black man in a curious dress. It shot out long arms and jumped up and down. William stood turned to stone, then with a shout began to run. "De ha'nt! De ha'nt! He done turned himself into de ha'nt—O Lawd, help dis niggah! O Lawd, help William Carlisle!"

He tore along the road. Behind him he heard the ha'nt, running after him, making uncouth sounds as he came on. They ate up the road. "Look out! Look out!" cried the frogs. The moon and the fireflies made a dazing kind of night. An owl hooted from a gum tree, "Who—You? Whooo—you?"

"O Lawd," prayed William, "I's gwine be er better church member. O Lawd, have mercy on dishyer po' William Carlisle! Jes' let me get dere, Lawd! Jes' let me get ter Cedar Hill en Captain Tony—"

He hurried and the ha'nt hurried.

Off from the road turned a yet narrower track leading at length to a county almshouse where dwelt in the shadow of the end a few old, worn out folk and an idiot or two. . . . William passed this lane mouth, but the ha'nt turned into it, dropping into a job trot but still waving his arms and making his doleful noise.

William's hair ceased to rise and his heart to pound. "He done turned off, jes' like de weasel turned off!—You get erlong, niggah, you most dere—"

Cedar Hill house, brick and columns like Wild Cherry, topped a green rise—a black and silver rise tonight—like Wild Cherry. Lamps shone at Cedar Hill as they shone at Wild Cherry. In the big old parlour at Wild Cherry a young man—Mr. Dick— sang at the piano to a young cousin's playing. He was in love with the cousin.

In his own room at Cedar Hill Captain Tony practised the flute, walking up and down in the lamplight. He, too, was a young man. Now he sent forth a shower of sweet notes, and now he laid down the flute and throwing himself into his chair before an ancient desk and running a hand through Byronic locks, reapplied himself to the verses he was writing. He was a master hand at song writing.

> "O Love that tieth all together.
> O Love that turneth never—that turneth never—"

The door opened. "Tony!" called his sister.

"Yes, Eliza, yes! I wish this house could keep from interrupting me when I write!"

"Oh, poets and such are so filled with importance! There's one of the Wild Cherry men downstairs with a note from Dick."

"Ah," said Tony. "He wants—he wants—

> *'that turneth never'*

I promised him—

> *'The jasmine, the rose and the passion flower—' "*

Putting down his pen he rose and stretched himself. "All right, Eliza—much obliged! Just send whoever it is up here."

William appeared in the doorway. "Ah, it's William Carlisle! Come in, William. Did you walk over?"

"I done come er foot, Captain Tony."

"You look kind of spent.—What's the matter?"

"A weasel crossed de road, sah. I hadn't no moh'n left Wild Cherry."

"Indeed, William? When that happens, you are supposed to turn back."

"Yaas, sah, I knows it. Mr. Dick, he say 'twas life en death, en ROME WILL FALL ef you don't get his message. Likewise he say he give me half er dollar."

"Ah, indeed! Mr. Dick is given to hyperbole. Let's have his note, for I suppose you brought a note."

William produced it. Captain Tony read, "Tony, send me that song that you promised right away! You've had time to finish a dozen! I'm staying over to set it to the piano and practise it with her. Please recognize that this is important. Oh, Sir, she's the darlint!"

"That's all he says," quoth Captain Tony. "Lovers are imperious!—Well, I can't finish that song before midnight. You can start with it tomorrow morning after breakfast, William. Aunt Dinah will give you something to eat and you can sleep in the quarter."

"All right, sah. I heard," said William, "de banjo pickin' as I come erlong."

"Yes. We all make music. It's nine o'clock," said Captain Tony. "You'd better be going."

William proceeded down the home hill to the quarter where candle and firelight and mellow voices and laughter and notes of the banjo yet proclaimed—yet proclaimed, "There's rest and balm, reward and pleasure in the old world—in the old world . . .although the weasels cross the road, although the weasels cross the road!"

Out of the brightly lighted cabin with a gush of banjo notes came the yallah gal. "Who dat?—Lawd, ef dat ain't William Carlisle!"

The Attic Room

She was so deaf she could not hear thunder. As a small child she had heard it, but then there befell an illness that left her deaf. It had been long now since she was a small child. Her acquaintances pitied her and when they saw too much of her considered her a bore. She was a slight, rather tall woman, with an eager face and a rose in each cheek when she was young. No one ever called her pretty, but there was that eagerness and color. The eagerness became with the years withdrawn or indrawn, but the color stayed a long time.

At one period of her life she used an ear trumpet. Then someone described to her a battery device and she procured one. But nothing served her very well. A tablet and pencil seemed truly the best, and at last became her real dependence. Summer and winter she carried, hanging from her arm, a black silk bag, and in it a school tablet and three sharpened pencils. Someone, perhaps, might be met at the gate as she stepped forth upon the shady old street. Smiles on that eager, pointed face.

"Good morning, Mr. Parton!"

"Good morning, Miss Janet!"

"Isn't it a beautiful day? Have you noticed the gossamers? The althaea is in bloom! Can you tell me who was Althaea—in mythology, I mean?" and the tablet and pencil were offered.

Her own voice was monotonous, for she could scarcely hear it, and somewhat too raised. Mr. Parton felt himself impatient over the beautiful day and the gossamers, but he liked to exhibit his learning and so, amiably enough but compendiously, he wrote for her the origin of Althaea.

She read over his moving arm, smiled and nodded. "Thank you! Have you ever thought----"

But Mr. Parton's own concerns awaited him. He wrote, "I'm sorry that I have an important engagement, Miss Janet," and, lifting his hat, departed.

Or it was snowing fast, and Mrs. Locke, the Presbyterian minister's wife, upon her weekly visit to her old friend, Mrs.

Strong, who was crippled with rheumatism, said:[1]

"Yes, that's what I think, too, Sarah! We ought to be able to get summer boarders in this town. Summer, spring and autumn, for that matter. It's a lovely country and a good climate. The trouble is it isn't distinguished or distinguishable from so many others. To ourselves, of course, but outsiders don't see it so. The Lord, He knows, I wish they would! Every other house has a couple of rooms it'd like to fill."

"I've three," nodded Mrs. Strong. "It would help us out mightily."

"Yes, the poor old town----"

"Mrs. Locke," interrupted the unhearing Janet with tablet and pencil held out, "may I borrow two or three more books?"

Mrs. Locke wrote, "Yes, indeed, Janet," and resumed her speech: "The poor old town is sweet to us, we know, and I do think there is really a kind of charm about it. If people were once started it might build up. Not industrially, I mean, for we could never compete with Parthia with its water power. But in other ways. To live in and come to."

Janet's deaf-person voice again interrupted. "It's a boon to have inherited all those books, and you and Mr. Locke have been angels to me. It's Sir Philip Sidney's Arcadia that I want now. Have you ever read it, Mrs. Locke?" Tablet and pencil.

Mrs. Locke wrote, "No, I haven't, Janet. You see, I don't have time for reading."

Janet said, "Time, now. That reminds me! I had a dream last night, mother. I was making time—spinning it, you know, like Clotho. I spun slow time and I spun swift time, I spun black time and I spun white time---"

Mrs. Strong took tablet and pencil and wrote, "Please, my dear, let Mrs. Locke and me finish our talk."

Janet colored. "Oh, I didn't mean----"

Mrs. Strong wrote, "Sally said that if you'd watch the baby, dear, she'd go over to Millicent's about that decision of George's."

Or the forsythia was out in yellow clouds and the blackbirds were returning. Mr. Ross, the merchant, was selling her nainsook, dimity, lawn and percale. "Anything more, Miss Janet?" asked Mr. Ross in dumb show.

"No. These are my summer dresses. I would like real Valenciennes to trim the nainsook with. But I can't have it, so I won't bother. Have you ever wondered, Mr. Ross, if the birds

and the flowers reckon up the cost of their wardrobes?" Pencil
and tablet.

"No, I can't say that I have, Miss Janet."

"And cycles. Cycles have always interested me. Have you
ever thought, Mr. Ross----"

Mr. Ross wanted her to go, now that she had bought nainsook, dimity, lawn and percale, and could not be expected to
buy Valenciennes, for her father was dead and her mother had
a struggle to keep the old brick house behind the five big box
bushes. Her voice was too loud, and that ridiculous tablet
and pencil----His two clerks were smiling. He wrote, and his
writing showed impatience:

"What I think of, Miss Janet, in this dead town, is how to
make people come and buy and bring others."

"Is it dead?" asked Janet, with a laugh. Unlike her speaking
voice, her laughter was musical. "I did not know it. I saw life
this morning in spangles everywhere!" She looked at tablet
and pencil as though she hoped for a real conversation.

But Mr. Ross was tired of her except as a purchaser. He
wrote, "Yes, I'll send your bundles. Excuse me now," and ges-
tured toward the three or four other customers and gave her a
perfunctory smile and bow.

Tablet and pencil went back into black silk bag. Her fellow customers slipped aside as she moved toward the doors.
Everybody in Courtfield knew poor Miss Janet Strong and black
silk bag and tablet and pencil.

At last she began to see that they stepped into byways
and hedges, leaving her the highroad. When she had this more
or less clear she began herself to take the byways and hedges,
leaving them the highroad. But not without returns to it. It was
her highroad also—and there must be talk among human beings,
exchange of likings and thoughts and imaginings! She wished
to have commerce with them—her townsfolk, her family and
acquaintance. She had no intimate, no personal, friends. One
day she saw with a shock that this was so.

Her family loved her; families must love their members.
But even her family----"I have about me a wall of ugliness! My
bag and my tablet and pencil are like an ugly and tiresome dwarf
to them all, and I myself am only a figure that had best be silent
and ask nothing!" She was twenty-eight before she saw this

fully.

In her memory the old brick house in Old Street first had sheltered her widowed mother and the three little girls, of whom she was the third, and Uncle Robertson. As she grew toward twenty, Sally and Deborah married. Then in five years Sally's husband died, and Sally, with three children and little income, returned to her mother's roof. After that, for years and years there were her mother and Sally, and Martin, Margaret and Marion, and Uncle Robertson. And in the cabin in the alley Martha and Dick and Young Martha, cook and gardener and housemaid. And of course herself. "I cannot forget myself. I wish I could either forget myself or remember myself, the one or the other! It's the half dead, half born, that I'd like to spew out of my mouth!"

She went to church on Sundays, to the Presbyterian Church with her mother until her mother was crippled, then with Sally and her brood to the Episcopal Church. She could faintly hear the singing, but not the service or the sermon. However, she knew the service and she could construct the sermon. Out of a wide reading and her own powers she turned the rector, a simple and imitative man, into the prophet or saint or expounder of her choice, and great or subtle ones she chose. Now she listened to Paul or Francis or Luther or Newman, and sometimes she put an angel into the pulpit. Out of the black silk bag she drew tablet and pencil and, shielded by Uncle Robertson, made stealthy notes.

It had early become a habit, this note making in church. Little notes, thoughts or images, or just lovely words that had danced her way in the deep silence of the cavernous building. Her thoughts were not orthodox, but as no one saw them it did not matter. As the years strung bead after bead upon the string there accumulated, in the old desk with many drawers in her room at home, a number of these notebooks.

Her room. Her mother had the big chamber downstairs, Sally and her young ones and the guest room and the little room took up the second floor. There was left the third floor, which was truly the attic, but with two rather large, dormer-windowed, sloping-ceilinged, many-cornered rooms. One of these was Uncle Robertson's, one Janet's. A poplar looked in at one of her windows, a cedar at the other.

Sometimes, up here, she talked to herself, or she repeated poetry aloud, or she spoke across the open attic space to Uncle

Robertson. While they were children, Martin and Margaret and Marion laughed at her voice coming down the stairs or out of the dormer windows, but when they were grown older they complained to their mother.

"It's so loud, mother! One can hear her in the parlor sometimes, or on the porch. We wouldn't mind, but it's hard on one's friends! And always to be explaining, 'That's our deaf aunt—she doesn't know her tones aren't like Cordelia's!' "

Sally spoke to her mother. Mrs. Strong wrote on the tablet for Janet, "Dear, I'm at you again about moderating your voice. Try and speak lower—ever so much lower, dear. Suppose you try, too, to talk a little less? It's not that we want you to be silent; of course not! But you can think and dream, and that's more than everyone can do. Just a little less appeal, I mean, to everybody to think and dream with you."

That year some wicked or incredible careless person sent her a comic valentine. It pictured an old maid, but an ear trumpet had been painted in, and the black silk bag, and the tablet and pencil, and out of the mouth went the legend, "I don't mean to bore you, but----"

By degrees she achieved it—less appeal and less appeal and less appeal. By the time she was thirty-seven, though she still carried the black silk bag, she did not at every encounter, nor at every other encounter, nor at every third or fourth encounter, draw out tablet and pencil. Nor did she speak, with her overloud voice that she did not know if she ever lowered successfully. Instead, she smiled and nodded, and stood by while others talked, or with a characteristic wave of her hand went her way.

The old town—she loved it. There were Old Street and High Street and Green Street. There were the warm, faded, brick houses, rather stately in their way—stately but decayed. There was the abundant green leafiness, or an amber-and-crimson leafiness, or the April mauve smokiness of folded buds, or the marvel of the outstretched limbs in winter. There were the gardens in bloom, the old-fashioned flowers. The church spires pleased her and the Doric pillars of the old courthouse. She loved her town and wished it well, but there did not seem to be anything that she could do for it. They said, too, that it was dead-alive, that it was sliding downhilll, that it was hard to get a living in it, or to keep up appearances.

She loved her family. Her mother died when she was thirty-

seven, and after that she loved her still, somewhere or everywhere, and loved Sally and Martin and Margaret and Marion
and Uncle Robertson and the colored folk. They loved her back,
of course, as families must and will—impatiently and critically
enough at times, or like a piece of the old furniture or a room
in the old home; but loved her. She was useful to Sally and to
Martin and the girls. From now a long time ago a number of
jobs that didn't need ears had slid into her hands. Martin was
her favorite. She mended and darned for him religiously, and
felt his foot upon the attic stair.

The simplest soul in the house might be Uncle Robertson.
He never criticized her, looking at her in that hostile and hopeless way, or demanding tablet and pencil and writing lacerating
words; and he was fond of long walks, and from when she was a
little girl had let her go along. Very early he had written one
day, "Don't let's converse! Let's let things converse inside."
She had agreed, and they had walked together ever since upon
that basis. It was with Uncle Robertson that she learned all the
truly lovely country around Courtfield. There ran sufficient
roads and more paths, and sometimes they left even these and
strayed through woods and over green or tawny hills. Year by
year she and Uncle Robertson walking together, and peace in
her heart at these times.

Peace in her heart alone, or so nearly alone as this, with
Nature; peace in her heart sitting, once a week, in church, covert-
ly making her notes, with her own angel in the pulpit; peace in
her heart up in her attic room, with the poplar and the cedar
looking in, with her books, borrowed or owned, with the butterfly flights and the rough statue blocks of her thought.

When she was yet under thirty she began in the attic room,
at odd hours, sometimes late at night, with the poplar and the
cedar sighing at her windows, to develop those notes into those
strange, short poems, the miraculous verses. Or sometimes
she drew them then and there out of the ambient, its upper
wards, its aerial palaces.

Her books. As everybody knows, the list is a strange one.
She had bought, out of a present of money, Plato and Plotinus
and Spinoza, Dante and Shelley and Blake, but she had rarely
been able to control what others came her way. There were
those that had been in the house immemorially and that her
mother had said she might have, and there were a round score

that Mr. Locke, the Presbyterian minister, had given her out of his inherited three thousand volumes, and which he had let her pick for herself. At Christmas and for her birthday it was "Janet wants a book," but never "What book do you want, Janet?" Only Uncle Robertson asked that. So there is in the room that is kept as nearly as may be as it was, a strange assortment. But first and last, in one way or another, many a seer was there, of old times and of new times. And who knows what she sipped, from the unlikeliest spring?

Sometimes she talked to Martin about unearthly matters. This youth had a good mind, but he was impatient of her impracticability and her peacock voice. And you could never really talk, never talk really of yourself, with her ridiculous black silk bag and tablet and pencil coming between! You couldn't expand. You always felt frozen and narrowed, despite her eyes and her eagerness. Stone-deaf maiden aunts----

Martin was growing a large grievance against the world. He wanted to go to college and it wasn't possible. He thought it strange that it shouldn't be possible. "We used to have the money. I don't see----There's been waste somewhere. But this town and everybody in it is dead! What's the use of having sense if there aren't any means? But I must say it's hard on a fellow!"

Janet would have given anything to have him have his wish and go to college. And after that he wanted to study medicine. But it all cost so frightfully! So they talked of his becoming a pharmacist. When Joe Albany, who evidently could not last more than a couple of years or so, was gone, there were his drugstore and his business—and Deborah, from her distant city, said that she would help, though she could not help much. It would be hard enough to send Martin to the nearest city and keep him there and pay his tuition while he was becoming a pharmacist. They scraped together the money and he went.

Then Margaret announced that it was no use just sitting still and watching the house crumble and holes come in the carpets, and she was going to be a trained nurse. Of course, for three years, you got nothing—hardly—beyond your keep in the hospital. She went, to another city than Martin's.

Marion's idea was that she wanted to marry, but she did not. After a year or two she began to teach in the public school.

Sally, Marion, Uncle Robertson and Janet in the old brick

house behind the box bushes that smelled so deep in the sunshine. Janet thought, "If only I could earn—if only I could do something for us all who are growing poorer and poorer. Teach school? I am deaf. Learn shorthand and typing and go to the city? I am deaf. Sew by the day here in Courtfield?" She could sew. She had done all the mending for the house, besides making her own underclothes for years. She went downstairs at once, and in her too-loud voice consulted Sally.

Martha heard her in the kitchen. "Lawd hab mercy! Miss Janet wants ter go sew for de rich folks!"

Sally shed tears. "Do you want to disgrace us, Janet?"

No, Janet did not want to do that.

Martin received his diploma as pharmacist and came home, and then in three months he married. Fanny Hope, who had beauty but not a penny. And Joe Albany continued to live. The opening at Courtfield did not open. Martin and Fanny lived in the little brick house in the yard behind the syringa and the yellow roses. Here Little Martin was born. When he was a year old Martin, returning from Parthia, where he had been to look over the pharmaceutical field, became involved in a railway accident and was brought home to the little brick house with a broken leg and an injured spine. The leg bone knit, but there was no recovery from the other injury, though he reached the wheel-chair stage. Now there were two families, and less and less means to live with. Margaret earned now as a nurse in the city of her choice, but must live herself as well as help the others to live. Marion had the munificent pay of a grade-school teacher. Uncle Robertson got a clerkship, but made absent-minded mistakes and could not keep it.

They were not an uncheerful cluster, for all that their anxieties racked them. They possessed, for the larger part of the time, the ancient Courtfield lightheartedness, and rested, not unlovable. Margaret made a good trained nurse, and Marion a good teacher, and Martin, though he could show himself sour and despairing, as a rule exhibited fortitude and a caustic wit. Fanny was no tower of strength, but she had amiability. Little Martin, and Little Fanny, who came three months after the accident, if they brought, each of them, a basketful of cares, brought likewise one of delights. Uncle Robertson remained Uncle Robertson. Dick and Martha stayed on for very little, but they let Young Martha go to a good place in Parthia.

Janet took three poems—it is not known which they were—
to Josephus Morgan, the editor of the Courtfield Herald. She
spoke in her overloud voice—and she thought she was whisper-
ing, "Mr. Morgan, I'd be more than glad if I could make a little
money. I've been thinking, and I had a dream, or maybe it was
a vision. Would you read these, and would you tell me if the
Herald could print them and if you could pay me a little for
them?"

Josephus took them with lifted brows. They were not tied
with blue ribbon; nor, on the other hand, were they typed.
They were in that strange, clear writing of hers, at once exquisite
and bold. When she had parted with them, she took from black
silk bag tablet and pencil.

With eyebrows still raised, he wrote, "I didn't know that
you were a poetess, Miss Janet."

Janet said hoarsely. "Read them, please."

He read them—they were short—he read them twice over
while he kept tapping the desk with his fingers and she watched
him. By now she was past mistress of faces, and he confirmed
her every impression of shortcoming, and she wished she had
never disturbed those year-by-year forming layers of writing in
the deep, bottom drawer, or had disturbed them only to lift
with both hands and give to the kitchen fire.

"H'm!" said Josephus. "H'm!" He wondered how he
could let her down easy, poor old Miss Janet Strong! He wrote—
he had a great distaste for that tablet and pencil, but he prepared
himself to write quite lengthly and kindly—he wrote, "The
Herald doesn't really pay anything, Miss Janet, and, if you've
noticed, it much oftener than not just copies for that column
out of the great poets. 'The bards sublime,' you know, 'whose
distant footsteps echo----' I don't believe----"

"It's all right," said Miss Janet hurriedly, reading as he
wrote, for she could read tablet and pencil backward or forward.
"It's all right, Mr. Morgan!" A rose was in her cheek; she wished
to spare him embarrassment; it was so painful to feel embarrassment—humiliation and embarrassment. "It's all right, Mr.
Morgan! I don't know why I thought—it just occurred to me—
but it's all right."

Josephus again considered the poems. He wrote, "I don't
exactly understand this one, Miss Janet. I doubt if anybody
would. It's too fine-drawn, isn't it? Rather cobwebby, what

you might call metaphysical? I wouldn't go so far as to say that it hasn't some beauty, but----"

"Oh, I know, Mr. Morgan, I know!" she answered. "There's nothing I can do rightly, God help me!"

"Now this one," resumed Josephus, "it certainly affects me curiously. It affects me—it affects me like a small bell, like a bell of a strange metal----" He broke off, sat for a moment as though he really were listening to something, then wrote with firmness, "The third one I don't understand at all—it's like birds flying. For your own amusement it's all right, Miss Janet, but I don't believe you could get them printed."

That night there arose a storm. She could not hear, but she could feel it. Thrill went up and down her spine and sideways through her body until she was like a quivering tree—like the ash Yggdrasil. She could see the lit splash of the rain against the windowpane, and the turmoil and exaltation of the cedar and the poplar. She sat up in her bed, propping herself with her long, thin hands. "I am out in it—I am out in it. All my boughs are waving, all my leaves are drinking! Hold fast, my roots, hold fast!"

The old house in Old Street grew older and began to crumble, there happened so little repairing. The box grew higher and thicker and was never trimmed; the grass became shaggy, the vines too heavy. Dick was so old now, his scythe and his pruning knife were rarely busy; he was waiting for another scythe. Indoors there had not been new carpets or curtains for many a long year. The roses in great wreaths upon the parlor carpet proved not fadeless. The ancient wallpaper exhibiting strange Chinese scenes became defaced; a great leak ruined a breadth behind the piano that had not been tuned since the wedding of Martin and Fanny—and now Little Martin and Little Fanny had changed to Young Martin and Young Fanny. The girandoles upon the mantel—gilt shepherds and shepherdesses—and the frame of the mantel mirror put on more and more tarnish, though the dangling, chiming prisms of the one and the glass of the other were maintained in brightness, it being one of Aunt Janet's jobs to keep them so. . . . Aunt Janet to Martin and Fanny and Margaret and Marion. Great-aunt Janet to Young Martin and Young Fanny.

Standing on a chair, wiping the mantel mirror, she looked

at herself in the glass. That eager, pointed face with a faded rose in the cheeks and crow's-feet around the eyes, and graying hair that grew into the point in the middle of the forehead called a widow's peak.

"Widow's peak. Widow's peak! To whom am I married to be widowed like this?" She wiped the glass, then she moved the chair and wiped the prisms of the girandoles. They shone and danced and chimed: "Lover in the heavens! Lover in the heavens!"

The old town was going downhill. It would have stopped itself, but it could not. The young men and then the young women of ability went away, went elsewhere. It began to grow old in the sense of decrepit. Not the lovely country in which it was placed could save it; not the really colorful Old Street and High Street and Green Street, and the mellow red-brick houses; not the climate, nor the accessibility of the region, nor the comparative refinement of the citizens; not the manifestness of its being in many ways a pleasant place to come to or to dwell in— nothing and no one, it seemed could say the "open sesame!"; nothing and no one could turn the head of attention Courtfield-ward.

The attic room caught the rain at night upon the old roof. She could not hear it, but she smelled it, knew it, pulsed beneath the multitudinous impact. She saw the lit blackness, and her flesh answered the eternal freshness and touched the slow waving of the world that yet had a motion besides the sideways and roundabout.

She did not sleep a great deal. Sometimes Courtfield, noticing the lighted lamp high in the poplar and the cedar, remarked, "Poor old Miss Janet is sitting up there reading."

Young Fanny, climbing there once in Aunt Janet's absence, took it in her head to open drawers. That night she reported to her father and mother, "That old desk of Aunt Janet's—the bottom drawer has stacks of tablets like those she carries in her black silk bag. I thought they'd have all the handwritings and all the answers to her questions for ages, and so I looked. But it's all her own writing. I think she's trying to write poetry—but there's prose too—and she must have been trying a long time!"

"Was she there?" asked Fanny.

"No, she had gone to the store for grandmother."

"You had no right to rummage in her desk," said Martin.

"I'm ashamed of you, Young Fanny!"

Young Fanny shrugged her shoulders. "I didn't have a bit of bad intention. I was just curious. She'll never know. I'm sure if scribbling's a comfort to her I hope she'll scribble on forever! It must be hard to be deaf and lonely and old!"

"She never seems to think of herself as growing elderly," said Fanny. "That's another of the queer things about her that divide her off from mother and Aunt Deborah."

Sally did know that she was growing elderly, and deplored it. Elderly and heavy, and nothing changed except to grow worse, apparently. But it can't be said that she was truly unhappy—Sally. She was large and slow of movement and placid. Uncle Robertson was old, and one brilliant autumn died from the other attic room and the old brick house and from Courtfield.

Courtfield remembered his funeral. He had been a landmark, old Mr. Robertson Strong. Everybody went to his funeral and the autumn flowers lay in heaps. In the church they sang what were said to be his favorite hymns, though nobody could produce how that was known. They sang "How firm a foundation," and "There is a land of pure delight, Where saints immortal reign." There was a throng in the cemetery on the slope of the hill, with the fairest kind of view, and the Virginia creeper reddening everywhere. Old Mr. Robertson Strong! He could remember everything in Courtfield and roundabout for a thousand years. He could remember when it was a prospering first-half-of-the-nineteenth-century town. He could remember the battle five miles away, the battle and the battlefield that apparently alone nowadays caused Courtfield ever to be mentioned.

Uncle Robertson. . . . His family stood around the grave; Sally and Deborah and Janet, Margaret, Marion and Fanny, Young Martin and Young Fanny; Martin, in his wheel chair, would not come. Martin hated curious eyes and pity.

Dust to dust. . .In the hope of a glorious resurrection.

Janet, standing beside the grave, knew that she was going to miss Uncle Robertson, but all the same and now indeed she and he were walking to Hunter's Rest, and the sumac was all red and the farewell summer all purple and lacy and the life everlasting had a warm and pungent smell and the white moon sailed in the sky. He had not walked that far for some years, but he was walking there now and she with him. Walking, and yet perhaps it was flying.

For several days Courtfield talked of Uncle Robertson's death and funeral. All details were gone over: The family, in the church and at the grave. "The Strongs have seen a lot of loss and trouble, but they've got quality. . . . Poor old Miss Janet, without black silk bag and tablet and pencil for that one day."

The attic room. She took the lamp and went into Uncle Robertson's room. It had grown like him, as her room had grown like her. "Uncle Robertson! Uncle Robertson! Keep on walking with me and I'll keep on walking with you." Her own room, and the poplar and the cedar. The poplar was almost bare of leaves, but the cedar held and would hold. She sat before the window with her head bowed upon her knees. "Lord of Being! Lord of Being! I'm willing to stay while You have any work for me. But call me soon—call me soon!"

Margaret came up the attic stair. "Aunt Janet, don't you want to sleep in mother's room tonight—or for one of us to sleep up here?" She spoke loudly into Janet's ear; the deaf woman answered as loudly.

"No thank you, dear! I'm fond of it up here. I don't mind Uncle Robertson. I never did. I like him and he likes me."

Margaret, sleeping with Marion and talking, the two of them, late into the night, said:

"By the way—Aunt Janet! Hasn't it ever occurred to you that she's a little crazy?"

Autumn fell away. Snow outside the attic window, falling thickly with large white flakes, furring the boughs of the poplar and given support by the cedar. It came Janet's birthday, and they forgot it in the house until it was a week gone by.

Then Sally remembered it. "Oh, Janet, I am sorry! I don't believe I ever forgot it before."

"It didn't matter. It didn't a bit, Sally!"

Young Fanny brought her a book that evening. It was Idylls of the King. "I think it's a shame that we all forgot, Aunt Janet—and I've got a gift for you anyway."

There fell more snow than usual that winter. Spring broke late, but when it came it was glorious. The poplar had a gown of pale green. Downstairs the doors stood open.

Fanny came in excitedly. "Mother! there's a young man— a gentleman—at the house. Martin knew his father in the city—

he was a little boy, then, and Martin used to play with him. He's remembered it all these years. Something's brought him to Courtfield, and he's hunted up Martin. He says he likes Courtfield—that it's just the place he's been looking for to finish some work in. He's a writer, I think. He's at the hotel, but it isn't quiet enough and he'd rather be somewhere else. He asked Martin if he knew where he might find a pleasant room and board with quiet people. I thought----"

"He could have the little room off the porch," said Sally. "Of course, Uncle Robertson's room is quieter."

From Uncle Robertson's windows flowed a rich view of housetops, budding trees and purple hills. The roof sloped delightfully, the furniture stood spare and quaint.

"I like this best," said John Albany.

Sally thought she must tell him. "The other room up here, Mr. Albany, belongs to my sister Janet. She means to be as quiet as a mouse, but she's stone deaf, poor dear, and she doesn't know how loud she speaks----"

"Do you mean she has company up here all the time?"

"Oh, no! She never has company. But she will speak sometimes, to herself or down the stairs, and her tread's heavier than she knows. However, the walls are thick. If she stops you too often and wants to talk, just tell her—you write it on the tablet she gives you—that you are very busy. She'll understand."

Albany hesitated a moment. It sounded as though it might prove a nuisance. But he loved this attic room and the view. He determined, "I'll risk the deaf lady!"

The next afternoon in he moved, with the play he had to finish. The supper bell rang—he stood back to let a rather tall, thin, gray-haired woman to down the stairs before him.

At the foot she paused and spoke in a loud voice. "It's Mr. Albany? I hope you'll like that room. It's likable. It was used by a likable soul."

Albany smiled and nodded, and she went on before him. "So that's the deaf sister! Well, she's got an interesting face!"

He settled to work, and to long walks through the increasing spring glory. The family rarely saw him save at mealtimes. Sometimes he was silent or abrupt and sometimes, when things were going as he wished, amiably expansive as to his own life and inviting as to theirs. He paid promptly, and said that he wished to stay through May and perhaps to return in the autumn, when he would be beginning another piece of work—if this present piece didn't kill him! Now and then he crossed the yard to the little brick house and talked to Martin.

Janet didn't annoy him. Sally and Martin both had spoken to her.

He worked, and swore at his work, and worked again. The attic pleased him enormously, and the view from Uncle Robertson's windows. "The other room has that poplar and cedar and the only really high mountain----"

When work would not flow he took his hat and stick and stretched his long legs. He had been in the old brick house two weeks when one day he found himself near the top of a wooded hill, and suddenly in an elfin scoop of earth. It had a floor of emerald moss and gray moss and three tall pines and two dogwood trees whitely flowering. Also there ran a ledge of rock for lying upon. A woman lay here who sat up as he approached. It was the deaf sister. When he had reached the dogwood she spoke:

"This is Hunter's Rest."

"Do you often come so far afield?" he asked. She could not hear him, but produced black silk bag and tablet and pencil. He wrote, "Do you often come so far afield?"

She answered, "No. It's mine for long keeps, but I haven't brought anybody here for a year." She smiled. "You can have it too. Because it is mine doesn't keep it from being yours."

That was the beginning. He could see through. Something helped him to see through. He walked back with her to Courtfield, and thereafter when they met on the attic stair or in the passage between their rooms they stopped to speak. This passage widened up here into a space something like a room, with a window and a view of Old Street, with an ancient press and table and a couple of chairs. Sometimes they stopped here for a few moments. He had with him a box of books, and he offered to lend her as many as she wished. The roses bloomed in her face. "Oh, will you?"

They walked together to Hunter's Rest, and the next week to Markham's Spring. The family couldn't make it out, but concluded that he was natively kind. Courtfield, passing them, thought, "Uncle Robertson's successor! How did that ever come about?"

It was the end of May, spring passing into summer, when she brought to him in the passage three or four tablets and copy-books from the bottom drawer of the desk. He took them from her and into his room. An hour later he came and knocked upon her door.

"Have you got any more of these?" he asked in a rather curious, strained voice.

The next day he wrote for her, "I am going to New York for a few days. Two men are there whom I want to see. I am usually sure of my own judgment, but some things are beyond little men's judgment. Will you let me take five or six of these books?"

"Take them? What for?" asked Janet.

"I want these men to see them. And if they think what I do, I want to come back and help you make up the first volume and get it published."

"If they think what you do? What do you think?"

"I think that you are a great poet," said John Albany, and kissed her hand.

Courtfield didn't profess to understand it, at least not at first. Later—much later—when many things had happened, Courtfield thought and said that it had understood it all the time.

The Courtfield Herald at once noticed, kindly and facetiously, the announced appearance of Hunter's Rest and Other Poems, by J. R. S. "We understand," wrote Josephus Morgan, "that J. R. S. equals Janet Robertson Strong. We all know this poetess. We have known her all our lives. She has known us. Courtfield, prepare to be proud of your swan! Miss Janet, may you find gentle critics and readers and buyers! The Herald will be proud to have a copy of Hunter's Rest (we all know the place) for review, and means to get you to autograph it."

The Herald's review is lost. Much later—oh, quite years later—Josephus Morgan, in an article entitled Courtfield and published in a widely read and highly paying journal, wrote: "As for the bright, particular star that has had its rising in our constellation and makes it marked—well do I remember that day, long ago, when she showed me a poem, an early flight. I said to her, 'Your wings are not yet strong enough, and the air is not yet ready for you.' "

Mr. Parton, writing, also rather deep in time, to a distant cousin: "You say, my dear Amelia, that the city grows too rough and crowded for you, and that you experience at times a desire to remove your establishment and your children to the country. Why do you not come to Courtfield? Once I could not have advised this, but the old town has suffered, or is in the process of suffering, a sea change. Individuals and families who are looking for an old-fashioned grace and simplicity of living set in an environment of much natural beauty, have at last discovered Courtfield. Swordgrass College, old and venerable, as you know, removed here some time since. There is a big, rambling, well-kept inn on Riven Hill. Very pleasant summer quarters with an excellent table after the old fashion may be had with many of our best people. Property generally is looking up. It has always been a pleasant place to dwell in, but we couldn't somehow get the fact over. But merit, like murder, will somehow out. Some little thing starts the ball, and then, if it has it in it, it rolls of itself. Of course we have a famous battlefield. And Janet Strong was born and lived here. It's amazing how the intellectuals eat up the least detail about her isolated but commonplace life."

But Mr. Parton, and Josephus Morgan in the magazines, are speaking after days and months and years.

Mrs. Locke, the Presbyterian minister's widow, an aged woman, but active, was walking up Green Street with the lilacs purple, white and tall above the fences, and talking to Sally Strong in the second spring after the first coming of John Albany to Courtfield. Mrs. Locke had been away for fifteen months, visiting her married son in the Middle West. The sun shone, the lilacs bloomed, the birds sang.

Mrs. Locke breathed deep. Truly, there's nothing in the world like home! She resumed her speech:

"Does she know that she's famous?"

"The money's more than we've looked at for a long, long time," said Sally. "Though of course it can't be a fortune, seeing, as Mr. Albany says, that it's poetry—the highest poetry, he calls it—and those prose 'arguments' that he says are impossible yet of full appreciation, though they are beginning to get it. But after all our straits, it seems a fortune to us. And he sends her reviews. They say what are to us the most extraordinary things, applied to Janet."

"I know," murmured Mrs. Locke. "You don't suppose they are mistaken, my dear? It seems a kind of dream. They say that people come to see her——"

"At first she didn't understand that—any more than the rest of us," said Sally candidly. "When they sent up their names —we have Young Martha back—down she came to see them and brought forward her black silk bag."

"Yes?" said Mrs. Locke sympathetically.

"Of course she sees now herself," said Sally. "We had a good talk about it. Some paper sent some smart aleck to 'interview' her." Sally flushed.

"Yes, we saw it," murmured Mrs. Locke. "Did she?"

"Yes. She wouldn't see the next person who came, and she wrote to Mr. Albany---- Now it seems that it's got about, away from Courtfield, that she's half an invalid. When a stranger rings Young Martha just says, 'Miss Janet is sorry, but she is not well enough to see anyone today.' "

"Well, that's sensible!" said Mrs. Locke kindly. "Janet has always had a very sweet spirit, you know, Sally."

"That's perfectly true," answered Sally, and paused for a whiff of the white lilac. Presently she spoke again. "It isn't possible to remember that she is what is called a genius. She is so exactly just Janet, poor dear! The last thing she would do is put on airs. And I suppose we don't really understand poetry— not yet. Martin and Young Fanny come nearer to it than the rest of us, but even they—And it isn't as though she had just begun to write these things. It turns out that she had been doing them for the better part of her life. Mr. Albany says she began to write when she was quite a young woman. He says they can bring out a volume every other year for ten years to come. And even now, when her light is burning up there late at night, I suppose she's writing. Mr. Albany says she's an enchanted princess dwelling in a guarded tower."

"Then he's a poet himself," said Mrs. Locke, exhibiting a little fine impatience. "Like you, Sally I'm not! Janet's just Janet to me—forever coming to borrow Mr. Locke's books, with that red in her cheeks and tablet and pencil. But I've always been fond of her, and of course one feels a great compassion----"

The lilac incense gave way to syringa incense, and the incense of calycanthus, with dark, inconspicuous blooms. "Sweet-shrub," the children and the servants called it. Old Mr. Ross, the merchant, was dead, but middle-aged Mr. Ross, his son, sold Courtfield summer goods. He was selling Miss Janet Strong dimity, lawn, linen and poplin.

"She hasn't bought four pieces at a time for years and years," thought Mr. Ross, and put out a hand for tablet and pencil. He wrote, "We've a very fine rose-and-purple print, Miss Janet."

But Janet shook her head. "I mustn't be extravagant, Mr. Ross. Sackcloth isn't a good lining for summer dresses." She had latterly achieved, after years of working upon it, the sinking of her voice. But as then, to her, it was like talking to herself, it often went too low and became a husky whisper.

Mr. Ross cut off the poplin, then wrote, "When are you going to New York, Miss Janet?"

"I am not going to New York," whispered Janet. "Why did you think so?"

"I thought you'd wish to taste your fame, Miss Janet," said pencil and tablet, "where there's more company than here."

The eyes that Courtfield had always found too brilliant—"like a cat's at night," said someone—considered it. "No. Have you never thought, Mr. Ross, that you can't truly drink 'fame,' except when you're dead alone? Then the mockery is only salty and the bitterness is clean."

Mr. Ross gave Miss Janet up, as, periodically, he had given her up ever since he began to keep this store, as his father had given her up before him. He wrote, "Do you want any trimmings, Miss Janet?"

His customer stood hesitating. The rose in her cheeks that would not quite fade deepened. That ridiculous whisper of hers sank so low that Mr. Ross had to lean across the counter to catch it. "Five yards of *real* Valenciennes—not very wide."

She went to church on Sunday. Some stranger was there, staring at her.

I believe in. . .the resurrection of the body.

Oh, the grave clothes—oh, the grave clothes!

And the life everlasting.

Amen! Amen!

She put an angel in the pulpit and sat hearkening to him.

That afternoon she walked to Hunter's Creek beyond Riven Hill. It was June. John Albany was coming tomorrow for a week.

She thought fondly of this, for he had become to her a brother and a counselor. Only he—only he and Uncle Robertson—— In recollection, quiet, profound and vivid, Uncle Robertson walked beside her.

Note

1, said: added.